Stephanie Baldi

MOBBED UP

A Novel by Stephanie Baldi

ISBN: 978-1-951543-20-4 — Print

ISBN: 978-1-951543-21-1 — eBook

Library of Congress Control Number: 2023900382

Front Cover Art by Mary Rogers
Cover Design and Layout by Colin Wheeler, PhD, MFA

Printed in
The United States of America

Dedication

Dr. Elyse Wheeler, whose friendship, love, encouragement, and hard work on my behalf, always inspires me to do my very best. I am forever grateful to Dr. Colin Wheeler, who dedicated his time to the completion of the *Mobbed Up* cover.

Acknowledgments

To my Mexican Train gals at Fairfield for their continued love and support. As always, my Brooklyn girls, Doreen, Marianne, & Pat. To all my devoted and loyal fans who have helped make my dream come true. To the talented Mary Rogers who designed and painted a canvas of the cover. And to the Carrollton Writers Guild whose continued support has inspired me to keep writing and telling my stories.

Chapter 1 — Monica
A Shot in the Dark

Monica woke to the sound of voices. She flung the covers off and padded to the window of her Staten Island townhome. Shafts of pale gold radiating from an early fall moon bathed the street below. Cool air rushed inside, ruffling the pale-yellow lace curtains. Her nostrils filled with the sweet scent of honeysuckle drifting up from the hedgerows bordering the house. Two dark shapes across the alleyway caught her attention as they vaulted over the neighbor's fence. Snatching her cell phone from the nightstand, she dialed 911.

A woman's voice asked, "What's your emergency?"

Screw it, she thought and hung up. Pete Mackey probably owes money to some bookie again.

Settling back into bed, she curled up underneath the floral comforter. A loud crack echoed outside. Monica bolted up. Tiptoeing to the window, she swept the tumble of long, ebony curls away from her face and peered out. The exact two figures leapt back over the fence, landing square on the sidewalk below a streetlamp. One of them glanced up, the light catching his face. Monica drew the curtains and inched away. It was Eddie. Eddie Marconi. What craziness did he get himself tangled up in?

Moments later, the doorbell rang. Monica's pulse skipped. The ringing grew quicker, more frantic. She slipped into her robe, dashed to the living room, and hit the wall switch. Cautious, she checked the peephole and drew back. Her full lips formed an angry pout.

"Come on, Monica, I know you're there," a male voice said. "Please open the door."

Her body tensed. A flush swept through her. After everything he had done, she vowed she would never speak to him again. Almost involuntarily, her hand turned the lock.

Eddie sailed past her, collapsing onto the sofa. "Thanks," he said between rapid breaths.

Her eyes swept over his black attire, the black knit cap on his head, and the gun in his hand. This couldn't be good. "Eddie, what the hell is going on?"

He glanced up, his face the picture of innocence. "Nothing for you to worry about."

"Nothing for me to worry about! Are you for real? You bang on my door at three in the morning, dressed like a ninja and carrying a gun."

"It's not what it looks like. Calm down, and I'll explain."

Monica cursed herself for letting him in. Eddie, the permanent thorn in her side, but also once the love of her life. Together for almost four years after high school, she tossed him out after it became clear she needed the ring, the house, and the kids. Eddie wanted free nookie and a place to hang out.

Hands on her hips, she said, "Well, I'm waiting."

"Pete's in deep with my Uncle Sal," Eddie blurted. "Owes him quite a bit of cash. He asked Brazo and me to give him a scare. You know, just a little one."

She motioned toward the gun. "Please put that thing down."

He placed it on the coffee table and got up. "Pete's dead."

"Dead?" Monica reared backward, picturing poor Pete, the neighborhood idiot. Every neighborhood has one. Skilled at getting himself into trouble, Pete might have been dumb, but he was harmless.

A nerve pulsed inside her chest. "You … killed him?"

"Hell no." Eddie faced her. "I didn't do it. Brazo didn't either. We arrived too late."

"Impossible. I heard what sounded like a gunshot. You were still over there."

"That's about the time we split."

"Then how do you know he's dead?"

"We got a glimpse into the window. Pete lay sprawled on the floor with some big goon standing over him." Eddie's brow furrowed. "Never seen the guy before."

"Eddie, are you sure? Maybe, Pete's alive. We need to call an ambulance."

"Oh, he's dead, all right." Eddie formed the shape of a gun with his hand, raised it to his temple, and pulled an imaginary trigger.

"For God's sake, Eddie!" About to tell him off, she stopped at the sound of police sirens outside. Gunshots were rare in this part of the borough. The front of her attached townhouse in the Sunnyside neighborhood faced the quiet of Clove Lake Park, one of the main reasons she chose this house.

Eddie crossed the room and killed the lights.

"What do you think you're doing?" Monica demanded. She stomped after him feeling for the switch. Eddie's hand caught hers.

"Keep them off, Monica. If the cops notice them, they'll figure someone's awake. Interviewing witnesses is one of their specialties."

"Witness? But I didn't see anything except you —"

"Exactly," Eddie cut in.

He trailed the tip of his finger across her lips. "Shush," he whispered.

She flinched and brushed his fingers aside. "Shush yourself."

The room, lit only by moonlight, cast a soft glow over his handsome face. Tall, lean, and olive-skinned, Eddie's skills in the art of lovemaking went above and beyond the ordinary. Knowing he was up to his old tricks, she stalked off.

Eddie came up behind her. "Come on, Monica," he pleaded. "Why waste the rest of the night?"

Monica spun around. "You just witnessed a man shot in the head, and you want to have sex? I think you should go, Eddie. Now." She strode to the door, flinging it open.

Eddie glanced down at his clothes. "Not dressed like this. Especially with the cops outside."

Leaning back against the doorframe, she eyed him for a second. He had made a good point. A flutter hit the pit of her stomach while her mind battled between wanting him to leave and wanting him to stay. Still uncertain, she found herself pushing the door closed.

"Okay, you can stay until they're gone. But no funny business."

Eddie pulled off his cap and dropped onto the sofa again. Watching him, the memory of his dark strands slipping between her fingers surfaced. She fought the urge to run her hand through his hair.

Wanting to change the subject, she asked, "So, working for your Uncle Sal again?"

He paused. "Well … kinda. No, not really."

"What is it then, you are or aren't?" Typical Eddie, never a straight answer.

"I was doing him a favor." His forehead wrinkled, and he let out a slow whistle. "Wait till he finds out about Pete. He's gonna be pissed."

Eddie's Uncle, known to most of Staten Island, was said to be 'mobbed up' or connected. Through no lack of trying, Eddie hadn't been able to work his way into the inner sanctum yet.

The sirens wailed louder before slowly dying out. Monica rushed to the window. Across the way, flashing red lights lit up the block.

Eddie jumped up and pulled her away from the window. He pressed up against her. His naked muscular body flashed across her mind. The way he used to move his lips along the hollow of her neck and… no, she needed to stop thinking about all that.

"I miss you," Eddie moaned. "Please, baby, let's cuddle. I want to hold you. Gaze into your beautiful green eyes. I promise I'll be good. You know you miss me too."

Knowing he spoke the truth, she hated herself for even entertaining the idea.

His hand trailed along her cheek. She almost caved. Mustering all her resolve, she said, "Not a chance." She stepped away and pointed her finger at him. "You stay put on the sofa." Without glancing back, she closed the bedroom door behind her.

Hours later, Monica woke to Eddie's body pressed up against hers. His arm draped over her waist, his palm resting on her breast, the way they used to sleep. All of it comforting, yet disconcerting at the same time. His bare chest's steady rise and fall against her back soothed the buried hurt. His warm breath fanned her neck. God, how she missed him.

Chapter 2 — Eddie
Big Tall Sal

Rock music blared. Eddie rolled over and hit the buzzer on Monica's clock radio. He leaned back against the pillows trying to shake off the recurring nightmare. The steady hiss of the shower perked him up. Grinning, he tugged off his underwear. Creeping cat-like over to the bathroom door, he opened it and slipped inside. Desire escalating at the sight of Monica's naked silhouette behind the steamy glass, he slid the shower door open. Monica whirled around.

She pushed him away with her soap-covered arm. "Oh, no, you don't."

Eddie laughed, grabbed her arm, and forced his way inside. "Come on, save some water. We can shower together."

His nautical blue eyes traveled the length of her body. Water raced down on her, beating a path between her breasts. Why did he give up on them? He should have tried harder. Pulling her close, he kissed the hollow of her neck. Steam swirled around them. He pressed her up against the beige tile while inhaling the fragrance of mango body wash. His hands explored until they found their mark between her thighs. She moaned, and her legs parted. Her eyes closed, and after a few minutes, she orgasmed.

"I love you, baby," he murmured. Drawing her closer into his arms, he tried to enter her.

Monica shoved him. He stumbled backward, almost falling onto the wet tiles as she charged past. Frustrated, Eddie steadied himself, grabbed some soap, and finished showering. He stepped out, swiping a towel from the rack.

Dressed in a bathrobe, Monica applied her make-up at the vanity. Wrapping the towel around his waist, his disappointment growing, Eddie inched up beside her. She hadn't answered him back with I love you, too. He rested his hand on her shoulder, but she shrugged it off and got up.

"Monica, please, talk to me." She wheeled around, and he cupped her chin. A tear splashed onto his hand, knocking the wind out of his sails. It killed him inside to see her cry.

"Baby, what's wrong?"

She swatted his hand away. Brushing at her tears, she said, "You're making me late." Without another word, she dried her hair and finished dressing.

"Come on, tell me what's wrong," he pleaded.

"I've got to go, Eddie."

He couldn't let her leave like this. "Baby, I'm sorry. I know I hurt you. I miss us, babe. I really do."

"You should have thought about that when you were out there screwing around."

Her words jabbed at his gut. The pain he had caused ran deep. She was right, and he needed to own it.

"I wish it never happened. It was one time, Monica. One time and I regret it. If you only knew how much."

"I can't forget it, Eddie. I don't trust you anymore."

He dug for a comeback. "Maybe if you hadn't taken that job in Maryland and gone away for so long, we could have worked things out. Admit it, Monica, you ran." She fell silent for a moment. He caught a trace of guilt in her eyes.

"Let's be real, Eddie. We never wanted the same things. Maybe I'm partly to blame for pushing us to get married. I'd never lie to you and say marriage wasn't what I wanted just to keep you." Her face clouded over. "But I never would have cheated on you."

Monica gathered her purse and charged toward the front door. Eddie followed close behind. With each step, her dark curls bounced, her long beautiful legs pumping fast in her black stilettoes.

"Give me another chance. I'll make it up to you," Eddie called after her. "You'll see." Begging wasn't his thing, but she was worth it.

"No," she said, slamming the front door.

Defeated, he trudged back to the bedroom and dressed. He checked his cell phone. Six missed calls from his Uncle Sal. Cursing, he left Monica's house. Twenty minutes later, exiting the Staten Island Expressway, he arrived at his uncle's house.

Salvatore Marconi lived large. The massive English Tudor standing in the Todt Hill neighborhood, one of the most exclusive areas of Staten Island, screamed money. Over the years, Todt Hill had been home to a few residents of note. Among them, Gambino crime family boss, Paul Castellano.

Eddie drove up to the gates in his white BMW X6. He waved at the two bodyguards stationed outside, who buzzed him in. He pulled onto the circular drive, got out, and rang the bell before going inside.

"Uncle Sal!" Eddie called out.

"In here, kid," a man's voice boomed.

Eddie proceeded down the hallway toward the kitchen. His uncle, hunched over an eight-burner commercial stove, stirred a huge stainless-steel pot. Polished cherry wood cabinets lined the walls and the sides of the enormous center island. On top of the Carrera Marble, a cutting board held fresh garlic, chopped onion bits, and a platter of sweet Italian sausages. The warm, deep tones of the terra-cotta tiles on the floor offset the pale coral backsplash.

Eddie inhaled the heavy aroma of tomatoes, garlic, and Italian herbs floating in the air. His stomach growled. Gravy. The pot would be on all day, the sauce thickening hour by hour until his Aunt Teresa spooned it over homemade pasta at dinner.

Eddie loved this kitchen. It bore so many memories of family dinners. Orphaned at five years old, after his parents died, he had lived with Uncle Sal. His uncle and aunt became surrogate parents, raising him along with their twin daughters, Gina and Antonia. Spoiled as a child, Eddie embodied the son his uncle never had.

Sal set the wooden spoon on the rest. He lumbered toward him, his six-foot-three frame towering above Eddie's five-foot-ten. Stocky and well-padded, with a full head of dark hair salted with grey, he wrapped his thick arms around Eddie's shoulders, giving him a bear hug.

"How's my favorite nephew?"

Eddie hugged him back, though his arms barely made it halfway around his uncle's body. "Doing great, Uncle Sal."

Sal stepped back. "So great you can't answer your phone."

"Sorry, I got distracted this morning." Warmth crept up his face.

Sal laughed. "Oh, I see, *fidanzata!* A girlfriend. Out of all your women, I liked…what's her name? Monica. Yeah, Monica. I liked her the best. Think you two might get back together?"

Eddie thought for a few seconds. "Maybe."

"You either will or you won't. There is no maybe." He gestured for him to sit at the large kitchen table. "We need to talk about last night. I believe there was trouble."

Eddie sucked in air between his teeth. "Yeah, big trouble. Pete's dead. You told me to get the money he owed, maybe rough him up a bit, but that's all."

Sal rubbed the stubble under his chin. "I know. I found out this morning." He rested his large hands on the table. "Tell me what happened."

Eddie described last night's events, what he and Brazo had witnessed through the window. He left out going to Monica's. Uncle Sal wouldn't appreciate that part of the story. Monica wasn't supposed to know about anything he did for his uncle.

"Did you recognize this man?"

"No, it was too dark. Everything happened so quick." Eddie waited, positive his uncle would explode.

"Are you sure he didn't get a look at you?"

"I don't think so," Eddie said.

Sal's face pinched. He cracked his knuckles, each pop filling the silence between them. This old habit usually surfaced when his uncle was anxious.

Eddie bit his lower lip. Should he confess? Tell Sal everything he didn't tell Monica. Pete struggling with the guy who shot him, both wrestling for the gun. The guy getting the upper hand and shooting Pete before turning and looking straight at him and Brazo? His uncle would realize he messed up. He'd never become a made man.

Sal's eyes pierced Eddie's. "You need to be certain. If he knows you can identify him, there could be trouble."

"I'm sure," Eddie lied. "As soon as we heard the gunshot, we split. But I don't understand who would want to kill Pete. Do you?"

Sal got up, returning to the stove without answering his question. "Let's leave this alone for now." He picked up the spoon and stirred. "I called Scalito's Funeral Home. I'm going to pay for Pete's funeral. The poor man had nobody. I forgave his debt. You must forgive the debts of the dead. We will all go to the funeral and pay our respects."

Eddie didn't pursue it. When his uncle wanted things left alone, the discussion ended. With the smell of the gravy fueling his hunger, he prepared to make his exit.

"You need anything else, Uncle Sal?"

"No, not now. Are you coming back for dinner later? Your aunt would be thrilled. Since you got your place, we miss you around here."

"I'll try."

"Well, if not, I'll see you at the funeral." He glanced over his shoulder, giving Eddie a sly look. "And bring that *fidanzata* of yours."

Eddie bear-hugged his uncle again before leaving. Was there something funny about this whole thing? Uncle Sal hadn't seemed too upset over Pete, plus he never said who he thought might want to kill him. Eddie pictured the man he'd seen through Pete's window, the light hitting his face just right. He didn't recognize the guy, so chances are the guy didn't know him either.

Deciding to forget about his conversation with his uncle, for now, he'd get something to eat before taking his best suit to the cleaners so it would be ready for the viewing. Afterward, he'd try to persuade Monica to come with him.

Recalling her tearful face, a heaviness settled in his chest. He needed her and needed to find a way to win her back.

Chapter 3 — Monica

Dressed in Black

Monica dodged the numerous potholes along the busy street. Native to Staten Island, potholes were a part of the ambiance of living in the so-called forgotten borough of New York City. A short trip anywhere around the island might blow a tire or destroy your shocks. She spotted an empty parking space directly in front of her store. Jackpot! No cruising the block today.

Before unlocking the front door, Monica admired the green awning above her flower shop on Victory Boulevard, a major thoroughfare chock-full of various businesses, including several well-known restaurants. The silhouette of a bride holding a bouquet and next to it in bold gold lettering the words, Brides, and Blooms, made her swell with pride. This was her baby.

She observed the windows, dressed for fall with various colorful mums, marigolds, and bright pink asters. Meaty orange pumpkins lounged among the maple leaves strewn about in patchwork hues of molten reds, golds, and rusts. A scarecrow sat in the middle, holding a small pot of begonias.

Three years of budgeting and saving enabled her to do it all on her own. After she found the perfect location, everything fell into place. But today, she found irony in the fact bridal flowers were her forte. She had dreamed of designing her wedding bouquet one day, her dream torn apart after Eddie cheated on her.

She shut off the alarm, switched on the lights, and flipped the door sign from closed to open. The spicy-sweet scent of lilacs and roses circulated in the air. Bright-colored hues mixed with soft pastels among the greenery. A round wooden table in the center held sample arrangements for customers to view. Monica gave them the once over to ensure the flowers displayed remained fresh. She checked the large glass coolers behind the cash register, making a mental note for future restocking.

Monica settled into the leather burgundy chair inside her office at the rear of the shop. She turned on the computer. Her fingers flying across the keyboard, she entered the purchases bought at the Flower Market on 28th Street in Manhattan the previous day. After several minutes, unable to concentrate, she stopped. She had a case of the 'Eddies'. Angry at herself for giving in too easily this morning, she wanted him to suffer. Wanted him to realize what he had lost.

After they broke up, she tried dating again. Forcing herself to go on numerous blind dates with guys she met on the internet or set-ups courtesy of her best friend, Carlotta "Cookie" Asante.

"Forget Eddie," Cookie had told her. "There's a whole big world out there packed with guys."

Cookie was right. Except most of the guys she dated were full of crap. They bragged about themselves, their jobs, and how much money they made. Puffed themselves up as a real catch. At the end of the night, they just wanted to get her in the sack, following up with the obligatory statement, 'I'll give you a call sometime.' But most never called, and the ones who did wasted her time.

Determined to forget Eddie, she left Staten Island altogether to try something different, surprising herself when she fell in love with her new career, until her world imploded and the unexpected happened.

Her cell phone buzzed, forcing her back to reality. "Hello."

"Hey, babe," Eddie said. "Look, I'm sorry about this morning. I didn't mean—

"Yeah, you never mean anything, do you?" she said, his voice rattling her.

"I really am sorry," Eddie said. "You know, about us … in the shower this morning. I shouldn't have done that, but you're so sexy, I couldn't help it."

She ran a hand through her thick curls. "Listen, I think we should stop communicating. It doesn't get us anywhere."

"Hearing you speak those words is like a knife to my heart, baby."

Monica inhaled to steady herself. Right now, she felt like twisting that so-called knife. "I think it's for the best."

"Well…if I agree, will you do one thing for me?"

Oh boy, here it comes. She braced herself. Eddie never made things easy. Why couldn't he say, yes, you're right and hang up the phone? "That depends."

"Go to Pete's wake with me."

"What?" He could have been asking her to dinner the way he said it.

"Yeah, Uncle Sal would like to see you."

"Oh, that clears things up. Is this a social occasion or a wake?"

"Come on. You know how we Italians are. Funerals and weddings are always special occasions for getting together."

Monica clenched her teeth to stop herself from screaming into the phone. "Ha, ha, very funny."

"Listen, babe, do me this favor. I won't ask you to do anything else. We're still friends, right?"

She cringed at the word friends. He was so cocky. "Is that what we are now, Eddie, friends?"

"Well, at the very least, I thought —"

"You thought what?" Monica exclaimed. "That's the trouble. You don't think." Trying hard not to lose it, she said,

"Look, if I do this for you, no more communication afterward. Am I making myself clear enough for you?"

"Crystal, baby."

Monica envisioned him smiling at the other end of the phone, claiming victory again.

"The viewing is at four this afternoon at Scalito's," Eddie said.

Monica sighed. "Where else would it be." Anybody well-known in the neighborhood, including half the dead mobsters, was laid out at Scalito's,

"I'll pick you up at three-thirty."

"No, I'll meet you there." Monica didn't want to give him the satisfaction of riding in his car. Experience had taught her he wouldn't keep his hands to himself.

"I'm just trying to be nice."

"Like I said, Eddie, I'll see you there." She hung up and slammed her cell phone down on the desk.

The bell on the front door of the shop jingled. Monica glanced at the clock hanging on the far wall. It must be Cookie. Best friends since high school, they shared a lot of history, and now they shared a workplace. Monica hired Cookie because she could trust her, besides being great with the customers.

"Monica!" Cookie called.

"Back here!"

Cookie's heels tapped on the tile floor, the sound echoing off the walls. She stuck her head in the office door. "Hey girl, what's up?"

Monica constantly amazed at how Cookie dressed, observed the tight sweater fitting snuggly over her ample breasts complemented by the shortest skirt Monica had ever seen. Her full lips were painted a brilliant ruby red. Doe-shaped eyes bore false eyelashes making her eyes look like bat wings when she blinked. Her long deep, auburn hair hung stick straight. A popping noise filled the room as Cookie's jaw worked the wad of gum in her mouth.

"You wouldn't believe what's up," Monica said. She told her about last night and, of course, about Pete's wake.

Cookie's face paled. "Poor Pete. He never hurt anybody. What a shame." She tossed her purse down and plopped into the chair across from the desk.

Monica squinted at the sight of Cookie's blue lace thong. "Cookie, not for nothing, but be careful how you sit. I can see your hoo-ha."

A sly smile crossed Cookie's lips. "I'm sorry, but that's kinda the whole point." She crossed her tanned legs. "Better?"

"Much." Monica rested her elbows on the desk, cupping her chin in both hands. "What am I going to do about Eddie?"

Amusement glinted in Cookie's eyes. "You know what to do, but you just don't want to do it. But I get it. It should be a crime for a guy to be that good-looking. But I can't understand how you still have feelings for him. He's a rat fink cheater."

"I know you're right, Cookie."

"You're wasting time. We ain't getting any younger."

Monica could almost hear the ticking of her biological clock. At thirty-four, she had envisioned herself married and already a mother.

The rest of the day flew by with customers coming in and ordering flower arrangements for Pete. Fan sprays of gladiolas, baskets of lilies, and red and pink carnations had her and Cookie struggling to finish and get them delivered. Afterward, Monica helped several more customers go through catalogs of wedding bouquets. She checked the time. It was almost two-thirty.

"Cookie, will you hold down the fort here? I need to get ready for the wake."

"Sure thing, not to worry. I'll go to the second viewing later tonight."

"Thanks." Monica grabbed her purse and left. On the drive home, she tried to push thoughts of her relationship with Eddie to the back burner for the time being.

After pulling a sexy black sheath plus matching pumps from her closet, she showered and dressed. Standing in front of the mirror, she had to admit the dress could go either way. It screamed a night out at the club with her high heels on. Maybe, her ballerina flats would tone it down a bit. She grabbed the flats and slipped them on. Better, but not quite satisfied, she took them off, slipping into her heels again. Did she feel guilty making it a priority to look drop-dead gorgeous at a wake? Hell no!

Let Eddie see what he was missing. She may be dressed in black, but she would make sure Eddie Marconi regretted ever letting her go.

Chapter 4 — Eddie
I Saw What You Did

Eddie sauntered into Scalito's Funeral Home dressed in his best navy suit, maroon striped tie, and shoes polished to a shine so high he could make out his reflection. The cloying scent of lilies among the many floral arrangements dominated the air. Without a doubt, most of those had come from Monica's shop.

He flipped through the pages of the guest book. Top-ranking mobsters appeared to be in attendance. Not that Pete was near and dear to their hearts, but because it presented the opportunity for them to meet to discuss business, common at funerals and weddings.

Eddie stood off to the side, waiting while the made men filed past the casket confessing their faith by genuflecting and making the sign of the cross. One by one, they disappeared into a private viewing room down the hall. Inside, the men would voice their issues regarding their respective territories to his Uncle Sal. They might also request favors which he would either grant or deny.

He made his way up the center aisle to the bronze casket flanked on either side by tall white candles. His uncle had spared no expense for someone, not a blood relative. It struck Eddie as odd.

Pete lay dressed in a grey suit and navy tie, hands folded neatly across his chest. Scalito's had done an excellent job hiding the bullet wound. Pete never looked this good alive.

Eddie said a quick prayer before stepping away. Scanning the room for Monica, he felt a tap on his shoulder. Tommy Brazenetti stood next to him. Brazo, as he was known in the neighborhood, wore a black pinstriped suit, his brown wavy hair deluged with so much hair gel it reminded Eddie of an oil slick. Reeking of cheap cologne, he almost overpowered the fragrance of the floral arrangements.

"Hey, Eddie."

He held out his hand, and Eddie reciprocated. Brazo motioned toward Pete. "Man, did you get a load of the casket? Your uncle sure shelled out some dough for that baby."

"I know," Eddie said. "Could be he felt bad about Pete having no family."

"Yeah, maybe." Leaning in closer, he whispered. "What was his reaction to Pete getting whacked?"

Eddie surveyed his surroundings before answering. "Nothing much. He wasn't too upset. He wanted to know if the man who shot Pete got a look at us."

Brazo's full brows arched, reminding Eddie of two furry caterpillars.

"What did you tell him?"

"I couldn't let him know the guy spotted us." Eddie pictured the man's face. His stomach muscles tensed while his palms leaked sweat. "I think we should save this discussion for later."

"Sure, whatever you say." His eyes focused on the doorway behind Eddie. He let out a low whistle. "Wow, she's hot. How did you ever give her up?"

Eddie swung around and spotted Monica signing the guest book. Without responding, he kept his eyes on her until she finished walking up the aisle toward the casket. She was hot, all right. He'd savor the vision of her in that black dress. Almost every man in the room had his eyes fixed on her.

She said a prayer before sitting down in the front row. Eddie left Brazo and eased down beside her.

"You look amazing, babe."

"Thanks. But I don't think you should focus on me right now. We're at a wake, after all."

He straightened up and put both hands in his lap. "Sorry, you're right."

The scent of her perfume drifted past. Eddie inhaled. He longed to bury his face against the soft skin on her neck. Trying to control the urge, he looked to his right and found himself staring into the eyes of Father Michael Martella, seated next to him.

"It's good to see you, Father Mike," Eddie said.

Father Mike adjusted his collar. He leaned in closer to Eddie. "Too bad I'm not good enough for you to come to see me at Sunday Mass."

Eddie's cheeks burned. "Nothing personal, Father. I've been a little busy lately."

"God is never too busy for you. He makes himself available twenty-four-seven. It's strange Monica doesn't seem to have any trouble getting to church."

Eddie tugged at the knot on his tie. "Oh, but we're not together anymore."

"I know. It's a shame. Someone like Monica could be a good influence on you. Mind telling me what happened? We could step outside for a few minutes."

"Well, it's kinda a long story. Something I'm not comfortable discussing here."

"You might feel relieved getting it off your chest. The longer you hold it in, the worse you'll feel."

"Come on, Father. We're here for Pete." Eddie could only imagine what Monica had told him about their break-up. Besides, he hadn't been to confession in over a year. Even if he had, he doubted he would have confessed to cheating. Certain things should stay between him and Monica. He didn't need Father Mike or God sticking their noses in it.

Father Mike shrugged. "No worries, we'll talk another time. See you at confession later this week."

Before Eddie could answer, he sprang to his feet. Standing in front of the casket, he caught Eddie's eye and winked. Everyone seated themselves. All heads bowed in prayer during the short ceremony. Two people from the neighborhood said some kind words about Pete. No one acknowledged the elephant in the room screaming, 'idiot.'

After they finished, a small gathering lingered outside in the hall. Eddie followed Monica to the end of the corridor away from them.

"Listen, Monica, thanks for coming. It means a lot to me and Uncle Sal."

She grinned and leaned back against the wall. "By the way, where is the dear man?"

"Oh, he's here. Just finishing up some business." He fidgeted with his tie before unbuttoning his suit jacket.

"You mean funny business?"

Eddie raised his brow. She could sure push his buttons. "Look, I get it. You don't approve of the family business, but there is nothing I can do about it."

"Family business," she smirked. "Is that what you call it?"

"Not here, not now, Monica. Okay?" He raked his fingers through his hair. "Did you tell Father Mike the details surrounding our break-up? The guy started grilling me like I was on trial or something."

Grinning, she pushed away from the wall and stood toe to toe with him. "That's not up for discussion, Eddie. Feeling guilty?"

Her eyes, hypnotic, deep pools of green framed by dark lashes, captured his. He resisted the urge to tell her to shut up, take her in his arms, and kiss her long and hard. Forcing those thoughts away, he said, "Never mind. I doubt you'd spill it, anyway."

"Getting back to your uncle," she said. "I can't understand why you want to be mixed up with him. You've been doing your uncle's bidding for years, and up to this point, it hasn't gotten you anywhere."

Giving her a dismissive shrug, he said, "Now that's where you're wrong. My uncle relies on me to get things done. He knows he can trust me."

Her voice softened. "Okay, don't get upset. I only want what's best for you. I think you can do better."

He reached for her hand, glad she didn't pull away. "Come on, let's go see Uncle Sal."

They walked down the hall towards the other viewing room. Eddie greeted his uncle's bodyguard, who slid the pocket door partway open, just enough for them to walk through, before sliding it closed. Sal stood in the far corner, shaking hands with several men.

"Looks like they're done," Eddie said.

A tall man in a dark suit looked in their direction, his hooded eyes glued to Eddie's face. Eddie froze. He squeezed Monica's hand. The man studied him a few seconds longer before turning back to face his uncle.

Monica tugged her hand away. "Eddie, you're crushing my fingers."

He ushered her towards the door. "We need to leave."

"What the hell is the matter with you? Let's say hello."

His heart bounced against his ribcage. "No...you don't understand. We have to go now." Eddie ushered her out into the hallway. He glanced around for Brazo before rushing out the front exit of the funeral parlor with Monica in tow.

"Eddie, what's wrong?"

They crossed the lot to Monica's car. "Listen, you drive straight home."

"Not until you tell me what's wrong. I've never seen you like this. You've gone pale." Her palm pressed against his brow. "You're on fire."

"Monica, please. Go home. I'll call you later. I'm fine."

"Okay, but you better. I'm worried about you." She got into her car and started the ignition. Her window slid down. "Promise you'll call me?"

He leaned toward the open window. "Promise." Not quite knowing what to do next, he waited until she drove off. Obviously, his uncle knew the man who killed Pete.

Eddie walked to his car, slipped in, and waited. From his vantage point, he could observe the entrance. He needed to get another look at this guy.

Twenty minutes later, the man stepped out of the funeral home. A tall, hulking figure, he climbed into a black Lincoln with dark-tinted windows. Eddie ducked as the Lincoln glided past. Deciding to drive over to Brazo's, he pulled out his cell phone and dialed.

"Hey, what's up?"

"Are you at home?" Eddie asked.

"Yeah, I left right after Monica came. Wakes are not my thing. Boy, I still don't understand how you let her go. If she—"

"Shut up and listen. We might have a problem. I need to come over."

"What kind of problem?"

"It has to do with Pete."

"You mean what happened the other night?"

"Yeah, I don't want to talk about it over the phone. I'll be there in twenty minutes."

Eddie disconnected the call and pressed the ignition. Punching the gas pedal, he sped out of the parking lot. So many scenarios played out in his mind. He needed to figure out the best move for him and Brazo.

Reaching the Staten Island Expressway, he weaved in and out of the lanes, leaning on the horn every time a car blocked his path. When traffic came to a crawl, he cursed. Forty minutes later, with daylight fading, he exited the highway, pulling onto Brazo's street.

Eddie's breath hitched. The black Lincoln was pulling out of Brazo's driveway. It made a left away from him before continuing up the road. Waiting until the car disappeared, he slipped into a spot across the street. He sprinted up the steps and rang the bell. Seconds passed with no answer. He rang the bell again and pressed his ear to the door. Nothing.

Eddie turned the brass knob and found the door unlocked. His heartbeat ramped up. Inching it open, he stepped into the foyer.

"Brazo, it's me, Eddie."

He took a few more furtive steps, squinting in the dim light. "Hey, man, where are you?"

Switching on a lamp, he continued into the kitchen. He peered out the window of the door leading to the attached garage. Brazo's car was inside.

He swept around the car's exterior, peering inside each window. Nothing appeared to be out of the ordinary. His fingers swept over the hood. The engine was still warm. Brazo couldn't have been home for too long before the Lincoln drove up. What did it all mean? Did he invite the man inside for some reason? A cold wave washed over Eddie as he pictured the man's face again. You didn't invite a man like that inside.

Moving on, he checked the main bedroom. There was no sign of his friend. Except for an unmade bed and some clothes strewn on the floor, everything seemed to be where it belonged.

He pulled out his cell and dialed Brazo's number. The ringer, made to sound like a freight train announcing a call, screamed nearby. Eddie followed the noise until it led him to a cell phone lying on the floor in the corner of the living room. The ringer stopped. Eddie picked it up and took one last glance around.

A glint of something shiny caught his eye. His knees grew weak. The gold cross that always hung from a chain around Brazo's neck lay on the floor. A gift from his mother before she passed away, he never took it off. Here it was, minus the gold chain.

Stuffing the cross inside his pocket, he placed the cell phone on the coffee table and hurried out the door. He turned the lock and then slid back behind the wheel of his car. Could they have kidnapped Brazo because of what he witnessed the other night at Pete's house? If that were the case, his life could be in danger too.

If something happened to Brazo, the man at Scalito's had played a part in it. Fear skated down his spine. It meant Uncle Sal could be involved too. Unable to rid himself of the angst growing inside him, he fingered the cross in his pocket. Dread clutched his insides, images of the man inside the black Lincoln haunting him.

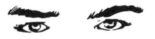

Chapter 5 — Monica

An Old Acquaintance

Monica collapsed into bed, waiting for Eddie to call. Hours had passed since leaving him in Scalito's parking lot. She couldn't remember ever seeing him so upset. Not even after she called it quits, and he tried to keep one foot in her door, believing someday they would get back together.

Reaching for her cell phone, she dialed Eddie's number. After several rings, his voicemail came on, his smooth tone making her go weak inside.

"Eddie, I'm worried. Please call and let me know you're okay." She tossed the phone onto the nightstand. Settling back against the pillows, thoughts of him lying in a ditch somewhere swirled through her mind. Not much could throw her off course except Eddie.

Monica spent the next few hours in a restless state until, exhausted from imagining all the horrible things that might have happened to him, she drifted off to sleep. She hit the alarm button when morning sunlight filtered in and grabbed her phone. No messages. Nothing from Eddie. Trying not to work herself into a frenzy, she got ready for work.

Arriving at her shop by ten o'clock opening time, she gave Eddie some slack. If he didn't call by noon, she'd allow full-blown panic to set in.

It was Cookie's day off, so she busied herself with the tall glass vases behind the register, removing several bouquets of wilted flowers and tossing them into the trash. She gathered fresh daisies, roses, tulips, and greenery.

The heady fragrance from the petals put her at ease while she tried several different combinations of flowers and formed new arrangements. Her keen eyes inspected each bouquet. The bell above the shop door tinkled. Engrossed in her work, she picked up another vase.

"Good morning. I'll be right with you."

"And good morning to you, Special Agent Cappelino."

Monica swung around and froze. Standing before her, six foot tall, with buzzed cut sandy-colored hair, dressed in a dark blue suit with a maroon tie, stood Daniel Gage, and along with him, all those ghosts from the past she had tried to forget.

He winked, spun the door hanger to closed, and flicked the lock.

She set the vase down. "That's former special Agent Cappelino. What the hell are you doing here, Danny?" She stepped from behind the counter. In three strides, she stood toe to toe with him. "I asked you a question."

"Whoa, Monica." He raised his hands in mock surrender and stepped back. "Still as ballsy as ever, I see."

Trying to keep her anger in check, she bit the inside of her lip, "If you don't start talking, I'll show you how ballsy. You have ten seconds, Danny." Squaring her shoulders, she jerked her thumb towards the door. "Otherwise, you can leave now."

Danny leaned in his face inches from hers. "I can't believe you're still holding a grudge after all this time."

She cut her eyes at him. "Don't flatter yourself. It wasn't that good. I was happy you broke off the relationship. But knowing you, you probably pictured me pining away."

His cheeks flamed a bright red making her smile inside at her small victory. "Now, for the last time, why are you here, Danny?"

He glanced around. "Is there somewhere else we can talk?"

"Right here is fine. It's only the two of us."

"Okay, I just thought we might be more comfortable sitting down."

"Unless you have news about the tragic death of someone close to me, I'll stand."

His brows drew into a hard line. "You mean, like Jack Wilson, or Froggy as you affectionately called him."

The bitter tone in his voice ripping open old wounds, her eyes locked on his face. She detested his smugness, the way he jutted out his square chin while he mocked her.

Monica crossed her arms. She looked him up and down. "Wow, Danny. I never thought you could stoop so low."

His shoulders slumped, the superior expression fading. "Monica, I'm sorry. I didn't mean that the way you think."

"Save it for someone who'll believe it. Now, I'm through being polite with you. Tell me why your sorry ass is here or get out of my shop!"

"It concerns Eddie. Eddie Marconi."

Monica shrunk back, her anger turning to fear. "Eddie? Did something happen to him?" She braced for the worst. All those awful images from the night before flashed in front of her.

Danny held up his hand. "Not that I'm aware of, but we need to talk about him."

Her body relaxed a bit. "Why?"

"The Bureau needs information, and Eddie Marconi might be the one to get it. I know how close the two of you are...were." He rubbed the back of his neck as a blush formed on the tips of his ears. "The Bureau wants you back, Monica. And they want you to turn him."

A tingling sensation coursed through her body, making it hard to speak. How could this be happening? She pointed her finger at him. "You, of all people, know the hell the Bureau put me through after Jack got killed. Come back? Turn Eddie? Hell, no!"

"Come on, Monica, as Special Agent, you know Jack shouldn't have been out there with you. He was hired purely as a profiler. I still can't fathom how you let it happen."

Monica took a tentative step forward. "So, all along, you blamed me for Jack's death, even though you tried to convince me it wasn't my fault."

He tugged at the knot in his tie. His lips pressed together, forming a thin white slash. "Look, none of it matters now. What happened can't be undone. Jack is dead. Let it rest."

"I wasn't the one who brought it up, Danny."

Tears formed, blurring her vision. She squeezed her eyes shut, holding them back. Old memories clawed their way to the surface. But she'd be damned if she'd let him see her cry.

"There will never be an end to what happened," she said. "I don't know why Jack followed me there that day. If I'd known he was anywhere near the scene, I wouldn't have pursued the suspect."

Monica pushed past him, unlocked the door, and flung it open. "I think it's best you leave."

"And what should I tell the Bureau?"

"Tell them no. I don't want to come back in. I won't try to turn Eddie into an asset. The Bureau refused to stand behind me when I needed them the most. Why should I agree to help them now?"

He edged towards her, his voice softening. "Because you would be helping one of our own."

"What do you mean?"

"That funeral you attended yesterday."

"Yeah, what about it?" She didn't wait for an answer. "You mean … Pete?"

"Known as Simple Pete out in the street," he said. "Brian Hanson to the Bureau."

Monica's heart jogged against her ribcage. Everyone in the neighborhood, including herself, had thought of him as the village idiot.

Since leaving the Bureau, she had ignored the sixth sense inside her, convinced she had no use for the thing that sharpened her mind … made her pay attention. Always being able to size someone up within seconds of meeting them had saved her life numerous times. Most people called it intuition, but with her, it ran much deeper, making her exceptional at her job. It explained why she learned so much from Jack with regard to profiling.

Ignoring it must be why she failed to recognize those telltale signs that might have given him away on those few occasions she encountered Brian Hanson. A sinking feeling engulfed her.

She studied Danny. "So, he was undercover."

"Deep under. I'm surprised you never figured it out, but Brian had done an excellent job making people think he wasn't that smart, about to come in until he was compromised."

She sighed, running a hand through her thick curls. "Are you saying Eddie's Uncle Sal had him eliminated?"

"Yeah, the big fancy funeral was a slap in the face to the Bureau. Salvatore Marconi put on a nice show playing make-believe."

Danny's chin dropped, his eyes focusing on the floor before meeting hers again. "Brian portrayed himself as a loner. Truth is, he left a wife and two kids behind. The Bureau has taken custody of his body as we speak."

"He was able to gather solid evidence on some of Sal's underlings. But we want the big fish. We want Salvatore Marconi. And we want him for the murder of a federal agent."

Knowing every undercover agent had a handler, Monica asked, "Who was the Case Agent in charge?"

Danny fell silent.

"Well, who, Danny?"

"Me, but none of the intelligence indicated Brian had been found out. I still can't understand how any of this happened. I've gone over the files and wiretaps a million times. Brian was one of the best at undercover work. The only thing we're certain of is, in all probability, Salvatore Marconi ordered the hit.

Searing hurt burned inside her at his words. Only someone in law enforcement or the military could relate to at the loss of one of their own. She had left the Bureau and all the bullshit behind her, but hearing about Brian brought it all back. No one close to her knew when she left home after graduating college with a Bachelor's Degree in Criminal Justice, she headed for Quantico to train. Eddie had fallen out of the picture by then. Her parents made their long-awaited move to Florida, where the rest of her close relatives lived.

As far as anyone else knew, she worked in an administrative job in Maryland before returning to Staten Island. With the Bureau no longer a part of her life, she focused on getting her shop, determined to leave the past behind, never imagining it would resurface.

Monica pushed the door closed and locked it. "Okay, Danny. What have you got? I need to know everything before I give you my answer."

Chapter 6 — Eddie
Moving Up

Eddie woke from the same nightmare-filled dream. Shaking it off as always, he checked his phone and cursed. Fifteen text messages plus frantic voicemails from Monica. Still drowsy, he dressed. Unsure of what to do next, he stopped by his uncle's house. Maybe the whole matter of the black Lincoln would be cleared up. He'd deal with Monica later.

Squinting at the glaring sun through the windshield, he flipped the visor down and hit the gas. He needed some time to think. Several scenes played out in his mind. What would Uncle Sal say if he asked about the man at Pete's funeral? Or should he not mention him at all but only voice his concern over what he found at Brazo's?

The closer he got to his destination, the more his confidence dwindled. Torn between loyalty to his uncle and wanting to know the truth weighed on his mind. But some things weren't meant to be questioned. Everything in this business was black and white. There was no grey.

He arrived, and the door opened before he could ring the bell. Lorenzo Barone's body blocked the doorway. Wide as he was tall, his protruding stomach bulged, threatening to pop the buttons on the vest of his grey three-piece suit. His Uncle Sal's brother-in-law and Caporegime winked and extended his hand.

"It's been a long time, Eddie."

His hand gripped in Lorenzo's vise, he tried squeezing back just as hard. A firm handshake was important. "Yeah, it's good to see you, too, *Zio* Lorenzo."

Lorenzo loosened his grip and continued down the steps. "We'll be seeing a lot more of each other real soon." His driver pulled up in a black Cadillac SUV. He climbed into the rear seat, the dark interior and tinted windows swallowing him up.

Uncertain about his remark, Eddie deliberated before going inside. A Caporegime or Capo could be compared to a lieutenant in the army who took orders from the Underboss, like his Uncle Sal, and directed the so-called soldiers or made men and associates underneath them.

His heartbeat quickened. Could this mean he would be moving up in the organization? Right now, he worked only as an associate for his Uncle Sal, taking care of certain businesses and, if necessary, roughing up those who failed to cooperate.

Stepping through the doorway, he called out, "Uncle Sal?"

"In here, kid," came the usual reply.

Eddie strode up the hallway, making an abrupt right into his uncle's study. Sal, seated behind an enormous mahogany desk, was engrossed in the stacks of paperwork laid out before him. Reading glasses perched on the tip of his nose, his eyes traveled down a page. A deep crease running from end to end across his forehead appeared to stretch, reminding Eddie of a rubber band about to snap.

"Hey, Uncle Sal."

Sal leaned back, letting out a chuckle. "Never thought there was so much money in the car wash business." The crease across his brow relaxed.

The car washes his uncle owned washed more than cars. The money he filtered through them came out sparkling clean.

He pointed to a chair in front of the desk. "Sit down, kid. So, what happened yesterday? You and your girl left without saying hello."

Eddie's gut knotted. He held back from wiping his sweaty palms down the front of his jeans. His uncle, like a bloodhound, could sniff out fear.

"Sorry. You were busy. I didn't want to interrupt."

Sal leaned forward, drumming his fingers on top of the desk. "I'm glad you came by today. You saved me a phone call. I've been meaning to talk to you about some things."

This was it. His uncle must have found out he witnessed Pete's killing. Now he'd have to explain why he lied.

"I know I've promised to move you up," Sal continued. "It's time I gave you more responsibility. You know you're like a son to me. My brother's only child, may he rest in peace."

The words he wanted to hear for so long sunk in at the same time the image of Brazo's gold cross swam before him. Best friends since grade school, and now he had no idea if he was alive. But Eddie believed in a different kind of loyalty—one bound by blood, the other by friendship. Blood most definitely the stronger of the two.

"Uncle Sal, I—"

Sal held up his hand. "Let me finish. You have always done what I asked without questioning why. I know you understand the intricacies of the business, how to conduct yourself, and make me proud. There is a meeting of all the families next week. I want you there with me."

Stern faced, Sal continued. "You've been an associate long enough. Handling the money from the car washes and the two pizzerias, plus turning a profit on some of your endeavors, has shown me how valuable you are to the organization and me. This gathering will allow you to get to know some of the soldiers from the other families."

Sal got up and motioned to him. "Come, proper congratulations are in order." The two men bear-hugged, but before Eddie could pull away, Sal whispered, "Your time will come soon."

Eddie, almost speechless at the invitation to a meeting of the so-called Commission, meant he would become a made man and take on all the responsibilities that came with it.

His uncle released him. "Thanks, Uncle Sal. I won't let you down."

"Now remember," Sal said. "The Bosses, Underbosses, Caporegimes, and Consiglieres will all be there. This is an important meeting. I want to show them how much I value you. They need to trust you, too, so I want you to sit with Jimmy before you go. He'll let you know what to expect and how to act." Sal held out his hand. *"Capisce"*

"Capisce, Uncle Sal."

Sal pulled his hand away. "Geez, kid. Why the sweaty palm?"

Heat rushed up Eddie's cheeks. "Just excited at the news, I guess." No way he could bring up Brazo now. He'd wait, bide his time a little. Maybe he could find out what happened with some digging on his own.

Sal lifted the receiver on his desk and punched a button. "He's here. Yeah, now's a good time." He placed the receiver down. "Go see Jimmy. He's in his office down the hall."

"Thanks again, Uncle Sal. I won't mess up."

The deep crease returned to his uncle's brow. "You better not, kid. You're about to step up and become an integral part of the Borgata."

Eddie strode up the hall and knocked on the wood-paneled pocket door.

"Come," a muffled voice called out.

Always off-limits, this was the first time he had been inside Jimmy's office. He glanced at the tall bookcases hugging two of the four walls. Dozens of leather-bound legal volumes with gold leaf lettering on their spines stood sandwiched together on the shelves. A massive oak desk held stacks of files.

Slim and diminutive in appearance, Jimmy Galante, Sal's Consigliere, stood in the middle of the room impeccably dressed in a dark blue custom-made suit. The tip of a maroon handkerchief peeked out from his breast pocket. Hazel eyes peered out from behind gold wire-rimmed glasses. Leaning in close for a firm handshake, Eddie detected the light scent of expensive cologne. Jimmy gestured toward one of the brown leather sofas flanking the fireplace.

"Nice to see you again. Take a seat."

Jimmy took a seat across from him. He adjusted his tie and crossed his legs. "Let's get right down to things."

"Sure," Eddie said.

"First, the rules. Never be late. It shows a lack of respect. Never introduce yourself to the top people you are meeting for the first time. There must be a second person to do it. In your case, this will be your Uncle Sal."

Eddie, hands clasped together in his lap, absorbed every word.

"If asked for any information, always answer truthfully," Jimmy said. "Never interfere with money belonging to one of the other families. You will have your own territory to worry about. When you're out on the street, no bragging. Always keep a low profile. Never disrespect any of the wives or girlfriends. Never associate or be seen with cops unless you know for sure they are or can be bought. Always make yourself available. No excuses. Immoral behavior that embarrasses the family will not be tolerated, and finally, always follow orders."

"Understood," Eddie said.

Jimmy uncrossed his legs and pointed his finger. "Above all, *omerta* at all times."

Omerta. The most important thing of all. It meant not cooperating with authorities and not interfering with the approved illegal action of others in the families. Above all, it meant a code of honor, a vow of silence.

Jimmy plucked the silk handkerchief from his breast pocket. He removed his glasses and wiped them.

"You must always do your best. Break the rules, and you'll be treated accordingly. Not even your Uncle Sal will be able to save you." He finished cleaning his glasses before returning the handkerchief to his pocket.

"You're young, still a bit cocky, but if you do the right thing, you'll move even further up, maybe even become a Capo one day." Jimmy got up. "That's it. The meeting is this coming Wednesday. After all the details are worked out, I'll contact you. You'll travel with your Uncle Sal."

Eddie thanked him and shook his hand again. Outside, alone in his car, he pumped his fist and smiled. At last, it was happening. Working for his uncle had paid off big. He sailed onto the Staten Island Expressway with thoughts of Brazo far from his mind.

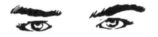

Chapter 7 — Monica
Decisions, Decisions

M onica rested her elbow on the desk. Chin in her hand, she listened to Danny. Still unable to digest the fact Brian Hanson had been undercover, her inner turmoil escalated.

"That's about all we have so far," Danny said. "Brian gathered sufficient evidence regarding Salvatore Marconi and his part in narcotics trafficking, weapons dealing, and extortion to put him away for a good while." He hesitated. "That is, maybe."

Her hands gripped the arms of the leather chair. "What do you mean?"

"The case could fall apart. They hire fancy lawyers, intimidate witnesses, and everything unravels."

Monica considered his words. It had happened numerous times before. The Bureau assembled what they thought to be a solid case, strong enough to hold up in court, and smartass lawyers would dismantle it brick by brick.

"You know, Danny, wiping out a federal agent is serious business in the Mob. The order might have come from the top, not Salvatore Marconi. If I recall correctly, he's an Under Boss."

"Right," Danny said. "But everything points to him giving the order. I wonder if he had permission or made the decision himself. We've got intel concerning an upcoming meeting. There are rumors that the heads of all five families will attend. I have a feeling Brian's killing is on their agenda.

"Where?"

"Unfortunately, we don't know. Even if we find out, there isn't much we can do at this point. The Bureau doesn't have anyone on the inside right now, just low associates who never get invites to those types of things. But Eddie is different. Even though he's only an associate, our intel says his uncle is going to move him up. Look, Monica, I'm not here to lay a guilt trip on you."

"No, the Bureau did an excellent job already," she said, her tone laced with bitterness.

Without warning, suppressed, unwanted emotions erupted. A painful lump formed in the back of her throat. Danny could never understand just how much leaving the Bureau cost her. After Eddie, it became her anchor. The thing she counted on to ease the pain of the past every time she walked through those doors. The camaraderie between her fellow agents and the knowledge of doing decent work for her country instilled a sense of pride nothing else could match.

"I'm asking if you'll help us prove Salvatore Marconi ordered the hit on Brian. If so, we can dump the other charges on top and ensure he's gone for a long time. But we can't do it without you. You're the only one who has a shot at turning Eddie into an asset. You need to do the right thing."

Monica's spine froze like a block of ice, knowing all too well how this worked. He was treating her as if she'd been a witness to a crime. Knowing their history made her resent him even more. Arms folded, she stared at him.

A flush crept up Danny's cheeks. "What?"

"Don't try to work me or play on my sympathy. I know what's at stake here. You think my moral compass is broken because I'm not with the Bureau anymore?"

He threw his hands up. "Okay, okay, my bad. Let me start over. It's your decision. I realize it's not an easy one."

Monica got up and glared down at him. Maybe she should cut him some slack, but she would not be played. "Listen, Danny, you're unaware of the history between Eddie and his Uncle Sal. The man raised him after his parents died. Their ties run deep."

"Ties can be severed."

"Yeah, but blood ties are strong. Especially when it comes to the Mob. I want to help. I really do. But this is personal. I must be honest and tell you I still care for him."

He studied her. "So, it's a no?"

"I didn't say that." Her stomach churned. "What will happen to Eddie? Will he get full immunity?"

Danny got up and came around the desk. "It's not up to me. That's a conversation for you to have with the Bureau. Talk to them, Monica. Let them know what your conditions are." He reached for her hand.

She drew away, ignoring his pained expression. "I can't agree with anything yet. I want a few days to think it over."

"Fair enough. I'll check back with you."

"If I'm even considering this, I don't want you showing up here again."

"Okay, you have my number."

"Actually, I don't. I deleted it quite some time ago."

Danny smirked. He grabbed a Post-it Note and pen off her desk. He scribbled his number. "You let me know." He eased open her office door. "I hope you'll consider everything I said for the sake of Brian's memory and the Bureau."

After he left, Monica paced her mind in turmoil. How could this be happening? Her life had settled. It might be far from perfect, but she had her shop, her friends, and sometimes she even had Eddie. No longer having to follow orders and endless directives, she relished making her own decisions.

But what if the Bureau hadn't let her down? Would she ever have come back to Staten Island? Lost in thought, the door chime startled her. Monica hurried to the front of the shop. Eddie stood by the counter, a wide grin across his face.

"Well, babe, I'm in," he said.

Monica pointed her finger at him. "Where the hell have you been, and what are you talking about? Didn't you get my messages?" She cringed at his all too familiar, 'I'm sorry' expression.

"You're right. I didn't mean to worry you. I should have called." The grin returning to his face, he said, "Uncle Sal realizes how valuable I am. I can't go into any details, but I've waited so long for this."

Her muscles tightened. What timing. Uncle Sal was pulling him into his inner circle. "I guess congratulations are in order. I know how much this means to you."

"Yeah," Eddie said. "I'm about to be mobbed up."

Monica forced a smile. His becoming a made man meant her facing what that really meant. Eddie would be expected to do more than oversee certain aspects of his uncle's illegal businesses. Murder could play a big part in testing his loyalty. He was in way over his head.

"By the way, who was that guy I just saw leaving? A customer or —"

"Of course, silly. He ordered flowers for his wife."

"Just asking. He had a certain look."

"What do you mean?"

"Never mind."

He pulled her into his arms. She leaned into him, trying to push away thoughts of Brian, Danny, and the Bureau. She'd think about them tomorrow. Right now, for whatever reason, she just wanted Eddie the way they used to be before he broke her heart.

She rested her head against his chest, but her anxiety grew. If she agreed to help the Bureau, things between her and Eddie could never be the same.

Chapter 8 — Eddie
Meeting Day

Eddie leaned into the supple leather seat in the rear of his uncle's Silver Cadillac Escalade, the soft purr of the engine soothing his nerves. Sal, busy on his cell phone, had only spoken a few words since the drive began. Seated up front with Mario Esposito, Sal's driver/bodyguard, Jimmy kept his silence. Another Cadillac tailed behind them with two additional bodyguards.

With the meeting scheduled in the Pocono Mountains of Pennsylvania, the car picked up speed, crossing the Bayonne Bridge and tearing along Route 80.

Dressed in a navy-blue suit, Eddie adjusted his tie, determined to be prepared if his initiation happened today.

Two hours later, they pulled up to a massive glass and cedar home jutting out of the mountainside. Numerous high-end automobiles lined the circular drive. The drivers and bodyguards huddled together in the cool mountain air, smoking cigarettes, and making small talk.

"Listen, kid," Uncle Sal said. "Wait until I introduce you, *capisce?*"

"Got it," Eddie said. He smoothed his tie again before plucking a scrap of lint off his suit jacket. They climbed out and went up the broad steps to the front porch.

Once inside, he followed his uncle toward the rear of the home. Male voices emanated from an enormous great room with floor-to-ceiling windows facing the valley below. Three long wooden tables configured in a horseshoe dominated the room where the heads of the five families, along with Under Bosses, their Capos, and Consiglieres, assembled.

Eddie's brain buzzed as he surveyed the scene. Some he recognized from essential functions like birthdays, weddings, and funerals. Others legends he had merely heard about on television or read about in newspapers, with names like Anthony 'The Hatchet' Ferranti, Tommy 'Bugs' Polizzi, Joey 'Knuckles' Carbone.

Several of them stood, embracing his uncle. Handshakes, bear hugs, and slaps on the back finished, Sal introduced him.

"This is my nephew, Eddie Marconi. My deceased brother's son now also a son to me. Sal's hand crept up Eddie's back, forcing him forward. Eddie moved along the tables, shaking hands with each man before returning to his uncle's side.

Sal winked at him. "Now, you go join the others downstairs."

Confused by his uncle's sudden dismissal, he remembered Jimmy saying, 'Always do what you're told.'

He withdrew and made his way down a series of stairs off the kitchen. The acrid odor of cigarette smoke mixed with whiskey drifted toward him. He arrived at the bottom and found himself standing in a large game room with about fifteen other guys.

Two men, suit jackets off, their sleeves rolled up, shot pool. Bright-colored balls smacked against one another as they slid across the dark green cloth. Several others perched atop stools by a long mahogany bar with drinks in their hands and smoking cigarettes. Eddie surveyed the room for a familiar face but didn't see anyone he knew.

One of the men slid off his stool. Short and stocky with red hair, pale skin, and puffy eyelids, he wore a dark green suit with a mustard-colored vest underneath, making Eddie think of a bullfrog.

After giving Eddie the once over, he stuck out his hand. "Oh yeah, we heard you were coming," he said. "You're Sally's boy, right? I'm Carmine Lonardo."

Eddie smarted at the word boy but forced a smile. He reciprocated the handshake. "Yeah, his nephew."

"Come meet the rest of the bums."

Eddie followed him, exchanging names and handshakes with the group.

Carmine slipped behind the bar. "Drink?"

"Yeah, sure, scotch will do." Eddie found Carmine's eagerness unsettling. Something seemed off about the guy.

Carmine twisted the top off a bottle of Chivas Regal and poured two shots. He handed a glass to Eddie and picked up his own. "Salud."

Eddie tipped his glass, allowing the warm whiskey to relax his body. He thanked Carmine before stepping away from the bar toward the guys playing pool. He leaned against one of the pillars and sipped his drink.

After the game ended, one of the players, a tall, muscular, dark-haired man, introduced himself as Tony Morello. Pointing his cue stick at Eddie, he smacked a C-Note down on the table. "Play?"

Eddie, no stranger to a game of pool, reached for his wallet and planted his money on top of Tony's. Evenings spent hanging around the neighborhood bars had made him quite good at the game.

"Sure, eight ball, okay?" Eddie finished his drink and set the glass aside.

"Rack 'em up," Tony said to one of the guys.

Eddie removed his suit jacket. Rolling up his shirt sleeves, he plucked a cue stick from the rack and chalked the tip. He gestured at Tony. Within minutes, the others gathered around the two men—all making bets among themselves as to who would win.

Eddie motioned at Tony. "Break?"

Tony swiped a hand through his dark hair. He moved to the end of the table, bent down, and scattered the balls across the table with his cue stick, sending a number three red one into a side pocket. He glanced up, flashing Eddie a grin. Over the next few minutes, he sunk two more balls,

All eyes fixed on Eddie whenever Tony sank a shot. But he kept his composure. His turn came, and he topped Tony by sinking five balls in a row.

As the game progressed, the room fell silent. Eddie finished sinking the designated balls. He smiled at Tony before chalking his stick one last time. "Eight ball in the corner pocket." Nervous tics hit the bottom of his gut, but he remained calm on the surface. As the new guy on the block, he needed to win this game.

Eddie leaned in and gripped the end of the cue stick with his right hand. Resting his thumb against his index finger, he let the cue stick slide back and forth. He sighted his shot and struck the cue ball, his aim perfect. It rocketed across the table and slammed into the eight-ball sending it into the corner pocket.

A couple of the men high-fived each other. It was apparent they had bet on the underdog. Eddie suppressed a grin as he observed money change hands. He slipped his cue stick into the rack.

Tony walked toward him and held out his hand. "Nice game. Didn't recognize you as a ringer." Before Eddie could respond, he tilted his head back and laughed. "No, seriously, man. You're good. Where did you learn to play like that?"

Eddie shook his hand. "Around the neighborhood."

"Staten Island, right?" Tony said.

"Yeah."

They retreated to the bar, where Tony handed Eddie two C-Notes. The rest of the men remained by the pool table with fresh players picking up cue sticks and making bets.

Tony poured two shots and handed one to Eddie. "Here's to a game well played." They downed their drinks and settled onto stools.

Muffled, angry shouts drifted from up above. A chair scraped the floor, followed by heavy footsteps pacing. Eddie glanced at the others. No one appeared to be paying attention to the noise, but Eddie knew better. They were aware of the commotion.

Tony poured himself another shot. "I hear your Sal's nephew. How come I haven't seen you around before?"

Eddie fidgeted with his shot glass. "I've been handling some minor stuff for him up until now."

Tony winked. "I get it. Someone's gonna be made soon."

Eddie struggled to remain passive at Tony's remarks. Getting made wasn't supposed to be common knowledge until after the ceremony.

"It took time for me to become made," Tony continued. "By the way, I work outta Jersey with Frank Uzelli.

Eddie set his shot glass down. He leaned in toward Tony. "You mean Frank, 'The Razor' Uzelli?"

Tony's brows drew together. "Yeah, I know what they say about Frank. But he's basically a decent guy. It's just sometimes he doesn't think before he acts."

Eddie swallowed the last of his scotch. Stories about Frank were legend. The Word was you needed to be careful around him because if he didn't like something, he'd whip out his straight razor. Frank had left many a scar on some poor innocent slob.

"Hey, can I ask you something?" Eddie said.

"Sure."

"What's the story with Carmine? I can't put my finger on it, but there is something about that dude."

Tony's face clouded over. "Carmine thinks he's somebody he's not. Works for Joey Russo. He's a soldier who pretends to be more important than he is. Don't pay him no mind." He pulled out a pack of cigarettes. "Smoke?"

"No thanks," Eddie said. "I gave those up a long time ago."

"Good for you." Tony stuck a cigarette between his lips and removed an old-fashioned Gold Zippo lighter from his pocket. He flipped the top open with his thumb.

Eddie smiled, the familiar sound evoking a memory. "Hey, I haven't seen one of those since my uncle Sal's when I was a kid before he kicked the habit."

Tony lit up. He took a deep drag. "Solid gold. A present from Frank." He held it up. "It's got my initials on it."

"Nice," Eddie said. He rolled his sleeves down and slipped on his jacket. They continued to make small talk until one of the guys whistled and pointed to the stairs. Tony stubbed out his cigarette. "Sounds like they're done."

They walked upstairs together. At the top, Tony said, "Nice meeting you, Staten Island. I'm sure we'll see each other again." He slapped Eddie's back. "I gotta practice my game."

Eddie pumped Tony's hand. "Sure thing."

As the men began to file out of the house, he searched for Sal. He found him at the opposite end of the room talking to a man whose back was to Eddie. As he approached, his uncle said, "I want you to meet someone."

The man turned. Tall, with dark hooded eyes and a broad face laced with a hint of mockery edging his mouth, he stared at Eddie and stuck out his hand. "Rocco Fischetti." His deep and guttural voice sounded as if he had a lump of gravel in his throat.

Rocco's palm swallowed his, squeezing it a bit too hard. Eddie struggled to speak. His words caught on the edge of his tongue. Heat shot through his body. Underneath his shirt, sweat raced down between his shoulder blades.

Sal slapped his back. "What's the matter? The man is speaking to you."

Eddie drew in a sharp breath. He needed to pull it together. Pumping Rocco's hand, he said, "Eddie Marconi, nice to meet you."

Rocco let go. He pointed his finger and said, "Have we met before?"

Eddie shook his head. "No ... I don't think so." His insides twisted. He couldn't take his eyes off the man who murdered Pete, his name legend. Rocco, 'The Reaper' Fischetti. If someone needed to disappear, you called Rocco.

Sal pulled his arm. "Time to leave, kid."

The hours dragged on the ride back to Staten Island, making Eddie restless. His uncle had informed him the meeting went well but didn't divulge any details. Only all the noise he had heard from upstairs might dispute what Sal said.

Sal dialed Eddie's Aunt Theresa, letting her know they were on their way home. After he hung up, he discussed some details with Jimmy regarding money laundering from his businesses.

Drained from the day's events, Eddie remained silent. He examined his hand, still feeling Rocco Fischetti's grip, the strength, and the power behind it. It was well over a week with no word from Brazo, the gnawing inside his stomach telling him the odds were he'd never see his friend again.

He glanced over at Sal. A question lingered on his mind. Did his uncle know what happened to Brazo, and if so, did he give the order?

Chapter 9 — Monica
Something Is Off

Ann Walsh burst through the door just as Monica and Cookie were taking a break. Her short, blond hair hadn't seen a comb. A navy sweater above dark jeans sagged on her thin frame. Bloodshot eyes and puffy lids added to her crazed look.

They knew Ann from high school, but she never looked this bad. She marched up to Monica, her leather purse sliding down her arm and landing with a thud on the floor.

"Where's Eddie?" she demanded, her right foot tapping rapidly up and down.

Monica, a little taken aback by the outburst, stared her down. "Well, hello to you too, Ann."

Cookie giggled. Snapping her gum several times, she reached and picked up Ann's purse. "I think you dropped something."

Without acknowledging her, Ann snatched the purse. "Well, where is he?"

Monica, arms folded, stepped closer to Ann. "Do you think I follow him around all day? How the hell should I know where Eddie is right now?"

Ann slumped, her rigid posture deflating like a leaky balloon. Tears pooled in her eyes, spilling over onto her cheeks. "I'm sorry, Monica. I didn't mean to yell at you. It's just … I haven't heard from Tommy."

Cookie's bat-winged eyes fluttered. "You and Brazo? You've got to be kidding me."

Ann, ignoring her again, wiped at her tears. "Tommy is missing."

"What do you mean missing?" Monica asked.

"He hasn't come around or called since the day of Pete's wake."

"Well," Cookie cut in. "Maybe he dumped you. Tommy's not known for staying with one chick too long. That man's pecker hunts females down like a dog in heat."

Ann balled her fists, her body rigid again. "Shut up, Cookie! You have no idea what Tommy and I have together. He's in love with me."

Cookie threw up her hands and backed away. "Okay, if you say so." When Ann faced Monica again, she twirled her index finger near her temple and mouthed 'crazy.'

"Look," Monica said. "I don't know where Eddie is. Did you go by Tommy's place?"

"Of course. I have a key." She unzipped her purse and pulled out a cell phone. "This is Tommy's. I found it in his bedroom. He doesn't go anywhere without it, plus his car is parked in the garage."

"What about his father or his sister? Did you check with them?"

"No. They weren't on speaking terms. His father and sister moved to North Carolina. I don't have their telephone numbers. But I know Tommy and Eddie are close. That's why I need to talk to him."

Monica grabbed her cell from the counter. "Let me try calling." She listened to the ringing on the other end. Eddie's voicemail came on. "Eddie, please call me as soon as you get this message. It's important." Her sixth sense started kicking in as if waking from a long rest. A slow burn hit the pit of her stomach. Tommy had been with Eddie the night of Brian Hanson's murder, and now Tommy had gone missing. Were the two connected somehow?

Monica studied Ann's tear-stained face. She reached out, touching her gently on the arm. "Here, enter your number in my cell. I'll call you as soon as I hear from Eddie."

Ann punched in her number. "Thanks, Monica. I just have this awful feeling about Tommy. He wouldn't leave me hanging like this."

Monica gave Ann a hug and a warning look at Cookie over Ann's shoulder. "Don't worry. I'm sure you'll hear from him soon."

The minute Ann closed the shop door, Cookie blurted out, "Seriously, Monica. Tommy Brazenetti? You know as well as I do the man can't keep his—"

"Stop, Cookie. Enough already. The poor girl is half out of her mind with worry."

"You got that part right," Cookie retorted. "She is half out of her mind if she actually thinks Tommy is in love with her."

"Jealous, maybe?"

Cookie stuck her finger into her mouth and made a gagging sound. They both burst out laughing. This was just one of the reasons Monica loved Cookie so much. She could put her at ease even in the middle of a serious moment.

Later, with Cookie gone, Monica prepared to close the shop. Her cell buzzed. It was Eddie calling.

"Wow, it's a good thing I'm not lying here bleeding," Monica quipped.

"Baby, I'm so sorry. I wasn't local."

"Where were you?"

"Just doing some business."

She gripped the phone tighter. "Yeah, okay, I know you can't tell me."

"I miss you, baby."

His voice, always so smooth, purred in her ear. "Listen, Eddie. I need to ask you something. Have you seen Tommy around?"

Silence greeted her. Seconds ticked by while she braced herself for his lie.

"Why are you asking about Brazo? I know he's not one of your favorite people."

"Ann Walsh came into the shop today hysterical. She claims he's missing. Do you know anything about that?"

"Ann and Brazo were tight for a bit, but he talked about breaking it off. He told me he wasn't ready to settle down with one person right now."

"Sounds familiar," Monica mumbled.

"What?"

"Nothing." She leaned against the counter, bracing herself for lie number two. "Ann went by his place. She even had his cell phone. You know he wouldn't just leave it there."

"Oh, that. Well, the truth is, he doesn't want contact right now. He's got a new phone and new number."

"In that case, give me the number so I can give it to Ann."

"Come on, Monica. You know I can't. If Brazo doesn't want to talk to her, I will respect that."

"Fair enough, Eddie. So, you're telling me he's okay?"

"Look, he skipped out for a bit, went to see his father and sister."

Monica bit her lip. Lie number three. "I thought they didn't get along."

"Seems they talked, and his father asked him to come for a visit."

"Then I guess he's in North Carolina."

"Yup," Eddie said. "Don't know how long he's gonna stay trying to make amends and all."

"Did he catch a flight?"

"Huh?"

"Ann said his car is still in the garage."

"Yeah, he flew."

"What should I tell Ann? She can't continue walking around in the state she's in."

"Tell her he's out of town and will be in touch soon."

Now he was turning *her* into a liar. But it was useless to keep pushing him. "Okay, but it probably won't make her feel any better."

"How about dinner tonight? Our special place. I need to see you."

"Sure. Meet you at Romano's in an hour." Romano's, the words had slipped out so easily. Memories of their many intimate dinners at the restaurant emerged. Once behind the wheel of her car, she pushed them away.

Instead, she thought about Brian Hanson and his untimely death. Eventually, Eddie would be ripe enough for her to turn him into an asset. If she had any chance at all to help the Bureau, she needed to dig and find something that would persuade him to go against his Uncle Sal.

It also meant agreeing to give their relationship another try. She would be the one he needed after things blew up.

A familiar sensation washed over her. A sense of duty and loyalty rooted within from the time she graduated training at Quantico. Those grueling weeks had made her forget everything else, including Eddie. Afterward, a new path was forged. One she was willing to follow and devote her life to until one awful incident swept everything away, making her swear she would never return to the Bureau even if they would have her back.

Her mind set, she dialed Danny's number. "I'll do it," she said. "We'll talk more tomorrow." She ended the call and drove to Romano's.

Chapter 10 — Uncle Sal
Taking A Hit

Sour expressions on their faces, Sal and Jimmy sat holding drinks their drinks. Jimmy knocked back the whiskey and got up from behind his desk. He poured another shot before turning to Sal.

"No disrespect, Sal, but I warned you. The Commission made no bones about how angry they were. Taking out a federal agent without permission goes against the grain with every one of the families."

Sal pinched the bridge of his nose, the tight band forming around his skull, squeezing harder. The feds had gotten one over on him and his crew. Their agent had made his way inside the organization by acting like a harmless idiot, leaving the associates and soldiers to trust him.

"What would you have me do? The guy had enough information to put me, my Capo, and some of my soldiers away." He gulped his drink and set the empty crystal tumbler aside. "I told them I needed to do it, but all I kept hearing was *aspetta, aspetta,* over and over again. Wait. Wait for what, Jimmy?"

"Rules are rules," Jimmy snapped. "They understand why you did it, but this puts us in a bad light. Things are not like the old days. We fly under the radar now. The other families would want you to keep your mouth shut and do time, just like anybody else."

"I ain't doing time for nobody." Sal huffed. "I acted in my defense.

His usually calm demeanor slipping, Jimmy got up and paced. "Yes, you did, but the icing on the cake was the funeral. The expensive casket, making a big show of things. That was a foolish thing to do, Sal."

"I disagree. The neighborhood sees me in a certain light. It wouldn't look right if I didn't do it for someone who was supposed to be one of my guys."

"I guess," Jimmy said, dropping down onto one of the leather chairs.

"The Commission will calm down. Any one of them would have done the same."

"Maybe, but what worries me is that we've heard nothing from the feds. I expected them to come knocking with an arrest warrant."

Sal stretched and cracked his knuckles. "That's because they got nothing on the hit. Could be a good thing."

"But there is no way they are going to let things lie," Jimmy countered. "Something's coming down the pike."

"What do you hear from your contacts?"

"Nothing, and I don't like it. Everyone has gone silent over this whole thing."

The sound of Sal's knuckles popping dominated the room. He hauled himself up from the sofa. "There is one other thing that needs taking care of … Little Frankie. He brought the fed in to work with his crew. Assured me he was a stand-up guy who wouldn't cause any trouble."

"Who do you want to do it?" Jimmy asked.

"Give it to Lorenzo. I can trust him to take care of things. One of his soldiers can be the button man."

Jimmy raised an eyebrow. "We talked about putting Eddie on Lorenzo's crew. You still want to go that route?"

"Definitely. Eddie needs to be in on this one. I have plans for him. This will tighten him up, make him a fast learner." Sal hesitated before continuing. "It's unfortunate he decided to go, rogue, the same night of the hit. I asked him to rough up Pete the week before I knew for sure he was FBI. Once it became definite, I had to act fast. Rocco did a decent job."

"Speaking of Rocco," Jimmy said. "No silencer? He's supposed to be a professional. The cops made a beeline to the place."

"I inquired about that. He said since the guy was an agent, he didn't want the hit to seem professional. Just a neighborhood robbery, you know, the noise from the gun and all."

"Not too smart, Sal. Anything that sends the cops racing to a scene isn't good. Eddie and Tommy were almost caught up in the middle of everything". Jimmy cocked his head. "Has Eddie inquired?"

"You mean about Tommy Brazenetti?"

Jimmy nodded. "Yes. They were very close."

"Not a word," Sal said. "Even after he came face to face with Rocco. It shook him a little, but he never said anything. I think it's a good sign. It means Eddie understands how things work."

"To some degree."

Sal's posture stiffened. "What do you mean?"

Jimmy got up again. "Come on, Sal. Sure, Eddie has broken a few bones and ruffed up some bums but nothing permanent."

"Eddie knows what comes with the territory," Sal said. "So, if you're asking, will he take someone out if necessary? My answer is yes. I wouldn't be moving him up if I thought differently."

"And Rocco? He's not the type to leave witnesses standing upright. Even this thing with Tommy could blow up if —"

"Never mind about Tommy. That's taken care of," Sal cut in. "As far as Eddie, Rocco knows he's my nephew. He gave me certain assurances."

Jimmy swallowed the last of his drink. "I hope you're right, Sal, for Eddie's sake."

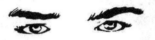

Chapter 11 — Eddie
Romano's with Monica

Eddie considered the day's events on the drive to Romano's. Becoming familiar with some other soldiers from the families was an eye-opening experience. He liked Tony Morello and hoped they would do some business together in the future.

Hearing the disturbance from upstairs had rattled him a bit especially after the others appeared not to react. But he guessed there were bound to be disagreements between the heads of the families. Moving up the ladder and becoming a soldier meant he needed to ignore such things, just as it had taken him some time to get used to obeying his uncle's orders. A beating when somebody owed money or needed straightening out soon became normal in his line of work.

At a red light, he tried to relax, but recalling his conversation with Monica about Ann Walsh and Brazo made it almost impossible. Ashamed he hadn't thought of his friend these past few weeks or what might have happened to him, he bit his lower lip and gripped the wheel. Should he have spoken up and asked his uncle about Tommy? But what then? Could he deal with the answer? Stop, he told himself. Enough. All he wanted right now was to be with Monica.

Arriving fifteen minutes early, he parked and went inside. The aroma of garlic, and onions, mixed with rich red gravy, greeted him. Dimly lit, the interior held tables covered in red checked cloths with candles in the center while soft Italian music emanated from speakers in the background. On a slow weekday evening, the restaurant was only half full. Delighted, Monica's and his favorite table by the window was unoccupied he seated himself.

His eyes rested on the long sleek bar on the far side of the room. Warmth spread through his body at the memory of the night he and Monica lingered at that bar for the first time.

They'd known each other since childhood and attended the same high school, but things didn't get serious until after graduation. The silly teasing between them slipped away. They had grown up overnight, and all he could see in front of him was the woman he wanted.

Lowering his eyes, he stared at the menu berating himself. Getting drunk didn't excuse how much he hurt her. After she left Staten Island for that job in Maryland, he almost lost his mind.

Surprised at her return, he had tried to convince her to give him another chance. His future included Monica. He didn't want anyone else. Once he was made and things settled a bit, he would buy her a ring. Show her proof of his commitment.

Eddie's thoughts were interrupted as Monica walked past the window and entered the restaurant. She smiled, shrugging off her light jacket, revealing a white silk blouse open at the neck, the front tucked into her tight jeans.

"I see you got our favorite table," she said, sitting across from him.

"Anything for you, baby." He reached for her hand, his fingers curling and kneading the soft skin beneath his fingertips before she pulled away. "How is everything at the shop?"

"Fine, except for that visit from Ann. I feel so bad for her."

"Yeah, me too. But I prefer to leave things between her and Brazo alone."

"But you weren't there. You didn't see how upset she was. I don't think she's going to let things go."

His muscles tensed. "What do you mean?"

"If she doesn't hear from him, I think she may report him missing. Get the police involved. You must try and get him to call her. Let him know how upset she is."

That's all he needed. Ann Walsh going to the police. "Sure thing. No worries. As soon as I hear from him, he can decide if he wants to reach out. If not, there's nothing I can do. Do you have her number?"

Monica dug inside her purse and pulled out her cell. "Here," she said.

Eddie entered the number into his phone. "I'll meet up with Ann and explain things."

Federico, a waiter familiar with the two, approached. He set a small basket of freshly baked garlic bread and a plateful of butter curls on the table.

"Nice to see you. It's been quite a while. What can I get for you tonight?"

"It's good to be back," Eddie said. He ordered a bottle of red wine and plates of pasta for the two of them. After the waiter poured the wine and left, he studied Monica's face. Flickering candlelight danced in her green eyes, those full lips beneath her high cheekbones captivating him. His gaze traveled to the hollow of her neck. Familiar territory, a path his lips had traveled so many times before. "I want us to be together again," he said, surprised at the hoarseness in his voice. "There is nobody else in this world I'd rather be with."

"What about Grace Scarfino?"

At the mention of Grace's name, his foot tapped the hard tile floor underneath the table. Why did she have to spoil things? He lifted his glass and gulped some wine. "Do you have to bring her up? It was one night. I got drunk. It meant nothing, Monica … you know that."

"So, what happens if you get drunk again and I'm not around?"

"Please, I'm trying to tell you how I feel. It will never happen again. I swear on my parents' graves."

"You can swear on all your dead relatives, Eddie. It still hurts. Did you know Grace came to me afterward, rubbing it in my face? I felt like a fool."

Unable to meet her eyes, Eddie glanced out the window. "I'm sorry she did that. I wish I'd never hurt you."

Federico set down two steaming plates of pasta and retreated. They both stared at the food until she broke the silence between them.

"Look, I'm willing to try again, but I want you to understand I still don't trust you."

Warmth radiated through his body. She had no idea just how much he needed to hear those words. The two of them together again was all he wanted. Elated, he said, "Baby, I promise you won't be sorry. I'll make it up to you. I'll prove you can trust me again."

This time she reached for his hand. "Okay, we start fresh … but remember, this is your last chance."

He brought her hand to his lips and kissed her palm. "I love you, Monica. Nothing will ever change that."

"I love you, too. Now let's eat before the food gets cold."

They ate and finished off the bottle of wine before ending up at Eddie's place. He closed the door behind them, pushing her up against it. Barely able to control himself, his lips pressed against hers, his tongue probing. She returned the kiss with such passion it almost took his breath away. He unbuttoned her blouse and cupped her breast. She moaned softly, and he led her to the bedroom. They tossed their clothes onto the floor. Lying naked on the bed, he trailed open-mouthed kisses down her neck and brushed his lips against her nipples. She arched her back and pulled him closer, his muscles tensing in anticipation.

"Oh God, how I missed you," he whispered, his body aching with longing. He could feel the heat from her skin against his own. He slipped inside her, their hips finding a familiar rhythm.

They made love twice that night, and a grateful Eddie slept peacefully for the first time in years, certain he could never be without her again.

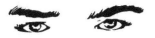

Chapter 12 —Monica

The Bureau

Monica exited the elevator onto the 23rd Floor of FBI Headquarters in Manhattan. Planting her feet firmly on the hard tile floor, she tugged at the collar of the black turtleneck attempting to strangle her and swore. Taking a deep breath, she proceeded to the reception area.

A middle-aged woman with streaks of grey in her dark hair sat behind a desk. "Monica Cappelino?"

"Yes."

"Assistant Director Acosta will be with you in a minute. Please have a seat."

"Thank you." Feeling her stature diminish at not being addressed as Special Agent, Cappelino, Monica shrunk down onto the stiff chrome and leather chair. The elevator doors chimed and slid open. Adrenaline shot through her body. For a split second, she considered fleeing back to Staten Island ... forgetting about the whole ugly business.

Her decision to try to turn Eddie had not come easy, and it wasn't set in stone yet. Regardless of his dealings with the mob, she still loved him. Changing how she felt about him was like trying to remove a tattoo. A faint scar would always remain no matter what happened. It all came down to what the Bureau offered in return. She was here to make sure they gave him the best deal possible.

"You can go in now, Ms. Cappelino."

Monica approached the heavy wooden door, its frosted glass panel emblazoned with 'Assistant Director in Charge Robert Acosta and stepped inside. The acidic smell of stale coffee from a small pot on a corner table greeted her. Light filtered in through half-open blinds trailing down the floor-to-ceiling windows on either side of a large desk.

Without glancing up from an open file, Robert Acosta waved his hand in her direction. "Please, sit." He stared at the file for a few more minutes before flipping it closed and smiling at her. "Sorry about that, Ms. Cappelino."

"No worries, sir," Monica said, noting this ADIC wasn't at all what she expected, his chiseled features and sculpted jawline catching her attention. Thick tufts of salt and pepper hair complemented his grey eyes. Bicep muscles bulged underneath the sleeves of his white dress shirt.

"We don't need to be that formal right now. Call me Bob, please. If you don't mind me addressing you as Monica, I'll do so."

"That's fine with me, sir … I mean, Bob."

He leaned back in his chair, lacing his fingers behind his head. "I was examining your file. Your Phase 1 testing results were off the charts. No problems at Quantico, but a very, if short, distinguished career. After reading the full report, I'm not so sure they treated you fairly."

A cold wave swept her body. She knew the deal. Be nice to the disgraced agent so you can reel her in and get what you want. "I'd rather not relive the past," she said. "I'm here about Edward and Salvatore Marconi. From what I was told, you're asking me to—"

"Please, stop right there." Bob's tone became stern. "I prefer we don't get off on the wrong foot."

"The wrong foot? Sorry, Bob, but I got the foot and the whole boot the day they let me go. Now, when you need my help, it seems perfectly fine for you to want me to come in and cooperate."

"I get it," Bob said. "You're bitter, and you have every right to be. After reviewing your file, I wanted to tell you something doesn't fit."

Monica fell silent. Had she judged him too quickly? "How's that?"

"You did an excellent job working your last case. Everything by the book. It doesn't make sense why you would have asked Agent Wilson to meet you in the field. Profilers work mainly inside. It's a rarity for one to be out in the field in pursuit of a suspect."

"That's just it," Monica said. "I never did."

"Only it says in your file the text message to Agent Wilson came from your cell phone."

"I believe my phone was hacked."

His gaze fixed on her, he said, "Yes, you claimed that in your report, but we couldn't find any proof."

Monica averted her eyes and waited. No use hearing old news again. They didn't believe her then, so why try to convince him otherwise?

"You and Agent Wilson worked closely together for many months. One of our best profilers, he enabled us to close an enormous number of cases. His passing was an immeasurable loss to the Bureau."

"Yes," Monica said. "But we were also good friends. My confidence grew partly because of Agent Wilson and what he taught me."

"About case work?"

"Yes, of course, but ..." How could she explain that Jack Wilson had helped her hone in on her sixth sense, teaching her to put it to practical use in the field, saving her life more than once.

"But?"

Stephanie Baldi | 67

"Nothing. Let's just say I still value what I learned from him," she said.

"There is something else I'm curious about. How is it that Eddie Marconi is unaware of your past as an FBI agent?"

"When we broke up, I wasn't with the Bureau. He had no idea I was even thinking about joining. I told him I was leaving Staten Island to take a job in Maryland. After the Bureau let me go, I returned home and opened my shop. There was no reason to discuss being a former agent with him or anyone."

Bob unlaced his fingers and leaned forward. "Look, I know our wanting Eddie to become an asset with you as his handler is a big deal."

His words struck a nerve. The image of Brian Hanson lying in a coffin flashed through her mind. "To be honest, at the time Special Agent Gage first came to see me, I was unaware of the circumstances surrounding Agent Hanson's death. I had no idea he was working undercover for the Bureau. A loss like his knocked the wind out of me, just as it did with Agent Wilson."

"But, before we go any further," Bob said. "I need to know where things stand between you and Eddie Marconi. Special Agent Gage has informed me of your history with him."

Just the mention of Danny's name made her want to scream, but she kept her emotions in check. "Until recently, Eddie and I were no longer in a relationship."

"Meaning?"

"I won't lie and say I don't have feelings for him, but my loyalty to the Bureau is still strong even after everything that happened. I want Salvatore Marconi to pay for what he did, and I want Eddie far away from him. The best way to accomplish this is to turn Eddie. It also means agreeing to a romantic relationship with him again, which I have already done, but I need certain assurances from the Bureau."

"Lay all your cards on the table, Monica. I'll see what I can do."

A tightness crept across her chest, causing her to shift uncomfortably in the chair. If he disagreed with her demands, there was no use in going any further.

"I want full immunity for Eddie and witness protection. If he succeeds, he'll have a target on his back both out on the street and inside."

"That's a big ask, Monica. We know all the illegal things Eddie's involved in for his uncle. A reduced sentence is a real possibility."

Monica shook her head and got up. "Sorry, that's not an option, Bob. Those are my terms. I know Eddie is a criminal, but he's also a bit naïve. I'm sure you know his backstory. Being pulled into Organized Crime when a mob boss raises you is almost a given. Eddie loves his uncle, but he's in over his head. I want to try and change the odds for him. Deep down, he's a good person. He just got swallowed up by Salvatore Marconi."

Bob pointed to the chair. "Please, Monica, sit down."

Monica eased into the chair, folded her arms, and waited for his response. No way would she negotiate anything less for Eddie. It was terrible enough lying and agreeing to give their relationship another try while knowing what she had consented to do for the Bureau if they met her terms.

"You're driving a hard bargain, Monica, but we need to make things right for Agent Hanson and his family. I'll draw up the paperwork and have it ready by next week. You can come in to review it. Everything will be in place."

"Thank you," Monica said. "You do understand this is going to take time. Eddie loves his uncle."

"Yes, I do."

Monica rose to leave.

"Wait a minute," Bob said, reaching into a desk drawer. He slid a small black leather badge holder across the desk. "I believe this belongs to you."

Monica's eyes watered as she picked it up. Feeling the smooth leather beneath her fingertips, she flipped it open. Her gold badge and photo ID were inside.

"Welcome back to the Bureau, Special Agent Cappelino."

Chapter 13 — Eddie
Secrets & Lies

Eddie strolled into the Sunrise Diner on Richmond Avenue. The pungent odor of greasy hamburger meat frying on the grill hung in the air. Servers scurried about carrying trays of food while the cook shouted ready orders. With the lunch rush underway, people occupied every seat at the long counter.

Ann Walsh was nowhere in sight, so he slid into the only empty booth and picked up a menu.

"Hey, Eddie," a woman called out.

He recognized that voice and could feel the flush sweeping across his cheeks. Of all the places he chose to meet Ann, he had to run into her. Keeping his face neutral, he glanced up.

"Oh, hi, Grace."

Grace Scarfino winked and gave him a wicked smile. A lock of her thick blonde hair fell seductively over one eye. "Haven't seen you around in quite some time."

"You work here now?" Eddie asked.

Without breaking eye contact, she trailed her index finger down the open neckline of her uniform to her cleavage, letting it linger for a second.

"Obvious, isn't it?"

He set the menu down. "Yeah, right. In that case, I'll have the pastrami sandwich and a coke."

She scribbled on her pad. "Why so cold, Eddie?"

"Look, Grace, let's not travel back in time. We were both drunk. It didn't mean anything."

She leaned down, exposing the scalloped blue lace running across the top of her bra. "I don't recall either of us being drunk all those other times."

Averting his eyes, he drummed his fingers on the table, white heat building inside his body. This was the last thing he needed right now. "Like I said, it didn't mean anything."

"But it meant something to me." She slid into the booth across from him.

He clasped his hands and leaned in. "Why are you bringing this up? It was a long time ago. I don't want to hurt you. We had fun, that's all."

"And what about Monica?"

"Yeah, what about Monica? She told me you confronted her. What did you say?"

Swatting away the hair covering her eye, a forlorn look on her face, she said, "I probably shouldn't have done that. It's just …."

"Just what?"

"I fell for you even though you were still seeing her at the time. I was jealous, so I told her we slept together that night you got wasted."

Eddie slumped and rested his palms on the table. "You do know she dumped me right after that."

"Yeah, I could have said it was more than once, but I didn't."

"What do you want, a prize for keeping your mouth shut?"

Her face pinched. She slid out of the booth. "No, Eddie, I just wanted you. I mean … for us to be together."

He caught her hand. "Sit back down a minute, Grace."

Sinking into the booth again, she swiped a napkin from the holder and dabbed at her eyes.

"Look, I never meant for things to get so mixed up. I wasn't willing to commit to one person. Sorry if I gave you the wrong impression. I don't like seeing you upset."

Her voice, almost a whisper, she said, "And now?"

"I care for Monica more than anyone else. I'm ready to commit to her. I hope you'll understand and respect that."

She let out a sigh before getting up again. "Okay, Eddie. I guess I hoped your feelings matched mine. I kinda always knew Monica would win in the end." She fished out the order pad from her pocket.

"Anything else I can get you?"

"Just the pastrami on rye and a coke," he said, his tension easing.

After she left, he exhaled and relaxed. One down and one to go. He checked his cell phone for the time. Ann Walsh was late. About to dial her number, he stopped as she came toward him and sank into the booth.

Sallow skin held faint blue smudges below each of her eyes. Pale pink stained the white insides. A jacket and jeans hung on her rail-thin frame. She removed the jacket, exposing a green silk blouse. Her shoulder bones jutted out, reminding Eddie of a partially stuffed scarecrow needing straw.

Horrified at her appearance, he tried to smile. "Hey, Ann."

Grace set his order down, a curious look on her face. "Can I get you anything else?"

"No, nothing, thanks," Eddie said.

She focused on Ann. "What'll you have?"

"Water," Ann responded, a dry crack in her voice.

"You're sure?" Eddie said. "You should have something besides water."

Her head bobbed from side to side. "No, just water, please."

Grace left, returning a few seconds later. She glanced at Eddie before setting the glass in front of Ann. After she retreated, he began, "So, I realize you're upset about Brazo ... I mean, Tommy. But I want you to know he's perfectly fine. Things between him and his dad weren't very good for a long time, so he made it a priority to make amends."

He stared at his sandwich. Too guilty to take a bite, he sipped his coke.

Giving him a bewildered stare, she opened her purse and placed Tommy's cell phone on the table. "I find it hard to believe he forgot this along with his car."

A flutter struck his stomach. Eddie remembered locking the door to Brazo's place. Apparently, she had a key. "Look, Ann, Tommy has a new phone with a new number. He knew you would try to contact him. If I'm being honest, he doesn't want to talk to anyone while he tries to figure things out with his dad. He didn't take his car because he flew to North Carolina."

She chewed her lower lip and stared, her deep brown eyes boring into him like hot coals. "Liar."

"What?" Her aggressive manner caught him off guard. This was supposed to be a simple conversation to calm her down before she did something stupid.

"I said, you're a liar. Tommy would never do that to me. He would have told me where he was going."

Eddie swallowed some more coke. "I can't help it if he doesn't want to talk to you. If you give him some space, he'll reach out when the time is right."

"Look, Tommy is missing, and I think you're keeping something from me."

Ann could cause more trouble than he thought. If only she knew half of what had taken place and that he had no idea where Brazo was.

"I haven't any reason to lie. I told Tommy before he left that he should call you, but …."

"But what?"

"Well, this is kind of hard for me to say. He wanted to break things off, but he was afraid of how you would react."

Ann's eyes watered. "Break up with me?"

"Just temporarily. Like I said earlier, he needed some space."

Hands trembling, she lifted the glass of water and gulped two long swallows before setting it back down. "Are you in contact with him?"

"Not lately." For the first time, he told her the truth.

"What is that supposed to mean?"

"I haven't heard from him in a while."

"I'm guessing you have his new number. I would appreciate your giving it to me."

"No can do," Eddie declared. "He asked me not to give it to anyone. As his friend, I will respect that."

Her face flushed a deep scarlet. Grabbing the cell phone and shoving it into her purse, she pointed her finger at him. "You are a real son of a bitch, Eddie Marconi! I still don't believe a word you said. Tommy and I were making wedding plans. He wouldn't just skip out on me."

Now it was his turn to be shocked. Brazo had never mentioned any wedding plans to him. Could she be lying? Or maybe he didn't know his best friend as well as he thought, but this could play right into his hands.

"Sure, he told me," he lied. "That's part of what scared him. Tommy's not certain he wants to get married right now. He was afraid to tell you. He knew how much it would hurt you."

Slowly, Ann slid out of the booth. "You have twenty-four hours to have Tommy get in touch with me. Otherwise, I'm going to the police to report him missing."

"You don't want to do that, Ann. Tommy would be really upset."

"Not as upset as I am. Twenty-four hours, Eddie. I'll be waiting to hear from him." She whirled around and stormed out of the diner.

Holy crap! Now, what? If he didn't produce a call from Brazo, he was sure she'd make good on her threat to file a report. If she did, the cops would come snooping around, and who knew where that could lead? Maybe he should tell his uncle about the night Pete was murdered and how he had spotted the Lincoln in Brazo's driveway after the funeral.

His appetite gone, he pushed his plate away and got up. He tossed more than enough to cover the check on the table. Pretending not to hear Grace call after him, he left the diner and drove home. Things were on real shaky ground now. Ann going to the cops on one side and his uncle on the other. Only Eddie knew who he feared the most. Hands down, it was his Uncle Sal.

Chapter 14 — Monica

And So It Begins

Monica scrutinized the paperwork granting Eddie immunity and witness protection if he agreed to cooperate, but it didn't ease the knot in her stomach. The word betrayal had never crossed her mind until now.

"Everything in order?" Bob asked.

Monica handed him the paperwork. "Yes, sir, it is."

He gathered the papers into a neat pile and slipped them inside a folder. "I know this isn't easy for you, but you'll be doing your country a great service. At the same time, you'll save Eddie from having to go to prison one day."

"I know, sir."

"There's still time to back out if that's what you want." He tapped the point of his pen on the desktop, his face turning serious. "Look, I need to know right now if you have any reservations. I don't want this thing blowing up in my face down the line. Before this goes any further, I want your assurance you'll remain laser-focused and handle this as you would any other case."

Hands in her lap, Monica relaxed into the chair. Of course, she had reservations, but keeping her body language neutral during this conversation was essential. Agents were trained to interpret it. She must not allow him to read into her true feelings.

"As I stated before, sir, my loyalty is to the Bureau first. Eddie and I were over before any of this began. I want to try to keep him safe and get justice for Special Agent Hanson at the same time. I believe I can accomplish that so long as I have the full backing of the Bureau."

"Good to hear. It alleviates some of my concerns." Lifting the telephone receiver, he punched a button and said, "Peggy, would you send in Special Agent Gage." He smiled at Monica. "You'll be reporting to him throughout this operation."

Her composure slipping, Monica said, "Sir, I don't think …."

Before she could finish the sentence, Daniel Gage dropped into the chair next to hers. He crossed his long legs and gave her a wink. Insides boiling, she restrained herself from slapping the Cheshire grin off his face. Her life had just gotten even more complicated.

"I know you two have worked well together in the past," Bob said. "Daniel will be the Case Agent for this operation." He nodded at Danny. "You'll file an FD515 STAT Sheet every ninety days, which I will personally review. Whatever manpower and resources you need, I will try my best to provide. We'll cover Monica's background story about a job in Maryland, just in case. The company, Renco, contracts with the Department of Defense and deals in government engineering. They assess the reliability of our nation's power grid. You worked there as an Administrative Assistant, Monica, dealing with their engineers. Do a little research on them."

"Noted, sir," Monica said.

"Thank you, sir," Danny said. "I'm sure between Special Agent Cappelino and me, we will be able to gather enough evidence to nail Salvatore Marconi."

Bob stood, signaling the meeting was at an end. "I am counting on the two of you."

They rode the elevator in silence. Stepping out onto the lobby, Monica made a beeline for the exit. "Wait," Danny called out, running to catch up.

Ignoring Danny, she moved through the automatic doors and out into the busy street, almost colliding with him when he stepped in front of her. Her hands curled into fists. "Move!"

"Look, I know you're not happy about my involvement in all of this, but you have to admit, as Bob said, we did work well together in the past."

"That doesn't matter now. I don't want to work with you on this case, but since I have no choice, I'm stuck." At her words, his eyes darkened with pain.

Danny shoved his hands into the pockets of his pants and rocked back slightly on his heels. "I'm sorry you feel that way, Monica. But we have to find a way to do this without ripping each other apart all the time."

Silent, she stared down at the cracks in the sidewalk. He was right. No matter the history between them, they owed it to Brian Hanson to build a solid case.

"Okay, you're right. No more bickering." She observed his body relax and remembered what they once had together. Danny had brought comfort at the time she needed it the most. Getting over Eddie and focusing on her career back in D.C. hadn't been easy.

They moved along a path with trees on either side away from the building and sat on a bench.

"I know you never really cared about me back then," Danny said.

"That isn't true. I did care only …."

His eyes glistened. "I get it, Monica. You weren't in love with me. That's why I broke things off. I was falling hard and knew you didn't feel the same way." His chiseled face drooped.

"But you became so mean, Danny. I never really understood why."

"I know. I was angry at you for *not* falling in love with me. I did some stupid things that looking back now, I regret."

A strange flutter hit the pit of her stomach. "Like what."

"Never mind," he said, avoiding her eyes. "None of it matters. I can't go back and change the past."

She grew uneasy. What exactly did he regret? But she could tell no amount of probing would make him reveal anything.

Easing up from the bench, she said, "Listen, Danny, I'm willing to put everything aside. I'll be under enough pressure just trying to turn Eddie." She held out her hand, but instead of shaking it, he stood and kissed her lightly on the cheek.

"I promise I'll help in any way I can," he said. "As former Case Agent for Brian Hanson, I need to make this a win. We'll get the son of a bitch."

Turning away, he walked back toward the building. Monica waited until he disappeared inside. Later, she stood against the railing on the Staten Island Ferry, salty air filling her lungs. Danny's words about having regrets haunted her. He was hiding something.

Chapter 15 —Ann

Trying to Find Answers

Ann took a sip of hot tea from a brown glazed mug. She glanced down at the plate of food in front of her. The sight of thick brown gravy sliding off mash potatoes, snaking its way toward the chicken and green beans, nauseated her. Unable to tolerate it any longer, she set her mug down, got up, and tossed the food into the trash, the empty plate landing with a clatter in the sink.

Her mother, father, and brother had gone out earlier. Thankful she was alone in the house, she grabbed the mug before retreating to her bedroom. Setting it on the nightstand, she collapsed onto the bed.

She didn't believe Eddie's story for one minute. Something horrible had happened to Tommy. No one would listen to her. Her parents had never liked him, so they brushed the whole thing off. Because of his involvement with Eddie and his Uncle Sal, they urged her to stay away from him.

How can I stay away from someone I love? Tommy was her first serious boyfriend. All the others before him didn't count. Sure, he had her promise not to tell anyone how serious their relationship was, about the future, of them getting married one day.

She missed his passionate kisses, the feel of his arms wrapping around her naked body after they made love and the unexpected gifts of jewelry and flowers along with weekends away. There wasn't any inkling of him having second thoughts about the two of them.

The last time they spoke, the morning of Pete's funeral, he even hinted at a ring. He talked of making things permanent between them, promising to sit down with her father to convince him he would take good care of her. Holding up her left hand, she scrutinized her naked finger. Tommy wouldn't lie. If there was a ring somewhere, it meant he was telling the truth.

Bolting up from the bed, she slipped on her jacket. Racing down the stairs, she left the house and drove to Tommy's place. Using her key, she slipped inside. Now, where would Tommy hide a ring? He wouldn't have wanted her to find it while the two of them were together. Starting in the kitchen, she checked every cabinet and drawer, even peeking inside a cereal box. She moved on to the main bedroom.

Throwing open his closet, she paused at the potent scent of his cologne lingering in the air. Her hands moved over the rows of shirts and suit jackets, checking pockets along the way. Too short to reach the shelf above, she hauled a chair from the kitchen. Climbing on top, she opened numerous shoe boxes but produced nothing.

Hopping down off the chair, she searched his dresser. She was about to give up until her fingers touched the smooth velvet of a small box in the bottom drawer. It lay underneath a pile of socks in the farthest corner. Sitting cross-legged on the floor, she lifted it out, her heart galloping so fast blood rushed to her head. Too scared to open the delicate burgundy box, she stared at the palm of her shaking hand. Minutes ticked by until, finally, she lifted the lid.

A nerve quickened in her throat at the sight of a large oval-cut diamond surrounded by rows of smaller diamonds set in a platinum band. Tommy *was* going to propose. All those talks about him wanting her to move into his house and her refusal to do so until he made things permanent had worked. She wouldn't live with him until she became his wife. A tear slid out the corner of her eye and down her cheek, blurring the ring. She snapped the lid closed and returned the box to its place beneath the pile of socks.

Convinced more than ever that Tommy wasn't visiting his father, she got up from the floor. Clearly, she was the only one who cared about him. She wouldn't let Eddie or anyone else deter her from finding Tommy.

Behind the wheel of her car again, Ann drove away and sped up the block. Fifteen minutes later, she pulled up in front of the 121st. Precinct. Uncle Richie would know exactly what to do.

Chapter 16 — Monica

Case Files

Monica collapsed into the chair behind her desk. It was after seven o'clock. The shop had been closed since six.

Turning to the computer screen, she logged into the FBI case files on Organized Crime in the Criminal Investigative Division and prepared for the worst. Gingerly, she typed in Salvatore Marconi's name. She had never pulled up his file during her previous time with the Bureau. Not being a part of the CID, she kept her curiosity at bay.

Too many memories of Eddie would surface. Besides his cheating, Salvatore Marconi had been another reason for her breaking things off with him. She never liked him working for his uncle but couldn't convince him to quit. If she had given him another chance, would his association with his uncle have broken them up anyway?

Over the next few minutes, the screen filled with file after file reaching back at least ten years. She huffed and tapped her chin. Opening the first file, she ignored his photograph and read.

Knowledge was power. She knew in order to turn Eddie, absorbing everything the Bureau had on his uncle was paramount to her success. Several hours later, blurry-eyed and with a pounding headache, she logged out.

It appeared Salvatore Marconi was up to his neck in illegal gambling, loansharking, extortion, racketeering, and suspicion of murder. So far, the Bureau had produced enough evidence to bring charges on some of those counts, but the murder of Agent Hanson had become a top priority now.

Monica understood tenfold how important it was that she turn Eddie into an asset. He would be the key to unlocking the evidence they needed to indict and prosecute his uncle. With a click of the mouse, she shut down her computer. Today she had peeked into Salvatore Marconi's world. But something gnawed at her. Monica studied the dark monitor screen. Almost involuntarily, she reached, switching the computer on again. She logged on for the second time, pulling up the Bureau's files on Organized Crime. She typed in Edward Andrew Marconi.

Several files popped up. Not nearly the number his uncle had, but nevertheless, there they were. She clicked on the first one. A black and white photo of Eddie's face stared back at her. Her eyes traveled down the screen. Eddie was listed as the nephew of Salvatore Marconi and a known associate of the Marconi Crime Family. Some background information concerning the death of his parents along with a few small details were also in the file. Tommy Brazenetti was also mentioned as one of Eddie's closest associates.

Monica clicked on the next page. With every word she read, a weight pressed tighter on her chest until she forced herself to stop reading. Pushing back from the desk, she stared at the computer screen and sucked in air.

Was this *her* Eddie? The man she still loved and cared for. How could he do such despicable things? There were reports of extortion and beatings. One so bad a man lay in a hospital unconscious for several weeks.

She had wanted to believe Eddie only did trivial things for his Uncle Sal, pushing away thoughts of what Eddie might be capable of doing. Her love for him made her ignore the ugly side of his life. Pain surged through her body. She stood, glancing around, looking for some form of relief. But there was none to be found. Why did she have to fall so hard for someone like Eddie? Dropping back down into the chair, she logged out and switched off the computer again, afraid if she read anymore, she would be unable to face him.

Her eyes closed as Agent Hanson's face appeared, along with memories of the night he died. Eddie had said he and Tommy were only going to scare him. Could they have had orders to kill him, not knowing someone else would get to him first? And where the hell did Tommy disappear to?

The wail of a passing siren outside the shop made her jump. She opened her eyes. Her cell buzzed, and she picked it up without checking the number.

"Hey babe, where are you?"

Her eyes misted over at the sound of his voice. Numb from reading files, she sank into a thick syrupy fog.

"Monica? Are you there?"

"Yes … yes, I'm here."

"What's wrong? You sound funny."

She thought of Agent Hanson again … what doing his job had cost him. Nothing was going to deter her from doing hers. Not even Eddie. "I'm fine, just a bit tired."

"Where are you? I miss you."

"Still at the shop. I had some bookkeeping to do. I'm leaving for home now."

"Okay, meet you there."

He hung up before she could answer. Monica grabbed her purse, set the alarm, and trudged out the door, locking it behind her. A bit unnerved, she thought she would have a day to let things settle before seeing him. When she pulled up, Eddie was sitting on the front steps. Grinning from ear to ear, he stood and walked over to her.

"I think you should give me a key," he said, planting a light kiss on her lips.

She needed her space, so giving him a key was out of the question. "We'll talk about a key after I see how things go."

His mouth drooped. He pulled her close, his arms tightening around her. "Things are going to go fine. You'll see.

Now, are you gonna invite me in, or should we give your neighbors a sidewalk show?"

"Very funny." Monica broke free and climbed up the front steps. Once they were inside, she went about switching on the lights.

"Had dinner yet?" he asked.

Realizing she hadn't eaten anything since early afternoon, she pointed to the kitchen. "No, all the meats frozen. I can offer you breakfast for dinner. Scrambled eggs, okay?"

"We'll order in. How about Chinese food for a change? I'll call Ming's Restaurant."

An hour later, they sat at the small kitchen table with plates of Kung Pao Chicken, steamed dumplings, vegetable fried rice, and two glasses of Riesling.

Monica studied Eddie as he slipped a dumpling into his mouth. Reading his file had forced her to accept that the Eddie she cared about was also the Eddie suspected of committing heinous crimes. But if any of this was going to work, she needed to get her act together. Training had taught her that in order to get the job done, she had to travel in Eddie's shoes and operate in his world. It was the only way to move forward.

"You must like what you see," Eddie said, breaking into her thoughts. He gave her a teasing smile.

"What?"

"You've been staring at me so hard, I almost feel like a criminal in a line-up." He burst out laughing before sliding his hand across the table, his fingertips touching hers.

"I like watching you," Monica said. "Right now, I'm happy knowing we're trying to work things out."

Eddie raised his wine glass. "Here's to working things out."

Monica followed suit. "Yes, to working things out."

They finished eating and retreated to the living room. Eddie stretched out on the sofa, his head in her lap. She swept her fingers through his dark hair. His eyes closed, and he let out a deep sigh.

"You know I love you more than anything else in this world," Eddie said, his voice a whisper.

"I love you too," Monica said.

Later, while he lay sleeping, she took comfort in the gentle whir of his steady breathing and the innocent expression on his face. He could have been anything else than the man he had become. In the past, she had tried hard to convince him he didn't need his Uncle Sal. Almost any career he wanted could be his if only he would apply himself.

But Salvatore Marconi had sealed Eddie's fate a long time ago. Sometime soon, she would make sure his would be sealed as well.

Chapter 17 — Ann

The Precinct

Ann's stomach pitched and rolled as she walked into the 121st Precinct. Pushing her hand through strands of unwashed hair, she marched up to the front desk.

A young red-haired officer glanced up from a computer screen. "How can I help you, Miss?"

"I'm looking for my ... I mean Detective Richard Walsh."

"What do you want to see him about?"

Her throat threatened to close, but she forced the words out. "I need to report a missing person."

"There is a twenty-four-hour waiting period before you can file. How long have they been missing?"

"I'm not exactly sure. Can you please see if Detective Walsh is here? I'm his niece, Ann."

Ten minutes later, Ann sat with her uncle in a small office down the hall from the main entrance. Teary-eyed and shaking, she told him about Tommy.

Six-foot-two Richard Walsh smoothed his thick mustache. His eyes sweeping over her, he leaned back into the hard wooden chair.

"Listen, sweetheart, I've heard all about you and Tommy from your folks. He's not the kind of guy they want you with. Unfortunately, I agree."

"But, Uncle Richie, you have to help. No one will listen. I love Tommy, and he loves me. I don't care what anyone else thinks. I need to know he's okay."

"You do know he's mixed up with some bad people. Anything could have happened to him, or maybe he's gone on the run."

Her frayed nerves jangled at his words. "No, Tommy wouldn't leave without telling me. I know that for a fact."

"How? You can't be sure, Annie girl."

Annie girl was what he used to call her when she was little. She could tell he wasn't taking her seriously. "Yes, I can. We were going to get married. I even found the ring he was going to give me."

His relaxed demeanor changed. "Where? What are you talking about?"

"I went to his house with the key he gave me. His car is still in the garage. I also found this." She reached into her purse and handed him the phone.

Richie glanced at the cell phone. "Do you know how dangerous that was? Going to his house when you know he might be missing was a foolish thing to do."

"But —"

"But nothing. Listen to me, young lady. You are not to go back to that house."

At his outburst, Ann's body shook. Her chest heaved. She let out a wail, tears flowing freely down her sunken cheeks.

Richie knelt in front of her. "Listen, sweetheart. You can't go on like this. I promise you I will investigate, but you must do something for me first."

Ann drew a tissue from her purse and wiped at her face. "What's that?"

"I need you to promise you'll stay away from Tommy's place." He held out his hand and motioned to her purse. "The key."

She dug inside, placing the key in his palm. "Are you going over to Tommy's?"

"Never mind what I'm going to do," he said. "Have you spoken to anyone else about this?"

"Yes. Eddie. Eddie Marconi." She caught him flinch but dismissed it at once. "Eddie claims Tommy flew to North Carolina to make amends with his dad. But I don't believe him. Tommy would have mentioned it to me. He hardly ever talked about his father and sister."

"Eddie is another person I'd advise you to steer clear of," Richie said. "He has a reputation in this neighborhood. We know for a fact that he's involved in some shady things. I don't want you talking to him anymore."

"I only spoke to him because Tommy is his best friend. I thought he might be able to help me."

"Like I said, stay clear of him. Don't talk to anyone else about Tommy until you hear from me." Richie stood. Reaching for her hands, he eased her up out of the chair. "You go home. Get some rest. You're not looking so good, and that upsets me."

"You'll let me know if you find out anything?"

"Sure thing."

"Please don't tell my parents I came to see you, Uncle Richie. They're already upset with me, and I don't want to argue with them over Tommy."

"Sure, Annie girl. This stays between you and me for now."

Outside the precinct entrance, Ann's spirits lifted. Uncle Richie wouldn't let her down. She glanced at her left hand. Yes, Tommy would be home soon to give her that engagement ring.

Chapter 18 — Richie

Two, Four, Six, Eight, Let's Investigate

Detective Richard Walsh pulled up to Tommy Brazenetti's house. Using Ann's key, he let himself inside.

A practiced eye told him things were okay—no signs of a struggle. Everything appeared to be in order, except for the fact Tommy was missing. He headed for the kitchen and out the door leading into the attached garage. Tommy's car sat idle.

Richie yanked the driver's side door handle, and it opened. His eyes scrutinized the empty interior. He reached and popped the trunk. He had witnessed first-hand numerous dead bodies of those connected to or on the outs with the mob.

Afraid of what he might find, he inched his way around to the vehicle's rear. The trunk was empty. His trepidation eased. After slamming it shut, he did one last sweep before leaving the house.

Back behind the wheel, Ann's teary face swam before him. As much as he cared for her, he found relief in the fact Tommy appeared to be missing.

"Poor kid," he said out loud. She thought she was gonna marry the guy. Neither he nor his brother would have ever allowed it to happen. Tommy was connected, making him a totally unsuitable groom for his niece.

Driving along Forest Avenue, Richie couldn't believe his luck when he recognized Eddie Marconi's white BMW X6 ahead. He tailed him up a side street before switching on his flashing red lights.

Eddie cruised to the curb. Richie pulled in behind him and got out. He motioned for him to slide the window down.

Eddie appeared to be one step ahead, handing him his license and registration. "Why the pull over? What did I do?" he asked, glaring at Richie.

"Nothing yet, wise guy. We need to have a little talk."

"What about?"

Richie loved seeing him squirm a bit. He handed back the license and registration. "Tommy Brazenetti, for one thing. Mind stepping out of the car?"

Eddie exited the car. Arms folded, he leaned against the car door. The two eyed each other. Richie took note of the Rolex watch, the expensive clothes, and shoes. Things he'd never be able to afford.

Richie flipped open his badge and flashed it in Eddie's face. Pocketing the badge, he said, "When was the last time you saw Tommy?"

"At Scalito's for a wake."

"Did you talk to him at all after that?" Richie observed him hesitate.

"Yeah. He called me right before he left town for North Carolina."

"Were you aware of the relationship he had with my niece?" Almost imperceptible, except to the trained eye of a cop, he spotted the hard tightening in Eddie's jaw.

"Your niece?"

Yeah, Ann. Ann Walsh. Don't play stupid with me. You do know Annie, don't you?"

"Sure, from way back in High School."

"Annie tells me she asked you about Tommy and why he left so suddenly. Not a phone call or a text. Doesn't sound right to me."

"Look," Eddie said. "I can't control what Tommy does. It was a crappy thing to do. He got scared, is all."

"Scared?"

"Yeah, of the wedding plans Ann kept talking about. No disrespect, but she was pushing his back against the wall, if you know what I mean."

"So, he didn't have the balls to tell her?"

"Guess not. He told me he was gonna fly to North Carolina. His father and sister are there. Things haven't been good between them. He wants to try and mend the relationship."

"Seems funny he left his cell phone behind. I believe you told Ann he has a new cell. What's his number Eddie?" He expected him to hesitate, but he never missed a beat.

"I never told her I had the number. She must have heard wrong."

"Come on, Eddie. You're telling me he didn't give his best friend his number?"

"That's right, and I respect him for it. If he wants to get in touch, he'll call me."

Unable to restrain himself, Richie grabbed him by the front of his shirt. "If I check with his relatives in North Carolina and your story doesn't pan out, you will see me again." He stared down at Eddie's balled fists. "Go ahead. I would love it."

Fingers slowly uncurling, he smiled at Richie. "I know better."

The two were beginning to draw a small crowd on the sidewalk. Richie let go and stepped back. "Sure, you do. But I bet you're good at using your hands on some poor sucker for your uncle."

"Look, if you're not gonna arrest me, then I think I'll be going now."

"Not before I say one last thing. Stay away from Annie. No more talking to her about Tommy." Richie stalked off and got into his car. He waited until Eddie pulled away before taking out his cell phone. Punching in a number, he waited.

"Jimmy, it's Richie. Tell Sal Eddie passed with flying colors."

Chapter 19 — Monica
Dinner at Uncle Sal's

Monica pulled on a pair of tight black jeans and a red silk blouse. Sweeping her long curls away from her face, she secured them with a silver clip. A few strands trailed loosely down each side of her cheeks.

Tonight, she would be going to Salvatore Marconi's for dinner. Eddie expressed surprise that it took such little persuasion to convince her, was overjoyed. Little did he know, Monica had begun to play her part. Getting Eddie to turn meant inserting herself into his world. The closer she got to his uncle, the better.

She reached into her bottom dresser drawer, her fingers searching. Clasping her leather ID case and Glock 19M, she lifted both out and brought them to her walk-in closet. A small safe stood in the far corner. Used for securing cash from her shop when she couldn't make the drop at the bank right away, it would hold these two items until she needed them. She trusted Eddie not to snoop, but this made more sense. At this point, nothing must jeopardize the operation. If it did, she could end up like Agent Hanson.

Keeping her regular routine, she arrived at her shop every morning. Danny, so far, had kept his distance, communicating only by phone.

Her cell dinged. A text from Eddie. He was parked out front. She grabbed a black leather jacket and slipped into her heels. Outside, leaning against the BMW, dressed in jeans and a grey pullover, he pecked her cheek before opening the car door for her. They pulled away, headed for Sal's.

Eddie beamed at her. "Babe, you look amazing. Thanks for agreeing to dinner at my uncle's house."

Giving him her warmest smile, she squeezed his thigh. "Sure. No worries. You might as well get used to it. There will be many other dinners if things work out between us."

"Please don't keep saying if. Things *are* going to work out. You'll see."

They drove through the gates, parking in front of the house. Monica made a mental note of the two bodyguards stationed on the property. Eddie reached for her hand, and they climbed the steps together. He rang the bell and led her inside. The ornate foyer with marble floor and gold leaf wallpaper mural of pale palm leaves took Monica by surprise, their leafy fronds trailing up the wall by the massive staircase. Much had changed since her last visit here.

Gone were the elaborate life-size Greek statues standing against bright red walls, their feet planted on large black and white checked linoleum. Evidence of a professional decorator's touch appeared everywhere. A familiar aroma surrounded them. Gravy, of course, Monica thought.

His Aunt Theresa came rushing toward them. Tall and slender, the opposite of Sal, she glided into the room dressed in a tight pink sweater showing off her ample breasts, her white palazzo pants billowing as she came toward them. Her voluminous honey-colored hair, layered and teased to great heights, reminded Monica of eighties movies when women wore big hair and shoulder pads.

"Monica, it's so good to see you again. It's been such a long time. I'm so glad you came." Before Monica could respond, she leaned in, kissing her on each cheek.

"I'm happy to be here." She imitated Theresa's greeting.

They moved into the dining room, whose walls were painted a soft pale pink. Flowered fine china place settings graced the oblong Cherrywood table. Tall crystal wine glasses stood at attention beside the plates.

Theresa led Monica to a seat and had Eddie sit beside her. "Gina and Antonia will be down in a minute. They're home from college this week."

"It'll be good to see them again," Monica said.

"Dinner will be ready in a few minutes. I'll get the wine."

After she left the room, Eddie grinned and nudged Monica. "See, isn't this nice? Aunt Theresa is great."

"Very nice." She couldn't help but wonder if Aunt Theresa approved of what her husband did for a living. How much of these opulent surroundings were paid for by the blood of others?

Theresa returned with a bottle of red wine and poured them each a glass. Sal lumbered in behind her like the Incredible Hulk, with a large plate of pasta swimming in gravy which he set in the middle of the table. Eddie got up, and they bear-hugged.

Sal grinned at Monica. "There she is!" His voice boomed across the room. "Why have you been such a stranger?"

He leaned and kissed her cheek. A sickening feeling washed over her as she called to mind the horrible things she had read in his file. All she wanted to do was see this man behind bars. "Just busy, I guess. It's nice to be here again."

Sal plopped down into a chair at the head of the table. Theresa left, only to return minutes later with two sliced loaves of garlic bread on a platter and a porcelain bowl loaded with meatballs, sausages, and green peppers.

Sal rocked back in his chair. He looked up at the ceiling. "Antonia! Gina! *Fretta, fretta!* Hurry before the food is cold."

Pounding footsteps proceeded their entry into the dining room. Identical twins, one could hardly tell the two apart if it weren't for the dyed short blonde hair Gina wore. On the other hand, her sister kept her long brown tresses. Both were dressed casually in t-shirts and jeans.

They greeted Monica and Eddie before seating themselves opposite them. Sal finished saying a short blessing and then frowned at Gina.

"I'm letting this hair thing go for now, but you had better dye it before you return home from college again." He gestured toward Monica. "See how beautiful she is. She keeps the hair God gave her. It looks healthy, not dull and brassy like yours."

Monica cringed. That wasn't exactly the truth. Once a month, she went to the beauty salon for added highlights.

Turning a deep shade of red, Gina swept her hands through her hair. "I wanted a change. I've gotten lots of compliments on it at school."

"You're not there for compliments, Gina," Sal bellowed. "You are there to learn. Do you have any idea what it's costing me for the two of you?" Grabbing a slice of garlic bread, he dipped it into the sauce on his plate before devouring it in two bites. "I said, dye it back."

Theresa quickly directed the conversation elsewhere. "So, Monica, how are things down at the shop?"

"Good. I have always wanted to be a florist. I especially enjoy helping brides pick out their arrangements."

"Speaking of brides," Antonia said, nodding toward Eddie. "What gives with the two of you? You've known each other for so long, and still no engagement."

Eddie smirked. "I've got plans. I'll know when the time is right." He gave Monica a wink.

Monica, silent during the exchange, slipped another fork full of pasta into her mouth. Great, Eddie has plans. She pictured him proposing and gulped some wine. That would be all she needed, him down on one knee with a ring. *Monica, will you marry me? Sorry, Eddie, no can do because I need you to help me put your uncle away for good.*

Silent as a serpent, Jimmy Galante slithered into the room. He gave Sal a nod, said hello to everyone, and eased into a chair. He eyed Sal. "Sorry to be so late. I had some pressing business to attend to."

Monica observed the look between the two men. It wouldn't be long before they excused themselves from the table.

"I remember when you were just a high school kid hanging around here, Monica," Jimmy said.

Monica drank the last of her wine and set the glass down. "Yeah, that was ages ago."

"Didn't you disappear for a while? Eddie was heartbroken. Where did you go?"

Monica's hands clenched the cloth napkin in her lap. He was poking the bear, but she couldn't let him get a rise out of her. As Consigliere, part of Jimmy's job included poking. It came naturally to him.

"I had an opportunity for a job out of New York State. It didn't work out. But it was just as well." She brushed her hand along Eddie's cheek. "I missed this guy too much, plus I saved enough to open my flower shop. Things ended up turning out for the best."

Jimmy stared at her a moment before saying. "Lucky you."

As she predicted, Sal and Jimmy excused themselves ten minutes later. Something was up. If only she could be privy to their conversation.

The rest of the meal was filled with idle chatter. The girls helped Theresa clear the table while Monica excused herself to go to the bathroom. A small powder room lay at the end of the hall. Monica slipped inside. To her surprise, although a little muffled, she could hear Sal and Jimmy talking. Leaning away from the sink, she pressed her ear to the wall.

"I told you this wasn't going to go away, Sal. The families are angry."

"They'll calm down after a while," Sal responded. "If necessary, I'll call another meeting. Convince them I was right."

"At least the news about Eddie was good," Jimmy said. "He kept his mouth shut."

"I had no doubts at all, Jimmy. Eddie is no snitch. I'm gonna make all the arrangements for the ceremony."

Monica's heart skidded. Unfortunately, she couldn't stay in here any longer before arousing suspicion. She washed her hands before easing out the door. Turning back up the hallway, she came face to face with Jimmy Galante.

Cold hazel eyes peered at her from behind wire-rim glasses while his false smile spiked her adrenaline. A shudder ran through her.

"Nice seeing you again, Monica. I'll have to come by your shop one day."

"You're welcome to come anytime."

"I should hope so." He adjusted his glasses and continued up the hallway.

She glanced over her shoulder—what a smug prick. If the Bureau got lucky, they might be able to indict Jimmy too.

"There you are." Eddie came toward her. "I was worried you fell in."

"Very funny."

They said their goodbyes and drove to her place. On the way, the conversation between Sal and Jimmy played over again in her mind, making her certain her hunch had been correct. The so-called five families were upset over the hit on Agent Hanson. Sal never had their permission.

But she wasn't so sure about the remark concerning Eddie keeping his mouth shut. That could mean a million different things.

"Why so quiet?" Eddie said, breaking into her thoughts.

"Just thinking how nice tonight was."

His face broke into a wide grin. "See, I told you my uncle's not so bad."

Later that night, after making love and unable to sleep, Monica padded into the living room while Eddie slept. She stood at the window overlooking the park, her fingers sliding along the pale green curtain. Everything was falling into place. The ceremony Sal mentioned meant Eddie was about to be made. His vision of becoming a soldier would soon be a reality, setting things up perfectly for her to turn him.

Chapter 20 — Eddie

The Jersey Crew

Given orders by Sal to drive to New Jersey and meet up with a member of the Jersey Crew made Eddie wonder about the connection. On his way to the Newark-Elizabeth Seaport in Bergen County, Eddie mulled over his encounter with Ann's Uncle Richie. Just his luck, her uncle had to be a detective. It looked like he was turning up the heat about Tommy going missing. Now, he would have to mention this encounter to Uncle Sal. It was way past time for answers.

Anxious to become a made man, the restlessness inside him intensified. He didn't want to be his uncle's errand boy any longer but a true soldier in the family business.

Arriving at his destination, he spotted multiple rows of shipping containers stacked atop one another. He pulled into the designated spot, cut the engine, and waited.

Ten minutes later, a silver Lexus LS glided to a stop beside him. Eddie was relieved to see Tony Morello climb out of the vehicle wearing jeans and a black leather jacket zipped all the way up. He opened Eddie's passenger-side door and got in.

"Hey, Staten Island, good to see you. I wasn't sure who was coming."

"Good to see you too," Eddie said.

Tony unzipped his jacket and pulled out a thick envelope. He handed it to Eddie. "Here's the cut."

Eddie opened it and peered inside at a thick wad of cash.

Tony gave him a wink. "You wanna count it?"

"No reason to." He stuffed the envelope under the seat.

"Got time for a drink?" Tony asked. "There's a bar not far from here."

"Sure. I'll follow you."

Fifteen minutes later, with mugs of beer in their hands, they seated themselves at a corner table in a bar called the Stingray. The pungent smell of whiskey and beer permeated the air. A big screen tv hung on the wall over a long dark mahogany bar. Tuned to a sports station, the commentator rattled off the latest football scores. Except for two other men sitting at the bar nursing drinks, the place was empty.

They made small talk, with Eddie noticing Tony's frequent glances at a closed door at the back of the room.

"So," Tony said, "You like working for your uncle?"

"Sure. He's like a father to me. Raised me after my parents died. I was just a little kid."

"That must have been rough."

"Yeah, but I don't remember too much about them anymore. Except for … "

"For what?"

"Sometimes, I have this dream, more like a nightmare. Feels almost real."

"Maybe the trauma of losing them is still with you."

"I guess," Eddie said, wishing otherwise as he swallowed some beer.

Tony gave him a sly smile. "Listen, your uncle sure has balls doing what he did."

Eddie narrowed his eyes. "What are you talking about."

"Come on, you must know. That's why they called the meeting. The Commission wasn't happy about him going rogue. They called him on the carpet. You can't do stuff like that without permission."

Growing more confused and uncomfortable by the minute, Eddie downed the last of his beer and got up. "I need to get going."

"Hey, wait a minute." Tony motioned to the chair. "Sit down. That's no way to leave."

"Look, I don't like where this conversation is going. Whatever my uncle did, he did it for a good reason."

Tony's jaw dropped. "You don't know, do you?" He pointed to the chair again. "Come on, sit."

Eddie eased down into the chair, his eyes fixed on Tony's. "What don't I know?"

Tony surveyed the room. Leaning in closer, he said. "Look, I like you, Staten Island. I get the feeling you're a stand-up guy. I could get my head handed to me by telling you. I just assumed it was something you knew."

"Stop beating around the bush, Tony. If you have something to tell me, spit it out."

Tony swallowed some beer and set the mug aside. "Word is your uncle had a federal agent whacked."

Eddie tried to absorb Tony's words. A sharp pain hit the inside of his gut. The only person recently deceased was Pete. A resounding *no* thundered through his brain. No way Pete was a federal agent. He must be talking about somebody else.

"Who told you this? How do you even know it's true?" Eddie asked.

"I keep my ear to the ground. I got it from a reliable source. Come on. You heard the squabbling upstairs at the meeting. It really pissed off the Commission. Doing something like that draws too much attention. Besides, it could mess up the side action between Frank and your Uncle Sal."

Eddie was about to speak when the door to the back room opened. Tony motioned for him to stay quiet. Several men in business suits shuffled out. He recognized two of them from the meeting he attended with his uncle. Without speaking, they disappeared out the front door.

The last man stepped out, closing the door behind him. Tony's expression changed. Eddie recognized him right away. It was Frank 'the Razor' Uzelli. A hulking figure, tall and broad-shouldered with a hook nose, he chugged toward them, his grey-green eyes focused on Tony.

"You do okay, today?"

"Sure, Frank. Everything's good."

He eyed Eddie. "Sal's nephew, right?"

"Yeah." Eddie held out his hand. "Eddie Marconi."

His grip squeezing harder than necessary, Frank said, "Tell your uncle I was asking for him." He nodded at Tony. "You do the thing yet?"

"Not yet. I was just getting ready —"

"Ready for what? Round up two of your crew and get it done. The guy clipped 5Gs."

"Right away, Frank," Tony said.

Frank signaled the bartender and dropped down onto a stool. Outside, Tony whipped out his lighter. He shook a cigarette from a pack. Eddie caught the slight tremor in his hand as he lit up.

"Listen," Tony said. "I can't say any more about what your uncle did. Just know I have no reason to lie to you. Maybe it's better you don't mention it, either. It's done, and if repercussions occur, so be it."

"Repercussions? What are you trying to say, Tony?"

"I'm not. Like I said, forget about it for now." He took a deep drag on his cigarette, releasing a cloud of smoke into the air. "If your uncle didn't want you to know, it's probably because you're not made yet. Let it lie. I shouldn't have brought it up."

Eddie shoved his hands into the front pockets of his jeans. "Yeah, but you did."

"Look, I need to call two of my guys." Tony crushed his lit cigarette beneath his shoe and pulled out his cell phone.

While Tony talked, Eddie paced back and forth, trying to digest the news he'd been given. He believed Tony was telling the truth. There was no reason for him to fabricate a story about his uncle. Plus, he did remember hearing shouts coming from upstairs during the meeting. Dare he say anything to Uncle Sal? He wasn't naive. Murder was a part of the business. Things were said among the associates from time to time when certain people disappeared.

"You wanna come along, Staten Island?" Tony asked, interrupting his thoughts.

"Where?"

Tony gave him a wicked smile. "I'll show you how we do things in Jersey."

"Sure, why not."

"Leave your car here."

They climbed into Tony's Lexus and sped toward the New Jersey Turnpike. Twenty minutes later, they exited and stopped in front of a low brick building. Tony opened the glove box and removed a revolver. He unzipped his jacked and tucked it inside his waistband. As he followed him inside, Eddie tried to remain cool. At the end of a long hallway, Tony opened a basement door, and they descended the steps.

Eddie took in the scene before him. A man was sitting on a wooden chair, his hands and legs tied, his head hanging down. Two guys hovered over him, both wearing jeans and sweatshirts. One held a club in his hand. Hearing Tony approach, they turned.

"He's with me," Tony said, pointing at Eddie. "Wants to see how we work."

One of the men nodded toward the man tied to the chair. "We picked him up trying to place another bet with a different crew."

Tony shook his head and stared at him. "Some people never learn, do they, Jack?"

The man in the chair looked up. A purple bruise swelled above his eye, and blood dripped from his lip. "Please, Tony, I'll make good. Tell Frank I'll get him his money."

Tony pulled out his revolver. "That's what you said last week." Frank doesn't want to hear your excuses anymore." He placed the barrel of the gun on the man's temple.

Jack reared back. "Please, please, don't shoot me!"

"Don't worry. I'm not gonna pull the trigger. How would Frank get his money if I killed you?"

Tony gestured at the guy with the club. He reared back and swung it down onto Jack's kneecap. Jack let out a scream amid the sickening sound of bones breaking.

"Now, you listen to me," Tony snapped. "You get Frank his money by the end of the week, or the next time I see you, I'll put a bullet into your thick skull."

Tony backed away. "Untie him," he ordered. "Drop him off outside the emergency room." He signaled to Eddie, and they left the building.

Back inside the Lexus, Tony said, "So, Staten Island. You think I let him off too easy?"

"Not my call."

"I know the bum will turn up next week with only half the money."

"And then what?" Eddie asked.

Tony eyed him slyly. "What would *you* do?"

Eddie dug for the correct response. "Depends. If your boss is willing to accept half, then nothing. If not, you follow through on your threat."

"Good answer," Tony said, gliding to a stop in front of the Stingray Bar. "You gotta know your Capo like the back of your hand. I know mine pretty well. He'd never accept half."

Later, on the drive back to Staten Island, Eddie ruminated over the day's events. What would it mean if there were repercussions for his uncle? Would he lose territories or his life as punishment, and what did Tony mean by the side business between the two Under Bosses? Loyalty meant he needed to tell his Uncle Sal what Tony told him. It would be wrong to keep something like this to himself. As for the show Tony put on in the basement. That was nothing new. He had taken part in beatings of his own for his uncle. But Tony was a soldier. Soldiers had power, and he was right about one thing. You needed to know your Caporegime inside and out. What he would tolerate and what he would not. He pictured his uncle, *Zio* Lorenzo, his soon-to-be Capo. How much would *he* accept?

Chapter 21 — Cookie
A Good Catch

Cookie balanced the food tray on her arm like an expert, the weight evenly distributed to prevent it from tipping over.

Grabbing a tray stand, she set it down and delivered the salads and sandwiches to the two couples seated inside a booth.

She often waitressed at her father's restaurant on her days off from the flower shop. The Hummingbird Bar & Grill offered a simple lunch menu of soup and sandwiches before a heavier dinner menu starting at five. Black leather booths dotted the perimeter, with tables running down the center. The sweet, fruity scent of the domed layer cakes lining the counter mixed with the aroma of fresh coffee and cold-cut layered heroes.

Although Cookie didn't mind helping out, she found most days boring with the regulars coming in and making small talk. She also hated wearing the stiff white buttoned-up blouse with the restaurant's name embroidered above the pocket. Her father rolled his eyes when she shortened the hem of the black skirt to several inches below the top of her thigh. 'This isn't Hooters,' he had bellowed at her. After a ten-minute argument, Cookie's hem stayed up. Her father simply shook his head and walked away.

While picking up the empty tray and folding the tray table, she spotted a good-looking man sitting alone in a corner booth. Not her usual type, she found him intriguing. She could tell he wasn't from around here. Setting the tray down on an empty table, she smoothed her hair and unbuttoned the top button of her blouse.

She approached the booth and said, "Hi there, what can I get for you?"

He looked up from the menu. His square jawline relaxed into a welcoming smile.

Cookie swore he was the handsomest man she had ever come across.

"What would you recommend?"

"Our roast beef special is excellent and …" For the first time in her life, she was at a loss for words.

"Guess I'll have the roast beef since I don't know what the and is," he said, handing her the menu. "A fresh cup of coffee would be nice, too. Just black, please."

Cookie could feel a flush sweep her cheeks. What was wrong with her? She always had a wisecrack or quick comeback. "Sorry, busy day today. I'll put the order in right away." Making a beeline toward the kitchen, she imagined him staring after her. She glanced back for a brief second, and their eyes met. She was right, could always tell when a man's radar was up.

Watching him through the pass-through window, she admired his profile as he texted on his cell phone.

Cookie hadn't had a meaningful relationship in over a year. She found the local neighborhood knuckleheads uninteresting and unfit for marriage. Online dating had proved disastrous, so she would wait until someone worthy came along. Well, he could be Mr. Worthy. Her mind blasted into overdrive, trying to come up with a plan. She couldn't let this one get away.

Scooping up his sandwich, she returned to the booth and set it down. "I'll be right back with your coffee, sir." Score, she thought—no wedding band on his finger.

Breaking out into that infectious smile again, he said. "Don't be too long."

Giving him a wink, she darted to the coffee pot and prepared a cup. Setting it down before him, she said, "Haven't seen you in here before."

"No. I'm not from the area, just a boring accountant. Paying a visit to some new clients."

Deciding to be bold with nothing to lose, Cookie leaned in closer. "Think you'll still be here around dinner time?" Catching herself, she added, "I don't mean this place. There are several great restaurants nearby."

His eyes crinkled at the corners. "I guess this isn't one of them."

"No, it is," she said quickly. "I mean, you might want to try someplace new for dinner." Toes curling inside her shoes, she tugged at the collar of her blouse. She sounded like an idiot.

He sipped his coffee and bit into the sandwich. "This is delicious. Thanks for the suggestion."

"Glad you like it." Had she read him wrong? Maybe he wasn't interested after all. She was about to walk away when he reached out and touched her bare arm, his fingers electric on her skin, hot and tingly.

"I'd be happy to go to dinner with you tonight. Shall we say seven?"

"Perfect." She took out her order pad, scribbled her address, and handed it to him. "See you then." Halfway across the restaurant, she stopped and returned to his booth. "I'm Cookie, by the way."

"Danny," he said and winked.

Chapter 22 — Eddie
Initiation Day

The call came well after midnight. Groggy from a heavy sleep, Eddie put the cell phone to his ear. "Hello, kid," Sal said. "Get up and get dressed in your best suit. Come over to the house. I'll be waiting."

Before Eddie could answer, the line went dead. Now wide awake, Eddie threw on his blue suit and bolted out the door. Sal was standing outside with Jimmy when he pulled up in front of his uncle's house. Both were formally dressed.

Sal pointed to the Cadillac. "Get in."

They climbed in, and Mario sped off. Eddie ignored the heat building inside his body. This was it. Tonight, he would become a made man. The car crossed over the Verrazano Narrows bridge and onto the Brooklyn Queens Expressway toward Manhattan, the silence between the men heightening Eddie's anxiety.

Half an hour later, the driver parked in front of an unnamed red brick building. Sal and Jimmy ushered him inside. Eddie recognized Paulie 'The Shiv' Martello, his uncle's Boss, seated at the head of a table in a dimly lit room devoid of decoration. All five families were present, along with their Underbosses. Several Caporegimes were there also, including his *Zio* Lorenzo Barone.

Sal sat to Paulie's right and Jimmy to his left. His heart thumping, Eddie absorbed the sight of all these powerful people. Memories of this night and what it meant would remain with him forever.

Paulie stood and motioned for Eddie to come forward. "Hold out your hand." Paulie took a knife and made a small cut on the tip of Eddie's finger. Droplets of blood hit the bare floor. "This is a blood oath," Paulie said.

Eddie cupped his hands. Paulie placed a picture of a saint into his palms, struck a match, and set it on fire. Heat warmed his flesh for a few seconds before the paper extinguished itself.

"Tonight, Eddie Marconi, you are born again into a new life, La Cosa Nostra, this thing of ours," Paulie said. "If you violate our code or betray our brothers, you will die and burn in hell just like the saint burned in your hands. Do you accept this life?"

"Yes, I do," Eddie affirmed. Paulie shook his hand. Sal and Jimmy got up. They pumped Eddie's hand before Sal leaned over and whispered. "You did good, kid. Go wait in the car. I need to talk with Paulie."

Outside, Mario lit a cigarette. Eddie's craving for one returned for the first time in years. Tempted, he inhaled the fresh air instead and pushed the thought away. The event he had waited so long for was over in a matter of minutes, but the meaning behind it was profound.

Sal came out of the building, his face flushed a deep red. Jimmy followed and motioned for Eddie to get into the car. Jimmy sat up front again with Mario.

"So, starting tomorrow, you will report to Lorenzo," Sal said to Eddie. "From this point on, the family comes before anything else. No matter where you are or what you are doing, if your *Zio* Lorenzo or I call, we expect you to drop everything." He squeezed Eddie's shoulder. "I'm letting you oversee the pizzerias, the car washes, and the auto dealership. Your responsible to keep up the take on these for Lorenzo and me. Don't screw it up. You must also kick up a portion of any other profits you make from your action. I'm expecting a lot from you. Keep your ear to the ground. Don't disappoint me."

Eddie considered his uncle's words. "Speaking of keeping my ear to the ground, Uncle Sal. I … heard something the other day from a soldier in the Jersey crew."

Jimmy turned his head. His eyes met Eddie's. "What did you hear?"

"That Pete was a federal agent." He glanced at his uncle. "And that you ordered the hit without permission."

Jimmy gave his uncle a look. "What else did this soldier say?"

"That my uncle could be in big trouble."

Sal let out a deep sigh, almost a groan. "Look, I'm glad you told me. You must let me know if there is any noise about our family." He squeezed Eddie's shoulder again. "Put it out of your mind. People talk about stuff all the time. Most of it a load of crap."

On the remainder of the ride back to Staten Island, Eddie, encased in stony silence, thought maybe he had made a mistake in mentioning what Tony Morello said. Regardless of his uncle's response, something was off about the whole thing. The look on his uncle's face as he came out of the building in Manhattan told the tale. His uncle reported to Paulie, and apparently, Paulie wasn't happy with him.

They arrived back at Sal's house at sunrise. Before Eddie got into his car, Sal said, "You start tomorrow. Don't make me sorry."

Driving home, his elation on being made evaporated. A heaviness lay in the pit of his stomach. In the unlikely event his uncle did order the hit without permission, a serious violation of the Commission, Eddie hoped there would be no retaliation.

He picked up his cell from the console and dialed Monica's number. He needed to hear her voice to stop the rumblings inside his head.

"Hey, babe."

She let out a yawn. "What time is it?"

"Sorry, it's only six thirty in the morning."

"What are you doing up so early?"

"I wanted to hear your voice."

"That's sweet. Where are you?"

Something stopped him from telling her about last night. It didn't seem like the right time. "Driving. I couldn't sleep. Mind if I come over."

"No, but I have to be at the shop by eight thirty."

"Be there in five. I'm close by."

Later, they snuggled together, his chest pressed up against her back. He nuzzled the nape of her neck and breathed in. His body relaxed. Slowly, his world fell into place again. Thoughts of the ceremony and his uncle faded. He focused on the upcoming afternoon. Today he would report to Lorenzo and begin to work as his soldier.

No matter what lay ahead, he could face it with Monica back by his side.

Chapter 23 — Cookie
Getting To Know Him

At precisely seven o'clock, Cookie's doorbell rang. Not used to her dates being punctual, she hurried to put the last finishing touch on her make-up. She straightened the tight cobalt blue dress with the plunging neckline and opened the front door to her apartment.

Danny, dressed in a charcoal grey suit with a black t-shirt underneath, gave her a broad smile. "You look beautiful," he said.

Cookie led him into the living room. "You don't look so bad yourself." She pointed to the sofa. "Give me another minute?"

"Sure. No reason to hurry."

Retreating to the bedroom for no other apparent reason than to make him wait a little longer, she checked herself one last time in the mirror. Taking a tube of lipstick from inside her purse, she swiped it across her lips and dropped it back inside.

"Ready," she said, coming into the living room.

Danny stood and faced her. Flecks of gold shot through his light brown eyes. He reached for her hand, pulling her closer. "I have a feeling we're going to enjoy tonight."

As he spoke, an odd sensation swept through her body. She sensed herself drawn to this man. It almost overwhelmed her. Resisting the urge to steer him to her bedroom, she ushered him towards the door.

Twenty minutes later, they were sitting in a booth at Anello's Steakhouse. Danny ordered a bottle of Merlot while she studied the menu. Growing uncomfortable with his eyes constantly on her, she set the menu down.

"Know what you want?" she asked.

"I can think of more than food, but I'll order the ribeye for now."

The waiter poured them each a glass of the Merlot and set the bottle down. Danny gave him his order.

"I'll have the filet," Cookie said. She might as well order a good cut of meat since she wasn't expecting to pay half like the last few dates she had gone on.

Danny sipped some wine. "So, tell me a little bit about yourself. I know you work at Hummingbirds, but that's about it."

"Yeah. My father owns the restaurant. I sometimes help on my days off from my other job."

"Mmm, let me see if I can guess your other job."

Cookie giggled. "You'll never guess." She finished her wine, and Danny poured her another glass.

"You seem like a caring person. A nurse, maybe?"

Having not eaten since breakfast, the wine rushed straight to her head. Still, she found herself sipping the second glass. "No, silly. You're never going to guess, so I'll tell you. I work at a florist shop. My best friend from high school owns it. She taught me how to do all kinds of flower arrangements. You might not think it's such a great job, but I love it."

For the first time, his expression changed. He shifted in his seat and stared at her.

"Mind telling me the name of the shop?"

"Why? You've probably never heard of it anyway."

"Humor me," he said, his voice tightening a bit.

Cookie set her wine glass aside while the waiter delivered their order. After he left, she picked up her knife and cut into the tender piece of steak. "Brides and Blooms," she said before inserting a piece into her mouth. Savoring the taste, she cut another small one, dipped it into her mashed potatoes, and stopped. "I love working for Monica." Danny stared at her, his food untouched. "What's wrong?"

"Nothing. How's the steak?"

"Great. But you haven't eaten anything." She set her fork down. Was this guy pulling her chain, or was he genuinely interested in her?

"Look, you don't know me, but I'm going to get real with you right up front," she said. When it comes to dating, I don't play games. When I first saw you at my father's restaurant, I was attracted to you because I thought you were different."

"Different, how?" he asked, finally picking up his knife and fork.

"Not some guy just jerking me around because he wants to get me into bed. I've been there too many times, so if that is all you're after, we can call it a night."

"No, Cookie. You're wrong about that. Would I like to sleep with you? Hell yes. What guy wouldn't? You're beautiful and kind—"

"Kind? How do you know I'm kind?" She leaned back and crossed her arms.

"I sense it, okay. I don't know how else to tell you. I'm good at reading people. My job has taught me ...." His expression changed again, became softer.

"Your job as an accountant?"

"Yes. All I'm trying to say is while helping people with their finances, after a while, you pick up on certain things."

"Then I guess we can move forward. That is if you want to."

"Yes, Cookie, I do. But I can't promise anything. I live in D.C., which would make this a long-distance thing."

She smiled and sipped her wine again. "Don't get ahead of yourself, Danny. We're not a thing … yet."

Chapter 24 — Monica

Eddie's Made

Eddie leaned into the open window of Monica's car. "Call you later," he said, his lips brushing her cheek before he walked away. During her drive to work, she reflected on their discussion over coffee that morning when Eddie informed her he was a made man.

She had caught the light in his eyes and an underlying fear. In her estimation, he wasn't cut out for what lay ahead. It meant nothing was off the table. Along with the usual criminal acts came the worst of all—murder.

Was Eddie capable of murder? Unable to imagine him killing someone, she pushed the thought out of her mind and unlocked the front door of her shop. Settling in her office, she dialed Danny's number.

Before he could say anything, she spoke. "Eddie was made last night."

"You're sure?"

"Trust me, I'm sure. He gave me the news this morning after he showed up at my place at dawn. Eddie is all the way in."

"Okay. This is great news for us."

"Us?"

"You know what I mean, Monica. The Bureau, of course."

Resting her elbows on the desk, she let out a sigh. "I need to find something that will make him want to turn. I'm going to start doing a little digging."

"What do you need?"

"Nothing, right now. I'll get back to you." The chime on the shop door rang. "I gotta go."

"Stay in touch."

"Of course." She ended the call just as Cookie strolled into her office. There was something different about her today. She wore her usual sexy clothes, skintight jeans, and a low-cut blouse, but her face appeared softer.

"What's up, Cookie?"

"Nothing much except …" She plopped down into the chair across from Monica. "I had the best date ever."

"Really? With who?" Monica's interest peaked. None of the usual Cookie complaints. Her date was too cheap, made her pay half, or he was too short, overweight, and boring.

"I'm not gonna say much until I see where it goes, but this guy is different."

"Where did you meet him?"

"At Hummingbirds."

Monica fidgeted with a pen lying on her desk. She didn't want to hurt Cookie's feelings. Probably some guy from the neighborhood. She had first-hand experience with them before she got tangled up with Eddie.

"I see that look," Cookie said. "He's not from around here. He came to Staten Island on business."

"Oh, an out-of-towner here on funny business." Cookie's face sagged. Monica regretted spitting the words out so quickly. "Sorry, all I meant was I don't want to see you get hurt by some guy just passing through here."

"You don't understand, Monica. I'm not sure I know how to explain it. Let's just say he wasn't the type to jump right into the sack before dumping me. He was genuinely interested in my life and what I had to say."

"So … you didn't sleep with him?"

Cookie's face flushed red. "I wanted to, but no, we didn't. There was no pressure on his end either."

"Good. Take things slow. Find out more about this guy before you get serious."

Cookie got up. "Well, I better start on those arrangements for Mrs. Canelo's baby shower."

After Cookie left, Monica dialed her mother's number in Florida. She had a hunch and needed to follow her gut. "Hey, Mom," Monica said.

"Hi, sweetheart. How are you? When are you coming down? We hardly ever get to see you. Florida's not that far away, you know."

She was used to this barrage every time she called. As an only child, Monica wished she had a sibling to share her parents with. "I'm fine, Mom. Is everything okay with you and Dad?"

"We're good."

"Listen, I have to ask you something." Monica chose her words carefully. "Do you remember Eddie Marconi's mother and father?"

"That's a silly question. Of course, I do. They were lovely people. Poor Eddie, I always felt sorry for him, you know, losing his parents in such a horrible way, but I never understood what you saw in him. Good looks aren't everything, Monica. And that uncle of his … I could tell you stories when it comes to him. He ruined everything for that family."

Monica gripped the phone tighter. "Ruined everything? What do you mean?"

"It doesn't matter anymore. It was years ago."

"I'm going to catch a flight."

"Wonderful. How soon are you coming?"

"I'll book a flight after I hang up and let you know the details."

"I can't wait to see you. Your father will be so excited. I'm going to call your Aunt Grace and Uncle Myron and let them know and—"

"Mom, please don't. I won't be staying long. I'll explain when I get there."

"You don't want to see them?"

"It's not that. Like I said, I'll explain everything." Before her mother could respond, she ended with, "Love you, see you soon."

Monica booked a flight for early the following day. She recalled her mother's words. Salvatore Marconi had ruined everything for Eddie's family. But how and why? Knowing the truth about the past might give her insight into handling Eddie in the future.

Later in the afternoon, with things slowing down a bit at the shop, she let Cookie know about her Florida trip.

"I'll only be gone a day or two."

"You can stay longer if you want. I can handle things."

"No, it's going to be a quick visit. I miss them and want to ensure they're doing okay."

At home, later in the evening, Monica packed an overnight bag. After zipping it shut, she dialed Eddie's number."

"Hey, babe, glad you called."

"Listen, I'm catching a flight for Florida tomorrow morning. I want to check in on my parents. Just a quick visit. I'll be back sometime late the next day."

"Need a ride to the airport?"

"No, I'll be fine. See you when I get back."

"Is everything okay? I mean, with your folks and all."

"Yes, I haven't seen them in a while, and I'm feeling a little guilty about it."

"Okay, baby, have a safe flight. You know how much I love you, don't you?"

"Sure, Eddie. I love you, too." Monica hung up and wandered over to the bedroom window. Glancing at the streetlamp below, she remembered the night Eddie had pounded on her door. Now, about to discover more about his family's past, her sixth sense was telling her she probably wouldn't like what she was about to learn.

Chapter 25 — Ann
Still In Limbo

Ann sat on the edge of her bed and dialed her uncle's number. After her visit to the precinct, he still had not contacted her. This whole situation was driving her mad. Didn't anyone care about Tommy besides her?

"Hello, Annie."

"Uncle Richie, I'm so glad you answered."

"Of course. I wouldn't miss a call from my favorite niece. What can I do for you?"

"I wanted to know if you found out anything about Tommy. Do you know where he is? Did he go to North Carolina like Eddie Marconi told me?"

"Slow down, Annie. I haven't gotten back to you because things like this take time."

"Things like this?" she could hear the shrill in her voice. "Is it bad news?"

"No, sweetheart. You need to calm down. What I meant to say is I'm still looking into things. I did speak with Eddie, and he confirmed what he told you about Tommy going to North Carolina. I've contacted someone I know there who will investigate things for me. I'm keeping this quiet because if Tommy did go to his dad and try to make amends, I don't want to ruin things or embarrass him. It wouldn't be smart to have the police knocking on their front door."

"Oh, I guess you're right about that." She forced herself to stay calm with the throb in her head about to explode. "How long before you hear something?"

"I really can't say. These things take as long as they take. But like I said before, you need to break this thing off either way. Move on, Annie. Tommy is no good for you. There are better guys out there. Promise me you'll think about what I'm saying."

"I can't promise anything, Uncle Richie. At least not before I know he's okay."

"Fair enough. Sit tight until you hear from me. It shouldn't be much longer."

Ann ended the call and flopped against the pillows. She was beginning to doubt her uncle's sincerity. How hard would he dig into things? He wanted her to stay away from Tommy. She sat up and grabbed her laptop from the nightstand. She typed in Brazenetti, North Carolina, and waited. Her eyes trailed down the screen, her heart skipping wildly against her chest.

There were only five people with that last name, two women and three men. One woman's name caught her attention. Elizabeth Brazenetti.

It was true that Tommy's family cut ties with him and moved away, but on occasion, he had mentioned his sister. How close they once were before the falling out. Could this be Tommy's sister, Liz, as he called her?

Having once had a telemarketing job, she called a friend who still worked at her old company. After a few minutes of forced chit-chat, Ann had her friend search for the name to see if it had ever been or was on the call list.

Her friend came back on the line. "Yes, yes. Thank you. I'll be in touch soon so we can get together," Ann said.

Staring at the number she had typed into the computer, she bit down hard on her lower lip. Blood trickled down her chin. She grabbed a tissue from the nightstand. Should she call? What if this Liz wasn't Tommy's sister? But if it was her, she hated to sound alarm bells without proof of a fire.

In reality, she couldn't rest until she called. Feeling like her cell phone weighed a ton, she dialed. On the sixth ring, a woman answered.

"Hello."

H… hello," Ann stuttered. "Is this Elizabeth Brazenetti?"

"Yes, whose calling?"

"I'm sorry. I know you don't know me. My name is Ann Walsh, and —"

"Look, whatever you're selling, I'm not interested."

"No, please wait. I'm not selling anything. I'm calling about your brother, Tommy." There was a pause at the other end of the line. Grateful she hadn't hung up, Ann continued.

"I'm your brother's girlfriend. I called because his friend told me he went to North Carolina to see his father. I need to know he's okay."

"Who told you that?"

"Eddie Marconi. Do you know him?"

"Sure, I remember Eddie. He caused enough trouble for our family."

"Trouble? What do you mean?"

"When my brother hooked up with Eddie, they began running the streets together. It caused nothing but heartache for my father and me. Tommy got arrested several times. My father would bail him out, but he would go right back to hanging around with Eddie."

"Is that what caused the rift between them?"

"Partly, yes. You see after my mother died, Tommy changed. He took her death harder than any of us. My father couldn't control him anymore, so he wanted to move away from Staten Island. They fought, and Tommy refused to go. That was over four years ago. We haven't spoken to him since."

"I'm so sorry," Ann said.

"Look, my father and I tried. We really did. Tommy wouldn't change his ways. Eddie won, and we lost. At this point, I don't think my father, or I would welcome any communication from him. Tommy made his choice a long time ago."

Ann grappled with what to say. Liz had made things clear. Tommy wasn't in North Carolina and wouldn't be welcome at his father's or sister's house.

"I don't want you to think we're cold-hearted people, Ann. You're telling me that Tommy hasn't been in touch with you doesn't surprise me. My brother does whatever he wants when he wants."

"But don't you care if he's missing?"

"As far as we're concerned, Tommy went missing from our family long ago."

Ann squeezed her eyes shut, the curt tone in Liz's voice adding to her desperation. "I understand. Thanks for speaking with me."

"One other thing, Ann. No matter how much you feel for him, you need to forget about Tommy."

"I wish I could, Liz." Ann ended the call, tired of people telling her to forget about Tommy. At least now she knew he wasn't in North Carolina. Her intuition was correct. Eddie lied. But why?

Her cell phone buzzed. Uncle Richie's number flashed on the screen. She put him on speaker.

"Hi, Uncle Richie. I need to tell you something."

"Well, before you do. I got great news. Tommy is in North Carolina. My sources confirmed he is at his father's house. So, you can stop worrying."

At a loss for words, Ann stared at the phone.

Chapter 26 — Danny

Cookie With a Tryst

Danny studied Cookie's sleeping face. Several long strands of her auburn hair lay splayed across the pillow. One of her fake eyelashes had come loose, the end curling entirely inward.

After this, their third date, they made the next step into her bedroom. Though not his usual type, he found Cookie charming and sexy. She amused him, and right now, amusement was something he needed. A nice distraction to help clear his mind of Monica.

Finding out she worked at Monica's shop had almost ended their date until Cookie assured him she wouldn't let anyone ruin things between them. She'd keep things to herself and see what developed. If Monica found out about them, he would handle her when the time came.

Lacing his fingers behind his head, he leaned back against the pillows. Reminiscing about the previous night brought a smile to his lips and a rise in his groin. Sex with Cookie had been more than satisfying. While she was adept at pleasing men, he returned the favor and enjoyed listening to her moans and cries of pleasure.

But nothing compared to sleeping with Monica because it wasn't just sex. At least not on his part. Falling hard for a woman who still pined for another man had cost him.

If Eddie Marconi still meant so much to her, she should have refused his invitation to dinner that first night. No matter how hard he tried, he could never bridge the distance she kept between them.

His love for her continued to simmer until it evolved into a burning anger, making him take the necessary action to protect himself. After all this time, he still harbored no guilt over his actions. Seeing Monica on a daily basis would have been torture for him if she had remained at the Bureau. A constant reminder of what he could never have.

Breaking things off just wasn't enough. Taking steps to ensure her termination became a matter of survival for him. After she left, the lingering pain was bearable. When they wrapped up this case, he'd make sure her reinstatement as Special Agent remained temporary.

Cookie stirred and opened her eyes. Squinting, she removed her false eyelashes, setting them on the nightstand.

"You don't need those," Danny said. "Your eyes are beautiful enough."

A lazy smile swept over her mouth. "If you say so."

"I do say so." He held out his arms. "Come here."

Cookie snuggled against him. She rested her head in the crook of his arm and sighed. "This is nice."

His lips brushed her forehead. "I agree."

Danny, I've been meaning to ask you. How long do you think you'll be staying?"

"I can't say for sure. I've been working with several clients on their investments. The good news is they gave me referrals, and I picked up some new ones. Guess I'll be around for a while."

"Sounds perfect to me," Cookie said, sitting up. "I need to get dressed. Monica is going away for a few days."

"Going away?"

"Yeah, to see her folks in Florida." Cookie grabbed her robe off the bench at the foot of the bed. With a wicked gleam in her eye, she said, "Shower?"

"Sure, I'll join you in a minute." Waiting until Cookie closed the bathroom door, he listened for the sound of the shower running. He dialed Monica's number.

"What, Danny? I'm busy."

The curtness in her voice annoyed him. "Just checking in. Any news?"

"It's way too soon for that. I'm looking into a few things. I'll call you when I get back."

"Back from where?"

"My parents in Florida. Believe it or not, they may have some background information from a long time ago I might be able to use. Talk to you in a couple of days."

The line went dead. Danny hissed and got out of bed. Same old Monica. She still had that edge in her voice whenever she talked to him. Could he trust her to do the right thing? He hoped her loyalty to the Bureau outweighed her commitment to Eddie Marconi.

When he opened the bathroom door, Cookie peeked out from behind the shower curtain.

"It's about time," she said. "It's lonely in here."

Danny moved toward her. "I know how to fix that."

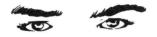

Chapter 27 — Monica

Florida Heat

Monica parked the rental car in front of a stucco ranch home that mirrored the others lining the street. Popping the trunk, she grabbed her overnight bag and glanced down the palm tree-lined sidewalk. This had been a good move for her parents. Growing old in New York was hard. Besides the frigid winters and rising costs, crime held every borough tight in its grip. They were much safer here in this gated, over fifty-five community.

Before she could reach the front door, it swung open. Her mother raced toward her. Lillian's silver hair was cut short into a bob that swept her cheeks. A sleeveless floral dress clung to her slight figure. Her sandals tapped against the pavement. Preparing for a hug, Monica dropped her bag.

"I'm so happy you're here," Lillian squealed. "It's been much too long." Her arms wrapped around Monica. She stepped back, her hand cupping Monica's chin. "Look at my girl. Beautiful as ever."

"Okay, Mom. I missed you, too." Leaning in, she kissed her mother's cheek.

"Come and get settled. Your father can't wait to see you."

Inside, a long sleek sectional graced the large living room beneath the vaulted ceiling. A glass table behind it held numerous family photos of the three. Monica often questioned why she didn't have siblings, but she had never asked.

Stationed on the fireplace mantle were several small potted plants, one with ivy trailing down to the hearth. Monica smiled. One never used a fireplace in Florida anyway.

"Ray!" Lillian called. "Raymond, Monica's here."

"Is that my favorite daughter?" Her father's voice boomed. He came out of the kitchen, his arms held wide, eyes crinkling above his grey mustache.

"You only have one daughter that I know of," Monica said, sinking into his embrace. She released him, noting his golf attire. "Playing today?"

"Only for a bit. Your mother has a nice dinner planned for later."

"Sure, no worries, Dad. You go on. We'll talk after."

He kissed her cheek and did the same to her mother before lifting his golf bag by the front door. "I want to hear all about your shop. Be back by four o'clock, Lilly."

After he was gone, Monica dropped her bag in the guest bedroom before going to the kitchen.

"Hungry?" her mother asked.

Monica surveyed the round kitchen table laden with cold cuts, bread, a mixed salad, and two glasses of lemonade. "How'd you guess?"

While they ate, Lillian asked if she was happy since leaving the Bureau, with leaving being the polite word between them.

"About that," Monica said. "I have some news."

Lillian's brow arched. "Good news, I hope."

"Well, yes and no." She proceeded to fill her mother in on her return to the Bureau. This was a safe space. Her parents had always understood they would never discuss her work with anyone outside the family.

"Oh, Monica. I'm not sure how I feel about all of this. I know how much working for the FBI meant to you, but I must admit, part of me was glad when you left."

"I know. But this case is important. The agent who lost his life deserves justice. If I can play a part in that, I'm more than happy to do so."

Lillian sipped some lemonade. Worry lines broke out on her face. "Salvatore Marconi is a dangerous man. If he were to find out what you're trying to do with his nephew...."

Monica reached for her mother's hand. "Please don't get upset. I can handle myself. I have a lot of training when it comes to working cases."

"I'll try not to," she said, patting Monica's hand.

"Mom, maybe you could be of some help. Remember when we spoke yesterday on the phone, you mentioned how Salvatore Marconi ruined everything for Eddie's family."

Lillian scowled. "Sure, I remember."

"What made you say that?"

"Because it's true."

"Please tell me everything you know from the past. It may help with this case."

Lillian's fingers curled around her pink linen napkin. "We used to be good friends with Matthew and Cathy, Eddie's parents. You were both small children at the time."

Monica smiled. "Yes, I remember how Eddie teased me, swiped one of my dolls, and swung it around by the hair, with me running behind him screaming. I should have known then how much trouble he'd be later on."

Lillian's features softened. "You two never got along back then. You would start whining whenever I said Matt and Cathy were coming over with Eddie."

"Yeah, but they stopped coming. Why? What changed, Mom?"

"Matt started to complain off and on about his brother, Sal. We all knew Sal was connected at the time. He wanted Matt in with him. But he was different. He didn't want any part of that life."

"So, what happened?"

"He … Sal started putting pressure on him. Matt was a union boss. The mob controlled the unions, and he wanted Matt to cooperate along with the rest."

The anguish on her mother's face caused Monica's stomach to dip. The words pressure and Sal in the same sentence couldn't be good. "Did he?"

"No. Matt refused. Your father told him how dangerous that was. But he insisted his brother wouldn't hurt him. Sal was family, after all."

"But then, late one night," Lillian continued. "Matt and Cathy came to our house. I remember I'd never seen them that upset. They brought Eddie with them. He was barely five years old. They wanted to know if anything happened to them, would we take care of Eddie. Matt didn't want him anywhere near Sal."

Monica imagined the scene playing out before her. The frantic parents afraid for their lives and desperate to keep their child away from a monster. A cold wave swept her body.

"Did you agree?"

"Of course. But we didn't think anything that bad would happen."

"You mean the accident?"

"Yes, if you want to call it that."

"Are you saying Eddie's parents didn't die in a car crash?"

"Car accident? No, absolutely not."

"But that's what Eddie said."

"Maybe Sal told him that, but it certainly isn't true. I don't think Eddie remembers much."

"What do you mean?"

Lilian's eyes filled. "It was no accident that killed them. I'm sure of it, and so is your father. The police found them in their backyard pool three days after they came to see us. The newspaper said they were intoxicated. Empty liquor bottles and glasses were found scattered around. Maybe one of them fell in, and the other one tried to save them. The medical examiner ruled it an accidental drowning. Eddie was upstairs asleep in the house at the time."

"What do you think really happened."

"I think the police, maybe even the medical examiner, was bought. Matt and Cathy didn't drink. Not even an occasional glass of wine. Plus, both had closed coffins. They claimed the bodies were too disfigured from drowning."

"What happened after they died? Did you try to get custody of Eddie?"

"No. We were warned."

"Warned? You mean threatened?"

"Basically, yes. Your father and I went to see Sal. We told him what his brother's wishes were. He laughed, said if we wanted to end up like Matt and Cathy, go ahead and file for custody."

Her insides boiling, Monica said, "That son of a bitch."

"Yes, he is a terrible person. We always felt awful for Eddie. But we couldn't try for custody. We had you to consider."

"I get it, Mom. You shouldn't feel bad. The two of you couldn't go up against a man like Salvatore Marconi and live to tell about it."

Lillian raised an eyebrow. "Now, maybe you'll understand why we never approved of your relationship with Eddie. And after what you told me about the case you're working on, we were right. Eddie has become just like his uncle."

"No, Mom. You're mistaken. Sal duped Eddie. Indoctrinated from when he was a boy … told becoming a mobster is an important achievement. He molded him into who he wanted him to be. But Eddie is in way over his head. If I can't get him to turn and help the Bureau, I believe in the long term, he won't make it out alive."

The Bureau's operation hit her full force at the word, alive. Eddie not making it was a reality. Assets who are discovered turn up dead.

Lillian's face softened. "Tell me something, Monica. Are you still in love with him?"

Heat surged through her body at her mother's words, the warmth spreading across her cheeks. "I won't lie and say no. I still care for him, but I want him out from under his uncle's clutches. But I don't think I will ever have a real relationship with him again. Too much happened between us in the past."

"But I'm assuming you will make him think you are."

"Yes. In order to work this case."

"Monica, be careful. We can't afford to lose you. You mean everything to your father and me. We would die if something happened to you."

Something *could* happen to her if things went the wrong way. But she needed to reassure her mother.

She reached for her mother's hand again. "Don't worry. I'll be fine. You have to trust me."

"I do trust you. Salvatore Marconi's the one I don't trust."

Chapter 28 — Eddie

Little Frankie

While late afternoon crept toward dusk, Eddie sauntered into Ruggiero's Italian Delicatessen on Forest Avenue. The chime above the door jingled, announcing his presence. Gus, the owner, stood behind an expansive glass case loaded with pastrami, turkey, sausages, and other cured meats. A variety of cheeses lined the far end. Displays of cookies and slices of cake wrapped in colored cellophane lay stationed across the top.

Eddie inhaled the sweet, yeasty aroma wafting off loaves of freshly baked bread lining two shelves behind the counter. He made eye contact with Gus, who grabbed a hunk of rare roast beef to slice for a customer. Its bloody juice dripped, leaving a trail inside the case. Several glass-doored coolers held soda, beer, and energy drinks along one wall. The sight of jars containing pickled eggs made Eddie wrinkle his nose. He stopped in front of a door at the rear and knocked.

"Come," a deep baritone voice called out. Eddie immediately recognized it as his *Zio* Lorenzo Barone.

Inside, he found Lorenzo seated at a small table. His bulk almost swallowed up the other three men sitting around him. Domenico, Pietro, and Little Frankie, soldiers in his crew, were all familiar faces.

A deep scar trailed above Domenico's left eyebrow, marring his otherwise handsome face. Eddie was aware of the stories that went along with it. He tipped his chair back and winked at Eddie.

Pietro could never be mistaken for Sicilian. His blond hair, blue eyes, and pale skin made him look more like a Swede. He gave Eddie a sly smile. Little Frankie was just that. Barely five-foot-four, his dimpled cheeks and boyish good looks had earned him his nickname.

Lorenzo squinted at Eddie, the puffy folds beneath his eyes like flattened marshmallows. "I want to welcome Eddie to our family as *Amico Nostro,* a valued soldier," he said.

Amico Nostro. A friend of ours. Music to Eddie's ears. An introduction used only between made men.

After a round of handshakes, Lorenzo pointed to an empty seat. "You will all work together to keep the current take on my businesses profitable. Each of you has your own action. I expect that income to grow along with any new enterprises you bring to the table."

Nodding at Domenico, he continued, "I need you four to go down to the storage unit. There are several boxes stacked in a corner. Get rid of the boxes. Come by my house after you finish."

"You got it, Boss," Domenico said.

Lorenzo pointed to the door. The meeting was over. The three men got up, and Eddie followed them outside to a black Cadillac CTS-V. Pietro climbed behind the wheel while Little Frankie took the passenger seat.

Eddie found himself next to Domenico in the rear. "So, how's it feel to be a soldier?" he asked.

"Feels good," Eddie said. "I waited a long time for this."

"We all did," Pietro piped in. "Now comes the hard part. Hope you're up for it."

Eddie shrugged. "Wouldn't be here if I wasn't."

While they drove, Eddie contemplated the contents of the boxes. They must have considerable weight to them. Otherwise, why would Lorenzo send all four men?

Located on the far side of Staten Island near the Goethals Bridge, the storage facility appeared deserted as Pietro drove down a lengthy line of units. He parked at the end of the second row, and the men got out. A set of keys jingling in his hand, Pietro inserted one into the lock on a unit. Domenico stepped forward, helping him lift the heavy steel door. Little Frankie switched on the light while Pietro closed the door behind them. The unit was empty except for four cardboard boxes stacked in the corner.

Before Eddie knew what was happening, Domenico came up behind Little Frankie and put the barrel of a 9mm handgun against the back of his head.

"What the fu —"

"You know what," Domenico said. "You brought the fed in. We could all go away because of you."

Little Frankie spun around. Hands up, he backed away. "Please, Domenico, I didn't know. I didn't know. You gotta believe me. I thought the guy was clean." His eyes locked on Pietro. "You know me better than anyone. I wouldn't do anything to hurt our crew."

Pietro slipped his hand inside his jacket pocket and pulled out a pack of cigarettes. He calmly took one out and lit it. He exhaled, smoke swirling around him. "Come on, Frankie, you know the deal. We gotta do this thing."

Little Frankie dropped to his knees. "Please, fellas, have mercy." Sweat poured down, mixing with the tears now dripping off his chin. "You could let me off. I'll leave Staten Island and go far away. You can tell Lorenzo it's done. No one will know except us." Little Frankie stretched out his hands toward Eddie. "Come on, Lorenzo's your *Zio*. Please call him, talk to him, tell him I didn't know."

Pietro cut in before Eddie could answer. "Lorenzo?" he mocked. "We have orders from the top. Now stop begging and die like a man."

"Sorry," Domenico said, his voice holding not an ounce of pity while Little Frankie continued to cry and beg, his body trembling uncontrollably.

Domenico stepped back. He squeezed the trigger twice, the loud crack of gunfire echoing inside the steel container. Two bullets entered Little Frankie's forehead. Eyes wide, he collapsed onto the cement floor, blood oozing out of his wounds.

Eddie froze. Saliva rose in his throat, his stomach ready to spill its contents. The odor of gunpowder stung his nose.

A weight pressed against his chest, threatening to cut off his breath. He willed himself to stay upright while Pietro opened the first box. He pulled out two meat and bone saws along with a tarp.

Together, the other two men rolled the body onto the tarp. Domenico removed Little Frankie's gold chain, watch, and clothes. Both men stripped down to their underwear. Domenico pointed at Eddie. "Unless you want your clothes ruined, you best take them off."

In a fog, Eddie followed suit. He stared, mesmerized, as the two men began sawing Little Frankie's arms. The sour taste of bile bit his tongue while the air inside grew thick, almost suffocating. Disturbing sounds of the tooth-edged metal cutting through flesh and bone made Eddie wince.

Pietro hit a major artery. A bright red stream of blood spurted out. He jumped back and cursed. "Son of a bitch."

Domenico laughed. "Stop it. You're not new at this. It can't be avoided."

Pietro raised his saw and pointed at Eddie. "Grab some garbage bags from one of the boxes."

Holding onto reality by a thread, almost unable to tear his eyes away, Eddie complied. The hit appeared carefully orchestrated. Everything they needed to complete the job was inside the boxes. He returned with the bags, and Domenico handed him one of Little Frankie's severed arms. As the scene progressed, the body parts, complete with cement bricks, were disposed of in trash bags. Eddie had to look away when they tossed Little Frankie's head into the last one.

Pietro tied the final bag while the sickening coppery scent of blood and intestines mixed with the odor of sweat from the three men.

Domenico grabbed towels from another box. He threw one at Eddie. "Wipe down and get dressed."

Clothing donned, Domenico lifted the steel door and peered out. Eddie helped stow the bags into the trunk of the Cadillac. Pietro pulled a bag of lime from the last box and spread it onto the unit's floor.

"We'll come back tomorrow and clean up," he said before closing the steel door.

It was already dark when they crossed the Verrazano Narrows Bridge and reached the dock in Sheepshead Bay, Brooklyn. All three carried the bags to a boat with the name Shark Bait painted on the back. They sped away from the dock and out into the open water of the Atlantic Ocean, Little Frankie's final resting place.

They dumped the remains overboard when they were far enough out with no other boats in sight. A full moon cast light across the slowly sinking trash bags concealing proof of their crime.

With Pietro at the helm, the boat swung around and sped back toward the dock. Eddie clung to the boat railing in an effort to stop his hands from shaking. He looked out into the vast darkness and then at the foaming wake streaming behind them.

"Rough one," Domenico said, lighting a cigarette and holding his pack out to Eddie.

Eddie lit one up for the first time in over five years and took a deep drag. The familiar nicotine rush soared through his body. "Yeah, it was," he replied, taking another hit.

"Look, I don't want you to think I'm heartless," Domenico continued. "Me and Little Frankie go way back. It's a shame he had to go." He threw up his hands. The tip of the cigarette glowed in the dark. "But what else can you do when the boss says someone has to get clipped? It doesn't matter how close you are to that person."

Domenico flicked his cigarette out over the water. "We weren't forced into this life. It was a matter of choice. Someday, it might be our turn. All it takes is one mistake, or someone higher up gets pissed at something you did or said."

Eddie shuddered inside at his words. All the talk of people disappearing or getting killed had never touched him personally until Brazo. Until tonight. He looked out over the ocean. Could Tommy be lying beneath those black waters?

By the time they reached Lorenzo's, it was almost two o'clock in the morning. After Pietro presented him with Little Frankie's gold chain and watch, Lorenzo seemed satisfied they had completed the hit.

Later, too wired to sleep, Eddie showered and grabbed a cold beer from the fridge. He collapsed onto the sofa and took two long draws from the bottle before setting it on the coffee table. Everything he'd learned about his uncle these past few days rang true. Sal ordered the hit on the federal agent. Little Frankie had paid the price for bringing him in. Another hit, courtesy of Salvatore Marconi. Here it was his first day with Lorenzo's crew, and he had taken part in a murder. Would *he* have pulled the trigger if asked?

He raised his still shaking hands. Clenching his fists, he willed them to stop. He was a soldier and needed to do everything necessary to remain in his uncle's good graces, or else he might be the one to suffer the same fate as Little Frankie.

Chapter 29 — Richie

Following Orders

Satisfied he had calmed his niece's fears, Detective Richard Walsh ended the call and drove toward Manhattan. A meeting with Salvatore Marconi was in order. If not for him, this thing with Tommy Brazenetti could have blown sky-high. Sal would appreciate his interference. He grinned and, out of habit, checked his rearview mirror for a tail.

One could never be too careful. Internal Affairs was always crawling up someone's ass. Richie wanted to make sure it wasn't his. Becoming indebted to the mob wasn't his original plan when joining the police force. Several years ago, a bust of an illegal gambling spot in the backroom of a restaurant on Staten Island had introduced him to Sal.

Sal wasn't part of the bust, but some of his guys were. Later, after his shift ended, he arrived home to find two men waiting across the street from his house. They said Sal had sent them, and he needed to talk to him about some things.

Richie was no fool. Growing up in the same neighborhood as Sal, he was well aware of his stature in the mob. Sal extended an invitation for him to become an associate long before joining the force, but Richie wanted no part of that life. With his Irish heritage, he could never attain the status of made man anyway. The police force appealed to him more, so he took the test and entered the academy.

Over the years, he accumulated a wife, three kids, a mortgage he couldn't afford, and a mountain of bills. Tired of working a second job while his wife stayed home raising their family, he took Sal up on his offer to be his eyes and ears at the precinct. A monthly payment of three grand in a brown envelope helped take care of things at home.

Richie drove past La Nona, the restaurant in Little Italy where he was to meet Sal. He cruised around the block a few times before parking several blocks away. Caution always on his mind, he proceeded to the back of the building and tapped on the door. Led inside by one of the male kitchen staff, the aroma of sausages sizzling in a pan jolted his senses. Several huge pots of pasta boiled on the commercial stove. A chef chopped garlic on a wooden cutting board while still another diced carrots.

The man led him through another door into a private dining room. Salvatore Marconi and Jimmy Galante sat at a table graced with a white linen tablecloth. A glass of red wine stood at the head of their plates, each heaped with linguini swimming in a white clam sauce.

Sal shoved a forkful of the skinny pasta into his mouth and pointed to a seat. Jimmy looked up and nodded. Richie sat down opposite the two. A waiter placed a glass of wine and a plate of the same pasta in front of him. Clam sauce wasn't his thing, but he needed to be polite.

"Thanks," Richie said before sipping some wine. "Good seeing both of you."

Sal wiped his mouth with a black cloth napkin and gulped some wine. "So, how's things going, Richie? What do you have for us?"

"It's been quiet," Richie said, twirling the pasta around his fork.

Jimmy set his fork down, his hazel eyes stern behind his wire-rimmed glasses. "That's what I'm afraid of. Look, Richie, none of this makes sense. A federal agent gets killed, and it stays quiet as a tomb. I don't like it. I've told Sal you need to look into this."

"Well, I don't exactly have access to the FBI."

"Yeah, but you hear things," Sal said. He finished the last of his wine and leaned back into the heavy wooden chair. "You can poke around. It happened in your district."

"Sure, but I have to be careful. It's not easy getting that kind of information. The Feds keep things pretty tight." He caught the glance between Jimmy and Sal. The pasta soured in his stomach. When Sal wanted something, you had best get it or else. After taking out a federal agent, making a detective disappear wouldn't be hard at all.

Sal pushed his plate aside. His hand wrapped around his fist. Knuckles popped in the silence. "I'm not asking, Richie. You get me the information I need. I don't grease your palm every month for nothing."

"No worries, Sal," Richie said. "Give me a little time, and I'll dig into it."

"Watch out you don't get buried in the process Richie," Sal shot back at him, his voice like bottled thunder.

"There is another matter we need to discuss," Jimmy said. "Your niece has been going around town blabbing about Tommy Brazenetti."

Richie swallowed some pasta. Ann was going to be the death of him if she didn't keep her big mouth shut. "I'm taking care of it. There's nothing to worry about."

"How is that?" Jimmy asked.

"I convinced her that Tommy has left town. His father and sister live in North Carolina. According to Eddie, there was some kind of rift between them. He wanted to try to make amends. Eddie's a good liar. He gave me what I needed to stop Ann."

Sal eyed him. "You're sure that's the end of it?"

"Positive," Richie said. "Don't worry. I can keep her in line."

"You better."

Richie paused, a question lingering on his tongue. The one he wanted to ask but didn't know if he should. He set his fork down and drank the last of his wine. "Mind if I ask something?"

"You can ask anything you want, Richie. That doesn't mean I'm going to give you an answer," Sal said.

Setting caution aside, Richie forged ahead. "Just between us. What happened to Tommy Brazenetti? I mean … is he still alive?"

Sal's face darkened. He appeared to double in size right before Richie's eyes. His fingers drummed the tabletop. "That's not your worry now, is it, Richie?"

"Just curious. I mean, everyone in the neighborhood knows Tommy. There might be others who start inquiring about him. If I knew for sure —"

"What difference does it make whether he's dead or alive?" Sal cut in. "I'm counting on you to shut them up."

Richie shifted in his chair. He had crossed a boundary. Nothing concrete would ever be said that could be used as evidence against Sal should Richie get caught. He rose to go, but Sal grabbed his arm. He sank into the chair again.

Sal pointed at Richie's plate. "You gonna let good food go to waste?"

"Of course not. I thought we were finished."

"Jimmy, did I say we were finished?" Sal asked.

Jimmy threw his hands up. "Not that I'm aware, Sal."

"Finish your meal, and then we're done," Sal said.

Richie picked up his fork, each mouthful making a slow crawl down his throat.

When Richie's plate was devoid of a single strand of pasta, Sal said, "Now we're finished, Richie. You can go."

A throbbing headache accompanied Richie on his drive back to Staten Island. His stomach remained nauseated from the rubbery texture and garlicky taste of clams. How long could he keep Ann at bay? She could cause him a lot of trouble if she didn't stop. He got the sense that whatever happened to Tommy, it wasn't good. What had he done to cause Sal to make him disappear?

He would have a final talk with Ann. Make sure she stops. Otherwise, Sal might make her disappear, too.

Chapter 30 — Eddie
A Dose of Cookie

Inhaling the fragrance from a profusion of bouquets, Eddie closed the shop door behind him and relaxed. He understood how much Monica loved this place. Brides and Blooms presented itself as a sanctuary from all the madness outside.

Cookie, focused on a computer screen, called out, "I'll be right with you." A few seconds later, she looked in his direction, her smile fading. "What do you want, Eddie? Monica's not here."

"I know. She's visiting her folks."

For some reason, Cookie always made him feel uncomfortable. Even back in high school, he tried to avoid her. Not something one could easily accomplish since she was Monica's best friend.

Hands planted on her hips, she said, "I know you didn't come to see me, so what gives?"

"Do you always have to be such a bi—"

"Don't go there, Eddie," she cut in. "If you're gonna resort to name-calling, I've got a few choice one's for you."

Eddie held up his hands. "Truce. I didn't come here to fight. I need to order some flowers for my Aunt Teresa. It's her birthday tomorrow."

"How nice. You're such a good nephew."

"Lose the smart remarks, Cookie."

"Can't stand the heat, can you," she smirked.

"What is it with you? I'm trying to be nice."

"Do you really want to know?"

"Enlighten me, please, so we can put things to bed."

"I'm not putting nothing to bed. Not after what you did to Monica. My girl was so hurt after you cheated on her that she left town."

"Old news, Cookie. Monica and I are past all that."

"Maybe, but I don't trust you. I think you're capable of hurting her again."

She stood toe to toe with him. Her lashes fluttered so fast that Eddie pictured her taking off and flying around the room.

"I'm warning you, Eddie Marconi. Don't ever do anything to hurt her again, or else."

Suppressing a laugh, he took a step back and folded his arms. She had no idea what he was capable of. "Or else what?"

Motioning toward his crotch, she said, "Just do it, and you'll find out."

"Yeah, I'm real scared, Cookie. Now, can I please order some flowers?"

Her face pinched. She pointed to the glass case behind the counter. "Anything catch your eye?"

Eddie studied the arrangements. "No, I need something more elaborate."

She grabbed a catalog and motioned to a seat by the round wooden table. "Look through this. I can make up anything you want."

Wanting to get away from Cookie, flipping through the catalog didn't take long. He pointed to a mixed floral arrangement titled Garden Pathway, a vibrant mix of sunflowers, hot pink roses, pink Stargazer lilies, blue delphinium, and orange Gerbera daisies accentuated with assorted greenery. "Here, I think this one is nice."

"Good choice," Cookie said, jotting down some notes. "When do you need it?"

"If you could have it delivered tomorrow, that would be great."

She got up and walked to the computer. Eddie finished giving her the address. More than glad to leave, he said goodbye and crossed the street to his car. About to pull away, he noticed a tall, sandy-haired man enter the shop.

Certain it was the same man from a while back, he waited. Ten minutes later, the shop lights turned off, and Cookie emerged with him. Eddie took a good look. No mistaking it was him. Didn't Monica say he had ordered flowers for his wife?

They walked up the block, and Cookie got into his car. A sly smile crossed his lips. "The pot calling the kettle black," he mused. She was dating a married man. A nice piece of information he could keep in his back pocket.

The next time Cookie Asante got smart with him, he'd take her down a notch.

Chapter 31 — Monica
Autopsy Clues

Sheets of rain pelted the tall glass windows outside ADIC Bob Acosta's office. He handed Monica a thumb drive. "What do you think you're going to find in here?" he asked.

Monica shifted slightly in the chair. "I'm not sure." With Bob Acosta's help, she had requested the autopsy reports for Eddie's parents ASAP before leaving Florida. They were sent electronically and downloaded onto a thumb drive. She drove straight from the airport to headquarters.

"Maybe a better question would be, what are your suspicions concerning the death of Eddie Marconi's parents."

"My parents knew them quite well before they died. Eddie's father was a union rep. Salvatore Marconi tried to pressure him into cooperating with the mob. According to my mother, he refused."

"So, you think their deaths were connected to the mob?"

"Maybe. But it's worth a shot."

"Well, I glanced through the files. The Medical Examiner listed the cause of death as accidental drowning due to intoxication. They were pulled out of their backyard pool. The Toxicology Report says they were way over the legal limit."

"Only my mother swears they never drank," Monica said. "Look, I need to find something to help me turn, Eddie. If I can do a little digging and his parents' deaths point to Salvatore Marconi, I know Eddie will never forgive him."

"I hope you find what you're looking for, Special Agent Cappelino. The sooner we move ahead on this, the better."

Monica rose to go. "I'm working on it, sir."

When she reached the office door, Bob said, "Remember how dangerous this assignment is. Not only for Eddie but for you, too. Stay on your toes."

"Yes, sir, I will."

Monica sat at an empty cubicle and typed in her password. She slipped the drive into the USB port of the computer. A copy of the death certificate for Matthew Marconi flashed on the screen, cause of death, accidental drowning. Next, she reviewed the toxicology report, followed by the summary of the medical examiner's observations and conclusions regarding the manner of death.

There was a general description of the clothing and personal effects. The external examination covered the entire body, including measurements and notations of all wounds, scars, marks, and current condition. There was a complete diagram listing any other findings or evidence of previous surgical procedures, plus a list of any prescribed medications.

Next came photographs. Mike's body lay on a stainless-steel table, a Y-shaped incision from both shoulders joining over the sternum and continuing down to the pubic bone, exposing the internal organs for examination. Her eyes fell on the last line, 'no further investigation is necessary'.

In her career as an FBI agent, she had seen photos like this and had even attended autopsies. But she had no connection to those poor souls. She was just doing her job. Seeing these photographs and knowing this man as a child struck something deep inside her. An overwhelming sense of loss enveloped her. She never got to know his parents the way her mother and father had. Eyes misting, she looked away, unable to continue for a minute.

She finished Matt's file and read Cathy's next, avoiding the photographs and pouring over every detail. Both toxicology reports were the same. Her intuition told her this was all too neat and simple. For two people who never drank to drown in a swimming pool did not make sense.

She skimmed the files one more time. The same medical examiner, a William T. Hoskins, signed off on both. Logging onto the internet, she searched for his name. A picture came up of a middle-aged gentleman dressed in a business suit. The article listed his educational background and specialty. It told of his illustrious career before his retirement several years ago. Searching further, she found an address in Old Westbury, NY, on Long Island, and jotted it down.

Paying Mr. Hoskins a visit might prove useful. She left FBI Headquarters, drove to the FDR Drive, and then took the Grand Central Parkway to Old Westbury. It would be an hour's drive if she didn't hit traffic.

She sped up the ramp just as her cell phone rang.

"Hey babe, are you back in town?"

"No," she lied. "Coming home later this evening. I'll call you as soon as I get in."

"Visit going, okay?"

"Yes, everything is fine with my folks."

"You sound like you're driving."

"I am. Picking up some last-minute groceries for my mom. You know, giving them a break. I'll be catching a flight after that. What about you? How are things going?"

"It's all good. My Aunt Teresa's birthday is today, and we're invited to have dinner with them at seven-thirty at Romano's. Think you can make it?"

That's all she needed right now, another dinner with the Marconi's. Brightening her voice, she said, "Sure, sounds good. I'll have to get a gift."

"Don't bother. I ordered flowers from your shop. I put both our names on the card."

"Perfect." Thank God she didn't have to go running around Staten Island looking for an appropriate gift for the wife of a Mafia Don.

"Yeah, but it wasn't a pleasant experience."

"What do you mean?"

"I didn't need Cookie busting my balls."

Monica stifled a laugh. "Sorry about that. You know she's harmless."

"Well, you need to talk to her about how she treats customers."

"No, you mean how she treats you. Cookie's fine with everyone else. She's very protective of me. Just let it slide. She'll come around eventually."

"I miss you, Monica."

"Miss you too."

"I'll pick you up at seven. Love you, baby."

"Me, too." Monica ended the call and tried to refocus. The last thing she wanted to do was sit down with the Marconis again, but she had to make everything appear normal. Portraying herself as Eddie's serious girlfriend required playing the part.

With the rain easing and little traffic, she had an easy drive to Old Westbury, where stately multi-million-dollar homes graced the tree-lined streets. Perfectly landscaped yards held deep, green bushes, trimmed to perfection. Rows of yellow and gold mums adorned each side of the brick walkways. Rain-soaked grass sparkled in the sunlight.

Monica parked in front of the Hoskins residence, a two-story mini mansion. A brick mailbox with their name embossed in gold stood at attention. She made her way to the ornate double wooden doors and pressed the bell.

Soft sing-song chimes echoed inside, and the door opened. A striking older woman with short, layered silver hair, impeccably dressed in a white silk blouse tucked into grey slacks, stared at her with emerald-colored eyes. A huge diamond wedding ring and band gleamed on her left hand.

"Can I help you?"

"Yes, Ma'am. Are you Mrs. William Hoskins?"

"Why yes, I'm Grace Hoskins."

Monica dug inside her sizeable purse, embarrassed, before holding up her ID. Thank God she only carried one this large while traveling. "I'm Special Agent Cappelino, and I would appreciate speaking with your husband."

The woman's hand brushed the hollow of her neck. "My husband?"

"Yes. Your husband. Is he available?"

"Listen, young lady, I don't know if this is some kind of joke, but my husband passed away almost month ago."

Trying not to let her disappointment show, Monica continued. "Oh, I'm so sorry. I wasn't aware of his death."

"You're FBI, aren't you."

"Well, yes —"

"Then you people should know these things," she cut in. "I had a feeling someone would show up sooner or later. You might as well come in."

A quick tensing seized Monica's body while she followed her inside. She didn't know what in the world this woman was talking about, but she decided to play along. "Yes, some questions remain about your husband's time as a medical examiner."

Grace Hoskins led her into a grand, opulent living room filled with expensive furnishings and artwork. A fireplace mantle held several different pictures inside gold frames. The familiar scent of lavender hung in the air.

She pointed to a pale blue damask-covered sofa. "Please sit." After Monica eased down, she sat opposite her in a wingback chair covered in the same fabric. Crossing her long legs, she leaned back in the chair, her mouth set in a grim line.

"First of all," Grace said. "I want to be reassured I will not be held responsible for anything my husband did illegally."

"So long as you had no knowledge of any criminal acts, you should be in the clear," Monica said. "We cannot hold you liable if he violated the law on his own."

"That is what I needed to know." She rose and motioned to Monica. "Come with me to the study."

They moved down a long hallway to a door at the end. Grace hesitated. "This is still somewhat difficult for me. William spent many hours in this room. I don't go in here very often."

"I understand," Monica said. "Take your time."

An audible breath escaped Grace's lips as she slowly opened the door. Inside, streaks of sunlight filtered through the blinds splaying across a large wooden desk. On top lay sticky notes, business cards, a drinking cup crammed with pens, and to the right, an inbox overflowing with stacks of files. A vintage antique brass desk lamp with a dark green shade sat to the left. An old-fashioned wall clock ticked, breaking the silence. A musty odor drifted up from the carpet. Evidence of a room kept closed to the outside world.

Grace went straight to a file cabinet in the far corner and opened the bottom drawer. She pulled out a small ledger. Placing it gingerly on the desk, she switched on the lamp and gestured to the chair behind it. "I think you may find what you're looking for in here. I'll be in the living room. Let me know when you finish." Without another word, she left, closing the door behind her.

Monica sat down and peered at the ledger. A cold tremor raced down her spine. Opening to the first page, she read the column headings. Written in what she assumed was William

Hoskin's handwriting was the date in the first column, the name in the second, cause of death in the third, and a monetary amount in the fourth. But the last column, the fifth, made her mouth go dry and her heart gallop. In red ink, he had written, 'Done for Blank.'

Monica could almost bet the names written in the second column all had fraudulent autopsy reports. She flipped the pages, going all the way back to the date Eddie's parents died. Her fingertip raced across each column and stopped at the cause of death, alcohol intoxication/drowning. For a mere ten grand, William T. Hoskins had fudged the report for Blank.

There was no doubt in her mind who Blank was. But why would Hoskins keep evidence that might incriminate him? Or was this his way of keeping insurance in case someone in the mob turned state's evidence and squealed?

Overwhelmed with questions, she closed the ledger and took it to the living room, where Grace stood staring out the front window. Turning when she heard Monica, she said, "I guess you'll be taking the ledger with you."

"If you are giving me permission, then yes. Otherwise, I would have to come back with a search warrant."

Grace adjusted the collar of her silk blouse. "No, that won't be necessary."

"Tell me something, if you would please," Monica said, slipping the ledger into her purse. "Did you come across the ledger after your husband died?"

"Yes and no. Impending death does strange things to people. They want to get their house in order, so to speak. William's illness was terminal. A week before he died, he confessed everything to me and said he had altered some autopsy results in exchange for money. I was shocked, to say the least. In retrospect, I found he wasn't the honorable man I thought I had married.

"But why did he keep a ledger?"

"Penance, my dear. He would go into his study and read through the ledger almost daily, asking for God's forgiveness. He carried all that guilt with him up until the moment he died." Eyes watering, she continued. "He wanted me to know what he had done, although now, I wish he never showed me that damn ledger."

"You could have destroyed it."

"I will be truthful and tell you, I thought about it. But I couldn't bring myself to do it. I always knew that one day someone would show up, and here you are, my dear. I'm not sure if giving it to you will help, but maybe it will be of some use."

"I need to ask you one more question before I go."

Grace's eyebrow shot up. She came toward Monica. "What's that?"

"Do you have any idea who Blank is?"

"Unfortunately, no. William said, if he told me, it might put my life in danger." Grace walked to the front door and opened it. "As I said, I hope my giving you the ledger will help. I'm glad you showed up today."

"And if I hadn't? Be honest, Mrs. Hoskins. Would you have turned the ledger over to the authorities?"

A smile crept across her lips. "Maybe." She ushered Monica out the door. "As they say, don't look a gift horse in the mouth."

The door closed softly behind Monica. She continued down the brick walk, feeling Grace Hoskin's eyes burning her back. After checking the time, she cursed and drove toward the city. There might be just enough time to return home and change before Eddie arrived. She glanced at her purse lying on the front seat. The ledger inside it could be the key to unlocking Salvatore Marconi's secrets and discovering what really happened to Eddie's parents.

Chapter 32 — Jimmy
The Making of a Consigliere

Jimmy Galante rolled his chair away from the desk and stretched. Exhausted after working on Sal's books for the last three hours, he buttoned his shirt sleeves before slipping into his grey suit jacket. He got up and poured himself a shot of whiskey. After draining the glass, he poured another. Looking out over the vast gardens in the backyard, lit by lanterns, they conjured up long-forgotten memories of his own boyhood home in the small town of Harmony in western Pennsylvania. A town he couldn't wait to leave behind.

His childhood in the tiny Italian enclave would have been unremarkable if it weren't for the bullying. Being small in stature invited all kinds of trouble from the bigger boys. So, he packed a suitcase on his eighteenth birthday, left for New York, and never looked back.

At the time, his knowledge of real life was scarce except for one thing, getting a good education equaled a promising future. Securing odd jobs, he put himself through law school, graduating with a law degree and a post-graduate MBA.

Time spent at a New York law firm introduced him to Salvatore Marconi. Sal walked through the door one day, asking for help. Jimmy was glad to oblige. Two weeks later, he quit the firm, becoming sole council to Sal. Working for a mob boss had its perks. Besides the money, he achieved the stature and power that had alluded him in the past. Jimmy relished Sal's dependence on his advice, which until lately, he followed most of the time.

Sal's obstinance could get in the way of common sense, as it did when he ordered the hit on a federal agent. Things still hadn't settled, and Jimmy worried about the aftermath. If The Commission agreed Sal had to go, where would that leave him?

There was a knock on his office door. Sal poked his head inside. "Ready?"

"Sure," Jimmy said, polishing off the last of his whiskey.

They climbed into the Escalade. Jimmy in the passenger seat, with Mario behind the wheel. Sal sat next to Teresa in the rear. Dressed in an elaborate peacock blue dress, her round diamond studs and matching necklace sparkled in the dark interior.

"Too bad the girls are away at college," Teresa said. "I would have loved for them to be here with us."

"Next year, maybe," Sal said. "Besides, they'll be home soon for winter break."

Arriving at Romano's, they went inside. Mario stationed himself by the front door. Joe Romano, the owner, greeted them. He kissed Teresa on both cheeks before exclaiming loudly, "Happy Birthday, my dear, and many more. Come, I have a private room all prepared."

Numerous patrons' eyes followed them as they proceeded through a door at the rear of the restaurant. Joe led them to a dimly lit room where fine china graced a table. Candles glowed at each end. A vase with long-stem pink roses sat in the middle.

"It's lovely," Teresa said. "Thank you so much, Joe." She looked admiringly at Sal. "I didn't want to make a big deal. A dinner with family and close friends is all I wanted this time around." Sal sat at one end with Teresa to his right, while Jimmy sat at the other.

Sal reached for her hand. "This is nice, but you deserve more."

A waiter poured each of them a glass of expensive red wine before placing an extra bottle on the table. A few minutes later, Lorenzo Barone rushed in with Rita, his wife, and Sal's only sister.

His face flushed crimson, and he bent and kissed Teresa's cheek. "So sorry we're late, but you know how long it takes this one to get ready," he said, gesturing toward Rita.

"No worries," Sal said. "We're still waiting for Eddie and Monica."

Rita's flaming orange lipstick all but matched her tight dress. Her platinum blond hair hung down the middle of her back. "Happy Birthday, sweetie," she said, sitting across from Teresa. She handed Teresa a long box wrapped and tied with a white bow.

"Oh, Rita, you didn't have to get me anything."

"Go ahead, open it," Rita cheered.

Teresa removed the bow and tore off the paper. Her eyes lit up when she lifted the lid. "It's beautiful." She pulled out a pale multi-colored silk designer scarf. "Thanks so much. This will pair well with so many things."

Eddie and Monica arrived fifteen minutes later, looking sheepish. Monica wore a black low-cut jumpsuit with an embroidered shawl draped over one shoulder. Her long curls swept up, exposed gold hoops dangling from each earlobe. Eddie's grey suit almost matched Jimmy's.

"Sorry," Eddie said. "Monica just got in from visiting her folks in Florida." He pulled a chair to Jimmy's right for Monica before sitting across from her.

Teresa gestured at them. "Thank you so much for the beautiful flowers."

"You're welcome," Monica said, resting her shawl on the chairback. "Happy Birthday."

"You took a late flight?" Jimmy asked.

"Yes. Unfortunately, I couldn't book anything earlier."

Jimmy surveyed the scene. Not for the first time, he wished for a woman of his own. Doing Sal's bidding had left him little time for outside activities. Plus, he needed to find someone who understood what her role would be in his life.

He glanced at Teresa and Rita. Both women accepted who their husbands were and what they did for a living. They never asked for details or questioned their place. His eyes swept over Monica. He wasn't so sure she would know her place. Monica was more the type to question everything.

Plates of mussels in a garlic and butter sauce arrived along with caponata, a savory dip consisting of olives, eggplant, and tomatoes. A basket of focaccia flatbread anchored each end of the table, and glistening pearls of mozzarella marinated in olive oil accompanied grape tomatoes.

Conversation around the table continued while Jimmy passed the focaccia flatbread to Monica along with the caponata. "So, tell me, how was Florida?" he asked.

She dipped some bread into the caponata. "Fine. I don't get to see my folks on a regular basis since they moved away."

"How are they doing? I remember them well."

"Oh? I don't recall them ever mentioning you," she said.

"No, they wouldn't," Jimmy said, a hint of maliciousness in his voice. He pried the meat out of a mussel, slipped it into his mouth, and pulled the meat out of the next one using the empty shell like tweezers. He repeated this half a dozen times before dipping his fingers into one of the small bowls of lemon juice to freshen them.

Monica's parents had been friends with Matthew and Cathy all those years ago. If only Matthew had listened and done the right thing, they would both be alive today.

If Eddie ever found out —he stopped his mind from going there. That will never happen, he told himself, just like Sal stopping Monica's parents from adopting Eddie. Besides, Eddie had everything growing up with Sal's family. Sal's guilt over his brother made him spoil the boy rotten.

Ignoring the conversation between the others, he focused on Eddie. "How are things going? I understand you did well the other night." Delighting in the fleeting look of anguish on his face, he continued. "It couldn't have been easy."

"I did okay," Eddie said. "Just part of the job."

Jimmy spooned some caponata onto a piece of the flatbread. "Good attitude to have. You'll do well to always remember that."

"What's part of the job?" Monica cut in.

Jimmy pointed to the mozzarella and tomatoes. "Please pass the plate, Monica."

Giving him a sideways look, she planted the plate in front of him. "Here you go," she said.

Eddie jumped, giving her a questioning look. Jimmy took notice and surmised she had stretched out one high-heeled foot and kicked Eddie under the table.

Never missing a beat, he smiled at her. "Boring stuff, Monica. I'm sure it wouldn't interest you. Right, Eddie?"

"Yeah, boring stuff."

The main course of Osso Buco, veal shanks braised in a red-wine reduction, was served along with sides of Spaghetti alla Carbonara. They all raised their glasses as Sal toasted Teresa's birthday.

At the end of the meal, Joe presented Torta alla Panna, an elaborate birthday cake consisting of sponge cake soaked in rum, filled with vanilla and chocolate pudding, and covered with whipped cream. They all sang happy birthday, after which Sal pulled out a velvet box and handed it to Teresa.

"You mean everything to me," he said, a sparkle in his eyes. "Happy birthday, my love."

Teresa opened the box and squealed. "Oh, Sal, it's gorgeous. Thank you so much, baby." She held up the box containing a diamond bracelet.

Jimmy caught Eddie's nod at Monica.

"Bet you could use one of those," Eddie teased.

Monica laughed. "Not when I have you."

Jimmy observed the interaction between them. The feeling in his gut that Monica posed nothing but trouble wouldn't go away. This girl was not good for Eddie. Ever since she moved back home, his head wasn't screwed on straight. He had warned Sal about her, but he shook it off and said she was alright, a neighborhood girl. One he had known since she was a child.

With dinner at an end, Jimmy stared after Eddie and Monica as they left the restaurant. Their relationship must not continue. He needed to work on convincing Sal to put a stop to it.

Chapter 33 — Ann
Why did Uncle Richie Lie?

Ann strode into Monica's shop. Glancing around for any sign of Cookie, she sighed with relief. Cookie Asante was one person she didn't want to talk to today or any other day. Even back in high school, she had avoided her like the plague.

Footsteps coming from the rear of the shop grew louder. She spotted Monica and breathed a sigh of relief. Ann blurted out, "Thank God, it's you and not Cookie."

"Hi, Ann," Monica said, walking past her to one of the glass cases behind the counter. "Don't worry. It's Cookie's day off. I know she can be a bit of a pain sometimes, but she means well."

Ann moved to the counter as Monica pulled various flowers, creating an arrangement. "What can I do for you, Ann?"

Sweeping a hand through her hair, she tried to remain calm. "I feel I can trust you. In any case, I have nowhere else to turn."

Monica stopped and laid a bunch of greenery beside a tall glass vase. "Is this about Tommy?"

"Yes, and no." She told Monica about her call to North Carolina. "You see, I was right. Something is terribly wrong. What makes things worse is my Uncle Richie lying to me. He said he confirmed Tommy was in North Carolina, but that isn't true."

Monica came from behind the counter. She flipped the door sign to closed. Turning to Ann, she said, "Are you talking about your uncle, the detective who works at the 121st precinct?"

"Yes. Why would he lie to me about Tommy?"

Monica took Ann by the hand and led her to the office. She pointed to a chair. "Please sit down." Taking a seat across from her, she rested her elbows on the desk and leaned in. "Listen, Ann. I'm going to be brutally honest with you right now. But you've got to promise me you will listen to what I have to say."

Ann, her eyes still liquid, replied with a shaky, "Y ... Yes."

"Tommy engaged in a bunch of illegal shit. You know he worked for Salvatore Marconi, don't you?"

Ann nodded. "But Tommy always told me not to worry. He said Sal protected him."

"Only up to a point, Ann. You were raised in this neighborhood. You know full well that man is connected. If Tommy did something Sal didn't like, or he stepped out of line, well ...."

Ann's body jerked. "Are you saying Tommy's dead?"

"No. I am saying you need to stop trying to find out what happened to him. I know this is hard, but you could be putting yourself in danger. People talk, and if that talk gets back to Sal, he may come after you."

Ann dipped her head, avoiding Monica's eyes. "I can't do that, Monica. It wouldn't be fair to Tommy or me. I don't care about Salvatore Marconi. I just want Tommy back."

Monica got up and knelt beside her. "Ann, please believe me. I don't know if Tommy is alive, but if he could contact you, I'm sure he would."

"And Eddie?" Ann asked.

"What about Eddie?"

"He knows something. I'm sure of it."

Monica stood and grabbed Ann's shoulders, lifting her out of the chair. "Eddie doesn't know anything. He told you about North Carolina because he thought it might put your mind at ease. But I can't have you harassing him, either. You'll be putting him in danger as well."

"But Sal is his uncle. He wouldn't hurt Eddie."

"No, you're wrong. Sal is all about business, and anybody that gets in the way will pay the price. Now you have got to promise me you will stop going around asking questions about Tommy. He's no good for you anyway. Tommy is a criminal."

Ann shook herself free. "How can you say that? You're back with Eddie!"

"Never mind about Eddie and me, Ann. I'm handling things with him."

She backed away, her eyes wild with rage. "Tommy's a good person. I will find out what happened to him even if I have to go and knock on Salvatore Marconi's door."

Fleeing from the office and out the front door, she ran up Victory Boulevard. People on the street stared after her as she flew by. Stopping blocks away, she leaned up against a brick building. Panting, she tried to catch her breath.

It didn't matter anymore what anyone else said. Even if it meant her own life, she needed to know what happened to Tommy. Her next stop would be Salvatore Marconi's house.

Fifteen minutes later, Ann pulled up to the gates. A burly man in a dark suit and sunglasses approached her car. He tapped on the window. Ann slid it down.

"Can I help you?"

"I need to see Salvatore Marconi."

"What's your name?"

"Ann. Ann Walsh. I need to see him. It's urgent."

"I don't think he's expecting you, but I'll check." He pulled out a cell phone and walked a few steps away. Staring intently at Ann, he shook his head and said, "Okay."

To Ann's surprise, he hit a button and the gates parted. He waved her on. She checked the rearview mirror as the gates closed behind her. Another man stationed on the front steps of the house motioned her forward.

Ann got out of the car. Legs wobbling, she climbed up the steps. The front door opened, and a man appeared.

"I'm Jimmy Galante. "I understand you want to see Mr. Marconi."

Chapter 34 — Eddie
To Confess or not to Confess

Eddie dipped his fingers into the holy water and made the sign of the cross before sitting alone in the polished wooden pew at Holy Cross Church. Sunlight filtered in through the surrounding stained-glass windows. The familiar scent of incense lingered in the air. Still, this church was a foreign place as of late.

Several people were going in and out of the confessional booths, each pulling the long purple curtain closed for privacy. Eddie was reminded of a photo booth in which he and Monica once sat at a carnival. But for sure, no one was taking photos inside these.

He focused on the ornate altar and life-sized crucifix hanging above it. Poor Jesus, he thought. Just like me, the poor guy didn't know what he was getting into. He tore his eyes away and focused on the rack containing the Bible and hymnal in the pew in front of him. Rubbing his sweaty palms down the front of his jeans, he fought the urge to cut and run.

Ever since the day of Little Frankie's murder, he had been unable to get a good night's sleep. Closing his eyes brought images of the frightened look on Little Frankie's face and the sounds of a saw cutting through bone. On top of that, his old nightmare returned with a vengeance.

Aware he remained the only person left inside the church, he rose. About to make his way out of the pew, he stopped at the sight of Father Michael Martella standing in the aisle.

"Well, to what do I owe the honor of your presence, Eddie?"

"Just a quick visit, Father Mike. I was about to leave."

"So I noticed." He pointed to the confessional. "Why waste it?"

"Come on, Father. I hadn't planned on spilling my guts."

Father Mike motioned for him to sit. "Amuse me. Let's talk a minute."

Regretting his decision to come to church, Eddie eased down. "About a minute is all I have."

"I saw Monica last Sunday."

"Oh, not that again. If Monica wants to come to church, that's up to her. I don't care one way or the other."

Father Mike focused on his face. "Those shadows under your eyes tell me you haven't slept much lately. What's going on, Eddie?"

Eddie looked away. "Nothing. I'm fine."

"No, you're not fine. You wouldn't be here if you were." He moved closer, his arm resting on the back of the pew. "You know I can't break the seal of confession. Anything you say is confidential."

Eddie remained silent. How could he confess to witnessing a murder and helping to dispose of the body? How many Our Fathers and Hail Marys would it take to wash away that sin?

"Eddie, you can trust me." He tugged at his collar and cleared his throat. "Look, I know about your uncle."

"What are you talking about?" Eddie asked.

"It's no secret that he runs things around here if you know what I mean. But what's most upsetting to me is the fact that he's pulling you in with him. Living his kind of life usually doesn't end very well."

Eddie snickered. "Yeah, but the church sure likes taking his large donations. They don't seem to have any problem doing that." A blush crept up Father Mike's face. He had struck a nerve.

"I can't control what the church does. Those kinds of things aren't up to me."

"Sure, sure, if you say so." Eddie rose to go. "Look, I appreciate you wanting to force a confession out of me, but there is nothing to confess."

Father Mike's eyes bore into him. "Everyone has something to confess. I'll be here whenever you're ready. Maybe you'll stop losing sleep over whatever is eating you up inside."

Eddie hurried up the aisle without looking back. His hands clenched and unclenched as he stepped outside into the sunlight. The word *Omerta* ran inside his head. No way could he break the oath he had made. Not even to a priest.

He pulled up in front of Monica's shop. just in time to see Ann Walsh scurry up the street. Inside, Monica was busy finishing an arrangement.

"Hey, babe," Eddie said, kissing her on the lips. "Was that Ann Walsh outside?" He caught the slightly annoyed look she gave him.

Finished with the arrangement, she set it inside the glass case. "Yeah, it was Ann," she said, coming from behind the counter.

"What did she want? Still crying about Tommy?"

"Yeah, but you know I can't figure out why you're not concerned about him."

"I told you he went —"

"Stop, Eddie. Please don't give me that North Carolina story again. Ann did some digging on her own, and Tommy is not in North Carolina."

"What do you mean digging on her own?"

"Apparently, she wasn't and still isn't going to let things lie."

Eddie swiped a hand through his hair. "Monica, you need to talk to her. She has to stop."

"I tried. She wouldn't listen. Everyone's been lying to her. Even that detective uncle of hers."

Eddie dropped down onto one of the chairs by the round wooden table. "Yeah, he stopped me a while back and asked about Tommy. I told him about North Carolina. None of this makes any sense. Why would he turn around and lie to her too?"

Monica folded her arms. Her face lit with fury. "So, you've been lying all along about Tommy." She slid onto the chair across from him. "Do you or don't you know what happened to him? Please, no more lying."

He couldn't tell her about the hit or what he and Tommy witnessed that night. But his answer was honest. "I swear to you. I have no idea what happened to Tommy. I wish I did."

"What about your uncle? Does he know anything?"

"Monica, you know I can't ask him." His eyes pleaded with her.

She reached for his hand. "I get it. But let me ask you this. How would you feel if you knew your uncle had something to do with Tommy's disappearance?"

Eddie gave her hand a gentle squeeze. "That's not a fair question."

"You know it's more than fair. I'll drop it for now. But I think you need to talk to Ann. Tell her you have no idea what happened to Tommy. With all the lying going on, she needs to hear the truth. Will you at least do that for me?"

"Of course. I don't want anything to come between us. We've been doing so good lately." They got up, and Eddie closed the distance between them, his arms enfolding her. "Please keep loving me, Monica. I can't live without you, baby."

"I will," she whispered.

Holding her in his arms, he wanted to believe, with time, their love would enable him to put all those awful images of Little Frankie and the loss of his best friend behind him. Otherwise, he couldn't face the fact it might not be enough.

Chapter 35 — Danny
Catching Up

Danny eased into the booth across from Monica inside a coffee shop on the upper west side of Manhattan. "Your call sounded urgent this morning. What have you got?"

Monica slid the ledger across the table. "Take a look."

She sipped her coffee while Danny thumbed through the pages. "What does all this mean?"

"I paid a visit to the home of one William Hoskins, former Medical Examiner. He performed the autopsies on Eddie's parents. He passed away recently, but I was fortunate to speak to Grace Hoskins, his widow. She's the one who gave me the ledger. It appears the dear departed Mr. Hoskins was up to his neck in filing false autopsy reports for the mob."

"Whoa, wait a minute, Monica. Are you telling me she just handed this ledger over to you?"

"More or less. It wasn't easy for her to do it. Apparently, she learned about all of this while her husband was coming to grips with his terminal illness. I'm guessing he was mulling over how to explain all this to his maker." She pointed to the ceiling. "You know, the man upstairs."

Danny leaned back in his chair and let out a slow whistle. "Wow." He opened the ledger again. His finger tapping a page, he said, "So, you think Blank is Salvatore Marconi?"

"Yes. At least in the case of Eddie's parents' falsified autopsy. But there could be others from the five families involved."

"And you're sure his wife had no knowledge of any of this?"

"Not until her husband was at death's door. I think she's grappling with the fact that she never really knew him. Giving me the ledger helped lift the weight she felt knowing what he did. I'm just glad she did the right thing. I guess it's time to subpoena Hoskin's bank records."

"Yeah, but I'm not sure we'll be able to trace where the money came from. I'm guessing most of it came in the way of cash," Danny said.

"Probably, but it's worth taking a look. Forensic Accounting needs to get involved in this one. If Hoskins was raking in cash from the mob, he had to deposit it somewhere."

"Under his mattress, perhaps?" Danny let out a chuckle. "Or a safe?"

"Having procured the ledger, it should be easy to get a search warrant."

"I'll get right on it. Excellent work, Monica." He rose to leave but hesitated, his eyes fixed on her.

"What?" Monica asked.

"I … I just wanted to say it feels great working together again."

"Work being the operative word. I'm still a bit pissed at you, Danny, so let's keep things professional."

Danny slid back down into the booth. "Look, I realize things didn't end well between us, but I want you to know how highly I regard you as an agent."

Monica caught a glimpse of something else besides sincerity behind his eyes. Guilt maybe? Or was it just her imagination? That day outside the Bureau, she had the same feeling. He was hiding something. Deciding to plunge ahead, she said, "When we spoke a while back, you stated something about regrets. What did you mean?"

His upper lip twitched. He stared down at the ledger before meeting her eyes. "I should have treated you better after

Jack was killed … come to your defense. Instead, I blamed you as much as the Bureau did. All the evidence pointed to you being responsible, so I never questioned it."

Monica measured her words. "I still think you blame me, and that hurts. You know I would never jeopardize a fellow agent's life. To this day, I have no idea how that message got sent to Jack from my phone."

"I don't want to blame you," Danny said. "But the evidence speaks for itself. Maybe you meant well by asking Jack to meet you. I'm sure you couldn't have imagined what would happen —"

Monica smacked her palm on the table and slid out of the booth. "Like I said, you still blame me. I never sent that message. At this point, I don't care what you believe. From now on, don't you ever bring up Jack again. Understood?"

His nostrils flared. "You don't have to go ballistic on me. I will never mention Jack or anything from the past again."

"Good. Let me know when you have the warrant for the Hoskins' residence. I want in on the search."

"You know that's not a good idea, Monica. Keeping your involvement with the Bureau out of the public eye is vital."

"I'll be careful."

"As Case Agent, I'm holding firm. This is not open for discussion."

Monica turned and stomped off. Several blocks later, her anger calming, she halted in front of a bar called Rudy's. Glancing at her watch, she strolled inside. Eleven thirty wasn't too early for a drink.

The dark interior soothed her frayed nerves. Only two patrons were inside, a man and a woman at the other end of the bar. Soft jazz music streamed from the overhead speakers. She hopped onto a bar stool and ordered a vodka tonic.

Danny could still rattle her. She sipped her drink, cursing at the thought of having slept with him. Theirs was one relationship she should never have gotten tangled up in. Loneliness can make people do things they wouldn't ordinarily do. She told him from the beginning she wanted to keep things casual. But in reality, it lessened the deep need inside her for Eddie.

Then came that awful night Danny said he loved her. After she wouldn't—no, couldn't answer him with I love you too, his anger had almost spiraled out of control. He accused her of leading him on, saying he always knew three people were in his bed.

That part was right. Why couldn't she get Eddie Marconi out of her head? The wound from his cheating had ripped her open inside. It didn't matter if it was only one time. The image of his being with someone else stayed embedded in her mind, yet she still loved him.

Her eyes watered, and she asked the bartender for another drink. She hadn't told Bob Acosta the truth when she said he didn't have to worry about her feelings for Eddie.

Swallowing the last of her drink, she paid the tab and left. Her ride on the Staten Island Ferry gave her time to gain perspective. Despite her feelings for Eddie, Salvatore Marconi must be put behind bars for murder. She clutched the railing and stared at the Manhattan skyline.

Eventually, Eddie would learn the truth about his uncle and, in the process, the truth about her.

Chapter 36 — Jimmy

A Visit to Sal's

Jimmy observed the young woman before him. The girl's gaunt appearance rattled him a bit. "I'm afraid Mr. Marconi is unavailable, but maybe I can help."

"I'm Ann … Ann Walsh. It's important."

He held the door open. "Come inside."

Ann glanced over her shoulder before looking back at him, but she didn't move.

"I won't bite, Ann," Jimmy urged. She followed him to his office. He pointed to one of the leather chairs across from his desk. Pouring a glass of water from a pitcher on the small corner bar, he smiled and offered it to her.

She hesitated a beat before accepting the glass. "Thanks." Raising it with trembling hands, she took a small sip.

Jimmy sat behind his desk, hands clasped together. "Now, tell me why you want to see Mr. Marconi. What is this all about?"

"Well … I think he knows my boyfriend, Tommy Brazenetti. I mean … I believe he works for Mr. Marconi. He's missing, so I thought he might know where he is."

"I believe you are mistaken," Jimmy said. "Mr. Marconi runs many different businesses, but I don't recall hearing that name. I would know because I do the payroll for those businesses. The name is not familiar."

Ann sprang up and set the glass of water on the edge of the desk. Through clenched teeth, she snarled, "Why do people keep lying to me about Tommy?"

With one pointed index finger, Jimmy pushed his glasses up the bridge of his nose. This unexpected outburst assured him this girl was not the type to let things go. Clearly, Richie had not done his job. "Please calm down, young woman. I can't speak for anyone else, but I am not lying when I tell you Mr. Marconi does not have a Tommy Brazenetti in his employ."

Tears spilled from her eyes. She crumpled down into the leather chair. "Why won't anyone help me?"

Jimmy extended a tissue from a box inside the desk drawer. "So, you say this Tommy is missing?"

"Yes. I need to know what happened to him."

"Tell you what, Ann. How about if I look into this? Maybe I can find something out."

"You would do that for me?"

"Sure, why not." He slid a piece of paper and a pen across the desk. "Write down your number. Give me a couple of days. I'll reach out to you as soon as I know something." As she scribbled, he said, "You said his full name is Tommy Brazenetti, right?"

"Yes, that's right. I wrote his address down too."

He ushered Ann to the front door, assuring her he would get to the bottom of things. Back in his office, he rang Sal.

"We have to talk," Jimmy said. "Richie's niece just left here."

"I'm out back," Sal grumbled.

Jimmy stormed down the hall, through the kitchen, and out the rear door to the yard. Sal, sitting inside the screened patio alone, frowned at him. "What the hell is going on? I thought this thing was being handled."

"So did I," Jimmy said, plopping down onto one of the floral-patterned settees across from him. Potted greenery surrounded the two men, along with several hanging baskets overflowing with colorful blooms. The terra-cotta tiles were in stark contrast to the woven rattan scatter rug beneath the glass coffee table—all of it Theresa Marconi's handiwork. The airy space appeared normal, but many deadly decisions were made in this very room.

Jimmy removed his glasses and rubbed his eyes. "Look, Ann Walsh is not going to let this thing with Tommy go. She needs to be stopped."

"I know, but if a girl from the neighborhood disappears, everyone gets involved. This needs to be handled carefully. No way can it lead to my crew or us."

"What are you thinking?" Jimmy asked, settling his glasses back in place.

"Joey Russo owes me a favor. It's time I called it in. The girl will become part of our stable."

"No. You can't do that, Sal. She'll see —"

"Since when do you tell *me* what not to do, Jimmy? As my Consigliere, I pay you to give me advice, not orders." A vein in Sal's forehead twitched. His face flushed a deep plum. "I'm going to have the girl picked up. This needs to end."

Heat licked Jimmy's skin. Sal was becoming increasingly out of control. Making rash decisions could lead to deadly consequences. But in this case, Jimmy was smart enough to back off. Once Sal made up his mind, there was no convincing him otherwise.

Sal pulled out his cell phone. "Joey, we need to meet. I'm calling in that favor. Be there in an hour." He ended the call and locked eyes with Jimmy.

"No long face. I need to do this. First, I got a fed infiltrating my crew, and now some mouthy girl may blow everything up. I'll meet with Joey, have him send one of his guys to grab her.

"But Sal, you can't have him bring her there. No one knows about that location except for Lorenzo and part of Joey and Frank's crew. It's a side hustle, a real money maker. We can't chance being found out."

"Don't worry," Sal huffed. "Of course, I'm going to make sure we stay good." He rose and stretched. "I got this, Jimmy. It will be over and done with."

"What about Richie?"

"Richie doesn't have any say in this. He should have taken care of business."

After he lumbered out of the room, Jimmy crossed his arms and leaned back into the cushions. Things between them had not gone well lately. There was a time when Sal always listened, took his advice, and was grateful to hear his opinion on matters.

What had changed? First the fed, now Ann Walsh. Did he have some kind of death wish? Jimmy returned to his office and poured a shot of whiskey, swallowing it in one gulp. He poured a second shot and slumped behind his desk.

He had become a part of this family these past years— his real one in that small Pennsylvania town just a distant memory.

Turning on the desk lamp, he pulled up several accounts on the computer. His fingers glided over the keys while he made the transfer of funds.

Insurance, he told himself. Should things blow up, the extra money in offshore accounts would come in handy. That is, as long as Sal didn't find out.

Chapter 37 — Eddie
Ann Walsh

Arranging to meet with Ann at Wolfe's Pond Park had been easy. The large public park on Staten Island's South Shore, bounded on the east by Raritan Bay, held a popular stretch of beach. With the late afternoon sun hidden by low-hanging dark clouds, Eddie parked and set out down the path toward the water. A breeze whipped up the salty air from the bay, mixing it with the scent of approaching rain. White caps licked the water's surface as a ghost-grey mist hovered above it.

Stopping short where the cement met the white sand, he leaned against a light pole. Pulling up the collar of his leather jacket, he waited. From this vantage point, he could still see the parking lot.

Thick clouds gathered overhead as the last of several parked automobiles pulled away, leaving only Eddie's car. He ruminated over how to convince Ann he knew nothing about Brazo's disappearance. This would be a daunting task. He missed Tommy and wished they had never gone out that night. The cost of one little mistake had proved deadly for his friend.

A car door slammed. Eddie pivoted around to see Ann, her back to him, digging inside her purse. A burgundy SUV careened into the lot, tires screeching across the black top.

Two men got out. Charging toward Ann, one grabbed her from behind, his arm around her neck, the other her waist. The second man waved a gun at a terrified Ann struggling to break free.

Eddie started up the path. His mouth went dry when he recognized the second man. Body-numbing panic set in. There was no mistaking the red hair and pale skin. It was Carmine

Lonardo, one of Joey Russo's soldiers. Confused, he moved off the path, ducking behind some bushes.

Amid a loud clap of thunder, the sky burst open, spitting out quarter-size raindrops. Ann's purse dropped to the ground as they dragged her to their car, flinging her into the back seat. Carmine picked up the purse before getting behind the wheel while the other man stayed in the rear with her.

Why was Carmine going after Ann? This wasn't his territory. Unless he had orders to grab her. Engine roaring, the SUV pulled away.

Eddie sprinted up the path, squinting through sheets of rain hammering against his face. He jumped into his car and peeled out of the lot, catching sight of the SUV as it rounded the exit. Following discretely behind, he swiped at his wet hair and the water running into his eyes. His jeans were completely soaked. Raindrops bounced off the hood, causing white puffs of steam to swirl up from the engine's heat.

An hour later, after traveling into lower Manhattan with the rain slowing, the SUV executed a right into an alleyway. Leaving his car, Eddie made his way up the alley. Crouching alongside an open dumpster, his stomach turned from the smell of rotting garbage. He held his breath and gulped.

Peering around the metal container, he watched Carmine drag Ann out of the backseat and into a tall brick building. A few minutes later, he came back out, minus Ann, and drove farther up the alley, disappearing around the bend.

Eddie took in the length of the alleyway. A camera was visible above the door Carmine had exited. What the hell was inside this place? Tall horizontal windows held thick frosted glass with thin wire running through them. Unbreakable for sure.

Eddie left the alleyway and returned to his car. About to pull away, a loud knock on the passenger side window gave him a jolt. Carmine's smiling face pressed close to the glass. He winked at Eddie and mouthed 'open up.'

Releasing the door lock, he waited while Carmine climbed inside. His stocky frame filled the leather seat while he attempted to suck in his protruding belly dipping over the top of his jeans.

"So, Eddie Marconi, what brings you to this neck of the woods?"

From the minute he met Carmine back at the meet in Pennsylvania, he had taken an instant dislike to the man. His feelings hadn't changed. No way he'd let this bullfrog intimidate him.

"I could ask you the same question," Eddie said. "I think you took something from Staten Island, and I want to know why."

His puffy eyelids blinked twice. "You need to be asking someone else that question. I'm just carrying out an order."

"Whose order, Carmine?"

"Come on. You know who. Joey—Joey Russo."

"Staten Island is not your boss's territory."

"Would you like to tell that to Joey? Or maybe I need to tell him how you followed me today. Sticking your nose where it doesn't belong could get you in a lot of trouble."

A surge of adrenaline rocked Eddie's body. Who the hell did this guy think he was talking to? Before Carmine could react, he reached over and grabbed the front of his shirt, pulling him closer. "Is that a threat, Carmine?"

Carmine wrenched away. His face flushed a deep purple. "Keep your fucking hands to yourself, Marconi. All I'm gonna say is I had orders, and I followed them. If you want any more information, you know who you need to talk to." Adjusting his shirt, he flung the car door open and got out. Turning one last time to Eddie, he said, "I won't forget this, Marconi. Go back to Staten Island where you belong."

After he was gone, Eddie pounded his fist on the steering wheel. He would love to give that guy a good going-over. He pulled away, the grid locked evening rush hour giving him time to ruminate over the day's events.

There could have been only one person who gave the order. Uncle Sal. Not using any of his soldiers meant no one inside his uncle's crew was supposed to know what happened. Mentioning this to his uncle would raise numerous questions as to why he had followed the SUV in the first place. Yet how could he remain silent in the face of Ann's kidnapping? First, Brazo, and now Ann.

Arriving just after seven o'clock at his uncle's house, he rushed inside. Jimmy Galante was waiting in the hallway, his steely eyes spitting lead. "Come," Jimmy said, pointing to his office.

Eddie followed Jimmy and slid the pocket door closed behind them.

Jimmy pointed to the sofa. "Sit down, please."

"I need to see my uncle. Something is going on —"

"Stop, Eddie. Just stop and sit," Jimmy ordered, dropping into the chair behind his desk.

Alarmed at the sharp tone in Jimmy's voice, Eddie eased onto the sofa.

"Look, I already know why you want to talk to Sal."

Eddie's brow shot up. "How's that?"

"I received a phone call about your little adventure."

"From who?"

"Never mind, that's not important. It would be best if you listened to what I say before you do something stupid. First and foremost is the protection of this family. Any attempt to jeopardize it must be dealt with. Ann Walsh needed to be stopped."

At the word stopped, a tingling crawled up Eddie's spine. He had always known disruptions were handled with severity. So far, none of it had touched him until Little Frankie's demise. Witnessing Ann's kidnapping added another layer to his already full plate of questions he couldn't ask.

"In this business," Jimmy continued, "You have to know when to walk away. Certain things need to be ignored. It's an unfortunate fact, but a fact, nonetheless. My advice to you, Eddie, is to walk away. Your uncle would not appreciate knowing you followed Joey Russo's soldiers when they took Ann."

"But I was supposed to meet Ann today," Eddie countered. "Convince her to stop running her mouth about Tommy, but before I got the chance to talk to her, all hell broke loose."

Jimmy's face flushed, his palm slapped the top of the desk. He got up and hovered over Eddie. "Don't you think others have tried to stop her? That girl has a hard head. No way were you going to convince her of anything. If you keep interfering with business, I guarantee you will be dealt with accordingly."

Heat surged through Eddie's body. Who the hell did Jimmy think he was talking to? No way would he continue to sit here any longer and be dressed down by his uncle's Consigliere.

He got up and met Jimmy face to face. "Back off, Jimmy," Eddie sneered. "Enough already. I got the message."

The pocket door slid open. Sal stood in the doorway, his eyes darting between the two men. "What the hell is going on in here?"

Jimmy moved away, his face still flushed a deep scarlet. "I got a call from Joey Russo," he said, turning to Sal. "It seems Eddie here tailed his crew after they took Ann."

Sal squinted. "Not a smart move, kid. How did you get mixed up in all this?"

"I was meeting her today … to convince her to shut her mouth."

"And if she didn't?" Sal asked. "How far would you have gone?"

Eddie knew the answer his uncle wanted to hear. Another test for him to pass or fail. "As far as I needed to," he lied. "Jimmy is jumping all over me for nothing. I only followed them because I wanted to see where they were taking her. I didn't interfere, Uncle Sal."

Jimmy locked eyes with Sal. "That's not what —"

Sal put up his hand. "Enough, Jimmy. I'll handle this. Come on, kid."

Giving Jimmy one last dirty look, Eddie followed his uncle through the kitchen and onto the rear patio. Sal closed the sliding glass door. Facing Eddie, he stretched and cracked his knuckles. "I can't have you and Jimmy going at each other."

Eddie's insides burned, hot coals hitting the pit of his stomach. "I don't like the way he talks to me. If he wants respect, he's gotta respect me, too."

Sal gave Eddie's cheek a light slap. "*Tutto bene*, okay, okay, I understand. I'll have a talk with him."

"Thanks, Uncle Sal. I would appreciate that."

"Now, it's time I brought you up to speed on my other operation before you trip over your own curiosity. Tomorrow, me, and you, we're gonna take a ride. All your questions will be put to rest."

"Where?" Eddie asked.

"Be here tomorrow morning at ten." He opened the slider. "Ten," he said again and disappeared inside.

Chapter 38 — Cookie
Could It Be Him?

Cookie loved lazy rainy days like this. Pulling the comforter up, she sank into the pillows piled up against the headboard. With the downpour outside, she had no desire to be outdoors on her day off. Too bad Danny wasn't around. Snuggling under the covers with him would be heaven.

From her point of view, their relationship had grown by leaps and bounds. He spent most of his free time — which wasn't nearly enough — with her. She couldn't imagine an accountant being that busy, but she hardly ever complained. Patience had never been her forte, although, with Danny, she tried hard not to lose it. The more she learned about his personality, she recognized her complaining would only drive him away.

So many times she had wanted to tell Monica about him. Keeping her word to Danny was tough. He claimed he didn't want anything to spoil their relationship, promising her he would eventually meet her friends and family. He even stopped coming into the Hummingbird.

At first, she thought he might have a wife hidden somewhere. Some guys never wore a wedding ring. It was the one question she did ask him. He insisted if that were the case, it wouldn't be possible to spend so much time with her. After reassuring her no wife existed, she dropped the matter. Later, as he took her in his arms, she couldn't help envisioning being his wife one day if things continued to work out between them.

Picking up the television remote, she clicked it on. Scrolling through the guide, she searched for a movie to watch. Finding nothing of interest, she switched to the news.

The anchor spewed out stories of murder and mayhem before announcing breaking news. "This just in," the pretty blonde-haired anchor, her eyes gleaming, announced. "The FBI has raided the home of former Chief Medical Examiner William Hoskins."

About to change the channel, Cookie sat straight up, all her attention on the television screen. A quick close-up of one of the agents carrying a box out of what appeared to be a stately mansion sent a jolt through her body. It couldn't be! No, but it looked like him. She hit rewind on the remote and froze the screen.

"Danny!" she cried. "Oh my God, it is *you*." With the remote still in her hand, she flung the comforter back and got out of bed, moving closer to the screen hanging on the wall. There was no mistaking his face. She pressed the forward button, and as he moved down the front walk of the house, FBI in bold letters appeared on the back of his jacket.

Danny was no accountant. Gooseflesh ran up and down her arms. She was dating an FBI agent. All at once, everything made sense. Him not wanting her to tell anyone about them because of his job. Unable to calm down, she paced the room. Should she tell him what she found out or wait until he was comfortable enough to say it himself? Until this point, she had kept her word, proving he could trust her.

Dropping down onto the bed, she envisioned a different life. Living in D.C. and married to Danny, maybe with a kid or two. Happy and relaxed, she drifted off to sleep, only to wake in the late afternoon with her phone blaring out Blondie's "Call Me," her ringtone.

"Hello," she said sleepily.

"Hi, how are you?"

Danny's voice swam in her ear as she sat upright. "I'm good. Will I see you tonight?"

"Sure. I'm just finishing up with a client. See you in about an hour."

Cookie glanced at the time. She had slept the afternoon away. After taking a quick shower, she fixed her hair and applied make-up. Pulling on a tight-fitting low-cut red cashmere sweater and black jeans, she took one last look in the mirror just as the bell rang.

She flung open the door. Her arms wrapped around Danny's neck.

"Whoa," he said. "What is all this?"

"Just missing you a whole bunch," she replied, looking into his eyes. She unwrapped her arms and led him inside.

"Wine?" she asked, heading for the kitchen.

"Sure. I thought we might ride over to New Jersey for dinner tonight. Something different."

Cookie returned with two glasses of red wine. Unable to wipe the grin off her face, she handed one to Danny, "Sounds good." They sat down together on the sofa.

Danny sipped some wine and studied her. "What gives, Cookie?"

"What do you mean?"

"I'm sensing something, but I'm not sure what it is."

She debated with herself. Why not tell him she found out he was an FBI agent? In fact, it would make things a whole lot easier for him. No more making believe he was an accountant.

Setting her glass on the coffee table, she said, "I found out something today, but I'm not sure whether to tell you."

His brow wrinkled. "You're … not pregnant, are you?"

"Pregnant! Don't be ridiculous. Of course not. You know I'm on the pill. I don't play around like that."

His face relaxed. "Then what is it?"

"Promise you won't get upset ... I mean, it shouldn't make a difference whether I know or not."

"Know what?"

"That you're an FBI agent." There she said it. A sense of relief washed over her.

Danny set his wine aside and got up. "I don't know what you're talking about."

"Okay, if you want to deny it, I'll go along." Cookie finished the last of her wine. She looked up and caught the scowl planted on his face. "What's the big deal, Danny? You know I would never tell anyone. I'll keep my word even though you've been lying to me all along."

He let out a deep sigh and sat back down. "How did you find out?"

"The news report today. Some raid you did. The camera captured you. I could hardly believe what I saw—I mean, there you were with the FBI."

"Shit," he hissed. "Those damn reporters. They're like ants, always crawling everywhere. Someone leaked the raid. They showed up while we were in the middle of things."

Cookie's hands cradled his face. Staring into his eyes, she said, "Don't worry, baby, no one will ever know. This stays between you and me. I promise."

He leaned in, kissing her lightly on the lips. "You do understand I can't talk about my work."

"I know," she said, taking his hand and leading him into the bedroom. "Are you packing tonight?" she asked, giving him a wicked grin.

"No. I left my firearm in the car."

She laughed, her hand traveling to the bulge in his pants. "Are you sure?" Her desire at a fever pitch, she quickly removed her clothes. "Come here," she beckoned, falling onto the bed.

Danny undressed, his hunger for her evident. His hands skimmed over her breasts, and she moaned. She melted into his warm body, their lips meeting again and again. Cookie fell hard. These past few months, she had held back, afraid to be hurt. But not anymore. This was the love she had waited for. Now, all she needed to do was say the words out loud. She hugged him tighter and whispered, "I love you, Danny."

Chapter 39 — Danny

All Screwed Up

Danny punched the gas pedal and swore. Cookie finding out he was an FBI agent could blow everything up. It was bad enough keeping their relationship from Monica. If she discovered that the two of them were dating, her anger toward him might steer her straight to Bob Acosta's office.

But breaking things off with Cookie now would be impossible. A brokenhearted woman was unpredictable, dangerous even. The 'I love you,' she blurted out, surprised him. Catching the hurt look on her face when he didn't respond was unsettling. He thought he had made things clear from the beginning. No promises.

Liking Cookie was easy, but love? No. It wasn't anywhere on his radar. Not since … Monica. If only she had loved him in return, so many other awful things wouldn't have happened. Jack Wilson might be alive today and still working at the Bureau.

Distracted by the day's events, he found himself driving past Monica's shop. Lights were on inside, but the closed sign on the door was in clear view. He cruised farther up the street, made a U-turn, and parked.

Minutes later, the shop lights went dark. Monica emerged with Eddie Marconi. After she locked the door, he pushed her against it and kissed her. In the fading light, Monica's arms wrapped around his neck, pulling him closer, making the kiss go deeper.

A hard knot formed in Danny's stomach. Was she doing more than just her job? Things were looking really serious between them. But then again, weren't they supposed to? As they got into Eddie's car, his eyes lingered on the two of them. He ducked as they drove past.

Needing to clear his mind, he pulled away, heading for the Verrazano Bridge, and onto the Brooklyn Queens Expressway. Work would keep him busy, get his mind straight. By the time he reached the Bureau and settled in to start going over the evidence from the day's raid, it was after nine o'clock. He made a beeline for the evidence room, where he logged out one of the boxes of material.

Alone under the buzzing fluorescent lights, he sat at his desk and began pouring over the files. Grace Hoskins had been more than cooperative. He got the impression she wanted all of her husband's belongings gone. Monica was right. The poor woman did not have any idea what her dear departed husband was involved in until, wracked with guilt, he confessed.

Yes, William Hoskins was guilty, but he was also afraid. Afraid to name those he falsified autopsies for, the ledger proving just how scared he was. He had to admit Monica obtaining that ledger gave the Bureau more leads to follow.

After about an hour of wading through old files and useless information, he spotted a manila folder lying flat at the bottom. It seemed to stick, catching on something. Giving it a final tug, the folder ripped open. A shower of black and white photographs fell onto the floor in a heap.

Danny gathered them up. One by one, he spread them out across his desk. The glossy black and whites appeared to have been taken from a distance away. The first one showed Salvatore Marconi passing an envelope to a man. Danny recognized the man immediately from his bio. There was no mistaking William Hoskins. He scrutinized the next one. Lorenzo Barone, Salvatore Marconi's Caporegime, and brother-in-law stood next to Hoskins in what appeared to be an autopsy room. A naked body lay on a gurney in front of them.

Heart hammering inside his chest, Danny grabbed the circular magnifying glass from his desk drawer, focusing it on the body. The face and body were bloated, almost unrecognizable. Familiar with the bodies of drowning victims from past cases, this one fit that description. Strands of long black hair appeared to be plastered to the face. He surmised it must be a female.

He flipped through the next set of pictures. Several more were of Lorenzo Barone. A side shot showed him face-to-face with William Hoskins. Hoskins held something in his hand. Danny focused the magnifying glass on what appeared to be a thick band of cash. His pulse raced as he pushed his chair back from the desk.

Here was actual proof Hoskins had some kind of relationship with Salvatore Marconi. Clearly an illegal one. Who had taken these incriminating photos, and how did they end up in the Hoskins residence?

Insurance was the only explanation that seemed to make sense. Hoskins might have asked someone to take the photos, keeping them in case things soured between him and Marconi. But how was the one in the autopsy room taken without Lorenzo Barone knowing?

Leaning forward, he flipped the photos over. Stamped on the back of each one was Albright Photography and a date. The autopsy photo went back over thirty years ago. His fingers flew over the keyboard by his computer. Google produced an address in lower Manhattan plus a phone number. Elated that the photography studio was still in business, he let out a satisfied sigh.

Tomorrow he would pay a visit to Albright Photography and find out who was responsible for taking the photos. Setting the files back into the box, except for the pictures, he returned them to the evidence room.

It was nearly midnight when he reached his apartment on the upper west side. Between the raid, Cookie, and going through files, Danny's exhaustion kicked in. He removed his suit jacket and tie before pouring three fingers of scotch.

Dropping onto the sofa facing a view of the city skyline, he gulped down the drink. A slow burn warmed his chest, loosening the tight muscles. Thoughts of Cookie and what she knew about him returned.

He banked on her keeping his secret. Getting involved with her in the first place had been a mistake, but in all fairness, at the time, he couldn't have predicted she worked for Monica. If he had known, would he have still asked her out? If he was honest with himself, yes. There was something so disarming about her feigned tough exterior on top of that slamming body of hers.

Danny pushed thoughts of Cookie away. Setting the empty tumbler aside, he stretched his long, lean body out on the sofa. He grabbed a throw pillow stuffing it behind his head. All he needed to do now was remain focused on getting enough evidence to charge Salvatore Marconi with Brian Hanson's murder. His eyes closed, and he drifted off to sleep only to wake hours later, blinking from the sunlight flooding into the living room. After a quick shower and shave, he grabbed the photos and left for Albright Photography. Whoever snapped these pictures did so at the direction of someone. Danny was determined to find out who and why.

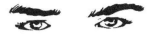

Chapter 40 — Monica
A Sinking Feeling

The aromatic scent of pink roses filled the room while Monica prepared an order for pick up later that afternoon. Setting the finished arrangement inside one of the tall glass cooler cases, she paused, letting the frigid air hit her full force, the cold breaching her beige cable knit sweater. She stepped away. The door closed with a gentle hiss.

Last night with Eddie had unsettled her. Arriving at her shop around eight, she could tell something was wrong. Shadows stained the skin below his eyes. The damp smell and wrinkled clothes told her he got caught in a deluge of rain.

Unable to pry any information out of him, she finally gave up. She cooked dinner, and they ate in almost complete silence. Later in bed, his restless stirring roused her, causing her to worry even more. Eddie didn't rattle that easily. Her sixth sense nudged at her. Whatever was causing his anxiety had to be pretty awful.

The bell above the shop door chimed. Instead of seeing Cookie, Detective Richard Walsh flashed her a smile. "Hello, Ms. Cappelino."

Just about everyone in the area knew Ann's uncle. But how many would know he was dirty? His name had appeared in the files she reviewed, along with several pictures of him with Salvatore Marconi and Jimmy Galante. Detective Walsh had no idea how fast his clock was ticking.

Monica came from behind the counter. "Hello, Detective Walsh. What can I do for you?"

"I was hoping you could tell me the last time you saw my niece, Ann Walsh. The man who owns the bar across the street said she left your shop a few days ago. He said she seemed upset and took off running down the street." He gave her a wiry smile.

"Yes, she was quite upset. Something about her boyfriend, Tommy Brazenetti."

"Are you and Annie good friends?"

"No, I haven't been around her since back in high school." The smile disappeared from his face. He folded his arms and leaned against the door. A message for sure. Did he think he could intimidate her?

"Then why did she come to see you?"

"Look," Monica said. "It's no secret my boyfriend, Eddie Marconi, and Tommy Brazenetti are good friends. Ann wanted me to talk to Eddie."

"And … did you?"

"Of course. But Eddie doesn't know anything. Unfortunately, Ann refused to believe that."

"Unfortunate for who? You or Ann?"

This jerk was starting to get to her. It was time for her to start asking the questions.

"What are you getting at, Detective?"

"I would like to know why she tore out of your shop so upset."

"I already told you why. If you need more information, maybe you should ask her."

"That's just it. Annie didn't arrive home last night. No one has heard from her, so any further information you could give me might help."

At his words, visions of Ann's tearful face flashed across her mind. Did she go to Salvatore Marconi's house after she left here? And Eddie, acting so strange last night. Did he have something to do with Ann's disappearance? Her stomach dipped before she replied. "I don't know anything else except …."

"Except what?"

How would he feel if she told him Ann threatened to see the very man Detective Richard Walsh was in bed with? "She said she was going to Salvatore Marconi's house."

Richie dropped his arms, his face paled. "She what?"

"I tried telling her it wasn't such a good idea, but I don't think she heard me."

Richie opened the shop door letting Cookie sail through before saying, "Thanks. I'll be in touch."

Cookie glanced after him. "Hey, wasn't that—?"

"Yes, Ann Walsh's uncle, the detective."

"What was he doing snooping around here?" She removed her jacket and hung it on a hook next to the door. Adjusting the hem of her low-cut forest green sweater, she looked at Monica, her face full of questions.

"It seems Ann didn't come home last night."

Cookie blinked. "Holy crap. First Tommy, now Ann. This is some scary stuff, Monica."

"I know." If she only knew how scary. "I'm going to my office to work on inventory." She left Cookie standing with a bewildered look on her face.

Closing her office door, she dialed Eddie's number. He was going to meet with Ann about Tommy. But last night, he said she never showed. Now her uncle was looking for her. Nothing was adding up.

"Hi babe, what's up?"

"You tell me. Ann Walsh's Uncle, the detective, was just here. It seems Ann is missing."

"Missing? Well, I guess that explains why she didn't meet me."

Alarm bells rang inside Monica. Eddie was lying again. The too casual tone of his voice gave him away. "If you know something about Ann, you need to tell me." A few seconds passed. "Eddie, did you hear what I said?"

"Sure … but why would I know anything?"

"Well, for starters, she left my shop vowing to go see your uncle to try to find out about Tommy. Do you know if she spoke with him?"

"Not that I know of. Come on, Monica, I don't think she had the balls to show up at my uncle's house. Besides, I would have heard."

"Okay, Eddie, let's get real. Besides all the tossing and turning in your sleep, you were awful quiet last night, Be honest for once."

"Look, ever since I got made, things have changed. I'm working harder."

"At what?" She imagined his body stiffening at her words, the silence on the other end confirming it. "I guess you're not allowed to tell me anything."

"Why are you pushing me so hard, Monica? I'm not going to let you turn this into an argument."

The line went dead, and she stared at the phone. The son of a bitch hung up on her. Pacing the room with the cell still in her hand, she dialed Danny's number.

"We need to meet," Monica said. "Yes, it's imperative. I think Salvatore Marconi may be responsible for kidnapping someone. And if he did, she might be dead already."

Chapter 41 — Eddie

The Women

At ten sharp, with Mario at the wheel, Eddie seated himself in the rear of the Cadillac beside his Uncle Sal. Still irritated at Jimmy, he was thankful he had not accompanied them today. Hearing the mention of another operation and having all his questions answered only confirmed his uncle's growing trust in him.

Sal's mood appeared lighter than usual, making him wonder where they were going. Eddie took in the darkening Manhattan skyline as they sped down the Brooklyn Queens Expressway, keeping his growing excitement in check until they reached lower Manhattan.

Traveling down the same street and up the alleyway Carmine Lonardo had taken Ann, quickly transformed Eddie's excitement into angst. A turbulent sky turned from grey to black, spewing a sudden shower of pregnant drops as the car stopped in front of the familiar brick building. Sal motioned for him to get out. A flash of lightning shaped like twisted barren branches streaked across the sky. Thunder boomed, filling Eddie with trepidation, as he followed his uncle through the soaking rain. Would the skies ever clear again?

Sal tapped on the metal door. It opened on command, and they stepped inside. Tony Morello's grin widened as Eddie approached. Nodding at Sal, who moved past him, he stuck out his hand, "Hey, Staten Island, good seeing you again."

Reciprocating the handshake, Eddie tried to hide his surprise. "Yeah, same here."

"Didn't know you were coming," Tony said. "Haven't seen you around this place."

Before Eddie could respond, Sal snapped, "Quit gabbing. I have things to show you."

"Sure thing, Uncle Sal." Relieved to get away from Tony, Eddie kept pace with his uncle.

They entered an elevator at the back of the first floor. Sal pressed six and then leaned against the wall. "What I show you today stays between us. *Capisce?*"

"Sure, no worries. You can always trust me."

Sal planted his index finger on Eddie's forehead. "I'm counting on it."

They exited the elevator onto a long corridor lined with doors on either side. As they passed, Eddie spotted padlocks on all the doors. Soft murmurs, voices, and what Eddie thought sounded like crying penetrated the walls. At first, he heard only female voices. They reached the last door on the right. A man's angry voice carried out into the hall followed by what sounded like a slap, and then a woman's shrieking cries for help. He glanced at the open padlock hanging from the doorknob and paused. The woman inside that room was in trouble. Hadn't his uncle heard her?

Sal halted, coming back toward him. "What the hell are you doing?"

"I … I heard a woman. She sounded like she needed help."

Without answering, Sal rapped his knuckles on the door. "It's Sal. Open up."

Relieved, Eddie heard heavy footsteps approach. The door swung open, revealing a red-faced Lorenzo Barone. Hands clenched at his sides, he said, "I'm sorry, Sal. This one just won't shut her mouth."

Sal moved past him. Eddie spotted Ann Walsh cowering against the far wall dressed in a white robe, a purple bruise marking her right cheek. The fear in her eyes intensified when she saw him.

"Eddie! Eddie! Please help me. Tell them to let me go. I won't say anything else about Tommy. I promise. I just want to go home." Legs collapsing beneath her, she slid down the wall onto the dark maroon carpet.

"Eddie is not here to help you," Sal spat at her. "You went too far. You should have known better and kept your big mouth shut." He nodded at Lorenzo. "I need her calm. Give it to her now."

Lorenzo pulled a syringe from his pocket. Grabbing Ann by the arm, he pulled her up from the floor, tossing her like a ragdoll onto the bed.

She recoiled at the sight of the needle. "Please, no, no. I'll do whatever you say."

Lorenzo hovered over her. Ann scooted up, pressing her back against the pillows, hands shielding her face. Her body shook uncontrollably. Taking a tourniquet from his pocket, he wrenched one arm away. He tightened it just below her bicep.

"Hold still, or else I'm gonna have to hurt you again." He tapped, searched for a vein, and plunged the needle into it.

Within seconds, Ann's eyes glazed over, and her body relaxed. She sank deeper into the pillows. Lorenzo removed the needle and tourniquet before stepping away. Droplets of blood dotted the sheet. "This one is a fighter. She's worse than that other one from Slovenia."

"The drug will keep her in line," Sal said. "But not too much. Otherwise, she won't be able to work."

Unnerved by the scene, Eddie stared at a drugged-up Ann. What the hell was this place? Surely, they didn't mean to keep her in this state forever. A firm hand rested on his shoulder.

"Come, and I'll explain everything, just like I promised," Sal said.

On leaden feet, Eddie walked out into the hall with his uncle. Lorenzo slowly closed the door. They continued down the hall and into a small office with a metal desk and two chairs.

Sal sat behind the desk and pointed to the other chair. "Sit."

Wishing he could erase the image of Ann from his mind, Eddie eased down onto the hard wooden surface. His mind, a jumble of nerves, he tried to focus on his uncle.

"Let me go back to the beginning. Then maybe you will understand what I'm about to tell you," Sal began. "The Bosses of the other families have been giving me, Joey Russo, and Frank Uzelli a tough time. They were cutting into our territories and our take. As Under Bosses, we had meetings and tried to reason with them, but it continued. Short of an all-out war between the families, we needed to come up with another solution. Cash was getting tight, so we started some side action."

"Side action?" Eddie asked. "What kind of side action are you talking about?"

Sal leaned back, arms crossed, before continuing. "Three floors of this building are where we keep the women. We've made European connections, so trafficking and keeping a stable is easy. But some women are not meant for that, so we put them to work, cutting and packaging the drugs."

Eddie's mind buzzed. Setting up deals with other Under Bosses and not sharing the profits with the heads of families was not allowed, and here his uncle admitted to doing it. "Uncle Sal, if they find out —"

Sal raised his hand. "They won't find out so long as we keep things tight. We don't deal in their territories, and we don't traffic there either. The girls, you know—the sex brings in a second cash flow."

At Sal's words, a pounding started inside Eddie's skull, jack hammering like it was going to explode. Frank, Joey, and his uncle were trafficking drugs and sex slaves.

"I can tell by the look on your face how shocked you are," Sal said. "But when things get tough, you learn to get creative. Things have changed since the old days. Now, it's a matter of survival."

Not knowing how to respond, Eddie kept silent, the image of Ann still raw and powerful. Never in his wildest thoughts could he have envisioned anything like this place. A loud boom of thunder shook the building. A flash of lightning illuminated his uncle's face. For the first time, Eddie glimpsed pure evil.

Sal got up and stood over him. "So, you have nothing else to say?"

Rain battered the frosted windows. The room grew colder. Gooseflesh crawled up Eddie's arms. He wished his uncle had never brought him here. But the reality was, he did see it and Ann. He looked up, his eyes meeting Sal's. "I'm just a bit shocked. I mean …"

"What? That you never thought I would ever deal in drugs and girls. I follow the money, kid. There is nothing wrong with what me, Joey and Frank are doing. If not us, then who? For sure, ours is not the only operation out there. "Come, I'll show you the rest."

In a fog, Eddie trudged back to the elevator with Sal. They rode down to the basement level and stepped out. Eddie shielded his eyes from the numerous blinding overhead lights. Below them, behind large plate glass windows, rows of naked women were stationed at long stainless-steel tables, bowls heaped with white powder in front of each one. Measuring carefully, they scooped some up, then added another white powdery substance before placing them in small aluminum squares. Folding each one with deft hands, they set them in piles. Several men stationed along the walls kept a watchful eye on the women.

Sal pointed to one of the tables. "The first bowl is pure heroin. The second is quinine and lactose. We mix the two. On the street, it's called Scramble. This way, we get more. If we leave it pure, we sell it to dealers who pay us a premium. Down the second row, we process the fentanyl. Fifty times stronger than heroin and in high demand on the street."

They moved farther down along the windows. Not one of the women looked up from their task. Like a factory assembly line without union benefits, Eddie thought. He squinted, focusing his eyes on the farthest part of the room where one man moved closer to one of the tables, his back facing Eddie. He leaned down and said something to one of the women, then turned, the bright lights catching his face.

Eddie's heart thumped. His body went numb as a hard knot formed in his throat. "Brazo," he said, his voice almost a whisper. "Brazo."

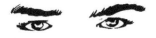

Chapter 42 — Monica
The Photographs

U nderneath her umbrella, Monica sprinted through the rain pouring down on Broadway toward the address Danny had given her. She spotted a black and white awning with Albright Photography printed on it across the street. A blast of wind swooped underneath the umbrella, almost turning it inside out. She hunched down, gripping it tighter. Danny stood under the awning, waving a large manila envelope at her.

Crossing over, she pulled up the collar of her trench coat with her free hand and huffed. *Blasted rain was making it colder than usual—buckets and buckets of it.* Closing the umbrella, she hovered beneath the awning with Danny.

"Sucks, doesn't it," Danny said, laughing. "You looked like you were going to fly away with that thing."

"Almost did," Monica said. She peered into the window of the photography studio. "Why are we meeting here?"

Danny showed her the photographs from the raid. "We need to find out who took these and why. It means there is a third party involved in all this somehow."

A prickling ran through Monica's scalp. The date on the back of the photo coincided with the same time of Eddie's parents' deaths. She'd keep that information to herself until it could be verified. "And the body on the autopsy table?" she asked.

"I'm guessing a drowning. I have people working on it," Danny said.

They entered the studio. A soft bell tinkled as Danny closed the door while Monica leaned her umbrella by the front entrance. Photographs hung from the walls, black and white, plus a variety of colored still shots of people and places stared back at them. An extended counter ran across the room's far wall, with more photographs hanging above it.

An older man with snow-white hair and a broad mustache to match appeared from behind a curtain at the rear of the counter. His stooped walk proof of years behind a camera lens. "How can I help you?" he said, staring at them through watery blue eyes dulled with age.

Danny held out his identification. "I'm Special Agent Daniel Gage with the FBI. And this is Special Agent Monica Cappelino. We'd like to ask you about some photographs taken by this studio. Are you the owner?"

"FBI? Sounds serious," he said, glancing at his watch. "Yes, Fred Albright. Been in the photography business close to fifty years." He pointed to the curtain. "Come with me. I'm afraid we'll have to talk while I set up for my next appointment."

They followed him through the curtain and into another well-lit space with a blank white backdrop. A variety of lighting equipment surrounded several cameras mounted on tripods around the room.

"As you can see," Fred said. "I don't run a Mickey Mouse operation here. No digital zoom like the cell phones use. I'm the real deal."

Monica smiled. She could relate to the pride he took in his occupation. "Yes, we can see that," she said. "I'm sure you're more than good at it."

Fred fiddled with the equipment, angling some cameras and adjusting the lights. Danny removed the photos from the envelope. "Would you mind taking a look at these?"

Reaching for the photos, Fred studied each one. "These are quite old," he said, handing them back to Danny. "I'm not sure I remember any details about them."

Monica noted the change in his expression, the slight tremor in his hand. More than likely, Fred didn't want to remember. "Listen," she said. "We would appreciate anything you can recall. An outside studio does not normally take photographs of this nature. If you need more time, we can take you to headquarters, where you can study them further."

Fred's face paled. "Look, this happened a long time ago. A fellow came in. He asked me to take some photos. Said he would pay good money if I agreed to do it, on the condition, I give him the developed shots plus the negatives and forget the whole matter." Fred's brows knitted together. The thin skin below his right eye twitched. "I thought it was kind of creepy. I didn't mind the outdoor shots but going to the morgue and hiding behind a one-way glass partition — I knew something was off. But I had just opened my studio. That money allowed me to buy all the necessary equipment I needed."

"Did you recognize the people you photographed?" Danny asked.

"No, no. But I guessed what they were doing wasn't exactly kosher if you know what I mean."

"Mr. Albright," Monica said. "Did William Hoskins pay you to take these photographs?"

"Hoskins?"

"Yes. He's the man in the white coat in the morgue and the person taking an envelope from another man in one of the other photographs."

Blinking rapidly, Fred shook his head, a puzzled expression on his face. "No, I never saw him until the day I went to the morgue. He's the one who had me hide behind the one-way glass. But he didn't ask me to take the photographs."

Monica and Danny exchanged looks. "Then who did?" Danny asked.

"Before I tell you, I need to know if I'm in some kind of trouble for doing this."

"If it helps our case, then no," Monica said. "Apparently, you were unaware of how important these pictures are."

Fred let out a sigh of relief, his body visibly relaxed. "The man who paid me to take those photos … his name was Jimmy. I think his last name was something like Gigante or—"

"Galante?" Monica asked.

"Yes, I think that was it. Galante."

Monica and Danny exchanged looks again before Danny inserted the photos back into the manila envelope. "Are you willing to put it in writing?"

"Is it safe for me to do that?"

"Listen," Monica said. "Even though we're in the early stages of this investigation, it might be wise for you to allow us to give you protection."

"Meaning?"

"After you finish up here today, we will move you to a safe house until the investigation ends, and we're sure you are not in any danger."

Fred spread his hands and glanced around. "But what about my business? I made plans to retire in six months. I have a buyer on the hook for this place."

"Then you might want to move up your retirement, Fred," Danny said. "Is six months' worth your life?"

"Well, in that case, I guess I can move things along. If the statement is all you need, let's get it over with. My appointment is due here in the next fifteen minutes."

Outside, torrential rain beat down amid clashes of thunder as Monica and Danny sprinted to Danny's car, Fred's statement tucked in with the photographs. Danny arranged for an agent on duty to take Fred to a safe house later that day.

"So, Jimmy Galante," Danny said. "He's been on our radar for a long time."

Monica swept soaking wet curls away from her face. "Yeah, but none of this makes sense unless …"

"Unless what?"

"Unless Hoskins and Galante formed an alliance somehow. Those photographs were meant to be insurance. It's the only thing that makes sense."

Danny drummed his fingers on the steering wheel. His face lit up. "Yeah, but Galante never figured Hoskins would kick the bucket or that the FBI would raid Hoskin's house."

"Seems so," Monica said. "But getting to the reason I called you in the first place. Detective Richard Walsh paid me a visit. It seems his niece Ann is missing. I have an awful feeling that Salvatore Marconi had something to do with it."

"Why?"

"She threatened to go to his house and ask about her missing boyfriend. I tried to convince her not to go, but I don't think she listened. How do you want to handle this?"

"I don't. At least not yet. If we arouse Salvatore Marconi's suspicion, it could blow up everything. I'm sorry about Ann, but she can't be our main focus unless we have proof that he did something to her."

The tightness in Monica's chest regarding Ann refused to ease, but Danny was right. Confronting Sal without evidence of a commission of a crime would jeopardize their operation. All she could do was hope that Ann was still alive.

"We can't put pressure on the detective either," Danny said. "From what we know, he's bought and paid for by Salvatore Marconi."

Monica nodded. "Then we wait and see how far he'll go to save his niece."

"Exactly. If he gets desperate …."

"Desperate people do desperate things," Monica agreed.

Later, back inside her car, away from Danny, she focused on the deluge of rain pinging furiously off the hood. She needed to talk to Eddie, feel him out again about Ann's disappearance. When questioned about his work, his uneasiness of late and short temper told her he knew much more than he was willing to reveal.

If the body in the autopsy photo could be positively identified as Eddie's mother, the next step would be to exhume the bodies and prove his parents' cause of death wasn't drowning. Knowing what lay ahead for her and Eddie, she sucked in a deep breath.

Her eyes filled, blurring the onslaught outside the window. If what she was doing was right, why did it feel so wrong?

Chapter 43 — Jimmy

The Raid

Downing his second scotch, Jimmy paced his office. Nothing appeared to be going right. The FBI raid on William Hoskin's house had rattled him to the bone. How could it have happened, and why?

The ultimate heinous crime, falsifying autopsy reports for Sal, had grown into a tremendous misstep. Hoskins had called him in a panic, said he couldn't do it anymore, and they met secretly. He needed Hoskins to continue to work for Sal. But he also needed to quell his fears and convince him they could have evidence against Sal if Hoskins were found out by the authorities. Striking a bargain with Hoskins seemed like a good idea at the time. Insurance for both of them. They could plead out if necessary.

He should have never let Hoskins hold onto those photographs, but living in Sal's house, it was too dangerous for him to keep them.

After Hoskin's death, he intended to wait and pay the widow a visit, never imagining the FBI would get there first. But how did they find out? That question bothered him more than anything else. There was no connection between their agent's death and Hoskin's. Coincidence? Maybe, but his gut refused to accept that answer.

He called Detective Walsh for a meeting. The bum had proved useless these past few months. He needed to start earning the money Sal paid him, or else Richie would have to go. They would find someone else on the inside.

Jimmy grabbed his car keys and left. Sal was out for the day with Eddie, a decision that led to another disagreement between the two. Jimmy believed Eddie wasn't ready to be let in on the side operation. But Sal had made up his mind. There was no changing it.

It was late afternoon when Jimmy pulled up to the small coffee shop just over the Verrazano Narrows bridge in Brooklyn. The rain had finally begun to turn from a steady discharge to a slow drizzle.

The aroma of freshly brewed coffee and the whir of expresso machines greeted him. The place was half full of people busy on their phones or tapping on laptops. He ordered an extra dark roast black and made his way to a small table in the rear. His coffee arrived at the same time Richie came through the door, a grim expression on his face. He guessed Ann Walsh would be the opening topic of their conversation.

Richie sat in the seat across from him. "I need you to tell me what happened to my niece, Ann."

Jimmy adjusted his wire rims and sipped some coffee. "You couldn't do what we asked, so we did it for you."

Richie blinked uncontrollably. "Are you saying—"

"Stop," Jimmy snapped. "Ann is very much alive. Just tucked away where she can't cause any trouble."

"But that wasn't necessary. I was handling things."

"How well do you think you were handling things? She showed up at Sal's house asking about Tommy Brazenetti."

Richie covered his face with his hands and slumped forward. Jimmy thought he was going to burst into tears. "Pull yourself together, Richie," he admonished. "I said Ann is okay. Besides, she isn't the reason I called you."

Richie dropped his hands. "Then why? What do you want?"

"I want you to do the job Sal pays you to do. You haven't given us one ounce of information on the feds. Sal had some dealings with someone in the past, and they're jumping on top of it like bloodhounds."

Richie gave him a blank stare. "The only thing I heard about was a raid on Long Island. But I didn't think that had anything to do with Sal."

"That's just it, Richie, you don't think. Any movement on their part should be communicated to us directly."

"But the raid … it was on some dead guy who used to be a medical examiner or something."

"Correct. As I said, Sal dealt with him in the past. I'm not sure why they're poking around. But the who is more important than the why. Someone gave them information that led to the raid. I want to know who that someone is."

Richie spread his palms face down on the table. "Look, Jimmy, I understand what you're saying, but the protection of FBI informants is ironclad. They don't broadcast that kind of stuff, even to us."

"Maybe it's not an informant," Jimmy said. "Could be one of their own started digging into things. Regardless, you need to bring me something on this. If there is going to be an indictment coming down, I have to be prepared for Sal's sake."

"What about Ann?"

"She's safe for now. All that could change if you don't come through."

"Please, Jimmy. Don't hurt her," Richie pleaded.

Jimmy glanced around. "Lower your voice."

"But what do I tell my brother and his wife? They're half out of their minds with worry."

Jimmy smiled. "Tell them the same story Eddie told you, only twist it a little. Ann is in North Carolina with Tommy Brazenetti. If you need her to confirm it, I will arrange for her to do so. A phone call should calm them— and you— down."

Richie nodded and got up. "One other thing," Jimmy said. "There better be no missing person's report filed on Ann. We don't want the neighborhood in an uproar."

"I'll talk to my brother tonight. Tell him she was afraid to call them, so she called me. But I need her to call home soon if you want things to remain calm."

"I'll talk to Sal. Let you know when. And one other thing."

"What's that?"

"You report directly to me with what you find, and I will take it to Sal. It's the way he wants things for now."

"Sure, Jimmy. Whatever Sal wants."

He stared after a deflated Richie. This thing with Ann put a fire under him. Sipping the last of his coffee, he bristled at the thought of everything being a bit off-kilter. The problem with Ann, his argument with Eddie, Sal not taking his advice, and the nagging feeling he had about Monica twisted inside his gut. It almost seemed like all this started after she hooked up with Eddie again.

Sure, she was pretty and smart, maybe too smart for Eddie. But she didn't fit into their world. Latching back onto him didn't make sense after their bad breakup. It was time to find out the real reason Monica Cappelino left and then returned to Staten Island.

Chapter 44 — Eddie

Tommy

Sal nudged Eddie's shoulder and laughed. "What's with the dropped jaw, kid? Shut your trap before something flies in."

Eddie snapped his mouth shut. He looked at Sal. "Sorry, it's just that I didn't expect to see Brazo … I mean, Tommy here."

"I said all your questions would be answered. We brought him here to test his loyalty. Rocco Fischetti told me what happened the night of the hit. You lied to me, kid," Sal said, his face an iron mask.

A quiver ran through Eddie's body. He should have known Rocco would tell Sal everything. "I'm sorry, Uncle Sal. I thought if I told you Rocco saw us that night, you would know I messed up."

"First of all, stop saying you're sorry," Sal barked. "If I hear that word one more time, I'm gonna make you sorry for real. You should have admitted the truth. It hurts me to know that you don't trust me enough to do that. In this business, there is nothing worse than lying. Lying gets you killed."

Fearful of saying the wrong thing, Eddie kept his silence. Muscles inside his chest clenched, proving just how afraid he was of his Uncle Sal. Always had been, even as a child.

Sal straightened his back and folded his arms. "I need to know, going forward, if I can trust you to tell me the truth. I can't have my nephew lying or hiding things from me. I vouched for you so you could become a made man, so I expect you to be a stand-up guy."

"I promise to always tell you the truth from this point on," Eddie said. "I swear on my parent's graves. Please believe I meant no disrespect."

Sal lowered his arms and stretched them out. "Come here." He wrapped Eddie in a bear hug before stepping back. "Remember, we're family. We take care of one another, always."

"Sure thing." Eddie's tension eased a bit. Things could have gone much worse for him.

Sal wrapped his knuckles on the window and beckoned to Tommy. "Now, talk to your friend. He's done well here. I'll see you back upstairs." He retreated into the elevator, but before closing the doors, he said," And Eddie, not a word about Ann Walsh."

Tommy stepped out of the room, a huge grin on his face. "Eddie, it's so good to see you."

Eddie surveyed his friend. The dark blue suit, white shirt, and maroon tie did little to hide his apparent weight loss. They shook hands and bear-hugged.

"I'm glad, too, Brazo," Eddie said. "I had no idea what the hell happened to you."

Tommy's brow furrowed. "Yeah, they nabbed me the day of the funeral. I thought for sure I was gonna get whacked. Rocco is a hell of a scary guy."

"How did you end up here?"

"Your Uncle Sal. He kept me alive but only if I agreed to work for him. I had to promise not to go back to my place or speak to anyone on the outside until he gave the okay."

"So, you live here, too?"

"Yeah. There's a block of rooms for us guys." He nodded at the women packaging drugs. "We watch them, make sure there is no funny business."

Eddie stepped closer to him and lowered his voice. "You do know the other families are totally unaware of this place. My uncle is going against them with all this." He pointed to the women and then up at the ceiling. "The others upstairs come from sex trafficking and—"

"Stop, Eddie," Tommy snapped. "I'm just glad to be alive. Things could have ended a lot worse for me. Sal says I can go home soon."

"You don't believe that do you?"

"What are you trying to say?"

"Think about it. You know too much about this place."

"But I would never say anything. We talked, and Sal knows."

Eddie debated telling him about Ann. His uncle's instructions had been clear. Not a word was to be said concerning her. But what if it was Monica? He damn sure would want someone to tell him.

"Listen," Eddie began. "Please stay calm. I need to tell you something. If any of those other guys in there see you react, it may not be good."

"First, I need to tell you I wish I had been a better friend. I watched the Lincoln pull away from your house before I went inside." Eddie dug into the pocket of his jeans. He pulled out the gold cross he had been carrying every day since Tommy's disappearance. "When I found this, I knew something terrible had happened."

Tommy visibly shook at the sight of the cross. Eddie placed it in the palm of his hand. "The cross my mom gave me," he said, his eyes filling as he continued to stare at it. "Thanks, man. This means a lot to me." He tucked the cross inside his breast pocket.

Eddie glanced at the men behind the glass again. "Listen carefully, but like I said, don't react. Ever since you disappeared, Ann has been looking for you."

"Annie?"

"Yes. But she ran all over Staten Island, running her mouth. She even went to the police and told her uncle, that detective. It riled up the wrong people."

Tommy's fright-filled eyes stared back at him. "Is she okay? Did they do something to her?"

"They kidnapped her and brought her here. She's upstairs as we speak. But you can't let them know I told you."

Tommy's breath came in spurts. "But is she alright? Tell me the truth, Eddie."

"She wouldn't stop carrying on. They injected her with heroin to keep her quiet." The color drain from his friend's face. "Listen, there is nothing you can do for her."

"Nothing I can do!" Tommy's voice had risen almost to a scream. Their attention drawn, two men inside the room stared at them through the glass.

"Quiet down, Brazo," Eddie said. "They're looking at us. Smile, make believe we're having a normal conversation."

Tommy forced a smile, nodding in the direction of the men. "What should I do, Eddie? I need to help her. Maybe if she knows I'm here and I'm okay, things will go better for her."

"I'm going to try and let her know, but you have to promise me you won't do anything crazy. Give me a few days. I'll get word to you somehow."

"But — "

"Brazo, you have to go on like nothing happened. If my Uncle Sal finds out, I told you, things will go sideways for you and me."

"What about Annie's folks and that uncle of hers?"

"I'm sure they covered that somehow. Look, I can't ask too many questions. I can only go so far. You have to trust me right now."

"Man, oh man, this is bad, Eddie." He shifted his weight from foot to foot.

"Please don't make it any worse. I gotta go. You'll hear something soon." Eddie pressed the button for the elevator. "Remember, I will try to do what I can for Ann and you."

Inside the elevator, Eddie slumped against the back wall. Still shocked, the thumping inside his head, like the beating of a drum, continued. Nerves jittered inside his body. He could never have imagined all the things his uncle revealed.

His good friend was being held hostage for witnessing a hit ordered by his uncle. Ann Walsh's only crime had been her love for Tommy Brazenetti. The women here were being bartered for sex or forced to work packaging drugs.

Joey Russo, Frank Uzelli, and his uncle had contrived this whole operation without permission from the five families. A cardinal sin that, if found out, would never be forgiven under any circumstances.

Deep inside, he was torn between helping Tommy and Ann or remaining loyal to his uncle. His future in the mob depended upon the decision he would ultimately make. When he spoke the oath, this was not the world he dreamed of. But once you were made, you couldn't just walk away. You either toed the line or ended up like Little Frankie.

Chapter 45 — Monica
Digging Up the Past

With Danny seated in the chair next to hers, Monica waited while Bob Acosta skimmed through the ledger and studied the photographs Danny had given him.

"You can see why we're asking permission to exhume the bodies," Danny said. "Monica and I believe we can find solid evidence to dispute the cause of death."

"Sir," Monica chimed in. "If I can convince Eddie by showing him proof that his uncle had his parents murdered, I know he'll cooperate."

"Well," Bob said. "With what I see here, you don't need to convince me. We need to convince a judge."

Danny leaned forward, hands clasped in his lap. "That is unless …"

A chill inched up Monica's spine. "Unless I get Eddie's permission."

Danny nodded. "He is the next of kin before anybody else."

Monica pictured asking Eddie permission to exhume the bodies. It would mean coming completely clean about the Bureau, herself, and the part she had played in everything.

"No, it won't work," she blurted out. "Eddie is the type of person who will not believe the truth unless we show him the evidence, give him proof his parents were murdered, and his uncle was involved. Besides, at this stage in the operation, I don't want to blow my cover or involve the Bureau until I get Eddie to agree to work with us."

"I agree with Monica, " Bob said. "I'll try to expedite things and have legal prepare the necessary paperwork to request the exhumation. If the court gives permission, we will move forward immediately."

Later the following evening, Monica made her way home from the flower shop. Due to meet Eddie soon at his place, she changed into a powder blue v-neck sweater and jeans. They had not seen each other for the past two days, Eddie claiming he was too busy.

Her mind wandered as she dried her hair before applying makeup. Exhuming Eddie's parents' bodies made her uneasy. What if the forensic pathologist couldn't find the actual cause of death? In rare circumstances, it was a real possibility. She believed everything her mother had told her and hoped they would find clear evidence.

Her cell rang, and she grabbed it off the nightstand. It was Eddie.

"I'm almost ready," she said, pumping a short burst of perfume on either side of her neck.

"I'm sorry, babe. Hard day today. Can we put tonight off?"

At the strange tone in his voice, Monica's intuition kicked in. "What's wrong, Eddie?"

"Nothings wrong. I'm kinda tired. Don't think I'd be much company."

"Have you eaten? I can pick up takeout. We could cuddle afterward if you like."

"Sorry. I know you're disappointed. I'm going to call it an early night. I love you to pieces. I'll make it up to you tomorrow night. Promise."

"No worries," Monica said. "Get some rest. I love you too." About to put her cell down, it rang again. This time it was Danny.

"It's a go, Monica. The judge approved the order. The bodies are in the family plot at St. Peters Cemetery. It's going to be an early detail, 7 A.M. sharp. We need to be careful no curiosity seekers are around, especially the press. I want to be sure this stays within the Bureau."

"I'll meet you there."

"You know you don't have to come."

"I said I'll meet you there." Monica ended the call. Fully dressed, she slept until five-thirty the next morning. She got up and hurried to the safe. Taught at Quantico to always be prepared, she removed her badge, Glock M19, and gun belt. After securing her weapon, she opened the blanket chest at the far end of the walk-in closet. Lifting out two heavy blankets, she placed them aside and removed her navy nylon jacket with the letters FBI emblazoned across the back. Grabbing a navy baseball cap from the shelf above, she wound her long hair into a tight coil at the nape of her neck, tucking it underneath the cap. Outside, she tossed the jacket onto the passenger seat and drove to the cemetery.

Hints of sunrise appeared, coloring the sky. Shades of pink tinged with gold painted the horizon. Monica lowered the window, letting in the cooing sound of morning doves. Thoughts of Eddie swirled inside her mind. Until the past few days, he had asked to see her every night. It wasn't like him to break a date. Had he gotten mixed up in something he didn't have the stomach for? She would be able to feel it as soon as he was near her again.

Wanting some time to herself, she pulled up to the cemetery at six sharp, her headlights beaming off the black wrought iron gates. A man peered out from behind them. Monica cut the engine, slipped her jacket on, and got out. Drawing her badge from her jacket pocket, she approached him.

"Special Agent Cappelino, sir. I'm sure you are aware we have business here this morning. Mind opening the gates?"

"You're early," the man said. "They told me seven o'clock."

Great. The guy was a stickler for time. "Sir, what is your name?"

"Martin. Martin Potts. I'm the manager here."

"Well, Martin, the rest of my team will be here shortly. I don't think there is any harm in letting me in a little early."

He glanced out toward the deserted street. "I guess it will be alright."

Monica got back into her car. The gates parted, and Martin waved her through. She leaned her head out the open window. "The Marconi gravesite, where is it?"

"Drive straight to the end of this road and turn left. You'll see two large angel statues, one at the head of each grave. Biggest ones in the cemetery. You can't miss them."

"Thanks." Following his directions, she turned left just as the sun began its ascent in a clear cobalt sky. Her breath hitched at the sight of the two enormous sculpted angels towering over the headstones. She parked and walked over to the graves, her eyes catching an object lying between them. A bouquet holding red roses, white peonies, and yellow lilies rested on the grass. She picked it up, inspecting the colorful petals. A white card fluttered to the ground.

She retrieved the card. Muscles coiled inside her chest, pushing hard against her ribcage as she read, 'I miss you every day. Love, Eddie.' How often did he come here? He had never mentioned visiting his parents' graves. Here was proof their loss lay sleeping deep inside him—something he had never admitted to her.

She studied the flowers again. Her shop was not responsible for the bouquet, but the flowers were fresh, indicating a recent visit.

Seeing Matthew and Cathy's names engraved on the headstones made her even more determined to get Salvatore Marconi put away for good. But most of it would depend on Eddie agreeing to turn against his uncle.

The sound of vehicles approaching made her look up. She stuck the card in her pocket and placed the flowers on a grave a few feet away. Evidence Technicians emerged from several white vans. Behind them, a compact excavator came into view, a lightweight machine that easily fits between grave markers. The team lost no time in cordoning off the area and setting up a tent while gathering the rest of the equipment needed.

Danny emerged from a black SUV and came toward her holding two styrofoam cups with lids. He handed one to her. "Brought you coffee. Light and sweet, if I remember right."

Grateful, Monica took the cup. "Thanks." She sipped, letting the warmth spread through her body. "Perfect."

"At least the weather is cooperating," Danny said.

"Yeah. I just want them to hurry and finish. Get the bodies the heck out of here before someone shows up."

Danny gave her a quizzical look. "You're jittery this morning. Don't worry. After we finish, we will make it look like nothing was touched. We've got turf and everything."

They walked several yards away as the digging began. "Listen, Danny. I need forensics to work fast on this. Something is off with Eddie. I can feel it. The sooner I can turn him, the better."

"You think he's ripe?"

"Pretty sure. He's antsy, not sleeping well. He's either involved in a mess he doesn't want to be involved in or uncovered the truth about his uncle's dealings. His best friend is still missing along with Ann Walsh."

"Have you pushed?" Danny asked.

"Of course. But he swears he doesn't know anything about either one."

Danny's eyebrow quirked upward."I find that hard to swallow."

"Look, I'm not saying I believe him. I think he's afraid to talk about any of it."

"Maybe," Danny said. "But I agree we need to move things along. I'll keep on top of forensics and let you know what comes up."

A few hours later, with the coffins loaded into the vans and the site cleaned up, Monica waited for Danny to leave before placing the flowers back between the empty graves along with Eddie's card. They had done an excellent job at covering up the disturbance. To the untrained eye, everything looked as it should.

Monica removed her jacket and hat, throwing them into the trunk of her car. By the time she arrived home and put everything back in its place, it was after ten o'clock. While she drove to her shop, she dialed Eddie's number.

"Hey, babe," His sleepy voice swam in her ear. "I'm sorry about last night."

"No worries. I'm just checking in. You sounded funny when we spoke."

"Tired is all. I will definitely see you later tonight. Wear something special. I'm taking you out."

"We could stay in," Monica said. "That is if you're still beat."

"No. I owe you a nice dinner. Pick you up at seven. Love you."

He ended the call before she could respond. Tonight, when they were face to face, she would pay attention, look for certain signs. Jack Wilson had taught her well. It was time for her to put those skills to work.

Chapter 46 — Cookie
What's Love Got To Do With It?

As Monica walked in, Cookie finished putting some entries into the computer by the register. "Got a bride coming in tomorrow to look at arrangements," she called out. Her ample breasts strained the buttons of her pink silk blouse, leaving just enough cleavage peeking out. Tight black jeans showed off her curves.

"That's great." Monica sailed past her toward her office. Cookie followed close behind, her white stilettos clicking with each step.

"Listen," Cookie said, plopping down into the chair across from Monica's desk. "I need your opinion on something."

Monica switched on the Keurig coffee maker. Inserting a K-Cup, she snatched a mug from a small cabinet above it. "Shoot. What's going on?" The coffee finished dripping, and she opened the small fridge below, adding milk and sugar to the cup. She sat at the desk and switched on her computer.

"Well, you know this guy I've been seeing."

"Oh, the mystery man?" Monica sipped her coffee.

"Yeah. The last time we were together, I said those three little words."

Monica set her mug down. "Cookie, no! You haven't even been seeing him that long."

She sucked in her lower lip and stared at Monica. How could she explain all this? Promising to keep the details about him and their relationship secret was beginning to weigh heavily on her.

"I can't help the way I feel. I'm falling hard for this guy. I just don't know what to do."

"What happened after you told him you loved him? Did he respond?"

She could hardly meet Monica's eyes. "No, he didn't."

"I'm not surprised. Men are really funny when it comes to those words. They are either all the way in or have one foot out the door. It can scare them away."

Tears built up, bluring Monica's face. "I think it did scare him. Things were going so good until I screwed it all up."

Monica handed her a tissue. "No, don't think like that. You were being honest. You told him how you felt. It's worse to lie. At least it showed you where he stands."

"Yeah, far away from me. That's where he's standing."

"When was the last time you heard from him?"

"It's been almost a week. I've left messages, but he's ghosting me."

"You said he was from out of town. Maybe he left. He might be married for all you know."

"No. He told me he wasn't. I believe him because …."

"Because what?"

"I can't tell you, Monica. It's something just between him and me. I promised I wouldn't say anything."

"Cookie, I don't understand you right now. Guys who keep secrets and make you keep them too will never be honest with you or anyone else."

Cookie stood up. This whole conversation was going nowhere. Monica had no idea what she and Danny had together. From their first date, she knew he was different. Even though she trusted Monica with Danny's secret of being an FBI agent, she would be breaking her promise if she revealed that information.

"I guess I'm just going to have to figure things out and decide whether or not he cares about me."

"Please, sit back down," Monica said. "I can see how much this whole thing has upset you. I have no right to judge you after what I've been through with Eddie."

Cookie slumped into the chair again. Why did everything have to be so hard with this one man? She had promised never to let a guy get close enough to hurt her. She needed to keep the upper hand. Meeting Monica's eyes, she said, "Well, tell me something then. How would you handle things in my situation?"

"Hell, I'm the last person who should be giving you any advice. But I think you need to continue to be honest about your feelings. If they aren't reciprocated, you need to decide whether you want to continue the relationship the way it is."

"You made a pretty quick decision back then concerning Eddie. I admired you for taking a stand and not giving in." She felt Monica draw back slightly, her face hardening.

"That was a different situation. I pushed for marriage, and Eddie wouldn't commit. His cheating played a part in our break-up, but if I'm being honest, the relationship would not have lasted anyway. We didn't want the same things, so I walked away."

She considered Monica's words carefully. "I guess I need time to sort out my feelings. If I don't hear from him, I'll have to deal with the fact he didn't really care for me in the first place."

"And if you do hear from him?" Monica asked.

"I'll be honest, just like you were with Eddie. If he can't handle it, then I'm not the woman for him."

Monica's face brightened. "That's the Cookie I know."

Forcing a smile, she got up and retreated to the front of the store, not daring to tell Monica her truth. In her heart, if Danny were to walk through the door, all her resolve would crumble, and she'd beg him to stay with her.

Chapter 47 — Jimmy
Who Do You Trust?

Jimmy looked up from the computer screen as Sal strolled into his office. His face appeared relaxed, something Jimmy hadn't seen in quite some time. He grinned and sat across from the desk.

"What's up, Sal?" Jimmy said.

"There was a slight hiccup when I took Eddie into the city the other day. But on the whole, I think things went quite well."

Jimmy leaned forward, hands clasped together. "Hiccup? What do you mean?"

"Seems Ann Walsh was giving Lorenzo trouble just as Eddie and I passed by. He had to settle her down."

"Eddie witness anything?"

"Yeah, the kid did good. Of course, he got rattled a bit, but we talked. I explained how things were. Afterward, we took a little walk down to the cutting room. He spotted Tommy, so I let them talk. I promised Eddie all his questions would be answered, so now he knows everything. No more wondering about his friend."

"I think this is all too soon, Sal. Eddie doesn't have enough experience to be let into that operation. As far as Tommy goes, you should have let Eddie keep wondering a little while longer."

"What is it with you and him," Sal huffed. "You got something against my nephew?"

"You know me better than that. Part of my job is to make sure the decisions we make protect the family at all costs."

"Who is we, Jimmy?"

Jimmy smarted at the comment. "I'm not going to get into a head-butting contest with you. If you no longer want my opinion, just say so."

Sal got up and poured them each a scotch. He handed one to Jimmy. "What bug crawled up your ass? You've been very disagreeable about a lot of things lately."

Jimmy swallowed some of his drink and set the glass aside. "I have always been honest with you, so I'm not going to change now. Several things are going on that have me unsettled."

"Like what?"

This was his chance, and he wouldn't hold back. If Sal didn't like what he had to say, then so be it. "First of all, there's Richie. He's not worth the money you pay him every month. I had a little talk with him."

Sal stared down into his whiskey, a thoughtful expression on his face. "Go on."

"He has got to bring us intel, or else he goes, and we find someone who will produce the results we need."

"I agree," Sal said. "What else has you all twisted up?"

Jimmy knew the next point needed to be handled delicately. If Sal found out he and Hoskins had a deal, his life would end for sure. "It concerns the raid on the Hoskins place. If we don't find out what caused the FBI to go on a fishing exhibition, we could be in trouble. When I met with Richie, I made things pretty clear."

"Anything else nagging at you?"

Jimmy removed his wire rims. He leaned back into his chair. "It concerns Eddie's girl, Monica."

"Monica?" Sal gave him a derisive laugh. "Now you've got me puzzled. Eddie and Monica have known each other since they were kids. They've been knocking around together since high school. On again, off again. You know how that goes."

"Why did she leave town in the first place?"

"Eddie was young and stupid. It seems she found out he cheated. He didn't know enough to keep things like that under wraps."

"Where did she go?" Jimmy asked.

"I'm not sure. I think Eddie mentioned something about her taking a job in Maryland."

"What kind of job?"

"Look, Jimmy. I'm not following you here. What difference does that make? I've known Monica for a lot of years. Besides, she's good for Eddie. He's different around her. Plus, she's beautiful and smart."

"It's just a feeling, Sal. I can't put my finger on it."

"So, Eddie is smart in his own way. Besides, opposites attract. I'm hoping they make things permanent."

Jimmy finished off his drink. "She doesn't seem the type to ignore Eddie's profession, and if so, that will become a problem."

Sal waved his hand, emitted a low grunt, and got up. "Trust me, Jimmy. You got nothing to worry about when it comes to Monica Cappelino. Snoop around if you want, but I doubt you'll find anything interesting."

"I just might do that," Jimmy said. "By the way, we need Ann Walsh to call her folks. Tell them the North Carolina story. Richie is frantic and I don't want him doing something stupid ofr cause an uproar."

"I'll arrange it," Sal said.

After Sal left the room, Jimmy picked up his cell and dialed. "Yeah, I know its been a long time. I'm in need of your services. I'll send you what I know. The name is Monica Cappelino. Find out everything you can."

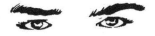

Chapter 48 — Richie
Trying To Get Intel

By the time he left his brother's house, Richie's guilt lay like a stone lodged in the back of his throat. As promised, Sal had produced a call from Ann. She reiterated the story about Tommy and North Carolina, which quieted his brother's family for the time being. Not having any idea of Ann's location, ate away at him. He believed she would remain safe so long as he could produce some intel about the FBI.

He drove to the precinct and went inside to his desk. Colleagues around him spoke into phones or tapped on computers, giving him an occasional nod as he sailed by. The door to Captain Toomey's office was closed.

"Hey Frank," Richie called to Detective Frank Reynolds, sitting across the aisle, his back to Richie. Frank swiveled around to face him, fingers brushing the bushy brown mustache on his upper lip. Nodding toward the door, Richie asked, "What gives?"

"Feds," Frank answered. "Not too sure what's going on."

The feds had made several visits to the station in the last weeks. For his own safety, he made the decision not to tell Sal. It would only infuriate him further since Richie couldn't produce any information.

Keeping one eye on the closed door, Richie flipped through his old-fashioned Rolodex, searching for a particular number. His fingers paused. He stared at the name. Special Agent Wanda Simmons, FBI. Forensics Unit.

A smile came to his lips. It had been a while since they last spoke. They met during Wanda's assignment to a case here two years ago. In a suspected serial killer case, Wanda was called in to review the latest crime scene, which Richie happily escorted her to.

Attracted to her long, shapely, model-like legs and full lips that formed a seductive pout whenever she was deep in thought, he made his move. To his surprise, they ended up in a New Jersey hotel for several wild nights of dinner and sex, followed by the customary shop talk.

On the day she left to return to D.C., she made it clear that she had no intention of continuing anything. After all, they were both married with families of their own to consider.

Before deleting her number from his phone, Richie had tucked it away in his Rolodex. Left with no other choice, he entered it back in. He would call and see if she could give him any intel, but he hesitated when the captain's door opened.

A tall, fairly young man with sandy buzzed-cut hair in a dark suit emerged. A stocky, dark-haired older man followed him. They shook hands with Captain Toomey and left.

Richie got up and strolled to the captain's office. He leaned against the doorframe. "Hey, Captain."

Toomey looked up from a desk piled high with manila folders, his broad face turning grim when he spotted Richie. "What is it, Walsh?"

Ignoring the storm brewing in the captain's eyes, Richie stepped inside and closed the door. "This may be none of my business, but the word is, the feds are in town. I was wondering if you could give me a heads-up."

Toomey's chin jutted out, and he eyed Richie. "A heads-up? What the hell are you getting at, detective?"

"Well, as you know, we had that little incident the last time they came to work a case. I just wanted to make sure we don't trip over each other working the same angles."

Toomey smirked. "Like you tripped over Wanda Simmons?"

Heat rose inside Richie's chest, climbing steadily up until he felt it sweep his cheeks. Captain, sir … I…."

"Save it, Walsh. If there is something my detectives need to know regarding a Federal Investigation, I'll inform them."

Richie backed toward the door. "Sure, whatever you say."

"I suggest you concentrate on clearing the pile of cases on your desk. That is your priority, Detective Walsh."

"Yes, sir. Working on it." Richie left, closing the door behind him. "Prick," he muttered under his breath. He should have known better than to ask Toomey anything. Retreating to his car, he dialed Wanda's number.

"Special Agent Simmons, here. How can I help you?"

The sound of her voice brought a rush to his loins. He pictured her legs, lips, and all the deliciously shameful things they had done together. "Wanda? It's me. Richie. Detective Richard Walsh from Staten Island."

There was a slight pause before she answered. "Why are you calling me detective?"

"Come on, Wanda. Don't be that way. We had a lot of fun together."

"Had being the operative word," she said, a hard edge in her voice.

"I know I promised not to call, but this is about work."

"Nothings come across my desk from your neck of the woods. What's going on?"

"Several agents have been here at the precinct a few times. You know how it goes. We don't want to step on any toes. I just need a little hint of what they might be working on."

"It could be something I'm not privy to, and if it is, there's a reason, especially if it's undercover work. Those cases are kept close to the vest to protect the agents involved."

"So, you think it's undercover work?"

"I didn't say that, Richie. You're not listening."

The brittleness in her voice made him try another tactic. "Listen, all that aside. How about I make a little trip to D.C.?"

"Boy, your skull is really thick. We had a good time, that's all. I'm not interested in a repeat performance."

His ego bruised, Richie slumped in the leather seat. He never thought she would turn out to be such a bitch. But he couldn't let her know she had gotten to him.

Making sure his tone sounded apologetic, he said, "Guess you're right, Wanda. I was just sitting here remembering how pretty you are, and I guess I got a little carried away. Hope you'll forgive me." There was a long silence. At first, he thought she may have hung up.

"There's nothing to forgive. I know I can be a little harsh sometimes. I'll do some checking, but I can't promise anything. Bye, for now, Richie."

"Thanks, Wanda. I appreciate it." With the call ending, he only hoped Wanda would come through with something. Sal and Jimmy were running out of patience, but most of all, there was Ann to consider. If anything further happened to her, it would be his fault.

If things came to a head, he would have to make a choice. Beg Sal for Ann in exchange for his own life, or get Sal and Jimmy off his back for good.

Chapter 49 — Monica

The Push

Monica woke to the sound of Eddie moaning in his sleep. She tapped his shoulder, but he failed to wake. She inched up against the pillows and waited. Late October moonlight bathed his face. His eyelids fluttered before he moaned for the second time.

After dinner in a fancy New Jersey restaurant, they returned to her place. In her mind, their lovemaking did not contain the usual passion but more of a clinging urgency on Eddie's part, like a drowning man trying to pull her under with him.

Easing out of bed, she put on her robe and entered the kitchen. She filled the tea kettle and waited. A hissing signaled the water was at boiling. She killed the flame before the pot could emit its whistle, pouring the water over the tea bag in her mug.

About to take it into the living room, Eddie appeared in the doorway dressed only in his jeans. Sleepy-eyed he ran a hand through his tousled dark hair and smiled. "What's going on? Why did you leave me all alone?"

She raised her mug. "For this. I couldn't sleep. You want some?"

"Naw, I need something cold." He opened the refrigerator and pulled out a container of orange juice.

Monica studied him as he poured a glass halfway full and then chugged it down. He wiped his upper lip with the back of his hand. "That's what I needed."

"Throat dry?" she asked.

"Yeah, very dry." He strolled over and kissed the top of her head. "Coming back to bed?"

"No. As a matter of fact, I'd like to talk. Let's go into the living room."

"Uh-oh, sounds serious."

Eddie seated himself on the sofa while she sat across from him. "I'm concerned," Monica said. "You're not sleeping well. You seem far away at times." She observed him fidget, his right foot repeatedly tapping the carpet.

"Like I told you before. Since I got made, things have been busy."

Monica remained silent. Her eyes focused on his face.

"Come on, you know I have more responsibilities now." He swiped a hand through his hair again. "My uncle expects a lot of me." His voice rose in pitch. "I don't even know why we have to have this conversation, Monica."

"We're having this conversation because I'm worried about you, Eddie. Did something happen over the past few weeks?"

"What do you mean? A lot of things have happened."

"For one, first, you lied and said Tommy went to North Carolina. You said you would talk to Ann, and now it seems she's gone, too. What happened?"

Eddie bolted up from the sofa. "Why do you care so much about Ann?"

Monica took several sips of tea. His body language and speech fit the mold. He was lying and keeping secrets. Secrets that were giving him nightmares. "Where is she, Eddie?"

"How should I know?"

He hovered over her, a menacing look on his face. One she had never witnessed before. One he probably used while intimidating some poor jerk who crossed his uncle. But it wasn't going to work with her. She was pushing, and with good reason. Eddie had to be dangling on the edge when she got the proof to make him turn.

"You said you were going to talk to her, but she didn't show."

His eyes blazed. "Why are you doing this, Monica? Why are you trying to start some shit between the two of us?"

She set her mug aside and got up. "I'm not starting anything. I just asked you a few questions."

"Yeah, ones you shouldn't be asking."

"Look, if we're going to be together, I should be able to ask you anything."

He threw up his hands. "Are you for real right now? You know what line of work I'm in. So, let's get something straight. You can't go harassing me about things you have no business knowing."

"Listen, Eddie, when not one but two people I know disappear, it's only natural for me to ask questions."

Without warning, he pulled her into his arms. His body gave off a slight tremor. "Please, baby. I don't want to argue about any of this. You have to understand the way things work in this life. I need you to do that for me, please."

She relaxed into his embrace, tilting her face to meet his eyes. "Sure. Let's not talk anymore tonight." Taking him by the hand, she led him into the bedroom. While her outside demeanor was calm, a quiet storm raged inside her.

He was there. She had done it. All of Jack Wilson's training had kicked in. Eddie's fight or flight response, the fidgeting, and verbal clues all told her that soon he would be forced to make a choice.

Jack had taught her to listen, participate in what she heard, to push but know when to pull back. Now all she needed was to show Eddie proof. Proof that Salvatore Marconi was the monster responsible for his parents' death.

Both she and Eddie rose early, he to go to so-called work and she into the city on the pretense of going to the flower market.

"Isn't Monday your usual day?" Eddie had asked.

"Yes, but I received a call some special greenery I've been hoping to find has come in," she told him.

Instead of taking the ferry and public transportation, Monica decided to drive to East 26th Street. Shrouded in Wednesday morning fog, she made her way across Manhattan to the Medical Examiner's office. Danny's text message had said to come as soon as possible.

Approaching the tall grey building, she entered the parking deck. Inside, she stepped off the elevator and was greeted by Danny pacing the hallway.

"Glad you could make it," he said. "They've found something."

Monica followed him down a long corridor through a set of double doors. They passed by several rooms where autopsies were taking place, their window curtains wide open. Monica glanced through the glass and quickly looked away as an attendant dropped what appeared to be an organ onto a scale. The eerie sound of a squeaky-wheeled gurney echoed behind them. They stepped to one side as an orderly pushed past with a body covered in a white sheet.

A technician greeted them farther down the hallway, handing them surgical masks and menthol ointment. She and Danny dabbed the menthol above their upper lip before putting on their masks. Inside the autopsy room, the sickly sweet smell of decomposing bodies mixed with antiseptic and bleach. Bright overhead lights lit the space, their glare captured on an empty stainless steel table on one side of the room.

A few feet away, an unusually tall man bent over an autopsy table. He looked up, an instrument in one of his gloved hands. Pulling his face mask down, he greeted them.

"Good morning, Doctor Brooks, Chief Medical Examiner. I have some fascinating findings regarding Cathy Marconi." He beckoned for them to move closer.

Monica had experienced autopsies before, had taken it in stride as part of her job, but this was different. There lying on the table were the naked, almost skeletal remains of Eddie's mother, Cathy. A person she had known as a child.

She felt Danny touch her lightly on her elbow. "I'm fine." Craning her neck to look up at Dr.Brooks, she said, "Please go on, Doctor."

Okay, then," he said. "We did a thorough examination and made some interesting discoveries. First, in this instance, the body's soft tissue is partially decomposed. Being in the water for a period of time didn't help, but in examining the hands—see here." He lifted one of Cathy's arms and pointed to her hand. "Several rough scrapings were found underneath the nails along with a piece of a nail broken completely off that doesn't seem to belong to this person. It indicates a sign of a struggle. We're sending the samples to Quantico's forensics lab to see if they find a DNA match."

"Did anything else show up?" Monica asked.

Dr. Brooks grinned. "It sure did. On both bodies, as a matter of fact. We used micro-CT imaging."

"I've heard of that," Danny said. "It's being used more and more in forensic pathology."

"Could you enlighten me, Dr. Brooks? I'm not too familiar," Monica said."

Excitement growing on his face, the doctor motioned them toward the body's head. "If you will, Micro-CT is a 3D imaging technique utilizing X-rays to see inside an object, slice by slice. It's similar to a CT or CAT scan, but it enhances the resolution. We scanned the bodies and found skull fractures on both."

"But," Monica interrupted, "Couldn't she have hit her head when she fell into the pool?"

"Certainly a possibility but not probable. Not with three separate, distinct fractures. I'm sure a type of blunt instrument was used in this case."

Visions of Cathy's vicious beating plagued Monica's mind. She could almost picture Cathy struggling, attempting to fight off the assault. How frightened she must have been.

"What were your findings on the other body?" Danny asked.

"Now, that's even more interesting," Dr.Brooks said. We found several leg fractures. To be more specific, knee fractures. Both kneecaps were almost completely shattered."

Shattered. The word jolted Monica's senses almost as if she herself had been struck. What happened the night Cathy and Matthew died was almost too painful to imagine. "Dr. Brooks, can we assume your findings will alter the original cause of death in these two cases?"

"There is no doubt in my mind that these two people were murdered before they were found in that pool. I don't understand how all this was missed the first time."

"I can assure you, Dr. Brooks," Monica said. "We know exactly why they were missed. It's the very reason we're all standing here today. The Bureau thanks you and would appreciate your expediting the final report." She motioned to Danny, and he followed her out. They both removed their masks, using them to wipe the menthol residue from their upper lips.

Monica walked a few paces up the hall with Danny. "This cements everything," she said. "Now we wait to see if the Bureau finds a DNA match."

Danny stuck his hands inside his pants pockets and leaned against the tiled wall. "I'm sorry, Monica. I know how hard this is for you. Having known these people personally makes everything so much more palpable."

"Yes, it does." They rode the elevator to the parking deck together. "Listen, Danny," she began. "I don't want you to doubt my handling this case. It is hard, but it's also driving me to stay on track."

He reached out, his hand cupping her chin. "If I thought you couldn't do the job, I would have made that clear long ago. I meant it when I said we have always worked well together."

She gave him a half-smile."Thanks."

Somewhat despondent over what she had learned, Monica drove back to Staten Island. Eddie's parents had suffered immeasurably at the hands of his uncle or someone directed to do the task. The final pieces of this ugly puzzle were coming together. Hopefully, soon they would know just who to blame, and Eddie would be hit with the stark reality of what really happened the night his parents died.

Chapter 50 — Danny
What to do about Cookie

Cookie had been blowing up his phone for the past week. Since she learned about his being an FBI agent, Danny started to back away. In a quandary over his approach, he sat at his desk, scanning text messages from her and listening to voicemails.

He set the cell phone down. The smart thing to do right now would be to stop ghosting her. If he continued to do so, she might go to Monica and spill everything.

He pictured Monica's face at the M.E.'s office earlier that day. Her eyes and body language revealed a lot. This new information had hit her hard. At the same time, his admiration for her had grown while working on this case. Her digging deeper, acquiring that ledger, was major.

Standing so close together in the parking deck, he wanted to do more than reach and cup her chin. He was a hair's breadth away from trying to kiss her. Memories of lying beside her, their bodies entwined, his fingers threading through her dark hair, were suffocating. He still wanted her so much. At times, he found it difficult to keep his composure.

Should he have waited for her to love him? Given things more time? Things might have worked out between them if he hadn't pressured her.

But instead, losing patience pushed him to do something rash. Something he never thought he would do to her. It was criminal, shameful, the act of a weak man. If he were found out, his career would be over, just as he had made it his mission to ensure Monica lost hers.

At least for now, Monica had her career again, and after everything was over, Eddie Marconi would be out of her life for good. A feeling of satisfaction welled up inside him. Maybe then, he could have a second chance with her.

He picked up his cell phone again. It was almost laughable to think Cookie was doing almost the same thing to him by telling him she loved him. Karma maybe? But he could handle Cookie for now. When this case was finished, he'd simply disappear. Tell her he was transferred overseas or something.

Danny dialed her number. "Hey, I'm sorry I haven't been in touch. If you're free later tonight, I'll explain." He waited through the silence on the other end. "Cookie, are you there?"

"Yes, I'm here. I've been going out of my mind. I left you messages, sent you texts. Why didn't you respond?"

"Geez, Cookie, you know about my job. That's how it is sometimes if I'm working on an important case."

"I didn't think responding to one little text would be such a big deal, Danny."

"Forgive me?" he asked. "I want to see you later."

"Come by around seven. We'll talk then."

"Seven it is."

"And Danny, just to be clear. Don't think you're getting any tonight. Not after what you put me through."

He held back a laugh. "Sure. We'll talk about everything." With the call ended, he leaned back, clasping his hands behind his head. "I bet I do get something tonight," he muttered.

Promptly at seven, Danny rang Cookie's doorbell. Surprised, she appeared devoid of make-up, her hair pulled back and clutching the collar of a pink bathrobe. He followed her into the living room. Without a word, she plopped down onto the sofa.

Danny sat next to her, hands in his lap. "I am truly sorry I haven't been in touch. But you need to understand the nature of my job. If I'm knee-deep in a case, that is where my focus is. It has to be this way, Cookie."

"It has to be, or that's your way of being," she huffed. "I was worried, Danny. One little response couldn't hurt anything. Besides, I don't believe that's the reason you stayed away from me."

"What do you mean?"

"I think you know. It was something I said the last time we were together, isn't it?"

Danny paused. Oh boy, she's looking for a commitment. He needed to handle this thing before she went crying to Monica. His arm came around her. His fingers swept across the back of her neck, and he smiled. "Listen, it was just a little too fast for me, but it had nothing to do with my not contacting you."

"So, you're not upset with my telling you how I feel?"

"No. Not at all. But listen, it will be honest when I say what you want to hear from me. I can promise you that."

She shook her head. "I don't know Danny, I—"

Before she could finish, he pulled her to him. His lips found hers. Her arms came around his neck as she returned the kiss. He pulled her up from the sofa and led her to the bedroom. "No more talk. Let's not waste the rest of the night."

Within minutes, they lay naked together, Danny confident he had the upper hand when it came to Cookie Asante. He would keep her under control until it was time to leave.

Chapter 51 — Eddie
In Need of a Friend

Eddie pulled up to the Stingray Bar and waited for Tony Morello. They were supposed to meet this afternoon at four o'clock. Yesterday's revelations had overwhelmed him. Not sure whether or not he could trust Tony, he decided to feel him out about his uncle's side action. Fifteen minutes late, Tony finally pulled up behind him. Dressed in a dark suit minus a tie, he greeted Eddie, and they went inside the bar. Only a few patrons sat on stools with drinks in their hands. Several gave Tony a nod hello. After ordering two beers, they grabbed a small table in the rear.

"So, Staten Island, why the call?" Tony took two long draws from his glass.

"Before I go there, I need to know if I can trust you."

"I've got the feeling this has to do with your visit to the building."

Eddie sipped some beer hoping it would dispel the knot that, since yesterday, had formed in his throat. "Well, can I?"

"That depends," Tony said. "Look, I will give you my word. You can speak freely as long as it doesn't have anything to do with my boss."

"I'm not here to talk about Frank Uzelli." Eddie leaned in closer. "My little trip into the city with my uncle was eye-opening."

"I thought as much," Tony said, eyeing him slyly. "The expression on your face gave it away."

"I'll start at the beginning." Eddie proceeded to tell Tony about Tommy. What happened that fateful night, how Tommy disappeared afterward, and about Ann."

"Let me ask you something," Tony said. "Where does your loyalty lie? To your friend or your uncle?"

Eddie spoke the answer Tony wanted to hear from him. "To my uncle, of course."

"Then what's the problem?"

He couldn't tell Tony he could barely think straight since seeing what they had done to Ann. He knew full well where his loyalty should be, but this was different. He grasped the mug with both hands, letting the cold cool his sweaty palms. "When you care about someone shouldn't you do whatever you can to help them?" he asked.

At his question, Tony's demeanor changed. An odd expression crossed his face. He looked at Eddie for a moment before speaking. "You may not believe me, but I had a similar situation a while back." He picked up the glass of beer. A slight tremor in his hand, he sipped and set it down again. "Someone I cared about got on the wrong side of Frank."

Almost afraid to ask, Eddie said, "What happened?" Tony's tough exterior started to disintegrate right in front of him. His posture slumped, and he stared off into the distance.

"This person was also my best friend. We grew up together, could always depend on each other." He leaned in closer, his voice just above a whisper. "I couldn't convince Frank to let things go. He took that as a sign of weakness."

Tony glanced around. Slowly, he unbuttoned the first three buttons of his shirt. The beginning of a deep red jagged scar appeared. Eddie's mouth fell open, and the air around him thinned as Tony quickly buttoned his shirt again.

"Frank did that to you?"

"And worse," Tony said.

"What do you mean?"

"To prove my loyalty, he ordered me to off the guy."

Capturing the deep hurt in Tony's eyes, Eddie didn't have to ask what happened next.

Muscles tightened in the pit of Eddie's stomach, squeezing, forming a hard band around his middle. Was there any possibility his uncle would order him to get rid of Tommy one day? And what about Ann? They would never let her go. Not with all the things she had witnessed.

"I'm sorry, man," Eddie said. "I can't imagine what you went through."

Tony looked up, his persona changing once again. "Don't be sorry for me, Staten Island. This is the life I—no, *we* chose. The sooner you come to terms with that, the better off you'll be."

Tony was right. He could do nothing for Tommy or Ann without paying a steep price. "I appreciate you coming to meet with me. I guess I have to get my head straight about certain things."

"I envy you in a way," Tony said.

"Why's that?"

"At least your uncle doesn't carry a straight razor."

Chapter 52 — Monica
Phantom

After trying to concentrate on the computer screen in front of her, Monica gave up. She picked up her cell and left the office. Cookie, upfront, putting an arrangement together of red roses, mini carnations, and white Asiatic and Peruvian lilies, grabbed some baby's breath, along with hypericum to insert among the assorted greenery.

Monica studied her work. "Wow, it looks great. I like your choices. You're getting better at this every day."

Cookie grinned. She continued to put the final touches on the bouquet. Monica was curious that she hadn't mentioned her mysterious man again. "So, tell me," she said. "Have you heard anything?"

Cookie's face brightened. A slight pale pink swept her cheeks. "As a matter of fact, he came by the other night. We talked. He explained certain things."

"Not buying it, Cookie," Monica quipped. "You slept with him, didn't you?"

She cut her eyes at Monica. "So, what if I did? I'm satisfied with what he told me. Everything's good."

"And the I love you?" Before Cookie could answer, Monica's cell phone buzzed. It was Danny. "I need to take this." She stepped outside. Bronzed acorns, unhinged from a nearby tree, littered the sidewalk. A slight breeze lifted her long curls as she pressed her phone to her ear.

"What's going on, Danny?"

"No DNA match in the CODIS database. We need more evidence in order to prove who was responsible for the deaths of Eddie's parents.

"Crap." Monica slumped against the shop door. She was so sure they would get a match. About to say something to Danny, another call came in. "Listen, Danny. Eddie's on the other line. I'll call you back."

Hiding her disappointment, she said cheerily, "I'm missing you today."

"That's nice to hear," Eddie said. "But you won't be missing me for long. I'll pick you up at four o'clock. We're invited to my Aunt Rita & Uncle Lorenzo's grandaughter Serefina's birthday party. It seems he's making a big deal over a seven-year-old. I picked up a card. I'll throw a couple hundred inside from the two of us. Kids like to buy their own stuff, anyway."

Monica's mind raced. Lorenzo Barone was in the morgue photograph. "Sure, Eddie. I'll leave a little early. Can't wait to see you."

"Me too, babe."

After he hung up, she dialed Danny's number. "Hey, I'm going to a birthday party. Guess where?"

"A birthday party? What's that got to do with anything?"

"It's at Lorenzo Barone's house. It's for his granddaughter. Can you say DNA?"

"Monica, this is not a good idea. If you get caught trying to swipe something from his house—"

"It's the only way," she cut in. "I'll be careful. Look, Danny, we need this. It may turn up nothing, but then again, who knows? I might find the final proof to convince Eddie."

"I don't like it, Monica. I'm going to set up surveillance down the street from his house. You need to be wired."

"What? Wired?

"We'll use the Phantom wireless technology, a smartphone app with remote hardware. You won't have a physical wire on your body. It will send audio to us through our Phantom box and decode it."

"I really don't think it's necessary."

"As Case Agent, I insist. It's my responsibility to keep you safe. If anything goes sideways, I need to be nearby to get you out of there fast. Meet me by the Brooklyn Heights Promenade at two o'clock."

At precisely two o'clock, Monica walked along the promenade. She leaned against the wrought iron railing. The sun, a golden disk against the blue sky, peaked through feathery white clouds. Seaspray showered the rocks below, filling the air with its briny scent. A flock of seagulls followed a fishing boat. They swooped and squawked in hopes of a nibble. Across the way, Lower Manhattan showed off its skyscrapers. Glass and steel shimmered in the sunlight.

She was so close to turning Eddie and needed a DNA match. Stubborn to the core, nothing short of absolute proof would convince him. She turned away from the railing as Danny approached. They sat together on a nearby bench.

"Put in your code and hand me your phone," Danny said. He proceeded to download the Report It app. "Make sure you leave the phone on. The app will run in the background without being seen by anyone. We'll be able to listen to the audio as it's being recorded. We can't use any of it to prosecute because we don't have prior court approval. It's strictly to keep you safe."

"Remember, Danny. I can handle myself. I don't want you busting in unless someone has a gun to my head."

"Speaking of guns. Is there any way to carry?"

She gave him an 'are you crazy look.'"Absolutely not. Eddie is hands-on if you know what I mean."

Danny smirked. "Yeah, his hands all over you,"

Feeling a rush of heat sweep her face, she looked away. "You know how this is. I have to make things real. The whole operation wouldn't work otherwise."

"Sorry," Danny said. "I shouldn't have said that."

Monica rose to leave. "No offense taken. After what happened with Agent Hanson, I know you're only trying to look out for me.

Danny got up. "I'm glad you see it that way."

"But no sending in the calvary unless absolutely necessary," she said. She walked a few steps up the promenade before turning back to Danny. "Don't worry, I got this," she said, smiling. Deep inside, she wasn't so sure.

Chapter 53 — Jimmy
Lorenzo's House

Jimmy ran a comb through his hair and adjusted his suit jacket. The missing necktie was the only thing that differed from his usual appearance. In order to attend a child's party, he had to do the bare minimum. Wearing jeans, polo shirts, or sneakers made him uncomfortable, so this would have to do.

He descended the two flights from his upstairs rooms and waited by the landing. His accommodations on the third floor, consisting of a bedroom, a small living room, plus a bath, suited him just fine—his respite from the family when needed.

Sal, casually dressed in slacks and a dark pullover sweater, lumbered toward him. "Geez, Jimmy, why the suit? You can relax. It's a kid's birthday party." Grabbing his leather jacket by the door, he motioned for Jimmy to follow him outside to the car. "Teresa went ahead to give Rita a hand."

They settled inside the rear seat with Mario at the wheel."Hear anything from Richie?" Sal asked.

"Nothing yet. I'll connect with him soon. He knows how serious we are about all this."

"Anything else I should be aware of?"

Jimmy almost told him about the man he had digging into Monica's past. Depending on what he found, there would be time enough to discuss it with Sal. "No, but I need to ask what are your plans for Ann Walsh?"

"She seems to be settling a bit, but I can't put her in the basement with the others. Too much potential for drama with Tommy there."

"What are you thinking?"

"No other choice but to put her to work upstairs."

"What if Tommy finds out?"

"He won't as long as we keep her locked up. And if by chance he does, then the two of them will have to go."

They pulled up to Lorenzo's house in the Todt Hill section of Staten Island. Though not as impressive as Sals, the two-story stucco stood out from the homes on either side of it. Lorenzo greeted them in the entryway to the sound of children laughing and squealing in the background.

They followed him down a long hall and through a kitchen bustling with activity. Caterers scurried about preparing trays of food, the aroma of baked goods mixing with Italian dishes. Rita, Teresa, and several other women were overseeing all the preparations.

"We got lucky with the weather," Lorenzo said. "It's unusually warm today, so we set everything up in the backyard."

Outside in the enormous fenced-in yard, pink balloons adorned with giant bows were everywhere. A group of children clapped and cheered as a magician performed tricks. Another group hunched over a slime table, pulling long colorful slime into different shapes, and several more were stationed by the outdoor pizza oven, sprinkling toppings onto dough.

Long tables around the perimeter, with servers at the ready, held large pans of lasagna, meatballs, sausage, and garlic bread. Another table showed off a five-tier birthday cake decorated with pink icing with rows of cupcakes surrounding it. Beside them, a chocolate fountain spewed as two little girls dipped marshmallows under the flowing lava.

The three men ambled toward the bar set up for adults in the far corner of the yard. They each ordered drinks from the man tending the bar before moving to one of the high-top tables.

"I love Serafina to death," Lorenzo said, pointing to a little girl in a flowery dress. "But I can't wait until this is over."

Stephanie Baldi | 259

Sal laughed. "You kidding me? I can't wait for one of my girls to marry and give me grandchildren. They both graduate from college this year. No serious boyfriends on the horizon." Sighing, he eyed the children. "Teresa had trouble getting pregnant, so we had them a little later. But I'm still grateful."

"What about Eddie?" Lorenzo asked. "Time for him to settle down, isn't it?"

"Yeah, I think that might be happening soon." Sal winked and gulped down some of his drink.

"You mean Monica?" Jimmy asked.

"Yeah, who else would it be? I know you don't care for her, but in this case, you might be wrong, Jimmy."

"Seems like a nice enough girl," Lorenzo said. "If they make each other happy, nothing else matters. As much as I complain about Rita, I don't know what I would do without her." His eyes focused on Jimmy. "What about you? No woman? Come to think of it. I've never seen you with one."

Jimmy could feel his face flush. "Haven't met anyone I'm interested in. Besides, Sal here keeps me busy. I don't have much free time."

"I could set you up," Lorenzo said.

"Don't bother. I've tried," Sal huffed. "I think Jimmy prefers being a bachelor. Less responsibility and aggravation."

Jimmy grinned. "That's right, Sal. My life suits me just fine the way it is." He finished his drink before drifting away from the two men to get food. As he filled his plate, he heard Sal call out, "Eddie, over here!"

Turning away from the table, he spotted Eddie walking hand in hand with Monica across the yard toward Sal. Jimmy tensed at the sight of the two. Eddie, dressed in jeans and a polo shirt, had his thumb hooked underneath the collar of a leather jacket flung over one shoulder. Monica's wide-leg black dress pants complemented the white silk blouse, making her look regal and put together. A breeze caught her long curls, lifting them off her shoulders before settling the dark waves down again. A large, expensive-looking purse hung from her shoulder. Nodding at the woman dishing out the food, he set his plate down. "I'll be right back." Walking toward the side of the house where it was quiet, he pulled out his cell and dialed.

"Got anything for me yet?" He listened intently, a smile forming on his lips. "Yeah, Maryland. Not one of the workers you spoke to at the company remembers her? Yeah, dig further. I knew something wasn't right." Suddenly ravenous, Jimmy finished the call and retrieved his plate. As he ate, he cringed when Monica laughed out loud at something Sal said. Once he found out the truth, she wouldn't be laughing anymore.

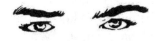

Chapter 54 — Monica

Searching

Gathered with the others around the high-top table, although outwardly she appeared calm, Monica's insides clenched. Either Sal or Lorenzo, maybe even both, had committed a heinous crime. Getting proof was foremost on her list. Her purse held several zip-lock bags, latex gloves, and swabs.

Watching the men sip drink after drink, she longed to collect their glasses but knew it was impossible. At one point, Lorenzo pulled a cigar from his shirt pocket. He placed it between his lips and lit up, puffing in and out, the tip forming a steady glow.

"Still with the stogies?" Sal asked, turning his nose up at the cloud of acrid smoke.

"Bad habit. I can't seem to give it up," Lorenzo said.

Without warning, Rita charged across the yard. She snatched the cigar from his lips. "No smoking around the children. You know better, Lorenzo."

Monica almost laughed out loud at the big man cowering back, a sheepish look on his face.

"Sorry, honey. I forgot."

"We talked about this," she retorted. "It's only for one day." She smiled at Monica. "Glad to see you again, sweetie. Come inside. I want you to meet some of the other women."

"Sure," Monica said. She pecked Eddie's cheek. "See you later." She followed Rita, her eyes glued to the cigar in her hand. Inside, Rita stubbed the tip of the cigar out in the sink. Pulling out the trash bin beneath it, she tossed the cigar inside.

Grabbing Monica's hand, she pulled her toward the living room, where five other women, including Teresa, sat with drinks in their hands. After introducing Monica, she asked, "Can I get you a drink? There's vodka and soda in the kitchen. It's what we girls like."

Monica smiled. "I'm sure you've been going crazy all day with the party. Just tell me where it is, and I'll get it."

"Oh, you're too sweet. Who knew giving a seven-year-old a birthday party would be this exhausting? There's a fresh bottle of vodka in the freezer. Soda on the counter next to it."

Monica returned to the kitchen. She eyed the cabinet beneath the sink while caterers hustled about carrying trays. The last one swept past her and out into the backyard. Opening the cabinet below the sink, she spotted the cigar and reached.

"What the heck are you doing, Monica?" Eddie stood in the doorway, a look of disbelief on his face.

"Just checking."

"Checking what?"

"Rita threw Lorenzo's cigar in the trash. I thought I smelled smoke. I wanted to make sure it was out." She straightened up and went to the freezer, pulling out the bottle of vodka. Grabbing a glass, she mixed a drink."

He eyed her before cracking a smile. "I don't ever remember you drinking vodka."

She finished mixing and lifted the glass. "It's what all the ladies here drink. See you later." Returning to the living room, she spent the next hour listening to the women prattle on about their husbands, children, and how much money they spent on various things.

At one point, Teresa turned to her. "So, when do you think you and Eddie will get married?"

Monica feigned a bit of shyness. "Oh, I think that's up to Eddie. I've been ready for quite some time." As soon as the words slipped out of her mouth, she regretted them. Sure Teresa would report back to Eddie, she finished with, "But between you and me, I think he's planning something."

Teresa clapped her hands in delight. "Really."

"Yeah, he keeps throwing little hints. I'm sure a ring is coming soon."

"Time to cut the cake!" someone called. The women got up and left while Monica lagged behind.

The cigar had been a good idea, but undoubtedly it had become contaminated with all the garbage thrown on top of it. She wandered out of the living room and eyed the stairs. Hearing the crowd singing Happy Birthday, this could be her chance.

Hurrying up the stairs, she poked her head into each room she passed, searching for the master bedroom. At the end of the hall, she found it. She crept inside and went straight into the bathroom. Switching on the light, she locked the door behind her.

A long Carrara marble-topped double sink vanity spanned one wall. She approached, assessing the items displayed on top, and immediately recognized which sink Lorenzo used. Pulling out her gloves, she slipped them on. Opening a zip-lock bag, she picked up a hairbrush. Strands of salt and pepper hair told her it belonged to Lorenzo. She removed some hair, placed it into the bag, and, taking a marker out, wrote his initials on the outside.

Eyeing a toothbrush, she grabbed it and placed it in a second bag, labeling it also. Pulling out a swab, she rubbed it around the rim of a glass sitting next to a tub of toothpaste. She spotted a waste basket. Nail clippings lay on top of tissue, and she gathered some and put them in another bag. Taking one last look around, she opened the vanity drawer. A fancy hair comb lay inside. She gathered some strands of hair from it.

Satisfied there was nothing else of use, she placed all the items inside her purse along with the gloves. Something among the items she collected should prove whether or not Lorenzo had killed Eddie's parents. Not looking forward to searching for DNA evidence concerning Salvatore Marconi, she hoped for a positive match.

Monica switched off the light and stepped out. Her heart skipped at the sight of Jimmy Galante standing on the other side of the door.

Chapter 55 — Ann

Trapped

Ann tightened the sash on her robe and stumbled into the bathroom. She splashed cold water on her face. Catching sight of her reflection in the mirror above the sink, she reared back. Her brown eyes were framed by sallow skin tinged with blue. She ran a shaky hand through tangled blonde hair.

Holding her arms out, she studied the red track marks imbedded in her skin. The poison they injected into her had left its proof. Her knees weakened. She lurched forward, grabbing onto the rim of the sink.

On wobbly legs, she made her way to the window. The heavy frosted, and wired glass blurred the outside world. Only a limited amount of light filtered into the small room. She hobbled to the bed and crawled beneath the covers. How long had she been here in this state? She tried to pull her mind out of the black pool it swam in for what to her felt like months. Vague images of Lorenzo's face flashed before her. She bit back a scream and sobbed into the pillow.

The lock outside the door clicked. Ann's stomach bucked. Her body shook uncontrollably. A man entered, someone she didn't remember seeing before. He was tall, fairly good-looking, and dressed in a dark suit.

Approaching the bed, he said. "Don't be scared. I'm not going to hurt you."

Her trembling dialed down a bit. "What …what do you want?" she said, her voice laced with fear.

"My name's Tony. Tony Morello. You don't have to be afraid of me. I came to check on you." He planted himself on the end of the bed. "A friend of mine told me you were here. He's worried about you."

Ann pushed up against the pillows. Her eyes met his. Could she trust him? "What friend, who?" she said, her voice husky, almost inaudible.

"Eddie, Eddie Marconi."

She scrunched up her face. "Don't you mention his name. Eddie doesn't care about me. He never tried to stop them." She held out her arms. "Look what they did to me. I'm not a junkie!" she screamed.

Tony glanced at the door. "Quiet down, please. We'll both be in trouble if they find me in here." He inched closer to her. "Listen, you may think Eddie doesn't care, but he does. He cares about you *and* Tommy."

Nerves rippled across her stomach at the mention of Tommy's name. "You know Tommy?"

"Well, sort of," Tony said.

"He's alive?"

"Yes. I can guarantee Tommy's alive."

His words struck her like a hard slap, waking her brain up from a bad dream. "Does he know where I am?"

Tony nodded. "Yes, he knows, but there is nothing he can do to help you right now."

"They made me call my parents," she sobbed. "They think I ran away with Tommy to North Carolina."

"Look, there is no way either of you can just walk out of here. You need to be patient and wait."

"Wait for what?" She glimpsed the frustration on his face, afraid of his answer.

"Until we can figure something out." Tony got up. "Cooperate. Things will go easier for you. If they think you're gonna cause trouble, they'll shoot you full of drugs again. And whatever you do, don't mention I was here."

"Please don't go, Tony. Stay a little longer."

"I can't. I'm already taking a big risk by being here. Remember what I said. You're not alone, Ann." He slipped out the door. Ann jumped at the click of the lock.

Tony's words planted themselves in her mind. Tommy was alive! Tommy was somewhere here in this awful place, being held prisoner like her.

For now, she needed to listen to Tony. She'd cooperate— no more drugs. So long as she knew her Tommy was alive and they would be together again, she could endure anything.

Chapter 56 — Eddie
Ask or Order?

Eddie followed Lorenzo and his uncle inside the house to an office at the far end of the hallway. A desk sat in one corner, an oversized leather chair behind it. Eddie surmised it could withstand Lorenzo's heft. Two wingbacks flanked a fireplace. Sal sat down in one and Lorenzo in the other. Eddie stood until Lorenzo pointed to a small sofa facing the two men.

"Sit down, Eddie," Lorenzo said. "Relax. We need to have a talk."

Eddie started going over the past week. His mind buzzed. Had he done something wrong? Easing onto the sofa, he clasped his hands and waited.

"You're a good earner. You've been making the cut so far," Lorenzo said. "I know I threw you right into the fire that first day with Domenico and Pietro. They told me you were a little shocked but came through. Domenico was the button man for Little Frankie, but that wasn't his first time. He's a good soldier, always reliable."

"It's just I wasn't aware," Eddie said. "I mean, if I had known ahead of time, I would have helped out more."

Sal and Lorenzo exchanged looks before Sal spoke. "I believe you, kid. Understand, there are no complaints here. Even when that detective stopped you a while back, you didn't budge on the North Carolina story."

His surprise must have shown on his face because Sal continued, "Yeah, he's on the take. Been that way for quite some time, although we're not too happy with him lately. But that's not for you to worry about."

Sal narrowed his eyes. "Now you know about Tommy and Ann. But I need to tell you, Rocco Fischetti was adamant, he wanted Tommy gone. He's lucky to be alive. I stopped Rocco from popping him."

Like a ghostly touch, a shiver ran over Eddie's skin. Rocco had almost killed Tommy. Anxiety growing, he clasped his hands tighter to keep them still.

"And in case you're wondering," Sal said. "He wasn't too happy with you, either. I explained how you weren't supposed to be there that night—bad timing. But I let him know you could be trusted and that he was not to touch you. Not under any circumstances."

Every nerve in Eddie's body buzzed. If not for his uncle, he would be dead.

"But there are a lot of things that come with being a made man," Sal said. "One of them is making your bones if you know what I mean."

Unease stirred inside Eddie's stomach. Everyone, from low associates to the big bosses, knew what it meant. A made man only stayed made if he killed someone. The thought had crossed Eddie's mind numerous times, but he always pushed it aside. How foolish he was to think his uncle would never ask that of him.

"You know your time will come. When it does, I need you to step up. It doesn't matter who. You need to follow through. I let you in on my side operation because I felt it was the right thing to do. But Tommy could still be a problem if I let him go. The same with Ann Walsh. That action is too important to be jeopardized by anyone."

Sal crossed his legs. His body visibly relaxed, making Eddie think he acted like they were having a normal conversation.

Interrupted by a tap on the door, Lorenzo called, "Come in."

Frank Uzelli and Joey Russo strode in, the air inside the room almost swallowed up by the power and strength of the formidable two men.

Today, Frank appeared more relaxed than last time at the Stingray bar. Even so, Eddie recalled the scar trailing down Tony's chest.

Broad-shouldered Joey Russo beamed at the men. His dark brown hair matched his neatly trimmed mustache. Muscles bulged beneath his knit shirt. After handshakes all around and knowing he should leave, Eddie moved toward the door.

"Wait," Sal called after him. "Stay a few minutes."

Sandwiched between Frank and Joey on the sofa, Eddie wished he could go. Every nerve in his body burned like it was on fire.

"So, Sal said. "I was just telling Eddie how important our operation in the city is."

"A big money maker for sure," Joey cut in. "We need to keep that going for as long as we can." He looked to the right, eye to eye with Eddie. "It must be kept under wraps at all costs."

Eddie nodded but didn't speak. All he wanted was to get away. Surely, there were things these men had to talk about without him listening.

"I mentioned Tommy Brazenetti and Ann Walsh to Eddie," Sal said. "He knows that they can't go blabbing."

Frank's hand closed on Eddie's shoulder. "Yeah, especially the girl. She's a little firecracker. If necessary, Eddie here will do whatever is right."

Reality struck. These men already had a conversation about him, Tommy, and Ann. He focused on Frank. His hawkish nose, like Pinocchio's, appeared to increase in size. "Sure," Eddie said. "I know the deal." Right now, he'd say whatever they wanted to hear.

"You can go, kid," Sal said, his face beaming. "Just remember, when the time comes, this is not an ask. It's an order."

Once outside the room, relief flooded through him. He let out a long breath. It all came down to him proving himself, making his bones. His uncle's words, this is not an ask, spoke volumes. There would be no discussion if he ordered him to kill Tommy or Ann. He would expect it to be done.

Wanting desperately to be near Monica, Eddie went up the hall and outside to the backyard, his eyes searching. She'd been missing since the cutting of the cake. Where the hell did she go?

Chapter 57 — Jimmy
She's Hiding Something

Jimmy waited outside the master bathroom door. Always vigilant, he noticed Monica was not in attendance as little Serafina cut into her cake. He walked back inside, catching sight of her climbing the stairs. After she had been inside the bathroom for ten minutes, his curiosity peaked. Leaning his ear against the door, he heard a bit of rustling but nothing else.

The light went out, and the knob turned. Jimmy moved back as Monica appeared. He caught the slip in her composure when she spotted him.

"What are you doing up here?" he demanded, blocking her path.

Giving him a frosty look, she said, "I might ask you the same question."

"You have no business upstairs in Lorenzo and Rita's private quarters."

A smile curled the edge of her lip. "Quarters? Come on, Jimmy, are we on a ship now?"

"You still haven't answered my question."

"And I don't intend to unless Lorenzo or Rita have a problem with me using their bathroom."

This woman was going to make his head explode. "You think you're so smart. But I've been checking up on you, and something doesn't add up."

"Oh really." Monica stood toe to toe with him. "I'm curious as to what you found."

"That so-called job of yours in Maryland."

"What about it?"

"I sent someone checking. Nobody there has ever heard of you."

"Depends on who you ask," Monica snipped.

"What do you mean?"

"Renco has government contracts. Some very sensitive ones. I worked pretty high up, directly with some of their engineers. A lot of stuff was top secret. So you see, it's not surprising I didn't hang out with the employees at the company. I had other friends in Maryland."

"I've had a feeling from day one you're hiding something, and I'm going to find out what it is."

Monica poked her finger into his chest. "First of all, who the hell are you to be checking up on me anyway? I'm sure Sal would find it interesting."

"I got news for you. Sal is aware." Jimmy grabbed her arm and reached for her purse. "What have you got inside there?"

Monica wrenched her arm free and jumped back. "Keep your hands to yourself, Jimmy."

"I said, let me see your purse." He lunged at her for a second time, but she was too quick. Her knee came up, landing hard between his legs.

Jimmy cried out and clutched his groin. He grunted and backed away.

"What the hell is going on in here?" Eddie came through the doorway, nostrils flaring, a look of pure hatred on his face.

"You're uncle's handyman is questioning why I used the upstairs bathroom."

"What the fuck, Jimmy?" Eddie snarled.

Jimmy pointed. "Check her purse. She took something. I just know it."

"You want to know what the hell I was doing, Jimmy?" Monica dug inside her purse and pulled out a tampon. "Inserting one of these. I just wanted a little privacy, so I came up here."

A flush swept Jimmy's body. Holding his aching groin, he pleaded with Eddie. "I'm telling you she's lying."

In two strides, Eddie snatched Jimmy up by his collar. "Listen, you little weasel, don't you ever go near her again. You got what you deserved. You're lucky I didn't come in here sooner. She explained what she was doing, so don't you say another word."

He dropped his hands and reached for Monica's. "Come on, let's go."

Jimmy plopped down onto the edge of the bed. Monica had been quick with her knee to his groin, maybe too quick, like she had been trained or something. She never flinched, never backed down.

His ache subsiding, he got up and went into the bathroom, not knowing what to look for at first. He checked the wastebasket. No used tampon, no wrapper from a fresh one. As a matter of fact, he had never even heard the toilet flush.

That bitch was lying, and he was determined to find out why.

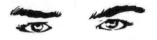

Chapter 58 — Eddie
The Cat's Out of the Bag

Upset at Jimmy, Eddie wanted to take Monica and leave Lorenzo's house but not before talking to his uncle. They reached the downstairs landing. Monica paused. "Listen, Eddie, "I don't want you to say anything."

"That prick is not going to get away with harassing you."

She caught Eddie's hand. "It doesn't matter. I took care of it." She burst into laughter. "Did you see his face when he was clutching his balls?"

"You think this is funny?"

"Yeah, sort of. You gotta admit he wasn't expecting that."

Unable to help himself, he started laughing, too. "You're right." He pulled her closer. "I never saw that side of you before. I kinda like it so long as you direct your anger at someone other than me."

"Come on, let's get out of here. I need to make a quick stop by the shop before we go to my place."

Twenty minutes later, they pulled up to Brides and Blooms. It was after seven o'clock. The lights were still on, causing Eddie to hesitate at the door.

"What's wrong?" Monica asked.

"Is Cookie inside?"

"Sure seems like it. She must have had a late order. Is there a problem?"

"She's always getting on my case. I'm not in the mood for her tonight."

"I won't be long, only a few minutes."

They entered the shop. Cookie looked up from the computer behind the register, her smile fading. Her eyes falling on Monica, she said, "I thought you were at a party?"

Monica moved past her toward the office. "We left early. I need to check on a back order real quick. It'll only take a minute," she called over her shoulder.

Deciding to ignore Cookie, Eddie stared out the front window at the passing traffic.

"Not even going to say hello?" Cookie asked.

He continued his vigil. "Yeah, hello."

"Wow, don't strain yourself."

Eddie swung around. "You think you're so smart. I know what you've been hiding."

Monica reappeared from the hallway. She looked from Cookie to Eddie. "Hiding? What are you talking about?"

Gleeful inside at what he was about to reveal, he grinned and said, "I know all about her dirty little secret."

Cookie came from behind the counter. Her fists clenched, and she moved closer. "You should be the last person talking about secrets."

Monica quickly stepped in between them. "Enough, you too. Do you always have to be going at each other?"

"Go ahead and ask her, Monica," Eddie said, his voice holding a bitter note. "Ask her how she can judge me when she's been seeing a married man?" Delighting in the rush of color to Cookie's cheeks, he continued. "I saw the two of them leave here together."

"Oh, so now you're spying on me?" Cookie's hands clamped her hips. "For your information, he is not married."

"If it's the guy Monica told me about, he most certainly is. He ordered flowers for his wife, and you know it." So intent on arguing with Cookie, for the first time, he caught the odd expression on Monica's face.

"What the hell is he talking about, Monica?" Cookie barked at her.

Monica took a step back. "I have no idea. Eddie, let's go. Between what happened earlier and now this thing with the two of you, all I want to do is go home." Before he could answer, she seized his hand and pulled him outside.

"What are you doing, Monica? You're always trying to protect her."

Silent, she continued to lead him to his car. Once they settled inside, she said. "Okay, enlighten me. Who is this guy you saw Cookie with?"

He poured out a description. "You're the one who told me he ordered flowers for his wife. Not too long ago, he came out of Brides and Blooms with Cookie. They got into his car together."

"Well, I might have been mistaken. Maybe the flowers weren't for his wife. You know we get so many customers, I can't remember everything about them."

"Don't try and cover for her, Monica." His throat pulsed, and a throbbing planted itself on his forehead. "Okay, look, I'm sorry if I upset you. This entire day has been a disaster."

"Agreed," Monica said. "Please, just drive to my place."

Eddie pulled away, a deep rumbling in the pit of his stomach. After the 'making his bones' discussion with his uncle and Lorenzo, Jimmy lashing out at Monica and arguing with Cookie, he was done.

He glanced at Monica, who stared out of the passenger side window. Something much deeper had upset her. He could feel it, like a cold wave washing over him. Maybe she was lying about the man Cookie was seeing, or there was something much more to it.

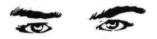

Chapter 59 — Danny

Caught

Danny removed the headset. "Let's get out of here," he barked to Steve Johnson, a fellow agent behind the wheel of the van. Arriving before the party began and parked a block away, he had been listening to Monica on the Phantom. Ready to make a move when Jimmy Galante questioned her, he heard him gasp. Laughing out loud, he concluded that Monica must have given him a swift kick to the groin.

Disappointed she had turned off the app after she left the party with Eddie, he would have loved to keep right on listening. Why not tell Monica that he still loved her and would do anything to be with her again? Cookie was only a deliberate distraction to keep his mind off her while they worked this case together.

He rubbed his temples, trying to dispel the ache beginning to form. The van jogged over a pothole, almost causing Danny to fall out of his seat at the controls. "For Christ's sake, Steve," he shouted.

"Sorry. What do you want from me? This is Staten Island."

His cell phone rang, interrupting his thoughts. The ache mushroomed. It was Cookie.

"Hey, what's up?"

"You tell me," she said.

Her voice had an edge to it. One he had never heard before. "I'm still working. Can we talk later?"

"I have one question for you, Danny. Did you come into Brides and Blooms and order flowers for your wife?"

Dumbstruck, he paused. What the hell was she talking about? "Didn't we go over this before?"

"Hey," Steve called out. "I need to stop at this gas station to take a leak. Want anything to drink?"

"Hold on," Danny said to Cookie. "No, you go ahead." After Steve left, he said, "Listen, I told you the truth. I'm not married. Why are you bringing this up again? I don't have time for games."

"Neither do I," she declared. "Monica told Eddie, that's Eddie Marconi, her boyfriend, that you came in here and ordered flowers for your wife."

His stomach dipped. Could Eddie have seen him come out of Monica's shop and questioned her? But he hadn't been there in quite some time. Not since Monica went to Florida.

"Who is this Eddie character?" he asked, trying to sidetrack her.

"I told you, he's Monica's boyfriend."

His jaw clenched. Freakin' Eddie Marconi must have been lurking around when he stopped at Brides and Blooms. He tried to focus, his mind scrambling to find an excuse before facing Monica again, but there was none. No way could he justify his dating Cookie Asante.

He needed to do everything he could to calm Cookie down. "Look, I don't know anything about all this. But you can easily find out if I'm telling the truth. Check your computer for my name. I have never ordered flowers from that shop. Someone has gotten this all wrong."

The van door opened, and Steve climbed inside, a can of coca-cola in his hand.

"I have to go." He ended the conversation with a full-blown headache hammering.

"Woman trouble?' Steve asked.

"No, what makes you say that?"

"The look of pure anguish on your face," Steve said, laughing.

"Just drive," Danny shot back. The only bright spot of the day was Monica obtaining DNA evidence. It was crucial to their investigation and the one thing that could not be disputed, even in a court of law.

How or why this thing with him and Cookie became a topic of conversation would have to wait until he faced Monica again. When he did, he would let her know exactly how he felt.

Chapter 60 — Eddie

Feeling the Heat

A ngry voices, shouts, and screams woke a startled Eddie. Drenched in sweat, he got out of bed and stumbled straight into the shower. Hot water streamed down his naked body easing the tension and erasing the vivid dream that haunted him almost every night.

These past few months, this dream had morphed into an all-consuming nightmare, the bits and pieces coming more into focus. What did it all mean?

It was getting harder to hide it from Monica. She questioned the restlessness and moaning in his sleep. He couldn't give her an answer when he didn't have one.

He finished dressing and checked his cell phone. Two missed calls, one from Tony Morello, the other from Lorenzo Barone. He called Lorenzo first.

"I need you to take care of something," Lorenzo's voice commanded his immediate attention.

"Sure thing, Boss," Eddie said.

"Take a ride to New Dorp. That mooch, Willie Banks, is trying to delay his payment. From now on, you're the bagman on this. You let him know I'm not gonna tolerate him paying late anymore."

"I got this," Eddie said. The line died, and he blew out a long breath. Another job added to his already long list. Between the car washes, pizzerias, auto dealership, and a few side things he had going, his plate overflowed with responsibility. Much more was expected of him now that he was made.

Determined to live up to those expectations, he left and drove across Staten Island to New Dorp. He pulled up in front of Banks Dry Cleaners. All four stores were well-known on Staten Island. Were it not for Willie's gambling habit, each one could easily turn a hefty profit. He removed a baseball bat from his trunk and stormed inside.

At the sight of Eddie, bald, pigeon-eyed Willie Banks dropped a bundle of clothing and tore off for the back of the store.

Eddie vaulted over the counter and chased after him. He plowed through articles of clothing covered in plastic hanging from multiple racks. Open-mouthed employees, eyes wide, jumped aside, clearing a path.

Arm stretched, Eddie caught Willie by the back of his collar, slamming him to the ground before he could escape out the rear door.

"Jesus Christ, Willie," Eddie said, hauling him up off the floor. "Do you have to make everything so damn hard?"

A beet-red-faced Willie shrunk back against the wall. His bald head gleaming with sweat, he pleaded, "Please, Eddie, tell Lorenzo I'll have everything by the end of the week."

Eddie stood toe to toe with Willie, his face inches away. "Not good enough, Willie. You know Lorenzo is not a patient man, and neither am I."

"I could give you half."

"All of it today, right now." He pressed the bat against Willie's throat.

Willie gagged, his eyes rife with fear. Those eyes awakened something deep inside Eddie. He lowered the bat. Flashbacks of Little Frankie pleading for his life invaded his mind. His heartbeat accelerated. His palms grew damp with sweat. What the hell was happening to him? He took a few steps back.

Trying to hide his growing anxiety, he said, "Listen, you own three other stores. Call your managers, have them drop off the cash."

"But I won't make this week's payroll if I do that," Willie protested.

"Not my problem. Your gambling has put you in this situation. I can't go to Lorenzo without the money. You know that." Eddie nodded at the bat still in his hand. "So, unless you want me to put you out of commission."

"Okay, okay," Willie squeaked. "I'll call them right now."

An hour later, Eddie left with Lorenzo's money. Needing to calm his mind, he ended up in South Beach on the boardwalk. Except for a few joggers, it was deserted. He slumped down onto an empty bench. The wind whipped across the beach gathering up nut-brown sand into small heaps. Foam-edged waves beat against the shore. Eddie closed his eyes and tilted his face upward toward the sun letting its warmth penetrate his skin.

He considered his earlier encounter with Willie. His bat had broken bones in the past for a lot less than Willie owed. What had stopped him from using it today? If Lorenzo or any other member of the crew had witnessed his failure, his standing in the organization would diminish.

Becoming a made man had cost him more than he could have imagined. For years he had wanted this. But there was no going back to being an associate. His uncle expected big things of him. Even, maybe someday, becoming a Capo. He would no doubt have to travel a treacherous road to get there.

Opening his eyes, he stared out at the ocean that used to calm him. How many bodies lie beneath its surface? He thought about Tommy and Ann again, locked away in Manhattan. Living with something dire happening to either of them would be unbearable.

He pictured his future with Monica. She had made it clear she never liked him working for his uncle. Would she still love him if she became aware of some of the things he had done already? Deep physical pain swelled up inside his chest, making his heart race again.

Hoping to calm himself, he got up and rushed back to his car. Leaning into the leather seat, he took slow, deliberate breaths until the panic subsided. He needed to stop and get hold of himself.

He drove toward home, dialing Tony Morello's number on the way.

"I see you called earlier. What's up?" Eddie asked. There was a pause on the other end. "Tony?"

"Yeah. I spoke to Ann. I tried to get her to stay calm. I think it helped her to know that Tommy is there."

"Good. I don't want them shooting her full of drugs again."

"Eddie," Tony said, his voice holding a hint of fear. "What are you planning to do?"

"I'm not sure yet. I need time to think."

"You understand, whatever it is, I can't be involved."

"I get it. You've done me a big favor just by talking to Ann. I really appreciate it."

"Just be careful," Tony said. "Some things are not worth putting your life in jeopardy. I know firsthand what it can cost."

Eddie let his words sink in. "I guess it comes down to what I can and can't live with. That's a decision I'll have to make. Thanks again, Tony." He ended the call, his mind in turmoil.

Chapter 61 — Monica
Results

Monica paced her office waiting for Cookie to arrive. With Cookie calling in sick, they had not spoken for the past three days. After the confrontation between her and Eddie, she almost wished she hadn't stopped to put the DNA samples in her safe. But it seemed to be the best solution at the time. Early the next morning, they were rushed to forensics at the FBI.

The thought of Danny dating Cookie was unimaginable. A violation of Bureau protocol for sure, which may account for his ghosting her. But before she confronted him, she had to be sure it was true.

The shop door jingled. Monica hurried to the front. A bleary-eyed Cookie, minus her false eyelashes, stood before her. She looked directly at Monica, her bottom lip trembling.

"You need to tell me what Eddie was talking about the other night."

"Come," Monica said, stretching out her hand. "Let's sit and talk in my office."

Refusing Monica's hand, Cookie locked the door and followed her. She eased down into the chair and waited.

Monica swept back a handful of curls and sat across from her. "I need to know that I can trust you with what I'm about to say because if I can't, lives may be in danger."

"Of course, you can trust me, Monica." She raised an eyebrow. "How can you even ask me that?"

"I'm sorry, but after I tell you, I think you'll understand." She began with her leaving Staten Island, training as an FBI agent, and her subsequent dismissal from the Bureau.

Cookie frowned. "Why didn't you tell me? I would never have judged you."

"I know, but I judged myself. I guess you could say I was ashamed of what happened to me."

"But you didn't send the text message to Jack Wilson."

"And I stand by that to this day," Monica said. "But there is still more I need to tell you." Leaving nothing out, she brought Cookie up to date on what had transpired so far concerning her trying to turn Eddie.

"He has no idea?" Cookie asked.

"None. I'm working for the Bureau again. The family of that slain agent deserves justice, and I will do whatever it takes to see Salvatore Marconi held responsible." Monica studied Cookie's face. More than friends, they had always been like sisters since way back in high school. The last thing she wanted was for Cookie to be hurt.

Monica took a breath. "Now, I need to ask you something. This man you're dating, what is his name?"

Cookie stared at her. She shifted slightly in the chair but didn't speak.

"Cookie, please tell me his name. It's important."

"He's working with you, isn't he?" she asked. "I know he's an FBI agent."

Monica's pulse shot up. "Did he tell you that?"

"No. I found out by accident, watching the news, something about a raid."

"Tell me his name, Cookie."

"Danny, his name is Danny Gage. But I don't understand what the problem is. I kept his secret all this time. I never told anyone, not even you. Last night, when Eddie said he was married, I became so confused."

Monica held up her hand. "It's okay. I know all of this is a lot to take in. Yes, Danny is working with me, but no, he isn't married. Eddie saw him come out of the shop and asked me about him, so I made up a story." She caught the relieved look on Cookie's face.

"So he didn't lie to me," Cookie said in a faraway tone as if reassuring herself.

"But you can't continue to see him. If the Bureau found out you work here and he was dating you, he could lose his job."

Cookie jumped up from the chair. "They won't find out unless you tell them, Monica."

Monica's stomach knotted. How could she convince her without appearing to be the bad guy in the picture? If Danny were standing in front of her, she wouldn't hesitate to do to him what she had done to Jimmy Galante.

"Okay, I'm going to get real with you," Monica said, getting up. "Danny never told you he loved you, did he?"

"Well, no, but —"

"And he won't, Cookie. He's not going to commit to a relationship."

"How do you know that? It could happen. We have something special between us. I don't care what you say, Monica. I love Danny, and I know somewhere deep inside he loves me too."

Her mind raced. She couldn't tell Cookie about her and Danny's past relationship, how he had been in love with her. One way or the other, this needed to fall in Danny's lap. The priority right now was making sure Cookie did not reveal anything to anyone about the case.

"I just don't want you to get hurt," Monica said.

"And I appreciate that." She frowned, her face turning serious. "What about you? I don't know what I would do if anything happened to you."

"I'll be fine," Monica said. "I can handle myself. But you have to promise me, not a word to anyone. And if you see Eddie again, you can't act differently towards him."

Cookie cracked a smile. "That's easy. I still don't like him. It makes me happy to know the relationship between the two of you is fake, at least on your part. I kept Danny's secret, and I can keep this one too."

Giving up for now, Monica said, "Okay, let's get back to work. Unlock the door."

After Cookie was gone, she closed her office door and dialed Danny's number, deciding she would keep calling until he answered. She imagined him scrambling to devise some excuse regarding Cookie. He had really screwed things up. Keeping a secret like this from her was unconscionable, not to mention unethical. Putting his own selfish needs before their case could have dire consequences.

To her surprise, he picked up on the first ring. "I was just about to call you," he said, his voice rising with excitement.

"Me, too," Monica said. "We need to talk."

"We sure do. Monica, we got a match. Some of the DNA you collected matched the samples taken from Cathy Marconi's body."

Her heart thumped. "So, we got Lorenzo?"

"No, not Lorenzo. We got Rita … Rita Barone."

Chapter 62 — Danny
Tensions Rise

A DIC Bob Acosta frowned at the two agents sitting across from him in his office. "Have I made an error in judgment putting the two of you together? Something is going on, and I'm sensing it isn't good. The tension in this room is almost palpable."

Danny looked directly at Bob. "Everything is fine, sir. There is no need for concern."

"I beg to differ, Special Agent Gage." Bob glanced at his watch. "Tell you what, I'm giving the two of you fifteen minutes to go and straighten out whatever is causing me to question, letting the two of you continue to work on this case."

Monica glanced at Danny. They stood in unison and went to Danny's office. As soon as the door was closed, Monica's steely eyes washed over him.

"What the fuck, Danny? Cookie Asante?"

"In all fairness, I didn't know she worked for you."

"And when you found out?"

"I was going to break it off—"

"But you didn't," Monica cut in. "You were having such a good time getting your rocks off at the expense of someone I care deeply about."

A flush swept over him, and he paced. "You're not so innocent either."

"What the hell is that supposed to mean?"

He stopped pacing and faced her. "You and Eddie Marconi. I saw how you can't keep your hands off him."

Bitterness rose in his throat. "Tell me something, Monica. Are you just playing along, or is there more to what's going on?"

"Oh no, don't you dare turn this around on me. What you did with Cookie is more than an infraction. You could lose your job, Danny."

Air seeping out his lungs, he collapsed onto the chair behind his desk. Monica was right. There was no excuse for what he did.

"Why, why did you do it?" Monica wailed.

He focused on her face, remembering what it was like to kiss her lips, hold her close, the two of them bare skin to bare skin, how he used to trace the soft curves of her body with his hands. Even now, in this heated moment, he wanted her more than ever before. "I did it because of you," he said softly. "I never got over us. I think secretly I wanted you to find out about Cookie and me." Ashamed, he swiveled his chair and gazed out the window behind him.

"Danny, look at me," Monica said. "Please turn around and look at me."

Ignoring the nervous tightening in his throat, he did as she asked.

"You have to let go of the past," Monica pleaded. "You will never be able to move forward unless you do."

His spine tensed at her words. "It was easy for you, wasn't it? To let go … I mean. Easy because you were not in love with me."

"I never meant to hurt you, Danny. Please, can we put this behind us?"

Dread rolled through the pit of his stomach. Nothing would be put behind them if she knew what else he had done. He got up and came around the desk. "I'm sorry about Cookie, and I'm sorry this caused so much turmoil between us. I'll talk to her."

"When you do, be gentle with her," Monica said.

"I'll tell her I'm being transferred after this case is finished, and I don't think a long-distance relationship is good for either of us. That I'm not ready to commit."

"Good, she'll still be hurt, but it's for the best." Monica nodded toward the door. "I think our fifteen minutes are up. Now, let's go work our case."

His heart breaking again, he forced a smile and followed her back to Bob Acosta's office.

Without another word about what had transpired earlier, Bob said, "Special Agent Gage, I understand the DNA results have come back, and it is not what we expected."

"That's correct, sir. We believed the DNA would match Lorenzo Barone since there are photographs tying him to William Hoskins, the medical examiner who performed the autopsies on Matthew and Cathy Marconi. We were surprised to find it matched his wife, Rita Barone."

Bob nodded at Monica. "Any thoughts, Special Agent Cappelino?"

"Well, sir, we now know Rita Barone was there on the night the Marconis'were killed. She may even have had a hand in it."

"So, what is the plan, Special Agent Gage?"

"We need to find out exactly how she was involved," Danny said. He turned his attention to Monica. "More important, I think it's time for you to present the facts to Eddie. We leave Rita on the back burner until we get a confession from Salvatore Marconi regarding the hit on Special Agent Hanson. If all goes to plan, we get Rita in here afterward to find out what transpired between the Marconis' and her on the night of the murders."

Bob looked at Monica. "You think you have enough to convince him?"

"Yes, sir, I do. He is already struggling with becoming a made man. But there is another concern I have. Jimmy Galante, Salvatore Marconi's Consigliere, is looking into my background. He confronted me after I finished gathering the DNA evidence. It seems no one at Renco vouched for me."

"Damn it," Bob said. "I'll look into it. We were supposed to have that covered."

"I gave him a story, sir. I'm not sure whether he believed me or not. But I can handle him if he pushes back again. I don't think I'll make any more trips into the Bureau unless necessary."

Bob nodded. 'I think that's wise. Keep me posted."

They left Bob Acosta's office and walked to the bank of elevators. "When do you plan on telling Eddie?" Danny asked.

"As soon as possible. He needs to understand what working for his uncle could cost him." The elevator door opened. Monica stepped inside."Let's stay focused, okay?"

"Absolutely," Danny agreed. After the elevator door closed, hoping he could keep his word, he trudged back to his office

Chapter 63 —Monica
The Reveal

Monica jumped up from the sofa at the sound of the doorbell. She had called Eddie and told him to come over right away. She had feared this day for so long. Taking a deep breath, she opened the door.

"Hey babe, what's so important that you needed to see me?" His lips brushed her cheek as he stepped inside.

Reaching for his hand, she said. "Come and sit down."

"Why so serious?" He sat next to her, his blue eyes full of questions.

"Things haven't been easy for you these past weeks. Becoming a made man has definitely affected you but not in a good way."

He avoided her eyes, his right leg bouncing up and down. "I told you before. I have a lot more responsibility."

"Listen, Eddie. I need you to stay calm and focused. I have something to tell you, and if you love me as much as you say you do, you will give me a chance to finish and not judge me."

He leaned back into the cushions. "Don't you know I would never do that?"

Monica steeled herself for the worst. "When I left Staten Island, I didn't leave to take a job in Maryland. I left to train at Quantico to become an FBI agent."

"You? An FBI agent," he said, laughing. "Come on, Monica. Why would you make up a story like that?"

Expecting this to be his first reaction, she reached into the end table drawer, pulled out her badge, and flipped it open. "It's not a story, Eddie. I'm telling you the truth."

He shot up from the sofa, his eyes wild. "I don't understand." He paced, running his hands through his hair and shaking his head. "Why would you keep something like this from me?" He stopped and drew back. "You know what I do for a living—what my uncle Sal does."

"Yes, and things are more serious than you know. Please sit back down and let me finish."

Slowly, Eddie sank onto the sofa, his eyes locked on her face.

"Let me start at the beginning," Monica said. Over the next half hour, she revealed almost everything to him, including how the Bureau had asked her to come back after Brian Hanson's murder. "I never expected to be working for the FBI again, not after what they put me through."

"You should have told me, Monica. For you to keep something like that from me ...." His voice trailed off, and he broke out into a sweat.

"I know all this is a shock," Monica said.

His breath came in spurts. Monica recognized he had gone into a full-blown panic attack. She grabbed his hand.

"It's okay. Breathe slowly in and out," she encouraged. "I'm here with you. You'll be okay." A few minutes later, after he appeared to calm down, she asked, "How long has this been going on?"

"It started after the thing with Little Frankie."

"Little Frankie?"

"He was the soldier who brought your agent into the crew. I believe my Uncle Sal ordered the hit on him."

A cold wave washed over her. "Eddie, did you ...?"

"No, no, not me. But I was there when they cut him up. I helped get rid of the body." He got up again and looked down at her. His breath shook. "What am I supposed to do now?"

Monica tried to imagine what it must have been like the day Eddie watched them kill and cut up Little Frankie, information she would keep from the Bureau. With so many things on his plate and a difficult decision ahead, she didn't want them questioning Eddie about all that.

"You need to do the right thing," she said. Your uncle has to pay for what he did to that agent."

"Monica, do you know what you're asking?"

"Yes, and when I tell you the rest, I think you'll feel differently."

"There's more?" he snapped. "How much more?"

"It concerns the death of your parents. It was no accident that killed them. They were murdered."

His face turned white, and he pressed a hand to his forehead. She thought he might collapse. "Please sit. I'm sorry, but you need to hear this." He nodded no and continued to stand.

She explained what her mother had revealed and the photographs they had found. How the medical examiner had falsified the cause of death on behalf of his uncle. She left out the DNA match. That would come later.

"How did they die?" he asked, his body trembling."

She got up and faced him. "Multiple fractures were found on their bodies."

"But you said the medical examiner fudged the cause of death. How do you know what killed them?"

Her pulse slammed in her neck. Answering this question was the hardest part. She took both his hands in hers. "The FBI had their bodies exhumed and re-examined."

He closed his eyes. Squeezing her hands, he asked, "Were you involved in that?"

"Yes. But please believe it wasn't easy for me. I remember your parents well. No one should have to die the way they did, but it's better to know the truth. They're back at rest now." She led him over to the sofa again, and they sat together.

"Eddie, you need justice for your parents and the agent who lost his life. It means getting your Uncle Sal to admit he ordered the hit." She proceeded to explain how the phantom recorder worked. "The Bureau has drawn up papers giving you full immunity from prosecution."

"How nice," Eddie mocked. "Do you have any idea what my life will be worth if I do this?"

Nerves fluttered in the pit of her stomach. "The Bureau is well aware of that. You'll be placed in Witness Protection."

His eyes watered. "You keep saying the Bureau. What about us? What about you and me and our future together?"

She debated on what to say. He had absorbed so much already. "Let's not get that far ahead. My main focus right now is to make sure your uncle pays for everything he's done. And it should be yours, too. Don't let him continue to hurt people, Eddie. His lying about your parents should be enough reason for you to agree to get that confession."

He took in an audible breath and blew it out. "I know you're right. But there are so many loose ends. Things you need to know."

"Like what?" She listened as he revealed his uncle's operation in the city and about Tommy and Ann."

"I need the so-called Bureau's help getting them out of there."

"I'm sure that can be arranged, but we must move carefully. First, your uncle's confession, and then we'll take care of Tommy and Ann."

Her heart broke as a tear fell from his eye. She moved to the end of the sofa and let him stretch out, his head in her lap. Her hands threaded through his dark hair to soothe his nerves. How could she ever live without him? She had loved this man her whole life. At the same time, she questioned if she could leave the Bureau and go with him. What did that future look like?

The two of them living in a different state under new identities. She would never be able to contact or see her parents again. She pushed all those thoughts away, wanting to concentrate on now instead of what lay ahead.

Eddie turned his head and stared up at her. "I'll do it. For my parents and for you. I'll do it, Monica."

Chapter 64 — Cookie

Friends

Cookie and Monica sat in a booth across from one another inside the Hummingbird Bar & Grill. It was late afternoon, way past the lunch rush, and only the two remained.

"Danny called me," Cookie said, dipping a french fry into the ketchup. After taking a small bite, she tossed the half-eaten fry back onto the plate. With little to no appetite these past few days, the hamburger sitting next to the fries appeared twice its normal size. Her stomach flipped at the thought of the cooked meat.

Monica poured dressing over her salad and stabbed at it with a fork. "What did he say?"

"That after this assignment, he was being transferred and couldn't commit to a long-distance relationship."

"I'm sorry things didn't work out." Monica reached and covered Cookie's hand with her own. "I know how much you cared for him."

As if singed by a burning flame, Cookie jerked her hand away. "I don't believe he was telling me the truth. I think this case you're working on with him is the real reason he broke things off." She caught a flicker of irritation in Monica's eyes, giving testament to her words.

"I won't lie to you, Cookie. Of course, the case plays a role in it. But at the same time, I can assure you Danny is not ready for a relationship right now."

Cookie blinked, her long false eyelashes glistening with tears. "Why? Because he used to be with you?" She caught Monica struggling to keep her composure. She didn't know for a fact they had slept together, but the gut feeling presented itself, refusing to go away. After all these years, was Monica truly her friend?

"Oh, Cookie, why did you have to go there?" Monica set her fork down. Elbows on the table, she leaned in. "It was a very long time ago. We trained together at Quantico. I had a hard time getting over Eddie, and you know, things happened. But I never fell in love with Danny."

"Why not tell me, then?"

"Because I didn't want him or anyone else getting in between us. You're the sister I never had. My one and only best friend. I was trying to protect you."

"Did you ever stop to think telling me the truth was a better idea? I might not have liked it, but I would have understood."

"You're right. I should have said something the moment I found out you were seeing him."

"Does Eddie know?"

"I told him everything last night. He knows who Danny is, but not about our past. I can't tell him right now, not with him having panic attacks. His mind is on overload."

"Panic attacks? Eddie? I can't even imagine that."

"It's true. I witnessed it for myself. The things he is doing as a made man are not sitting well with him. But he has agreed to work with the Bureau."

"Well, that's one good thing, I guess."

"Listen, I'm sorry if I hurt you in any way," Monica said. "Trust me on this. Danny is not the right guy for you."

She gave Monica a teasing smile, "And Eddie's the right guy for you?" Her friend's face paled. For the first time, she caught the worry in her eyes. "This whole thing is dangerous for Eddie, isn't it?"

"Very. If he were to get caught working as an informant, his life wouldn't be worth a nickel."

"If things go okay, what happens to him?"

"He goes into the Federal Witness Protection Program. It's the only way to keep him safe."

"And what about you, Monica? After Eddie is gone, will you still be here?"

"I haven't made that decision yet, and I won't until this case is finished." Her fingers tapping gently on the table, she asked, "Are we okay, Cookie?"

Cookie shrugged. "I could never stay mad at you. All I want now is to move on from Danny. It won't be easy, but he's left me no choice." This time she reached and grabbed Monica's hand. "Promise me you'll be careful."

"Don't worry, I promise," Monica said, smiling.

Somewhat relieved after their talk, the knot inside Cookie's stomach slowly unraveled. She'd never forget her time with Danny. He woke something inside her, making her realize that she could fall in love after all.

Chapter 65 — Richie
Wanda Comes Through

The phone lying on the nightstand buzzed. Richie rolled over and glanced at the time on the old clock radio his wife refused to part with. Who the hell was calling him after two in the morning? It had better not be a spam call.

He squinted in the darkness and picked up the phone. "This better be good," he grumbled.

"It's Wanda, and believe me, this is good."

Richie inched away and up from his sleeping wife. "Hold on a minute." Wearing only underwear and socks, he crept out of the bedroom and down the hall. "Geez, Wanda, this couldn't wait until morning?"

"Look, I just finished working a double over here in the lab. I didn't have to call you at all."

Richie caught himself. Changing the nasty tone of his voice, he said, "Sorry, you're right. You woke me up from a deep sleep, is all."

"Sleeping at this time of night? I can remember all the things we were doing at two in the morning."

Despite the late hour and the call, Richie felt himself go hard. This woman could get to him so easy. "I thought you didn't want a repeat? I did offer to fly down there."

"Just teasing," Wanda said, her low giggle tickling his ear.

"Too bad. What have you got for me?"

"It seems one of our UCA's got shot and killed in your neck of the woods. Believe me. Agents will go through hellfire to get justice for that agent."

Richie sank onto the recliner in the living room. A fed gets killed, and no one in the precinct is told anything about it. How is that possible? "So, the two agents I saw in my captain's office are here on Staten Island investigating the case?"

"This is a highly sensitive matter. They haven't even released the name of the agent that got killed. But yes, those agents you saw plus one more are all working the case."

"Who are they looking at?"

"My guess is Organized Crime."

"You mentioned a third agent."

A heavy sigh came through the phone. "You need to promise me you'll keep this intel to yourself. This female agent used to work for the Bureau. I'm not sure why she left. That information is under wraps. Now, it seems she's working for us again."

"Do you know who she is? I need a name, Wanda, so I can steer clear. My captain already warned me. He knows about our past."

"I only have the last name. Cappelino. Remember you didn't hear this from me. I gave you one for old time's sake."

Before he could answer, the line went dead. He stared at the phone, his mind fully awake. It all made sense now why Sal and Jimmy were so hopped up on him finding intel on the feds.

Richie let out a low whistle. Sal put a hit on an FBI agent. Could he have been stupid enough to do something like that? He would have needed the permission of all five families, a nearly impossible task. If that agent had gotten the goods on him, they would tell Sal to keep quiet and do his time. And in the middle of it all was the chick from the flower shop, Monica Cappelino. Who would ever have thought she worked for the FBI?

Here was leverage he could use to get Ann back. Fuck Jimmy Galante. He needed to deal with Sal directly on this. But first, he needed to confirm a few things.

The next morning, with a pep in his step and whistling a tune, Richie walked into the Homicide Division.

"Hey, Garrett," he called out to a young man sitting at one of the desks.

Garrett waved his hand. "Let me finish making this call."

Impatient, Richie sat at an empty desk and drummed his fingers on the hard surface.

"What's up, Richie?" Garrett asked. Placing the receiver down.

"I need to look at some of your files?"

"What for?"

"Any unsolved shootings from the last four months."

Garrett turned to his computer, his fingers racing over the keyboard. "Have at it," he said, getting up from his chair. "I need a coffee break anyway."

Richie sat scrolling through the numbered files. There were eighteen in all, the details in some pointing to gang-related or possible domestic violence. Nothing caught his eye until number twelve. He clicked on the file which was red-flagged. It refused to open.

Garrett returned with a coffee in his hand. "Find what you were looking for?"

Richie pointed to the screen. "What does this red flag mean? I can't seem to open this file."

"Oh, that," Garrett said, taking a loud gulp of coffee. "It's a restricted file. We don't work those. It usually means the feds or some other government agency is involved for whatever reason."

Richie got up. "Thanks. I appreciate your help."

"Sure. Anytime, Richie."

Richie left the building and got into his car. He had made a mental note of the date of the shooting. His next stop was Scalito's Funeral Home. If the mob was involved in a death in any way, Anthony Scalito would know.

Arriving at Scalito's twenty minutes later, he went inside and down the hall to the office. A rotund Anthony Scalito sat behind a desk, his double chin grazing his shirt collar. He looked up, fleshy pockets of skin clinging to his deep-set eyes.

Couldn't find a coffin big enough to fit him, Richie thought, disgusted by the sight of the man. He put on a smile and flipped open his badge.

Anthony glanced at it. "What can I do for you, Detective Walsh?"

"I need some information regarding a funeral service that occurred here a while back."

"What kind of information?" Anthony pushed away from his desk, exposing his enormous stomach. He clasped his hands together, his fingers like fat sausages.

"The name of the deceased and who paid for the funeral?"

Anthony shifted his bulk, the chair squeaking in protest. "Are you related to the deceased?"

"No, I'm not, and I can promise if you give me a hard time, I'm coming back with a search warrant. Who knows what we might find."

"Are you kidding me, detective?"

"No, absolutely not. It's a simple request." He noted the anxious expression, making him wonder what could he possibly be hiding? But he aimed to get the information he needed. If Scalito was hiding something, Richie wasn't interested.

"Give me the date."

Richie gave him the information. Anthony Scalito typed into his computer, grabbed a piece of paper, and scribbled. "Here, Detective. Is there anything else?"

Richie got up. "No, I appreciate your cooperation. Have a good day." Richie hurried to his car, not looking at the paper until inside. A smile edged his mouth. The name Peter Mackey and paid by was written on the paper. He pounded his fist on the steering wheel. "Son of a bitch!" Salvatore Marconi had covered the cost of the funeral. Could this man have been the undercover agent? If so, Sal had made a big mistake.

Chapter 66 — Sal
Where is the Proof?

Mario opened the rear door of the Cadillac for Sal and Jimmy and then got behind the wheel.

"La Nona," Sal said.

While they sped toward the Manhattan restaurant, the noon sun glaring off the tinted windows, Sal noted the grim expression on Jimmy's face. "What gives with you? You've been moping ever since the party at Lorenzo's."

Jimmy set his briefcase on the seat between them. "I wasn't going to say anything until I knew for sure."

Sal frowned and crossed his arms. He was losing patience and had started to think his Consigliere was not focused enough. Considered a part of the family all these years, he expected more than his constant complaints of late. "Why do you always have to make a big show out of everything? Just spit it out, Jimmy."

"Something happened at Lorenzo's concerning Monica. I caught her coming out of the master bathroom upstairs. I questioned her. She claimed it was more private for what she had to do. You know, lady stuff, that time of the month."

"Is wanting a little privacy in the john a crime?" Sal asked.

"That's just it. I think she was doing something else. I checked, and there was no discarded wrapper or anything, if you know what I mean. Plus, I never heard the toilet flush."

"So, Sherlock, what conclusion have you come to?" Sal snapped.

"Look, you can make fun all you want, but when I asked to see her purse, she...."

"She what?" Sal stared at the deep shade of pink creeping across Jimmy's face. He chuckled and jabbed his arm. "Well?"

"She kicked me."

Sal produced a full-blown belly laugh. "I'm not going to ask where? I knew there was a reason I liked that girl."

"She's hiding something," Jimmy exclaimed. "I already found out no one has ever heard of her at that job in Maryland. She claims it's because she worked on some top-secret stuff for the government. I'm telling you, Sal. It's a bunch of bullshit."

"Okay," Sal said, regaining his composure. "What do you suggest I do?"

"Humor me. Put a tail on her while I keep on digging."

"If it's going to make you feel better, I'll get one of the crew on it."

"No," Jimmy said. "Not someone on your crew. It may leak back to Eddie."

"Okay, I'll talk to Joey Russo. He still owes me a few favors. I still think you're reaching, Jimmy. Until I get proof that Monica's against the family, I won't believe it."

By the time they reached La Nona, Sal, famished, was glad he set the meeting with Frank Uzelli and Joey Russo at one of his favorite restaurants. Inside, they entered a private room, the table already set. He removed his light jacket and sat opposite Jimmy.

A young waiter set two bottles of expensive red wine on the table, pouring a glass for Sal and one for Jimmy. He returned a few minutes later with two baskets of fresh-baked garlic bread and an antipasto platter. The pungent aroma of provolone, parmigiana and cured meats filled the small room.

Sal swallowed back the saliva forming in his mouth, knowing it wouldn't be polite to start without the others. He gulped down a glass of wine, finishing just as Joey and Frank walked in.

After handshakes all around, the two men sat at the table. Sal had never cared much for Frank and sensed the man felt the same about him, but sacrifices were made for the sake of business. His feelings toward Joey were different. He considered him a *pasiano,* someone he could trust as a friend.

Sal filled a small plate with mortadella, capicola, and provolone. The others followed suit, pouring themselves a glass of wine each.

"So," Joey said, turning to Jimmy. "How are the books looking?"

Jimmy reached down, removed some papers from his briefcase, and passed them around the table. "Here are the latest spreadsheets. You can see how profitable things have been."

Frank studied the information before him. He frowned, his eyes locked on Jimmy. "Sure you're not skimming off the top? Cause you know what happens if I find out." In a flash, he grabbed Jimmy's arm. Pulling a straight razor from his pocket, he held it a hair's breadth above his wrist. "Cheatin' hands get cut off," Frank snarled. The waiter, about to enter with plates of pasta, slowly backed out of the room.

Sal and Joey set down their forks. A tomb-like silence filled the room. A shaky Jimmy gave Sal a pleading look.

"Come on, Frank," Sal said. "Enough."

Frank let go of Jimmy's arm. He slipped the razor into his pocket and burst out laughing. "I was only fooling around." Reaching out, he slapped a shaken Jimmy on the back. "Don't you trust me, Jimmy?"

"That wasn't very funny," Jimmy said, his voice suddenly hard as steel. "Besides, you should know where my loyalty lies." He motioned toward Sal. "Do you think I would try to cheat my boss, never mind you?"

"Relax," Frank chided, digging into his antipasto. He wolfed down a mouthful, followed by a half glass of wine.

The young waiter returned. He set the plates down with trembling hands, disappearing without a word.

Frank let out a chuckle. "Poor kid. I think I scared the crap out of him."

Joey leaned back in his chair, a frown creasing his brow. "You have a habit of doing that, Frank. I find it so unnecessary."

"I beg to differ," Frank said. "Keeps people in line when they know the consequences. Just ask any of my guys. They know what happens if they cross me."

Sal waved his hand. "Okay, enough of all this ridiculous talk. We have a new shipment coming in from overseas."

"What's it worth?" Joey asked.

"Street value of 5 mil," Sal said. "We should be looking pretty good for the next few months."

Frank shoved a forkful of pasta into his mouth. He finished chewing and then licked his lips. "As long as it gets through without a hitch. You never know if it's going to get busted."

"That's in your territory. We pay enough for that not to happen," Sal said. He was becoming more and more irritated with Frank's behavior. If it were left up to him, he would never have let Frank in on the action, but Joey insisted they needed Frank and his contacts at the seaport in New Jersey.

The talk turned to other things as they finished their meal. Sal was relieved after Frank excused himself to leave early for New Jersey.

Once he was gone, Sal nodded at Jimmy. He could tell the man was still shaken by what had happened to him earlier. "Sorry, Jimmy. I won't let anything like that happen again. Frank can be a real jerk."

Jimmy removed his wire rims and wiped them on a napkin but didn't respond.

"Listen, Joey," Sal said. "I need a favor. It seems Jimmy has some suspicions about my nephew's girl. Can you get one of your guys to tail her?"

"Sure, no problem. Give me the info, and I'll put Carmine Lonardo on it. He did well grabbing the girl."

Sal cleared his throat. "I don't want her hurt. He needs to be discreet. My nephew can't find out about this. He can report back to Jimmy."

Joey smoothed his mustache and looked at Jimmy. "What are you thinking about her?"

"I'm not sure. A few things have come to my attention. Trust is a big factor."

"Okay, give me the information, and I'll get him on it."

Later, on the car ride back to Staten Island, Sal observed Jimmy's silence. He would love to have Frank taken out if it wasn't for keeping the peace. The man and his razor were the dangerous part of doing business with him. He had heard dozens of stories over the years, most of them true. Sal liked things done the old-fashioned way with a quick bullet. There was no need for torture.

He glanced over at Jimmy again. This thing with Monica had really crawled up his ass. Better to put the whole thing to bed and let Carmine report back. If he found something, he'd handle Monica accordingly. Sal leaned back and closed his eyes, certain the whole thing was a wild goose chase.

Chapter 67 — Eddie
Wired Up

Eddie exited the Staten Island Ferry and headed for Battery Park in Manhattan. He was to meet Monica near the Seaglass Carousel at noon. Arriving early, he strolled over to the carousel. The aroma of sweet, buttery-soft, roasted chestnuts from a street vendor wafted past. Through the large windows, he viewed the thirty massive fiberglass fish. Each one illuminated internally with color-changing LED lights. Lacking a center pole like a traditional carousel, children perched inside each fish as they rotated, the lights creating a beautiful under the sea effect. Their smiles and squeals of delight put him at ease. He pictured his and Monica's child here some day.

His eyes glued to the colorful fish, his ease slowly dissipated. He may never see his beloved New York again. Agreeing to try and get a confession from his uncle meant living somewhere new, somewhere unknown.

Turning away from the window, he sat on one of the long metal benches. Most of the surrounding trees had shed their leaves, leaving crooked branches stretching upward like twisted veins. A gust of keening wind off New York Harbour tickled the nape of his neck. A shiver ran through him. He pulled up the collar of his leather jacket and then stuck his hands inside the pockets.

Monica's revelations had hit him like a punch to his gut. Keeping secret about her becoming an FBI agent was tough enough, but his parents' cause of death was even worse news. According to Monica, they were beaten to death. Knowing his uncle might have played a part was hard to swallow. Was he capable of killing his own brother and his wife?

Eddie's shoulders drooped. He stared at the ground and tried to push back the hard wedge forming inside his throat. He needed to know what happened the day they died.

"Eddie, this is Special Agent Daniel Gage."

He looked up. Monica and the guy he saw Cookie with were standing over him. He rose and shook Danny's hand. "Yeah, I've seen you before."

"I want you to know how grateful the Bureau is that you agreed to work with us," Danny said.

"I'm not doing this for the Bureau. I'm doing it for my parents."

Danny glanced at Monica. "I understand, never the less, they appreciate it."

Eddie got the sudden urge to take Monica by the hand and flee. He wanted to forget everything he had learned these past few days and return to the way things were. But he couldn't imagine doing that, either. Not after all he had been through since becoming a made man.

"Come," Monica said. "We'll go to the van. Danny needs to show you how all of this will work."

The three of them climbed inside a white van parked up the street. Danny loaded the app for the Phantom into Eddie's phone. "It works in the background so long as your cell is turned on."

Eddie stared at him and then at his phone. "I don't need to do anything?"

"No," Monica said. "It will record, interpret and send it back to us."

"Do you have any other questions?" Danny asked.

"None," Eddie said. All he wanted was to get on the ferry with Monica and return home. "We done here?"

"Sure," Danny said. "Try to give us a heads up when you get ready to talk to your uncle. If anything should go wrong, we'll be close by."

"How comforting," Eddie muttered. He held up his cell phone and turned it off. Looking at Monica, he said, "Ready to go?"

"Sure. Let's catch the ferry."

A half-hour later, they sat huddled together inside the ferry. Eddie's arm draped around Monica's shoulders. The feeling he couldn't get close enough to her spiraled through him.

"Are you going to be all right?" She asked. "I'm worried about these panic attacks."

Eddie removed his arm from around her. "Did you tell that clown about it?"

"If you mean Danny, no. But in all honesty, I should have."

"It's not necessary. I'll be okay. The more I think about the situation, the madder I get. I just want the whole thing over with."

She reached for his hand. "I know all this is still a shock. Just remember you're doing the right thing."

He gave her a wry smile.

"What's so funny?"

"I was thinking about how you kicked Jimmy in his balls. Your FBI training came in handy, didn't it?"

Monica chuckled. "No, not really. It was a gut instinct. I can't stand that snake."

"When it comes to Jimmy Galante, we're definitely on the same page," Eddie said.

Monica proceeded to tell him how Jimmy was digging into her background. "He suspects, but so far, he can't prove anything."

Eddie grew uncomfortable. "Watch out for him, Monica. When he puts his mind to something, he doesn't let go until he gets what he wants."

"I'll be careful." She rested her head against his shoulder. "I saw you standing by the carousel earlier. What were you thinking about?"

"The future."

"What about it?"

"How someday one of our children would ride that carousel. But I know it will probably never happen." He leaned and kissed the top of her head.

They rode the rest of the way in a comforting silence. Once they arrived at Monica's, the urgent need between them surfaced again. Eddie's hand moved across the back of her neck. He pulled her closer. Their lips met as they exchanged hungry kisses. She led him to the bedroom, and they were naked within minutes. She ran her hands down the front of his chest. He emitted a sharp inhale at her touch. His fingertips tingled as they skimmed over her soft curves.

"Baby, I love you so much," he said softly. "I never want to be without you."

Later, as they lay together and with Monica fast asleep, he studied her face in the moonlight streaming in through the window. No matter what the future held, he couldn't leave here without her. He would get that confession for the Bureau, find out what happened to his parents, and then the two of them could leave Staten Island together. No matter where the government sent him, he'd still have Monica.

Chapter 68 — Monica

Somebody's Watching Me

Armed and on her way to Brides and Blooms, Monica glanced in her rearview mirror for the third time. Certain she was being tailed, instead of driving straight to Victory Boulevard, she made an abrupt right turn and checked again. Cautious, since her run-in with Jimmy Galante, she had spotted the tail. The same white Acura SUV was two car lengths behind her. She pulled over in front of a neighborhood grocery store and parked.

Not wanting to alarm Eddie the previous day at the carousel, she opted not to tell him about her ride into Manhattan. Once she was sure about the tail, she deliberately took the ferry, hoping to get a better look at the man. But he was late boarding, and the boat left without him. Whoever chose him to follow her had picked the wrong person.

Once inside the grocery, she grabbed a basket and pretended to peruse the produce situated by the front window. The SUV inched its way past. Seated behind the wheel was the same pale-faced man with red hair she had seen yesterday. She made note of the license plate and sent a text to Danny.

Monica placed some fruit into the basket and checked out. Back inside her car, her cell phone rang.

"Hey," Danny said. "I ran the plate. It belongs to a Carmine Lonardo. He's one of Joey Russo's soldiers. I don't like this, Monica. It doesn't make sense."

"Well, it kinda does."

"What do you mean?"

Monica told him about the side action Salvatore Marconi had going in the city and who was in with him, plus how the man following her missed the ferry.

"Why didn't you tell me any of this before?" Danny said, his voice harsh.

"Because I promised Eddie we would take care of the illegal business after we get the confession from his uncle. I want to try and get Tommy Brazenetti and Ann Walsh out of there safely."

"So, how do you want to play this?"

"I have a feeling this is all Jimmy Galante's doing. I'm not sure if Salvatore Marconi gave him permission or not. I'm just going to leave things as they are. I'll get back to you." Monica hung up before Danny could answer. She had no intention of leaving things alone.

The SUV kept tailing her until she reached the shop. Inside, Cookie was busy helping a customer. She said hello and then exited through the back door. Creeping around the side of the building, she surveyed the street and spotted the SUV across the way, a few car lengths up the block. She sprinted toward it and wrapped on the driver's side window. A startled Carmine looked up at her, his face turning almost as red as his hair.

He slid the window down. "Can I help you?"

"I think I should be asking you that question," Monica said. "Who the heck are you, and why are you following me?"

"I don't know what the hell you're talking about. I'm waiting for a friend."

"Is that so. Then you won't mind if I call my boyfriend. You might know him. Name's Eddie. Eddie Marconi. I think he would be real interested in talking to you."

His eyes blazed up at her, their puffy lids appearing to swell larger. "I don't know anyone by that name." He punched the ignition and gunned the engine. "You best move out of the way."

"What about the friend you were waiting for?" Monica asked, snickering.

"Just move, lady." He put the car in drive and cut the wheel.

Monica jumped back as he peeled away from the curb. "Idiot," she muttered.

At least she wouldn't have to worry about being tailed for a while. Poor Carmine Lonardo had a lot of explaining to do to his boss.

Back in her shop, Monica removed her weapon and placed it in the top drawer of the desk. It was time for her to carry whenever possible. If she or Eddie were found out, she needed to be prepared.

Now to deal with Jimmy Galante, she mused. She dialed Teresa Marconi's number. Teresa had given her the number at Lorenzo's grandaughter's party. "We're practically related," she had said.

"Hi, it's Monica. I was wondering if your husband is home. I'm a little shaken up."

"Why? What happened, Monica?"

Luck was with her. She heard Sal's voice in the background. Teresa put him on the phone.

"I'm so sorry to bother you," Monica said. "But some guy … well, I think he's been following me. He's kind of scary looking." She heard Sal clear his throat. "I'm really upset," she went on.

"What's the guy look like?" Sal asked.

She gave him a description of Carmine and his car.

"Okay, you listen to me, Monica. You don't need to worry about a thing. I'll take care of it. He won't bother you again."

"Thank you so much. I couldn't reach Eddie. I wasn't sure if I should call you or not."

"Of course, you can call me. I already consider you a part of this family."

"Thanks again. I appreciate it." After Monica hung up, she sat in her office with a satisfied smile, wishing she could be a fly on the wall when Sal confronted Jimmy Galante.

Chapter 69 — Sal
Suspicions

Monica's call rattled Sal for several reasons. Joey Russo hadn't selected the right man for the job. Monica discovering the tail and calling him made him suspect Jimmy might be right. The girl was sharp, maybe too sharp.

"I told you, Sal," Jimmy said. "Something doesn't sit well with me when it comes to her." He removed his wire rims and stared at Sal.

"I get it, Jimmy. I'm wondering how she nailed the tail so quick. Maybe a trained eye or just coincidence. Her actions towards you upstairs in Lorenzo's house just might mean more than I was inclined to believe."

"No way was she going to let me see what was inside her purse," Jimmy declared. "I've had a gut feeling about her from the beginning. I still have someone working on her background. If I was to bet, he's going to find out what she was really doing after she left here."

Sal rubbed the stubble on his chin, got up, and paced. "It would really disappoint me if what you find out is bad. Eddie has pined over this girl for years. He went with others, but nothing serious. It will break the poor kid's heart."

"She's not the only thing I'm still worried about," Jimmy said.

Sal stopped pacing and eyed Jimmy. "What else?"

"The raid on the Hoskins residence. If anything is traced back to us, it will put you away for sure."

"Not just me, Jimmy. You know your involvement as well." Sal's jaw clenched. Did he think he was immune from prosecution? Lately, he had grown increasingly mistrustful of his Consigliere.

Jimmy went pale. His fingers fidgeted with a pen on his desk. "Of course. I'm an accessory, if nothing else. But you know I would fight like hell to protect you, Sal."

Not wanting to respond to Jimmy's last statement, he changed the subject. "My worst fear is Eddie finding out what really happened to Matthew and Cathy. Things should never have gone that far. I loved my brother."

"How much do you think he remembers? I mean, he was just a kid."

"I'm not sure. He's never mentioned anything, but it doesn't mean it's not locked away somewhere in his mind waiting to reappear."

"Tell me something," Jimmy said. "I've always been curious. If Rita hadn't gone over there that night, how different do you think things would have turned out?"

Sal got up, poured himself a shot of whiskey, and downed it. Despite his best efforts, he felt powerless as he thought about his brother's death, the sorrow left behind surfacing, steadfast and uncontrollable. It gripped him like a vise.

"In answer to your question," Sal began. "Matthew held on to his union post with an iron fist. Always honest to a fault, I don't believe he would have changed his way of thinking no matter what I said." He walked to the tall windows and stared out at the bleak early November sky. "So, if I'm being honest, in the end, things probably would have turned out the same with one big difference."

"What's that?"

"Matt and Cathy's deaths. They suffered way too much. You've known me for a long time, Jimmy. It wasn't my way of doing things."

"But you let Rita and Lorenzo off the hook. I never understood why."

"Although Lorenzo isn't blood, he's married to Rita, the only sibling I have left." Sal threw up his hands. "I had to make a decision, more bloodshed in the family, or try to move on. I chose the latter."

Sal turned and walked out of Jimmy's office. He grabbed his jacket off a hook by the back kitchen door and stepped outside. A battleship grey sky hung overhead. He left the screened patio, ambling along a stone path to a pair of benches, and eased down.

Thoughts of Matthew clawed at his brain. His decision to forgive hadn't come easy. He had made a bargain with the devil years ago. A bargain too late to be broken, his oath to the Mafia, and his own pride denying him the right to repent his sins. Adding Eddie to the mix wasn't difficult at all. The kid had always wanted in. Who was he to deny him that right?

He rose from the bench just as a black crow swooped, cawed, and then flew into the bare branches of a maple tree. Trudging up the path toward the house, he stopped. His eyes locked on the stones underneath his feet. Solid and steadfast in their place, the same as he. There was nothing else to do but continue this life.

He pulled out his cell phone and dialed Eddie's number. "Listen, kid. I need to see you. It's time for you to make your bones."

Chapter 70 — Eddie
Choices

Eddie dialed Monica's number. "I'm going to turn it on," was all he said and hung up. Uncle Sal had made things pretty clear. Making his bones meant he would be ordered to kill someone. His stomach pinched as if a line of barbed wire were jabbing at his insides. In order to avoid what lay ahead, he needed that confession from his uncle today.

Determined, he pulled up to his uncle's house and went inside. Keeping his cell phone in his hand, he went up the hall and found Sal and Jimmy in Sal's study. Today, for whatever reason, his uncle appeared twice as large as he sat behind the desk and beckoned him forward—a spider welcoming him into its lair.

"Come in, kid. Take a seat." He pointed to the chair opposite Jimmy. His eyes sweeping over Eddie, he said, "You don't look so good. Everything okay?"

Eddie nodded. "Yeah, I'm good." He eased down and placed his cell on the end table next to his chair. "Things are keeping me busy."

"You like working for *Zio* Lorenzo?" Sal asked.

"Sure. He looks out for me," Eddie lied. These past few weeks, it had become perfectly clear the only person his uncle looked out for was himself. Only interested in profits, he made little small talk with any of the soldiers but seemed to love giving orders.

"Good," Sal said."

Eddie nodded toward Jimmy. "Does he have to be here?"

Sal let out a long breath. "I know you two have a beef with each other concerning Monica."

Jimmy shifted uncomfortably in his chair. "I want to apologize for that day at Lorenzo's. I shouldn't have questioned Monica."

"You're damn right," Eddie snapped. "You'd be wise to mind your own business when it comes to me or her."

A grin spread across Sal's face. "I like this, you standing up for yourself." He motioned at Jimmy. "You can leave us."

Without a word, Jimmy got up and left, leaving the two of them alone. Afternoon shadows played on the opposite wall—uninvited ghosts. Eddie had been in this room so many times before, but today it felt different, almost tomb-like. There were so many things he wanted to ask his uncle.

He studied the man's face, aching to find out what really happened to his parents. Learning the sordid details from Monica had tilted his world, making him no longer sure of his place in it and what his life meant.

"So," Sal said, breaking into his thoughts. "There comes a time when loyalty is tested. How far will you go to protect this family and your oath?"

He looked directly into his uncle's eyes. "As far as I need to."

"Good. There is the matter of Tommy Brazenetti. He needs to leave this world."

Eddie's jaw clenched at his words. There was no need to ask his uncle why. Tommy was not a threat. It all came down to him following orders. He thought about Tony Morello, and what Frank Uzelli had made him do, his protests ending in a razor cut down the center of his chest.

"I understand," Eddie responded. Meanwhile, deep inside, he wanted to cry out, leap over the desk and grab his uncle by the throat.

"I'll make it easy for you," Sal said. "I'll have them put him in a separate room, a quiet place for you to say goodbye and do what must be done."

Before he could stop himself, Eddie said, "What about Ann Walsh?"

"Ann?" Sal's voice rose in octave, becoming almost savage. "Why the hell are you worried about her? She's a working girl now. I'm going to keep her around for a bit longer."

Eddie's voice met his uncle's tone. "I'm not worried about her. I'm just surprised, is all."

"About what?"

"I thought you might want me to get rid of her, too."

His uncle's eyes widened. "Well, I never expected you to want to be the button man for both of them."

"I do whatever you ask me to do. I understand that's the way it's supposed to be."

Sal leaned back into the chair and studied him. His brow forming the familiar long crease.

"Look," Eddie said. "My first day with Lorenzo's crew prepared me. I'm just a little disappointed."

"Disappointed about what?" Sal asked.

"That you didn't trust me when I told you someone from the Jersey Crew said you ordered a hit on a federal agent without permission from the families. It felt awkward like everyone knew except me. It made me look bad."

"And if I did?" Sal asked.

"I'm sure you had a good reason."

"Yeah, the bum had enough evidence to try and put me away. The Commission was moving too slow. I did what I had to do."

"So, Rocco Fischetti took care of it for you. But I can't believe you let him go after Tommy. We would have never said anything. You talk about loyalty and trust, but it works both ways."

Sal slapped his palm on top of the desk, his face crimson. "I saved you from Rocco. After I ordered him to take out Pete Mackey, I stopped him from whacking you and Tommy."

"I understand that, Uncle Sal. I'm just letting you know how I feel about the whole thing."

"Listen, kid. Don't make me have to straighten you out. You don't get to feel one way or the other. You take orders and do what you're supposed to do." Sal stood up. "Now, I'm gonna make the call about Tommy. You need to get to the city and take care of things."

Eddie rose and grabbed his cell. "Sure. I know what's expected of me." As he reached the door, Sal called out. "You let me know when it's done."

Eddie turned, took one last look at Sal. "I will. Just don't call me kid anymore."

Eddie got into his BMW and charged down the driveway, his body shaking so bad it was hard to control the wheel. He had never spoken to his uncle like that. But he got what the feds wanted. Now he needed to go and save Tommy and Ann. His undoing would be complete.

His cell rang. It was Monica calling. He let it go to voicemail before turning off his phone and driving to the city. Forty-five minutes later, he parked across from the brick building. Opening the glove box, he pulled out his 9mm and tucked it behind him into his waistband.

Every step he took toward the door brought him clarity. He knew who he had become, but he also knew who he wanted to be.

Chapter 71 — Monica

Gone

Frantic, Monica tried Eddie for the third time. His conversation with his uncle had come through loud and clear as she sat parked in the van with Danny and Steve. "He's not answering," she said to Danny, who was ending a call.

"He's turned off his cell. Where do you think he is?" Danny asked.

"Probably on his way to the city. I'm afraid he's going to try and rescue Tommy and Ann. I told him we would help after he got the confession. We need to get to Manhattan,"

"I just called the Bureau. They'll be drawing up the arrest warrant for Salvatore Marconi for the murder of Brian Hanson and one for Jimmy Galante for his involvement in the false autopsy reports," Danny said. "They're also trying to track down Rocco Fischetti."

He gave Steve the address in Manhattan, and they sped off in the van, Monica's heartbeat pounding in her ears. If Eddie tried to do this alone, his chances weren't good. If only he had listened to her. She continued to call his cell phone, leaving message after message.

When they were halfway there, Danny's phone rang.

Monica saw the expression on Danny's face. Gooseflesh crawled up her arms. "What is it?"

"Agents are getting ready to raid the building in Manhattan."

"No!" Monica cried. "Have them stand down until we get there and see what's going on. I don't want Eddie caught up in the middle of anything."

Danny hesitated. "You know, as Case Agent, it's my ass if anything goes wrong."

"Please, Danny. Do this for me."

"Just this once, Monica. But if I feel we need to send them in, it's a done deal."

Monica pictured Eddie's face, her mind scrambling. She could never forgive herself if anything happened to him because of what the Bureau asked him to do. It surprised her how much she still loved him—never wanting to admit that nothing had changed since she left all those years ago.

The awful things he had done no longer mattered to her. She had pushed him to this point and needed him to stay alive.

As the van swerved in and out of traffic, the blue light on the dashboard flashing, she could only hope they would reach him in time.

Chapter 72 — Ann

Trying to Survive

The lock clicked, and the door opened. Ann tightened the sash on her robe and moved away from the window. It was him. He was back again. A wave of nausea swept over her. How much more could she endure?

"Miss me?" he said, his puffy eyes glaring at her. He removed his suit jacket and hung it on the back of a chair. His tie came next. He loosened it, slipping it up and over his red hair.

Carmine held out his arms. "Come here."

Her words barely audible, Ann said, "I … I can't."

"Don't make me come and get you. I said, come here."

Terror welled up inside as she remembered the last time. His hands had squeezed her neck until she almost passed out. The rough sex left her sore and broken. Carmine always made her swear she wouldn't tell anyone about his visits.

Left without a choice and afraid to anger him, she took a few furtive steps forward. When she was within arm's reach of him, he grabbed her by the hair.

Ann screeched as he flung her down onto the bed. "Please, don't hurt me," she wailed. "I'll do whatever you want."

"Of course you will," he said, unbuttoning his shirt. "You be a good girl for me so we can have some fun."

Carmine continued to undress until he stood wearing nothing but his underwear. "Open your robe," he ordered.

Ann fumbled with the sash on her robe, her trembling fingers unable to work the knot she had tied.

"Do I have to do it for you?" he sneered.

"I'm trying."

"Well, try harder before I rip it off of you."

Tears welled up and spilled down her cheeks. When would all of this end? Tony had told her to be patient and cooperate, plus Tommy was somewhere in this awful place, and she had yet to see him.

"Don't start bawling," Carmine barked. "I can't stand that whiney stuff. Wipe your face and open the robe."

She worked the knot again until the robe came open. His eyes, like a hungry animal preparing to devour a meal, swept over her. He moved to the bed and lay down beside her. Ann closed her eyes. Carmine's hands traveled up and down her naked body, his breathing heavier, his voice hoarse.

"That's a good girl. See, this isn't so bad, is it?"

Ann refused to answer. His fingers grabbed her chin, forcing her face toward his, "Open your eyes, bitch. I want you to look at me."

She slowly opened her eyes as Carmine Lonardo climbed on top of her.

Chapter 73 — Eddie

Rescue Me

Eddie wrapped his knuckles on the metal door. It swung open, and Tony Morello, looking handsome in a blue pin-striped suit, cracked a smile. "Good seeing you, Staten Island."

"It may not be," Eddie said as Tony closed the door.

"What do you mean?"

"I'm going to be honest with you, Tony," Eddie said, reaching for the gun in his waistband. "I came here to get Tommy and Ann out."

Tony stared at the gun in Eddie's hand. "Are you crazy? Put that thing away." He glanced up the long hallway. "Geez, Eddie. Do you think you're gonna just walk out of here with them? You have to have a plan."

"No, no plan, Tony. My uncle sent me here today to kill Tommy, and I'm not gonna do it. So I have no choice but to get him and Ann out of here."

Tony's eyes narrowed. "You could have given me a heads up."

"Frank or Joey here?" Eddie asked.

Tony nodded toward the ceiling. "Both upstairs."

Eddie lowered his gun, tucking it back into his waistband. He went and pressed the button for the elevator.

"Where are you going?"

"To get Tommy."

"He's not in the basement anymore. Joey brought him upstairs."

Eddie hesitated. Of course, Frank and Joey would know the decision his uncle had made for Tommy. The elevator arrived, and he stepped inside. He removed his 9mm again.

"Wait!" Tony called. "I'm coming with you." He pulled out a weapon of his own and got in. "We might as well do this together."

"What about, Frank?" Eddie said, his flesh crawling at the thought of the straight razor.

"I'm done with him. This has been a long time coming."

Eddie pressed six, the two of them silent as the elevator rose. The doors opened, and they walked out together, each surveying the long hallway.

"Do you know where they're holding Tommy?" Eddie whispered.

"I have an idea. Follow me."

He followed Tony down the hallway in the opposite direction of Ann's room and the office. Tony made a sharp right at the end and pointed to a door. It looked the same as all the others until they got closer. Eddie noticed a keypad instead of a lock.

Tony approached the keypad. He punched in some numbers and opened the door. Tommy lay on a steel-framed bed with a sliver of a mattress. One of his eyes appeared swollen shut, and a deep gash ran down the right side of his face.

He reared up when he saw the two men. "Eddie, what is this all about? They brought me up here and beat the hell out of me."

Tony put a finger to his lips. "Shush," he hissed.

"It's okay, Tommy," Eddie said, hearing the catch in his own voice. Seeing his friend in this condition made him even more determined. "We've come to get you and Ann out of here."

Eddie and Tony helped Tommy up off the bed. "Can you walk?" Eddie asked.

"Yeah, they hadn't gotten to my kneecaps, yet."

Tony peeked around the doorframe. "All's clear."

The three men left the room and went up the hallway and around the corner. As they approached Ann's room, Tony pointed to the lock. "It's open. Be careful. Someone is inside. His voice went soft, almost dangerous.

Weapons in their hands, Eddie and Tony, entered the room. Adrenaline surged through Eddie's body at the sight of Carmine Lonardo laying on top of Ann. He pointed his 9mm at Carmine. "Get the fuck off of her!"

Carmine rolled to one side and got up, his eyes wide at the sight of the three men. "Look, fellas, I was just having a little fun."

Tommy ran over to a frightened Ann as she pulled on her robe. "Oh, baby, I'm so sorry."

Carmine moved to get his clothes. Eddie stepped closer. "No, I don't think so." He motioned to Ann and Tommy. "Get to the elevator." He tossed them his car keys. "I'm parked right up the block."

Tommy, hesitant, looked from Eddie to Ann. "Come on, Tommy." Ann grabbed his hand, and they dashed out the door.

"You're out of your mind, Marconi," Carmine sneered. "You think the Capos are gonna let this go?" He focused on Tony. "I can't believe you let him talk you into this."

"Eddie didn't have to talk me into anything," Tony said.

"So, now what?" Carmine snarled. "The three of us just go on our merry way? Pretend we don't know what happened."

Tony raised his weapon. "Who said anything about the three of us?" He pulled the trigger, planting a shot in Carmine's forehead.

Eyes wide, Carmine went limp and collapsed onto the floor.

Eddie and Tony backed away. Footsteps sounded from the hall. Before they could turn around, Frank Uzelli charged through the door with Joey Russo. Frank grabbed Tony from behind, his straight razor slashing across his neck.

Eddie sprung to the side, lifted his weapon, and shot Joey Russo.

Joey clutched at his chest. "You son of bitch! You'll die for this." Blood seeped through the front of his shirt. He leaned back against the doorframe and slid to the floor.

Eddie raised his weapon again, but Frank was nowhere to be seen. He rushed over to Tony, who lay, eyes wide open, blood pouring from the wound on his neck. He made a gurgling sound as his arm reached up towards Eddie, then fell back down. His voice a mere rasp, he said, "Go after, Frank." His eyes closed and his body went limp.

"No, no!" Eddie cried. But Tony didn't respond.

Holding tight to his weapon, he stepped out into the hallway in search of Frank. He crept farther down to the office, but it was empty. He went over to the desk and began pulling open several drawers until he found a ring of keys.

The gun still in his other hand, he crept back down the hallway again. He reached the opposite end with still no sign of Frank. The elevator doors opened behind him. Eddie spun around.

Monica stepped out, her gun drawn. She ran toward him. "Thank God you're alive."

Chapter 74 — Sal

The Commission

Sal poked his head into Jimmy's office door. "I'm going out. Richie called, says he got information for me."

"Want me to come?" Jimmy asked, looking away from the computer.

"No. I'm going into the city afterwards." Outside, he climbed into the Cadillac SUV and told Mario to take the Bayonne Bridge to the seaport in New Jersey.

Winding their way along Richmond Terrace, Sal stared out the window at the sun's rays glistening off the Kill Van Kull channel. The calm sea reminded him of growing up not far from here. He and Matthew would fish along the banks, teasing and play fighting with each other. When Rita married Lorenzo not long after their father died, it was Matthew who walked her down the isle.

If only Matthew had agreed to let the mob have control of his union. It was a known fact back then. Cooperate or suffer the consequences. But would he have gone all the way with Matt if things hadn't gone off the rails? He'd never know. Rita and Lorenzo made sure of that.

His thoughts turned to his conversation with Eddie. The kid was really growing balls. After he followed through on getting rid of Tommy, with his loyalty set in stone, big things were in store for his future in the organization.

His cell phone rang, and he glanced at the number. It was Frank Uzelli calling. Disgusted by Frank's behavior toward Jimmy, he declined the call and put his phone on vibrate. He would catch up with Frank later after his meeting with Richie.

They cruised over the bridge and made their way to the Bayonne Container Yard. Mario drove through the opening in the iron gates, waving to the security guard who they knew well. After driving past a long line of shipping containers, Mario pulled over and cut the ignition.

The meetings between the two never took place on Staten Island due to Richie's paranoia about being followed. Minutes ticked by. Sal drummed his fingers on the leather seat. He didn't tolerate people being late.

There was a knock on the opposite rear window. Mario released the locks. He placed a cigarette between his lips and stepped out of the car while Richie slid inside next to Sal.

"Can't you ever be on time?" Sal snapped. "You're ten minutes late."

Richie murmured an apology and then dug his hands inside the pockets of his wool jacket. "I have some information for you."

"It's about time," Sal said. "I hope it's worth my making the trip here." Sal's phone buzzed repeatedly.

Richie gave him a questioning look. "Do you need to answer that?"

"Don't worry about it. Tell me why this meeting was so urgent."

"The FBI is here investigating the murder of one of their undercover agents." Richie stopped as if waiting for a response from Sal.

"Is that all you got?" Sal asked. This guy was really trying his patience.

"No, of course not. It appears they're looking at Organized Crime. This is a really big deal, Sal. This one is not going away."

"They have to prove we were involved, right Richie?"

"Well, sure, but …."

"But nothing. If they can't get proof, then we don't have to worry. But I need you to stay on top of this. Find out exactly who they're looking at."

"There is one other thing," Richie said. "But I need certain assurances first."

"Assurances?"

"About my niece, Ann. I need your word that nothing will happen to her and that you'll let her go. I'll make sure she stays quiet. I can send her to relatives out of state."

Sal glared at him. "Since when do I bargain with you?"

"Please, Sal, you can stop paying me. I don't care about the money. I just want Ann back."

Sal stretched and popped his knuckles. "If I do this, you promise to take her away from here?"

"Absolutely," Richie said. "You'll never hear from her or see her again."

"Okay. What else have you got?"

"It's about Monica Cappelino. She's a fed. She's working on the case."

Sal's gut spasmed. "Monica? A fed?"

"Yes. I got it straight from a source inside the FBI."

"Get out, Richie," Sal bellowed, his face crimson.

"What?"

"You heard me. Get out of the car, now."

"Remember you gave me your word about Ann. I'm holding you to it." Richie opened the door and left.

Sal sat in stunned silence. Jimmy had been right all along. That bitch was trying to get information by leading his nephew on. He needed to talk to Eddie right away. Sal pulled out his cell.

Ten missed calls from Frank Uzelli flashed on the screen. He dialed Frank's number.

"What's with all the calls?"

Sal listened, a blinding rage building within. Eddie had betrayed him. He hung up, staring at the phone in disbelief, until another thought hit him like a thunderbolt. His conversation with Eddie about loyalty. He had confessed to ordering the hit on Pete Mackey. Eddie was a rat working with the feds! This man he had raised like a son put a knife right through his heart.

Wanting to return to Staten Island as soon as possible, he slid the window down and called out to Mario before raising it again. A hail of bullets bombarded the car, shattering the window.

Sal ducked, to no avail, as several struck him in the side of his neck and chest. Gasping, he reached for the door handle and swung it open. He caught sight of Richie lying a few feet away on the ground. Where was Mario?

He fell out of the car and onto the pavement. Burning pain ripped through his body. He blinked and tried to clear his vision. The last thing he saw was Mario putting out his cigarette. Rocco Fischetti stood next to him with an automatic weapon in his hands.

Rocco walked over and looked down, his smile leaking acid. "The Commission has spoken."

Salvatore Marconi's world went black.

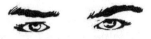

Chapter 75 — Jimmy
What Goes Around Comes Around

Jimmy finished transferring a portion of Sal's profits to his overseas accounts. These last few weeks had left a nagging feeling he just couldn't shake. Between the hit on the federal agent, the side action in Manhattan, the tension between him and Eddie, and his suspicion about Monica, his nerves were raw.

Maybe it was time for him to get out. He had accumulated enough money to live quite a luxurious life outside the United States.

There was a light tap on his door. "Come," Jimmy called.

Teresa stepped in, a coat over her arm and carrying a purse. "Do you know what time Sal is coming back?"

"Not too sure. I think he went into the city. Is there something you need?" He really liked Teresa. Over the years, she had always looked out for him, made him feel like he belonged.

"No, not really," she said. "I couldn't reach him. Just let him know I went out to do a little shopping and to meet some of the women for an early dinner."

Jimmy chuckled. "Oh, a girls' night."

"Yeah, something like that. Sometimes I wish I still *was* a girl. Those days are far behind me."

"Well, enjoy yourself. You deserve it. You always take good care of everyone here."

"Thanks, Jimmy. You're a peach."

After she left, Jimmy pulled up a map of Europe on his computer. The Swiss Alps might be nice, he thought. A beautiful country, Switzerland. He had been there on vacation twice. A second home in a warmer climate tempted him also. Singapore, or Malaysia, he could live like a king in those countries.

His cell rang, interrupting his meanderings. "What have you got?" Jimmy asked. He removed his wire rims and leaned his elbows on the desk. "Are you one hundred percent sure?"

The air in the room thinned. He pinched the bridge of his nose as a slamming headache formed. "Yeah, don't worry," he said. "You earned your money. I'll send it tonight."

Jimmy hung up the phone. He massaged his forehead and set his wire rims back in place. It turned out Monica trained as an FBI agent after she left Staten Island. All his suspicions were correct about her.

A million questions presented themselves. Could she still be working for them? Was the shop a cover for her job with the FBI? He got up and poured a shot of whiskey. It all made sense now. Her snooping around Lorenzo's house, creeping up the hall after dinner that first time and the raid on the Hoskins' residence. Her cozying up to Eddie was all a cover. Monica was a fake. Sal needed to hear this right away.

Jimmy picked up his cell and dialed. The call went straight to voicemail. "Sal, call me as soon as you get this message. It's urgent."

He gulped down his drink and poured another. Footsteps sounded in the hall. Jimmy swung around. It must be Sal. The glass in his hand dropped to the floor, shattering the crystal tumbler.

Frank Uzelli stood in the doorway.

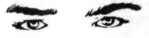

Chapter 76 — Monica
Fair Game

Taking in Eddie's pale face and wild eyes. Monica asked, "Are you okay? Why didn't you wait for us?"

Eddie lowered his gun. "I couldn't. My uncle ordered me to come here and kill Tommy. I got you your confession. This part I had to do for me."

He led her up the hall to Tony and Carmine's bodies. Tears welled up in his eyes at the sight of Tony again. "He was only trying to help me, and look what happened to him."

Monica bent down. Lifting Tony's wrist, she searched for a pulse. Weak and thready. "He's still breathing, but barely." Pulling out her cell, she called for an ambulance, directing them to the proper floor. She removed her scarf and put pressure on the wound.

Frantic, Eddie asked, "Will he make it?"

"Maybe," Monica said, "Unfortunately, with things like this, there is always collateral damage. Tell me exactly what happened." Sirens wailed outside as she listened to Eddie. After he finished, they heard the elevator doors open. Danny, along with several agents, rushed into the room. Behind them, two EMTs wheeled in a stretcher.

"He still has a pulse," Monica said releasing the pressure on the wound. The EMT took over. She grasped Eddie's hand and led him to the elevator. Danny followed and she brought him up to date. "Frank Uzelli is on the run."

"We already cleared out the basement and seized the drugs," Danny said. "We've got agents searching the rest of the building."

Eddie handed Danny the ring of keys and his gun. "You need to check these rooms."

"We need to get you into protective custody," Danny said.

Eddie shook his head and backed away. "Not yet. There's one other thing I have to do. I need to talk to my uncle one more time before you arrest him. Call it closure. You owe me that much for what I did to help the Bureau."

Seeing the determined look on Eddie's face, Monica said, "I'll go with him."

Danny hesitated. "Agents are on their way to take Salvatore Marconi, Jimmy Galante, and Rita and Lorenzo Barone into custody. Keep me updated. We'll finish things here. I'll contact the agents and let them know."

They left the building and got into Monica's car. "Are you sure you want to do this?" she asked.

"It's not a question of want. It's what I need."

Monica, behind the wheel, glanced sideways at Eddie every so often. The ordeal he had been through today would stay with him for the rest of his life. A life she might never be able to live with him.

Eddie broke the silence between them. "What about Tommy and Ann?"

"I know how much you care about them. You need to convince them to go into witness protection the same as you. We can't guarantee, after what happened, that they'll be safe."

Eddie stared out the passenger window. "Okay. I'll talk to Tommy. At least they can be together the same as us."

Monica took a deep, steadying breath. How could she tell him she was not going? She had wrestled with this decision ever since she agreed to rejoin the Bureau. Her throat closed, the words refusing to come out. Now was not the right time. But would there ever be one?

They pulled up to Sal's house. The gates were wide open. Several agents waited at the bottom of the driveway. One of them signaled Monica as they got out of the car. She looked at Eddie. "Wait here."

Monica walked over, relieved to see it was Steve Johnson. "What's up, Steve?"

"We just got word. Salvatore Marconi's body was found along with a Detective Richard Walsh."

Her heart gave a slight twist inside her chest. "Where?"

"New Jersey. A shipping container yard. It was definitely a hit. Both men had more than one bullet hole in them. One good thing, though, we have Rita and Lorenzo Barone in custody."

"That's good news. Give me a minute with Eddie before you go inside after Jimmy Galante."

"Sure," Steve said. "He did a great thing for the Bureau."

Monica turned. Eddie was nowhere in sight. He had gone inside without her. She hurried up the driveway and through the front door. She followed the sound of voices up the hallway. They were coming from Jimmy Galante's office.

"Let him go, Frank," she heard Eddie say. "Enough killing has been done tonight."

"I'm not letting this weasel go," Frank growled. "He's been cooking the books. Stealing money."

"That's not true," Jimmy whined. "Tell him, Eddie. I would never cheat anyone."

"And you, Eddie," Frank spat. "What you did tonight when Sal and the other families find out, you're dead meat. Nobody tolerates a rat, Eddie. Nobody."

Monica drew her weapon and crept toward the door, her back against the wall. A gold-framed mirror hanging on the wall directly across from the doorway gave her a clear picture. Frank

Uzelli stood with one arm wrapped around Jimmy Galante's shoulders. His other hand held a straight razor.

"You see, Jimmy. I kept a set of books of my own," Frank said. "The figures you've been giving me don't match up to mine."

Monica pushed away from the wall and whirled around. She stood in the doorway, arms outstretched, gun in her hands. "Put the razor down, Frank. This is over."

"He stared at Monica, his mouth open. "You? A cop? I saw you at Lorenzo's."

"No," Eddie said. "She's FBI."

Frank nodded toward Monica. "You put that gun down, bitch, or I'll slit his throat."

"That's not going to happen, Frank." Monica took a step closer. "There's dozens of agents outside. You'll never get away. We raided your little operation in the city. So, it doesn't matter to me whether we take you in or I shoot you."

Frank's arm shot up. Monica squeezed the trigger. The bullet sped from the chamber, striking him in the arm that held the razor. It dropped from his hand, and he fell back against the wall of bookcases. An ashen-faced Jimmy collapsed onto the floor.

At the sound of the gunshot, agents swarmed inside. Steve rushed over to Monica. "Are you okay?"

Monica lowered her weapon. "Fine."

Steve and several agents went over to Frank who lay moaning on the floor. "Call an ambulance," Steve barked at one of the agents.

Monica nodded toward Eddie. "Please wait outside. I'll be out in a few minutes."

"But ..."

"Please. I'm okay. I need you to go."

After he was gone, she walked over to Jimmy. He grabbed the edge of the desk and slowly got onto his feet. "I knew it all along!" His voice shook with fury. "I warned Sal about you, but he wouldn't listen. Now he'll see how right I was."

Monica smirked. "Sal isn't going to see or hear anything. Sal's dead."

Jimmy's mouth gaped. "Dead?"

"That's right. Your dear Sal and Detective Richard Walsh, who we know was on the take, were shot multiple times."

"Killed by the FBI?"

"No, Jimmy, not by us. I believe the Commission wasn't too happy with him. Going rogue and killing an FBI agent didn't sit very well with them. And if I were to guess, you will probably be next."

Monica holstered her weapon and took a step closer. "You thought you were so smart, Jimmy. We know all about your dealings with William Hoskins, how the autopsies were fudged to cover up numerous murders. You see, Hoskins kept a ledger. Oh, and then there were the photographs you had Fred Albright take. Thank goodness his memory is intact."

Jimmy's eyes shot daggers at her. His fists clenched and unclenched at his side. "I'll bury the legal system in lawyers and appeals. I'll never see the inside of a cell."

Monica delighted in watching him squirm. Jimmy Galante had it coming for a long time. "No matter what you do, Jimmy, the end result will be the same. You'll just prolong the inevitable." She turned to one of her fellow agents. "Take this prick into custody."

"Wait," Jimmy said. "I need protection. You know they'll try to get to me."

Monica turned away and called back over her shoulder. "Not our problem, Jimmy."

Outside, Monica breathed in. The air felt crisp, cleaner, somehow. She made her way over to Eddie. "I have something to tell you."

"I have a feeling it's about my uncle."

"Yes, you're right. He's dead, Eddie. Taken out by the Commission along with Detective Richard Walsh."

His eyes filled, and he stared off into the distance. "I guess things turned out the way they were supposed to. I could never picture my Uncle Sal in a prison cell."

"There is one other thing I need you to know, "Monica continued, touching him lightly on the arm. "The Bureau did their DNA testing with regards to your parents, and the results weren't what we thought they would be."

"What do you mean? Was my uncle involved or not?"

"Well, that's something we're about to find out for sure. If I can get permission, do you think you're up to listening in when we conduct our interrogation?"

"I *have* to be there, Monica. I need to finally know the truth."

"Good, then I'll arrange it."

Chapter 77 — Rita

The Confession

A tearful Rita Barone sat inside the interrogation room. Her once perfectly styled platinum blonde hair hung in a tangled mess. Her signature bright orange lipstick matched the jumpsuit she wore. Eyes red from crying, she glanced up at the camera mounted in the corner of the ceiling. Monica sat across from her with Danny.

"Rita," Monica said. "Is it my understanding that you have agreed to cooperate with the FBI's investigation regarding the deaths of Cathy and Matthew Marconi in exchange for a lighter prison sentence?"

"Y…yes," Rita replied. "I agree to cooperate."

"To the best of your recollection, can you tell us what happened on the night of July 12th, 1993?"

Rita stretched out her arms, laying her hands palms down on the table. Her fingertips tapped against the wood. "I called Cathy about eight o'clock that night. I told her I wanted to come over and talk."

"About what?" Monica asked.

"I knew that Matthew, my brother, was giving Sal and Lorenzo a hard time."

"Sal being Salvatore Marconi and Lorenzo Barone, your husband, correct?" Monica asked.

"Yes."

Danny leaned forward in his chair. "A hard time about what?"

Rita hesitated and bit her lower lip. "Matthew was a union boss in the construction industry. I overheard him and Lorenzo arguing. Lorenzo told him Sal was furious at him for not having some of the union members pull slow downs on particular jobs."

"How did Matthew respond?" Monica asked.

"He said he wanted to stay legitimate, that he wanted no part of the family business. But Lorenzo told him he would pay the price if he didn't do what Sal wanted. Then, the shouting began. Matthew said nobody, not even his brother, was going to force him to do anything he didn't want to do. Matthew stormed out of the house, and I overheard Lorenzo make a call to Sal."

"What did you hear?" Danny asked.

"Lorenzo told Sal that Matthew was being difficult and sooner or later something needed to be done." Rita's eyes filled, tears spilled down her cheeks.

Monica handed her a tissue. "So, you went over to Cathy's."

Rita dabbed at her eyes. "Yes. I thought I could persuade her to convince Matthew to cooperate with Sal. You have to understand. I knew things were going to get very bad."

"Rita," Monica said. "You need to tell us exactly what happened after you arrived at Cathy's."

Rita's body shook, her eyes pleaded with Monica. "I didn't mean to hurt her. I should never have called Lorenzo."

"What did you do, Rita?" Monica asked. "We need to hear every detail if you want your deal to go through."

"I … I got to Cathy's, and we went outside to the backyard by the pool. We were alone. Matthew wasn't home. I told her she needed to talk to him. Tell him how bad the situation was becoming. At first, she laughed. She said she couldn't tell Matthew what to do. That I should mind my own business, let the men work it out. I think she believed Sal would never hurt him."

"I got angry. I screamed at her, begged her to listen to what I was saying. She told me to get out of her house, that she didn't want to talk about it anymore. I … I pushed her. I didn't mean to hurt her. I was trying to get her to listen."

Rita buried her face in her hands and sobbed, her shoulders shaking uncontrollably. Danny looked at Monica and then back at Rita. "Do you need to take a break?" he asked.

Rita dropped her hands and shook her head no. "I need to get this over with."

"What happened next?" Monica asked.

"Cathy fell backward onto the pavement and struck her head. I tried to help her get up, but she fought me, and we struggled. I ended up on top of her. I was so angry that she wouldn't listen to me. I could barely see straight. I remember grabbing her head and banging it against the cement. Seconds later, I realized she was unconscious, and I couldn't wake her up."

"I panicked. The only thing I could think of was to call Lorenzo. While I waited for him to come, Matthew came home. When he saw Cathy lying there, he screamed at me, wanting to know what had happened. I told him it was an accident and that Lorenzo was on the way. But he shouted at me to call an ambulance. So, I got on my phone and pretended to call."

"Then, Lorenzo and Sal arrived just as Cathy was coming around. Matthew pointed at me and started screaming, saying, look what she did to my Cathy, look what she did. I don't know why, but I didn't notice it at first," Rita continued.

"Notice what?" Monica asked.

"The bat in Lorenzo's hand. Sal grabbed Matthew from behind, and Lorenzo swung the bat at Matthew's knees. I heard his bones crack as he screamed and collapsed to the ground. By this time, Cathy was trying to get up. She managed to stand just as Lorenzo swung the bat again, and she fell backward into the pool.

"Matthew wouldn't stop yelling. Lorenzo swung the bat at Matthew's head and then pushed him into the pool. I just stood there. I couldn't believe what had happened. They told me to leave, that they would take care of everything."

"But, then I saw him. Oh, my God! I saw him." Rita began sobbing again. "He was standing dressed in his pajamas in the living room, looking out the sliding glass doors."

"Who? Who did you see?"

"Eddie. I saw Eddie. I didn't know how long he'd been standing there. I called out to Sal, and he came running. He told me to take Eddie to Teresa and that I was not to say a word to her about what happened. He told me to tell her there had been a car accident and that Matthew and Cathy were dead. I did what he asked. The whole time, Eddie was silent. He never said a word about any of it. Later, I was with Teresa after Sal and Lorenzo arrived. Teresa couldn't stop crying. She believed the accident story. Later, Sal took Eddie into a separate room. I have no idea what he told the boy. From that day on, none of what happened was ever mentioned again."

Rita fell silent as Monica stood up. "I have to go," she said. "Have them take her the hell out of here and back to her cell."

Chapter 78 — Eddie

Penitence

After Rita Barone finished, Eddie bolted out of the room where he had been viewing the interrogation on a computer screen. With two FBI agents tailing him, he drove to Holy Cross Church, the need burning like a fire within his soul. The trembling in his body refused to cease.

He entered the church, dipped his shaking fingers, made the sign of the cross, and trudged up the aisle to the first pew. It was late afternoon, and the last of the people who had come to confession were leaving.

Staring at the crucifix behind the alter, his eyes watered, blurring the image of Christ. The uncle he once loved had sanctioned the murder of his parents. His nightmare was real. The yelling, the screams were all witnessed by him. He had blocked it out all these years. Listening to Rita brought it all back.

He had woken up to shouting outside his open bedroom window. His mother's voice rose, and then a second woman's voice rose even higher. Tiptoeing over to the window, he peered out into the backyard.

Aunt Rita and his mother were standing near the pool. They were arguing. His mother shouted at her to leave. He remembered turning away from the window and going downstairs. Through the open living room sliders, he could see his mother lying on the ground struggling with his Aunt Rita. Frightened and not knowing what to do, he backed to the corner of the living room.

Aunt Rita was crying and talking to someone on her phone. He remembered hiding behind the recliner. His Uncle

Lorenzo and Uncle Sal arrived and went outside. Creeping out from behind the chair, he watched Lorenzo swing a bat. All of it like a dream, when he heard his father cry out, the splash of the water in the pool, and then silence.

He recalled his Aunt Rita taking him by the hand. He had no recollection of the ride to his Uncle Sal's house. His Aunt Teresa's face just a hazy memory as she held him close before his Uncle Sal came later and took him into another room.

"What did you see, Eddie?" he asked.

Frightened and confused, he looked into his uncle's dark eyes. Those eyes signaled a warning. "Nothing," he remembered saying. "I didn't see anything."

"That's a good boy," his uncle replied.

After that, his Aunt Teresa put him to bed upstairs. The following day he was told he would be living with them for good.

Why didn't he try to save his mother and father? But, at just five years old, what could he have done? Eddie let out a breath, with the realization his repressed memory had been a blessing in disguise. His Uncle Sal might have done away with him, too, if he said anything about what he witnessed.

Eddie thought about the events of earlier that day. At least Tommy and Ann were safe. He would never forget Tony Morello as he tried to digest the enormity of Tony's sacrifice. As for the hit on his uncle, the Commission had not forgiven him for what he did. They had meted out their own form of justice. Others, like Jimmy Galante and Frank Uzelli, would also pay a price.

Sitting here now, overwhelmed by memories and shamed over the things he had done in the name of Salvatore Marconi, he bowed his head and tried to pray. But the words stuck in his throat.

A tap on his shoulder made him look up. Father Mike, a somber expression on his face, eased down next to him. "Talk to me, Eddie. I'm here for you. God is here for you."

"Don't talk to me about God," Eddie declared. "Where was he when my parents were getting beaten to death? Can you tell me that, Father?" The damn inside him burst. Tears poured down his face, dripping off his chin. An endless flow he couldn't control.

Father Mike placed his arm around Eddie's shoulders. "Nobody, other than God, can understand the pain you're going through. Whether you want to believe me or not, you need to open your heart and talk to him. If you're mad, then let him know."

Eddie stared at the crucifix again. He raised his hand and shook his fist in the air. "Why didn't you help them?" he cried. "Why didn't you stop it from happening?" He collapsed back into the pew and slumped against Father Mike's shoulder. His chest heaved. He tried to catch his breath. The two remained that way for the next ten minutes until Eddie controlled himself. He sat up and looked at Father Mike. "Will I ever feel close to God again?"

"You will, with time. That is if you make an effort to reach out to him." He stood up and beckoned to Eddie. "The confessional is waiting." He left and disappeared into the booth.

Minutes passed. Eddie wrangled with his thoughts until he followed Father Mike inside. He made the sign of the cross and began, "Forgive me, Father, for I have sinned."

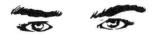

Chapter 79 — Monica

The Truth Reveals Itself

Monica left FBI Headquarters in Manhattan intending to catch the ferry back to Staten Island. Eddie's abrupt departure after the interrogation did not surprise her. All of it information overload, he needed time to process everything. It was her job to allow him to do that.

Halfway up the block, she heard someone call her name. She stopped and turned around. "Jasper?"

Jasper Walton came toward her. A sudden breeze caught his unbuttoned tan trenchcoat, making him look like he was about to take flight. His grey hair dipped below his collar, and the same large red frames he had always worn still sat on his face. She smiled to herself. The IT guys were always so diverse looking.

"I thought you retired from the Bureau some time ago," she said, hugging him.

"I did. But accounting screwed up enough of my checks to warrant a personal visit."

"I'm glad we ran into each other. I never got the chance to say goodbye to you."

"Me, too. You were always one of my favorite agents, Monica. By the way, how did that sim thing turn out on the case you were working with Agent Gage? I left before you finished the case." He ran a finger up the bridge of his nose and adjusted his glasses.

"Sim thing?"

"Yeah. Agent Gage came to me. He explained you were working on a case together. He asked if it was possible to clone a SIM card from a cell phone."

A flutter hit the pit of Monica's stomach. She pointed to a bench along the path. "Do you have time to explain it to me?"

"Sure." After they were seated, Jasper began. "I'll try to put it in the simplest language possible. Cloning a cell phone SIM card is done using smart card copying software. It enables someone access to, say, a victim's mobile subscriber international identity known as IMSI and their master encryption key. Since the information is burnt onto the SIM card, physical access is required."

"So, they would need the person's cell?" Monica asked.

"Yes. It means taking the SIM card out of the mobile device and placing it into a card reader attached to a computer where the duplication software is installed."

A ripple crept across Monica's chest, the dread inside her growing. "Did Danny give you an actual phone or a SIM card?"

Jasper rubbed his chin. "Let me see. I believe it was a SIM card. It happened the day before I retired, so I never did know the outcome. At the time, it was innovative technology I was experimenting with." He winked at Monica. "I didn't have the okay from the Bureau, yet."

"Let me see if I understand you correctly," Monica said. "If you clone a person's SIM card, you can make it look like a message came from their phone?"

"Absolutely. In the criminal world, it's known as SIM swapping."

Monica got up from the bench. She pulled out her cell phone. "I'd like to stay in touch. Can I have your number?"

"Sure thing." Jasper rattled off his number. "Tell me something before I go."

"What's that?" Monica asked.

"Did the SIM cloning work?"

Monica smiled. "Yes. It worked really well." She gave Jasper a final hug before hurrying back to the FBI building.

She rode the elevator, thinking back to when she and Danny were together. Working on a kidnapping and murder case, she traced the suspect to an old, abandoned warehouse. A few days before, she had made it clear to Danny that their time together was ending. She had also forgotten her cell phone at his apartment.

Down with a bad cold and not thinking too much of it, she retrieved it late in the afternoon the following day. Danny's attitude was cold. He told her he wanted to cut ties immediately. At the time, she was relieved, never thinking he was out for revenge.

Monica stepped off the elevator and charged straight for Bob Acosta's office.

Chapter 80 — Eddie
Leaving On A Jet Plane

With two FBI agents outside, Eddie and Monica sat together on the sofa. She glanced at Eddie's suitcase sitting by the door.

"Before we leave," Eddie said. "I need to tell you something I've been keeping from you for a long time."

Monica shook her head. "You don't need to tell me anything. I'm just glad to see you're handling things so well after finding out the truth."

"No," he insisted. "If I'm going to become the man I want to be, then I have to come clean all the way." He reached and took both her hands in his. "When I told you Grace Scarfino, and I were together the night I was drunk, that was true." Looking into her green eyes, a heaviness settled inside his chest. He didn't want to hurt her again.

"Go on," Monica said. "You can tell me the rest."

"Well, Grace and I were together off and on."

She closed her eyes, opened them again, and looked down at their hands. "I suspected as much."

"Monica, baby, it didn't mean anything to me. I was just playing around."

Drawing her hands away, she said, "But I bet it meant something to Grace. I could tell the day she came to see me. You can't go around taking people's feelings for granted, Eddie."

"I know that now. I'm trying to be better. After everything, I want you to know that you're the love of my life, and I can't wait to start over with you."

Monica got up and walked to the window, her back to him. "I'm not coming with you, Eddie." She spoke the words, her voice barely audible."

"What do you mean?" He went over to her. "I thought you loved me."

She whirled around and faced him. "I do love you. I love you so damn much. That's the problem."

"Then why? Why won't you come with me?"

"There are things I can't explain and stuff I still need to finish here at the Bureau."

"The Bureau! I would never have agreed to help the Bureau if I knew I would lose you." He stared at her, burning the memory of her face into his brain.

"If you truly want to change, you need time to find yourself again and begin a new life. One you can be proud of."

He cupped her chin with one hand and trailed his finger along her cheek with the other. "How am I supposed to do that without you?"

"I have always had faith in you. Even when I knew what you were doing for your Uncle Sal, I saw the good in you, and now you have to use it to your advantage."

She wrapped her arms around his neck, the warmth of her body against his almost unbearable. He ran a hand down her dark curls, his palm resting on the nape of her neck. He pulled her closer and kissed her, knowing his hunger for her would never again be satisfied.

Their lips parted, and he gazed into her eyes for the last time. "I love you, Monica. Please don't forget me."

"Never," She said softly.

He walked to the door and picked up his suitcase. Turning around for one last look at the woman he would love until the day he died, he opened the door and stepped out.

Chapter 81 — Monica
Danny's Undoing

The doorbell rang, letting Monica know Danny had arrived. The grey skies outside her window were an appropriate backdrop for what was about to happen. She opened the door with a smile and let him in.

"So, we did well working together on our last case," he said, grinning. He removed his jacket and laid it on the arm of the sofa—his broad shoulders and muscled arms outlined by the navy polo shirt complementing his khaki's.

Monica, dressed in jeans and a sweater, pointed to a chair. "Have a seat, Danny."

"Why so formal?" he asked, easing into the chair. "Oh, I forgot. Eddie's gone, isn't he? Still pining away?"

"Let's not talk about, Eddie," she said, sitting across from him. "I'd much rather talk about you and Jasper Walton."

The amused look on his face evaporated. He shifted uncomfortably in the chair. "I have no idea what you're getting at. Jasper left the Bureau a long time ago. What does he have to do with me?"

"Funny you should ask," Monica quipped. "I ran into Jasper the other day. He told me a fascinating story about you, him, and a SIM card."

His face turned crimson as he rose from the chair. "Look, I don't know what Jasper may have told you, but whatever it is, it has nothing to do with me."

"I beg to differ," Monica said, standing up. "You know what you did, Danny. The day I left my phone at your apartment, you took it to Jasper. He duplicated the SIM card, and you made it look like I messaged Jack Wilson."

Danny took a step back. "Bullshit. How could you even think I would do something like that?"

"Oh, you did it, all right. I lost everything because of you, and Jack ended up dead. You knew how dangerous it was for him to follow me to the warehouse. But you let it happen anyway. Jack walked into a trap. He arrived before I did, and the suspect shot him. Even though I was able to bring his killer down, do you have any idea how I felt seeing Jack laying there dead?"

Danny's face flushed. He swept a hand across his forehead and paced. "I was angry with you, Monica. The thought of coming to work every day, seeing you there, and knowing you didn't love me. I just wanted you gone!"

"How could you do it at the expense of someone else's life, Danny? Jack was a good man. He didn't deserve to be used in your game."

"I know. After I realized what I had done, it was too late." Danny moved toward her. "So, now what. Are you going to turn me in? They'll put me in jail, Monica. I'm sorry about Jack, but is it worth ruining my life? My career?"

"You mean the way you ruined mine, Danny?"

The bedroom door opened. Bob Acosta stepped out. "Agent Gage, I'm afraid I have to take you into custody."

Danny bolted to the door and swung it open. Two agents appeared on the other side, their guns drawn. The color drained from his face, and he backed away.

"Take him," Bob ordered.

After they cuffed Danny and removed him from the apartment, Monica collapsed onto the sofa. All this time, she couldn't understand how the message to Jack had come from her phone. Danny would have gotten off if she had never found out the truth. At least Jack Wilson would get some form of justice.

"Are you okay, Agent Cappelino?" Bob asked.

Monica looked up at him, her lips forming a slow smile. "More than okay, sir."

"See you first thing tomorrow morning, then."

Later that evening, alone in her apartment, Monica poured herself a glass of wine and drifted to the bedroom window. As much as she missed him, she had made the right decision in letting Eddie go without her. He needed to find himself to become the man she always knew he could be.

Her job with the FBI was secure. The career she had lost now waited for her return. Poor Danny would end up incarcerated, exactly where he should be after what he had done. As for her shop, she decided to make Cookie a full partner, leaving her to run it while she went to work for the Bureau again. Ann and Tommy had gladly taken the opportunity for a fresh start under The Witness Protection Program. Jimmy Galante and Frank Uzelli would soon go to trial. Unfortunately, Rocco Fischetti remained a fugitive at the top of the FBI's most wanted list. Tony Morello had survived, though a long road to recovery lay ahead of him.

Monica pulled back the sheer curtain. Moonlight bathed the sidewalk below. The memory of Eddie all those months ago under the streetlamp rose to the surface. On that fateful night, she couldn't have imagined where his coming back into her life would lead.

She raised her glass. "Here's to you, my love."

Epilogue — Monica
Two Years Later

Rays of sunshine beat off the hood of Monica's rental car. The flight from New York to Scottsdale, Arizona, yesterday had felt like an eternity. Located in the beautiful Sonoran Desert at the foot of the scenic McDowell Mountains, it was worlds away from Staten Island.

For the second time, Monica pulled up the address from the GPS on her cell phone. During the drive to her destination, she again questioned her decision to open up Eddie's file and find out his whereabouts. A clear violation of Bureau regulations.

The burning desire inside her to see him one last time refused to abate. These past few years had brought many changes. Her life turned upside down in a way she never thought possible.

With Eddie gone and her strong will to move forward with her life, she had recently accepted a new assignment working for the FBI's Joint Terrorism Task Force, first returning to Quantico for further training.

Late at night, in her new apartment in Washington, D.C., memories of her life back home in New York refused to yield. The only solace was knowing Eddie was safe from those who would do him harm.

There were rumblings from the five families about his being a rat, a $500,000 contract put on his life. With a new identity, she hoped his whereabouts would remain unknown.

Close to her destination, she shut off her GPS. She cruised down the appropriate street, taking in the row of stucco homes and neatly landscaped yards for the first time in daylight hours. She parked a few houses down from the address on the opposite side of the street and waited.

His handsome face swam before her. She studied her hands and remembered how her fingers used to sweep through his dark hair. The fierce lovemaking they shared between them, bodies always in sync with one another. She'd give almost anything to feel him close to her again.

A gurgling sound came from the rear. She reached for the door handle. Andrew was waking up. She got out, removed him from the car seat, and brought him up front.

His eyes opened. A grin appeared on his face. "Mama," he said softly, almost crooning the words. She ruffled his curly black hair. Andrew slapped his tiny hand on the steering wheel, looked up at her, and laughed. His eyes were the same nautical blue as his father's.

A mail truck drove past, stopping at each box along the street before disappearing around the corner. Monica waited. Minutes ticked by until the front door of the address opened. A man came out of the house and walked down the stone pathway. Her heart beat wildly against her ribcage. His features, tanned by the Arizona sun, made him even more handsome than before. He stopped at the mailbox and dug inside.

Couldn't he tell she was near, feel her presence somehow? She tried to will him to look her way. But seeing her and the baby would only cause him grief, the last thing she wanted him to feel. This visit was a selfish one on her part but necessary.

Still standing by the curb, head down, Eddie thumbed through the mail. She almost gasped when he turned a brown envelope over in his hand, the one she had placed in the mailbox the night before.

He glanced around and then opened it. His eyes grew wide. A smile appeared on his face. He held the picture to his chest for a moment before looking at it again.

Monica stood the baby up in her lap. She stretched out her arm and pointed. "See, that's your daddy, Andrew. That's Da Da."

Andrew's eyes lit up, and he clapped his hands. He stared at Eddie as if contemplating what she had said, and then, without missing a beat, he blurted out, "Da Da."

Tucking the remainder of the mail under his arm, Eddie went up the walk and back inside the house. Monica had no regrets about sending the photo of Andrew and her riding on the Seaglass Carousel back in New York City.

She sat the baby back down on her lap. Hugging him tight, she said. "He's okay, Andrew. Your daddy's okay. And we'll be okay, too."

Nominated for Georgia Author of the Year for her novel *Redemption*, Stephanie is dedicated to giving her readers fast-paced, high-stakes, page-turning stories that keep you on the edge of your seat and are full of surprising twists! Stephanie's second novel in her trilogy, *Retribution*, was released in 2019, followed by *Reckoning* in 2022. The collection makes up the *Sicario Files Trilogy*. Her new novel, *Mobbed Up*, features a cast of new characters and, though she claims there will not be a sequel and that she is taking a break, the next tangled web will soon enthrall her.

You can find her online at **www.stephaniebaldi2.com** or follow her on Facebook and Twitter at **sbauthor7.**

Other Titles by Stephanie Baldi

The Sicario Files Trilogy
REDEMPTION

Murder is the catalyst pushing Carrie Overton headlong into the arms of the hitman sent to kill her.

Determined to escape her alcoholic and drug-addicted mother and distance herself from the memory of the son she lost, Carrie leaves home with Travis Montgomery, a man twenty years her senior who harbors shocking secrets connected to her past.

After Travis forces her to help him steal two million dollars from a drug lord, leaving two people dead, Carrie decides to add a third victim to her list, and Travis is left lying on the floor.

Eager to start over, she takes the stolen money and travels to the small mountain town of Laurel, Pennsylvania. Carrie lies about her past and relaxes into her new life. Before long, Carrie's lies are piling up, and her crimes are about to catch up to her.

Nicholas D'Angelo is known as a ghost, a contract killer for one of the biggest drug lords in Miami. His assignment is simple. Find the people, who stole the two million dollars, recover the money and eliminate them.

With a hitman on her trail, Carrie is forced to make a choice. Trust the hitman who vows to disobey his orders and protect her. Or stay in Laurel and face the drug lord determined to end her life. Either one might kill her.

RETRIBUTION

Almost six long years have passed since Carmela Santiago witnessed the hitman she loved assassinate her father. Now she is ready to exact her plan of revenge against him and the people he loves. Carmela will stop at nothing to tear his family apart. Running her father's drug smuggling empire, she will use every resource at her disposal, including money, sex, the men in her life, and her very own cold-blooded sicario, to help her carry out her deeds.

Nicholas D'Angelo, the contract killer, once employed by Carmela's father has his family safely tucked away in a compound in Tuscany, Italy. Many times, he has regretted his decision to let Carmela live. Forced by the government to return to the United States and resume the life of a killer, Nick knows will put his family in jeopardy.

Carmela Santiago has the means to destroy him and all those he holds dear. Carmela moves forward with her plan of revenge, but her closest allies are fast becoming her enemies. As she pushes things to the limit, Carmela gets caught in her own web of lies, murder, and deceit. With the stakes rising higher, she is determined to win. Nick will use everything at his disposal to stop her.

RECKONING

One terrible night in Tahoe left Carmela Santiago dead and a visible scar on Miguel Medina's face. After three long years, a still open wound lies hidden inside his cold heart. Once Carmela's trusted Sicario and lover, he is determined to exact vengeance on the man responsible for her death. Miguel knows going up against such a man as Nicholas D'Angelo, will not be easy.

Both ghosts, hitmen at the top of their game, their past confrontation in Tahoe has proven they possess the skills to eliminate one another. Only Miguel's plans run much deeper.

Vowing to reclaim Carmela's daughter, Natalia, and raise her as his own, Miguel has struck at the heart of Nick's family by stealing away something they love.

With pressure mounting and time running out, Nick must find a way to take back what rightfully belongs to him and destroy Miguel Medina once and for all.

Available in paperback and eBook

and

on Audible

CPSIA information can be obtained
at www.ICGtesting.com
Printed in the USA
LVHW111109050223
738542LV00003B/3